"*Real Vampires Live Large* is an outstanding sequel . . . Equal parts humor and spice, with mystery and adventure tossed into the mix. Glory's world is a place I look forward to visiting again, the sooner the better."
—*Fresh Fiction*

"Gerry Bartlett has created a laugh-out-loud book that I couldn't put down. *Real Vampires Live Large* is a winner."
—*The Romance Readers Connection*

"Glory gives 'Girl Power' a whole new meaning, especially in the undead way. What a fun read!" —*All About Romance*

Praise for
Real Vampires Have Curves

"Full-figured vampire Glory bursts from the page in this lively, fun, and engaging spin on the vampire mythology."
—Julie Kenner, *USA Today* bestselling author

"A real winner. Bartlett brings a fresh spin to paranormal chick lit in this clever combination of suspense and humor and wonderful style. Hang on to your seats—this book is a wild ride." —*Romantic Times*

"Fans of paranormal chick lit will want to take a bite out of Gerry Bartlett's amusing tale. Glory is terrific."
—*The Best Reviews*

"A sexy, smart, and lively contemporary romance . . . The plot is engaging, the characters are stimulating (not to mention, so is the sex), and the writing is sharp. Glory St. Clair is one hot, curvaceous vampire! She's sassy, sexy, and somewhat single . . . a breath of fresh air." —*Romance Reader at Heart*

"A vampire who even smart . . . plenty of quirk from MaryJanice Davidso Charlaine Harris' Southe *Real Vampires Have Curves.'*

Titles by Gerry Bartlett

REAL VAMPIRES HAVE CURVES
REAL VAMPIRES LIVE LARGE

Real Vampires Live Large

GERRY BARTLETT

BERKLEY SENSATION, NEW YORK

THE BERKLEY PUBLISHING GROUP
Published by the Penguin Group
Penguin Group (USA) Inc.
375 Hudson Street, New York, New York 10014, USA
Penguin Group (Canada), 90 Eglinton Avenue East, Suite 700, Toronto, Ontario M4P 2Y3, Canada
(a division of Pearson Penguin Canada Inc.)
Penguin Books Ltd., 80 Strand, London WC2R 0RL, England
Penguin Group Ireland, 25 St. Stephen's Green, Dublin 2, Ireland (a division of Penguin Books Ltd.)
Penguin Group (Australia), 250 Camberwell Road, Camberwell, Victoria 3124, Australia
(a division of Pearson Australia Group Pty. Ltd.)
Penguin Books India Pvt. Ltd., 11 Community Centre, Panchsheel Park, New Delhi—110 017, India
Penguin Group (NZ), 67 Apollo Drive, Rosedale, North Shore 0632, New Zealand
(a division of Pearson New Zealand Ltd.)
Penguin Books (South Africa) (Pty.) Ltd., 24 Sturdee Avenue, Rosebank, Johannesburg 2196,
South Africa

Penguin Books Ltd., Registered Offices: 80 Strand, London WC2R 0RL, England

REAL VAMPIRES LIVE LARGE

A Berkley Sensation Book / published by arrangement with the author

PRINTING HISTORY
Berkley trade edition / July 2007
Berkley Sensation mass-market edition / April 2008

Copyright © 2007 by Gerry Bartlett.
Cover art by Chris Long.
Cover design by George Long.
Interior text design by Kristin del Rosario.

ISBN: 978-0-425-22122-8

BERKLEY® SENSATION
Berkley Sensation Books are published by The Berkley Publishing Group,
a division of Penguin Group (USA) Inc.,
375 Hudson Street, New York, New York 10014.
BERKLEY SENSATION and the "B" design are trademarks belonging to Penguin Group (USA) Inc.

PRINTED IN THE UNITED STATES OF AMERICA

10 9 8 7 6 5 4 3 2 1

Thanks to:

Sarah Thigpen, for making me laugh;
Kenneth "Bicycle" Collins, for making me mad;
And Nina Bangs, for making me stretch.
I couldn't have done it without you.

Finally, this book is dedicated to the memory of the original
Valdez, the Wonder Dog, and all the other wonderful companion animals who have gotten to Heaven ahead of us.

One

"You're a blood-sucking vampire, Gloriana St. Clair. When are you going to start acting like one?"

I snarled and showed some fang. "Careful, fur face. You really don't want to make me mad." Yeah, I'm a vampire. Forget stereotypes. I'm blond, blue-eyed and twentysomething with a, uh, voluptuous figure. Vamps are everywhere and you won't have a clue. We're pretty good at blending with mortals and if we're caught in a compromising situation, like say with our fangs in your neck . . . ? Well, there's always the whammy. We can make fang marks disappear along with your memory. Hmmm. Makes you wonder, doesn't it?

"Come on, Glory. I'm hurting here." Valdez talks in my head. A lot.

"You're my dog-slash-bodyguard, Valdez. You're supposed to be taking care of *me*."

"I will. I am. Now turn around."

"I'm not going back to the store. Forget it. I got the essentials—cream rinse and flea shampoo." I gasped when my stomach cramped again. "Those damned Cheetos almost killed me."

"I'm not asking you to eat any. You expect me to give them up just because you can't handle them?"

"I had a near-death experience." Who knew a Big Grab of Cheetos could be so *lethal*? If you know anything about vampires, you know we can dish it out, but we can't or *won't* take it. I'm an old vampire. Like, "I hung out with Billy

Shakespeare" old. I knew better, but just once I'd wanted a little crunch in my diet. I gave up biting mortals, mostly, ages ago. But chugging the bottled fake stuff just hadn't been cutting it for me for a long, long time.

I wheeled my aging Suburban into the parking lot behind my apartment building where I have my shop, Vintage Vamp's Emporium (cute, huh?) on the ground floor. The security lights were out again. Not a good sign. Valdez had taken an arrow in the hip back here. An arrow intended for me. I slowed down to a crawl, fought another pain, this one in my head for a change, then pulled into my parking spot.

Crunch, thump and the car lurched to a stop. Oops.

"Now you've done it. Stay here and lock yourself in." Valdez opened the passenger door (don't ask) and hopped out, obviously on high alert. Was this a trap? Everyone *I* know realizes that's *my* parking spot. Was some stake-happy vamp hunter waiting to get me when I checked out whatever I'd hit?

"I'm not picking up on a threat. But we're in deep shit anyway." Valdez stopped next to my door. *"Back up a foot, then come see."*

As soon as I turned off the engine, another sharp pain hit me right between my eyes. What the hell? I never have headaches unless I'm trying to block one of my mind-reading friends. And the Cheetos didn't mess with my head. Instead I'm stuck with what I'll call the Cheeto bulge. I'm curvy anyway, but since I did the dirty with the snacks, I've developed a new curve in my tummy area. I unlocked the doors and got out.

Thanks to my superior vamp night vision I could see that the Suburban looked undamaged, but the crushed metal between the car and the fence had once been, gulp, a motorcycle. And not one of those cheap bikes, but, double gulp, a classic Harley. And I know about these things. Had a boyfriend once who'd been into those. Mortal. And very last century. One thing I try to do is stay current. I may be ancient, but I don't ever intend to look or act that way.

"What the hell have you done, Gloriana?"

I turned around, fully prepared to do some kind of vamp whammy until I could figure out how to make this right without the involvement of law enforcement or insurance adjusters. One look at the furious Harley owner and I knew the whammy wasn't going to cut it.

Richard Mainwaring is a vamp too. A friend, sort of, but also a scary dude. Anyway, he was staring at the mangled mess like, if he'd been any less pure macho male, he would have shed a few tears. I wanted to cry too. Maybe I could entice him upstairs for a bottle of Fangtastic (my blood substitute of choice lately) and an all-out sob fest.

"I didn't see it. And this is my parking spot." Yep, I was defensive.

"There's no assigned parking here." He tenderly set the fallen motorcycle back on its wheels, the effort doing nice things to his biceps. The Harley wobbled for a moment and I held my breath until it seemed steady.

"But it's for residents only. You don't live here, do you?" He'd been an item with my roommate, Florence da Vinci, until recently, but the last word on that subject was that Flo had dumped him. Had they made up and he was moving into Flo's bedroom?

"No. And I'm not with Florence." He had a grim look. And don't you hate the fact that he'd read my mind? It's a bad vamp habit that I refuse to acquire, at least not on a regular basis. And I'd had run-ins with Richard before. His thoughts are never up for grabs.

"Then you have no business parking here. Visitor parking is in front of the building."

He knelt down to examine what had been the rear wheel of the Harley. Hmm. He did fill out a pair of jeans nicely. Not that I should be noticing that right now. More to the point, he had a set of shoulders on him, clearly showcased in a sleeveless leather vest, shoulders that would have done a linebacker proud. I have vamp strength, but this guy could have thrown me across the parking lot without breaking a sweat.

He turned and gave me a measuring look. Oops. I think I came up short. I unzipped my jacket, a cozy velour hoodie that matched my turquoise sweat pants and sleeveless tank. He could outmuscle me, but I've got a few weapons of my own. Maybe if I flashed a little cleavage . . . Mainwaring's a former priest turned vamp, but I know for a fact that he's very into women.

"Gloriana, how could you do this? Didn't you see the space was already occupied?" Mainwaring has a slight British accent, white blond hair and the kind of eyes that make you think of clear skies. That is, if you can remember that far back. Me, I haven't seen daylight personally since 1604. Sigh.

"It's dark back here." I looked down at my dog, pressed against my right leg. "And Valdez and I were having a discussion . . ."

"Don't lay this off on me, Blondie." Valdez chuffed and stepped away. *"You were driving this heap, not me."*

I'm not the only one who can hear Valdez and Mainwaring gave the dog a look, like—who's the master here? Good question. Instead of growling at Mainwaring like a good guard dog, Valdez sat down and scratched his left ear. We really needed that flea shampoo.

"Look. The Harley is, I mean was, black without a lot of chrome or anything. Plus the security lights are out. Maybe we should hustle our butts inside to discuss this. Hunters could be stalking us as we speak." I did feel . . . something out here.

Mainwaring stood and scanned the area with a narrow-eyed look that meant business if anyone dared make a move on us. Finally he shook his head. "We're safe enough. But perhaps you'd like to go inside, closer to your checkbook."

"Ha. Ha." I put my hand on his bulging bicep, fluttered my eyelashes and leaned in to give him a cleavage close-up. Mainwaring just glared. Ever try charming an uptight man with a wounded Harley? But charm was all I had at the moment. Unlike a lot of vamps, I'm not rich. I work for a living. This century I started my own business, and it got off to a great start, but there's overhead, stock to buy, my own living expenses . . . Well, you get the picture. Obviously, I don't have enough in my checking account to pay for Richie Rich's Harley. Hey, I buy generic cream rinse. What does that tell you?

"Now, Richard." I smiled what I hoped was sweetly. Not easy to do when your head feels like it's about to split open. "I'm really, really sorry, but be reasonable. You know I didn't mean to hit the motorcycle. And I'm sure you can afford—"

He turned and squatted next to the downed bike. I knew enough to shut up. For a long moment, he just stared at it, then he picked up a piece of metal that had fallen to the ground. He finally stood and walked closer to me, too close. I held my ground, even though I could practically feel the hostility coming off of Mr. Motorcycle.

"You need to be held accountable, Gloriana. Whether or not I can afford to replace a 1946 Knucklehead is not the issue."

"Excuse me?" I knew better than to grin, but it was a struggle. "Did you just call your bike a knucklehead?"

"That's the model. A 1946 Harley Davidson Knucklehead. Rare. Valuable." He was *really* in my space. "Maybe even irreplaceable."

Oh, jeez. Heaven forbid I should have mangled a vintage cycle. And I *did* feel bad, especially with Richard looming over me. I eased around him to check out the damage.

"Look. I think it can be fixed. It's mainly the back end that's crunched. Why don't you get an estimate or two and then we'll talk?" And maybe I could win the lottery in the meantime.

"It isn't the money, it's the principle." Richard was right behind me, peering over my shoulder. He smelled like all vamps do, it's a yummy scent that mere mortals can't even pick up. But Richard also had a nice sandalwood kind of thing going on and a male musk that was having an unfortunate effect on my sex-starved libido.

I swore off men after my on-again, off-again maker and mate, Jeremy Blade aka Angus Jeremiah Campbell III, and I faced death at stake-point together on Halloween. I'd expected a little post-action celebration, one-on-one. Instead, Jerry played hero to his best friend's widow, who's thin and beautiful, and, well, thin. You get the idea. Okay, so I'd only been celibate a little over a week, but vamps are sensual creatures. Sometimes that's a blessing, sometimes a curse.

So I was noticing Mainwaring's male attributes. For a former priest, he was surprisingly built. Though I'd heard he'd been a crusader back in the day.

"Crusader then galley slave." His open vest brushed my back. "And I gave up celibacy a long time ago."

His breath stirred my hair, which should have been washed two days ago. I inhaled and licked my lips. I'm *really* not good at celibacy.

I turned to face him. Diversion time. "Yeah? Bet that's an interesting story. How'd you escape? I've heard most galley slaves die at their oar."

"Long story. And don't change the subject." He stared at the bike for a moment, shook his head, then reached down to pick up his saddle bags.

Gee. He may have given up celibacy, but he wasn't exactly falling under my spell, either. Well, what did I expect? His last girlfriend had been my roommate, Florence da Vinci, ancient vampire and certified sex goddess. Of course Flo isn't her real name, she's paying homage to her favorite Italian city and one of her former lovers. Flo is a love 'em and leave 'em kind of gal. How could I compete with a woman who'd talked Leonardo into painting her into the Last Supper at you know who's right hand?

"I've got an appointment. We'll discuss the Harley later." With a glance at Valdez, Richard strode off into the night.

"Well, you weren't much help." I fussed at Valdez while

I grabbed the grocery sacks out of the car. Most of the stuff was for the dog anyway. I order the Fangtastic online. It's not exactly a beverage you find at your local mini-mart.

"The guy was pissed. You can't blame him." Valdez looked mournfully at the motorcycle. Even in dog form, he is such a guy. *"You're lucky he didn't try to knock you on your ass. If he'd raised his hand, then I'd have made my move."*

"Your move. Yeah, right." I was being bitchy. Valdez did have some pretty scary moves, which he's saved me with more than once. But Mainwaring dripped power like my old car did oil. I locked the car and headed for the back entrance to the building, stopping when my head screamed again.

"Gloriana. Come to me." A husky whisper made me drop my groceries and grab my head. Who or what was this?

Valdez growled and looked around. *"Something's going on. Your head is killing you. Because someone or something is trying to send you a message."*

"Not Blade."

"Nope. This guy's one bad actor, trying to get you to go somewhere. I'd like a piece of him." Valdez growled again and paced in a circle around me.

I held onto my head, queasy with pain. Obviously my dog reads my mind too. I'm used to it. I'm also used to letting him take care of me. Like now.

"What's wrong with a cell phone?" This didn't make sense. Blade sent me mental messages all the time and it didn't hurt.

"Gloriana, come here." Same damned compelling voice. I fought the urge to follow it.

"I tell you. It ain't Blade." Valdez growled, deep and dangerous enough to give me goose bumps. *"Cut it out, whoever you are. Gloriana's goin' nowhere and you don't want to mess with me."* Valdez backed up until his tail brushed my legs. *"Suck it up, Blondie. Punch in the code. I figure you'll be okay once we get inside."*

I managed to grab my bags and deal with the code. Believe me, vamps only live where there's great security. We both scooted inside. As soon as the steel door slammed shut, I did feel better.

"*You okay now?*" Valdez nudged me.

"Yeah. That was weird though." I trudged up the stairs. You get that Valdez isn't really a dog, don't you?

"*Careful, you're smashing my Twinkies.*" Valdez is into junk food and the occasional steak. I get him what he wants since I know he'd lay down his life for me. Previous Valdezes have. And isn't that hellacious?

Not my idea, of course. But when Blade and I parted company the first time, centuries ago, he'd insisted I needed a bodyguard. Jerry *made* me, so I give him a certain amount of respect. Respect, not obedience. I do have my pride. But I caved. Of course I sure wasn't going to be saddled with a male guard, even a cute one. That would've cramped my style, big time. And, trust me, Jerry wasn't going to send in a hunk of the month to be with me twenty-four seven. Remember my celibacy issues?

So we'd settled on guard dogs, always named Valdez for some reason. Recent ones have been shape-shifters, though Jerry forbids the guards to be anything but dogs around me. Think Jerry's jealous? Works for me. Anyway, he's got some kind of hold over the guys, this Valdez for sure. I don't know what kind of debt the V-man owes, but it's made for some really fierce and loyal protection.

"I'm okay. You think Mainwaring was doing that to me? Giving me a headache?"

"*He's one tough dude and neither one of us needs to be making him mad. But you had that headache before we hit the Harley. Remember?*"

"Good point." I threw up a block so Valdez couldn't read my mind. I remembered a night when Mainwaring showed me his scary side right here on the stairs to my apartment. The worst part? He'd wiped Valdez's memory. Poor pup didn't realize he'd been whammied into sitting meekly at the bottom of the stairs while I'd fought off the Mainwaring mojo all by my lonesome. "So it wasn't Mainwaring."

"Mainwaring? You've seen Ricardo?" Florence met us at the door and took one of the bags from me. "Not that I care. I'm through with him."

"You sure? Because he parks like he lives here."

"Not in this apartment." Flo pulled out nail polish remover and a sack of cotton balls. "I hate mysterious men. He keeps secrets. Pah! I have a secret for him. He's the worst lover I ever had." Flo's cheeks were pink, which meant she was really agitated. Vamps don't have enough blood to flush unless they've just fed. I saw three empty Fangtastic bottles on the table. Okay, so Flo had been hitting the red stuff pretty hard.

I can never read Flo's mind, though I sure as heck try. She reads mine, of course. Everyone does. Unless I block them. Unfortunately, blocking brings on another kind of headache. But I knew Flo was lying anyway. I mean, even *Sex and the City* reruns turned up full blast hadn't completely drowned out her shrieks of ecstasy when she'd been doing the wild thing with Richard. And, trust me, Flo doesn't fake it for anyone.

I let it go. She needed to vent. Neither of us had a decent boyfriend at the moment. And we live forever. Not a situation conducive to self-denial of any kind.

It was almost dawn and I felt it. All day I'd be dead to the world, literally. I threw on a comfy nightgown, glad to be safe inside, no weird voice in my head. I let Valdez into the bedroom and he hopped on the foot of my queen-sized bed. You didn't think I slept in a coffin, did you? That would be so cliché.

TWO

Whump, whump, whump, whump.

"Please remain calm. The fire is out. The fire is out. Firemen are on their way and are clearing the smoke out of the building."

I was wet, cold and lying on concrete. My baby dolls were tangled around my hips and Valdez was barking into my ear.

"Fire?" I took a breath. Smoke. Oh, shit.

"Yeah, fire. I dragged you up here." Valdez bumped me with his cold nose. *"But you're okay now, Blondie. Right?"*

"Fire!" I swallowed and sat up. A helicopter sporting the logo of a local TV station hovered overhead. Nice. My chubby thighs would be on the evening news.

"You dragged me up here? Flo! Diana!" I jumped up and looked around. I may sleep like the dead, but once the sun goes down, I'm operating on all cylinders. I saw the other resident vamps—Flo, Diana and a guy I knew lived on the third floor—laid out on the roof. They were all wet and all in various stages of stirring. The sun had obviously just slipped below the horizon.

"Yep. I'd say our old buddy Brent Westwood decided to take a parting shot." Valdez growled and leaned against my leg. *"Somebody threw a firebomb into your shop and the fire spread from there. Whoever did it had a hell of a nerve pulling that in broad daylight. Of course it's Monday and the shop was closed. Mugs and Muffins was probably open though. I wonder—"*

"Shut up, Valdez. I . . . My God!" My legs folded and I sat hard on the concrete again. Just about anything, from a wooden skewer to a chopstick could take a vamp out while she's sleeping. And a fire . . . No amount of healing sleep could bring a vamp back from being a crispy critter. I rubbed my dog's ears. He'd *saved* me.

"How do you know this was Westwood?" We'd been fighting off the big-game hunter, who thought vamps were the biggest game of all, ever since I'd arrived in Austin. After a recent showdown, we all figured he'd move on to easier prey. Parting shot.

"Who else? People love your shop. Only an asshole like Westwood—"

Whump. Whump. Whump. Whump. "Medical assistance is on its way. Please wave if you're all right."

"Yeah, right. Smile for the camera, you mean." I picked up my sodden sheet and threw it over my head.

"How are the others?" I pushed to my feet again and wobbled over to Flo like Casper the not-so-friendly ghost, Valdez at my heels. Of course my roommate *would* sleep in the raw. Valdez had draped a wet sheet over her but the rotors were blowing everything on the roof all to hell. Flo sat up, giving the camera a nice shot of her boobs.

"We're on camera, Flo. You might want to wrap your sheet a little tighter."

"What's happened?" She pushed back her dark hair and looked around, then up. "They'd better not be taking my picture. I need my hair dryer, my makeup."

Hopefully, they didn't have audio. I could hear the lead-in now. "Fire victim runs for blow dryer as rescuers battle blaze."

I looked at Valdez. "My shop?" My voice cracked. I'd built Vintage Vamp's Emporium from nothing into a thriving business that actually supported me.

"I figure it's probably gutted." Valdez sat down and scratched his ear. *"Of course I was pretty busy. When the smoke alarms went*

off, I had to clear you guys out. And the stairwell was solid smoke." He coughed, sneezed, then looked at me for sympathy.

"My hero!" I dropped to my knees and threw my arms around his neck. I sniffed wet fur, a mix of dog and smoke. Valdez coughed again and I looked at him, really looked at him. "Seriously. Are you all right?"

"Yeah, I'm okay." Cough, cough.

Okay, now he was faking it. I sat back. Maybe he deserved a little slack. "How did you manage to get all of us out?"

"It wasn't easy. It was still daylight. So I had to pile you guys up inside the stairwell with the door open for ventilation until the sun went down. I had a hell of a time keeping all of you from frying."

"Frying. Oh, my God."

"We are alive, no?" Flo sat down and put her arm around me. Her Italian accent comes out when she's stressed. "And once again our puppy has saved the day." She patted the dog's head. "We are dead without you, signore."

Valdez puffed out his chest and looked up. *"You think I'll be on the evening news? You know they're going to want an interview."*

"Sure. Right. Talking dog saves sleeping vampires. Sorry, but you'll have to settle for a bag of Cheetos."

"Now you're talking."

I gave him a final ear rub, then walked over to check on Diana. She ran the coffee shop downstairs. If my shop was toast, so was hers.

"Di, are you okay?"

She coughed and sat up. "What happened?" She wore cute red plaid flannel jammies and her sheet, wet of course, coordinated in navy blue.

"Fire. Someone firebombed my shop, probably yours too if Westwood did it." I reached out and pulled her to her feet.

"What?" She glanced up, then shot the finger at the

helicopter. "Buzz off, vultures." She headed for the door to
the stairs. "I've got to check on the shop." Mugs and Muffins.
Like me, Diana has to support herself. If her shop had been
hit too . . . Well, this was really, really bad. For both of us.

I grabbed her before she could open the door. "Wait. The
firemen are working their way up here. The building's full
of smoke."

"My shoes!" Flo was on her feet, her sheet wrapped into a
strapless sheath.

*"I don't think the fire got that far. The building's security sys-
tem went off as soon as I heard something crash through Blondie's
shop window. The fire trucks got here pretty quick after that."*
Valdez spent my sleeping hours on hyper alert. Thank God.

"I say, how did we get wet?" The third floor vampire had
joined us. He was a sight in an old-fashioned nightshirt but
good looking in a college professor kind of way. His British
accent was cute. We'd met him at some vamp meetings. Den-
nis, David, something like that.

*"Sprinkler system in the halls. You got wet when I dragged you
out of bed and up the stairs to the roof."*

"But my door was locked. Double dead bolts." The prof
stared at Valdez.

*"So I did a little damage. I couldn't just let you guys go up in
smoke."*

I swallowed a lump the size of Valdez's food bowl.

"Brilliant! You don't even know me." The male vamp
had obviously just found his new best friend.

"I saved all the vamps in the building." Valdez was visibly
preening, and why not? *"It's my thing. You'd think some of those
shifters would have been around, but no such luck. So I handled
it."*

Shifters. Shape-shifters, that is, live in a couple of the
apartments. A werecat, my friend and employee, lives right
across the hall. I took a shaky breath and felt sick again.
This time I couldn't blame it on Cheetos or an evil mind-
meld. If Valdez hadn't been who or what he was . . .

The stair door slammed open and three firemen dressed

in full, bright yellow gear appeared on the roof. The first one threw off his helmet and ran his hand through his short brown hair.

"Anybody hurt? You folks okay?"

We stayed huddled together, looking appropriately shocked and disoriented.

"The fire. It didn't spread to the apartments, did it?" If I had lost everything I owned . . . I've had to start over before, but it's hard, really hard.

"No, ma'am. Sprinkler and alarm systems saved the day." The fireman sounded pure Texan. "You got good response time too. The fire itself didn't have a chance to spread upstairs. Just the smoke."

"The sprinklers didn't go off in the apartments, did they?" Flo was suddenly right beside the fireman and grabbed his arm. "I have a most valuable collection that will be ruined if it gets wet."

Flo's collection of Ferragamos, Pradas, Manolos, et al. The fireman looked down at her, obviously liked the way Flo's sheet was slipping, and patted her hand.

"No, ma'am. Only the hallways have sprinklers. Fire's out now. Smoke's just about cleared. Do any of you folks need the paramedics?" The fireman whipped out his walkie-talkie when Diana coughed.

"No! Really! I'm fine. Just the night air and wet clothes." Diana managed a smile. "Can we go in now? I'm freezing."

Actually we were lucky for early November in Austin. It was fairly cool, but not even close to freezing. Maybe I was being too literal. I'd almost been fried. Okay? A vamp doesn't feel heat and cold like a mortal does. So I faked a shiver.

"Yeah, let's move inside if that's all right."

"One minute." The fireman spoke into a walkie-talkie. "Let me get the all clear." Another fireman showed up in the doorway with a stack of blankets. We each took one gratefully.

Whump. Whump. Whump. Whump. Channel whatever

was getting this all on tape. Flo decided to take advantage and planted a big wet one of thanks on cute fireman's lips after he announced we were good to go. Then we all hustled into the stairwell and out of camera view.

"What started the fire?" I glanced at Valdez.

"Arson." The fireman had a grim look as he stopped at the top of the stairs. "Someone broke the windows in the stores downstairs and tossed in incendiary devices." The fireman couldn't take his eyes off Flo. She was busy rearranging her sheet again, flashing the entire crew. Probably unintentional. She was really anxious to check out that shoe collection.

The fireman's walkie-talkie squawked again. "How'd you folks get up here? The smoke alarm wake you?"

"Sure. Who could sleep through that?" Professor Vamp patted Valdez. "This fellow barked too, though. Just to be sure we knew to take it seriously."

"No kidding." The fireman, Flo attached to his side, gave Valdez an admiring glance. "But why are the doors knocked down? And who the hell could do that? I mean, three apartments look like a battering ram . . ." Flo looked up into the fireman's eyes and he was under the whammy.

As damage control, it was a Band-Aid. We'd have to whammy every fireman who'd seen the doors Valdez had obviously knocked down. I looked at Di and the professor and they went to work on the other firemen coming down the stairs behind us. Before we got to the bottom, the guys had no memory of anything other than knocking the doors down themselves because they were looking for victims.

We stepped outside and I got my first look at what used to be a pretty cute vintage clothing shop. Thank God for sprinkler systems. The windows were shattered, the area right in front of them totaled. It didn't look like the fire had penetrated the closed door into the back room, though. I felt wobbly as I picked my way around broken glass. Diana cried out and I saw that Mugs and Muffins had received the same treatment. If Westwood had done this . . .

"Folks, you've got to let the paramedics look you over. It's our policy." Cute fireman led Flo over to an ambulance. You can bet she wasn't letting anyone put a stethoscope to her barely beating heart. And, sure enough, the men around her smiled and nodded and let her walk back to us without a checkup. The whammy at work again.

"They won't bother us now. Let's go upstairs." She sniffed. "The whole building smells like smoke. My shoes had better not be ruined."

Diana looked at her with red eyes. "Your shoes? Your *shoes*? Excuse me? Do you see my shop? Glory's shop? We're out of business!"

I grabbed Diana's arm. "We'll be fine. Damian's bound to have insurance." Hope. Pray. Damian Sabatini was Flo's brother and owned the building. "Upstairs. Get a shower and some dry clothes."

"Electricity will be off for a while, people." Another fireman, a captain according to his helmet. "Here are some flashlights. But please just gather what you need for the night and make plans to sleep elsewhere. Until the building inspector gives the go ahead to occupy the residences."

I realized we were lucky no one had asked why we all were ready for bed at what must be seven in the evening. We were a pretty strange looking group.

We heard a shout and I saw Diana grabbed by two of her employees. I caught some snatches. Slow time of day. No customers so both workers had been in the back area making up a batch of the muffins the place was famous for. At least neither of them had been hurt.

A car pulled up behind the fire engine and a man jumped out. Damian aka Casanova. He's a sexy vampire, but I'm now immune. He'd played some dirty tricks on me while trying to add another notch to his bed post.

Did I mention he's our landlord? I was actually glad to see him and his look of concern. Please let him have insurance. I sure didn't. I know. I know. But the premiums! I looked back at the shop. Maybe I'd rethink my priorities if my business survived this.

"Florence, Gloriana, are you all right?" He grabbed Flo and looked her over. "Diana?"

"We're all fine, Damian." Flo hugged him before we all turned to head upstairs.

"Wait!" Someone grabbed my arm. "Donna Mitchell, Channel Six News. The fireman said this is your shop?" A female reporter dressed in a blazer and running shoes thrust a microphone near my mouth. I started to brush her off, then glanced at the front of my shop again.

"Yes. This is, *was* my place. Vintage Vamp's Emporium, offering fine clothing and accessories from the past at bargain prices." Okay, so I had to plug it, even if I had no idea if I even had a shop anymore. Tears filled my eyes and the camera zoomed in. Nothing like a tragedy to boost ratings.

"Any idea what happened, Ms. . . . ?"

"Gloriana St. Clair." I hitched my slipping blanket up on my shoulders. My wet hair dripped into my eyes. I was damned mad and looking pitiful worked for me right now. Valdez pressed himself against my legs and looked up at me soulfully. "We all work night shifts, so my dog here helped wake us up." I patted him on the head and he showed his teeth in a doggy grin. "Someone did this on purpose."

"Are you saying this was arson?" The reporter was all business now, gesturing at the cameraman so he could pan to the broken and blackened windows.

"Absolutely." I looked directly at the camera when it was aimed at me again. "And I want to put whoever did this on notice. I *will* reopen. I will *not* just disappear."

"Gee, you make this sound like a hate crime. Are you, um, a minority?"

Blond, blue-eyed white girl a minority? I smiled and read the reporter's mind. Hmm. I could set her straight, ha-ha, but why bother?

"I'm a woman, trying to support myself. Some people"—maybe I was digging a hole here—"don't like independence or people who are different."

The reporter thrust the microphone at Flo who had somehow managed to pull her hair back into a chic ponytail, her sheet now a toga that Julius Caesar himself had probably taught her how to wrap.

"Are you Ms. St. Clair's partner?"

Flo grinned, obviously reading the reporter's mind too.

"Glory and I haven't been together long"—she linked her arm through mine—"and the business is all hers. Me, I'm into new. I have a wonderful shoe collection, spared by the fire, thank God. I just hope Glory's business survives this." Flo actually kissed my cheek and I swear I jumped a foot.

"We're not—"

"Hush, Glory. Let me tell Donna about my shoes." Flo began rattling off designer names until the reporter's eyes glazed and she signaled the cameraman to cut.

"I think we have enough. Excuse me, I see an arson investigator has arrived. Good luck with your business, Ms. St. Clair. Here's my card. If you need to contact me for a follow-up."

Follow-up. I took one more long look at my shop, shook my head then went inside the apartment building. The halls were wet and the smell of smoke made my nose run and my eyes sting. I climbed the stairs, then stepped over the door Valdez had knocked down to get me out. The frame was broken, the locks shattered. I felt him beside me.

"You really are a hero, Valdez." I dropped to my knees and buried my face in his damp fur. Oh, great. *Now* I cried. I held onto him and felt Flo patting my back. I know blood-sucking vampires are supposed to be tough, but we're still human, sort of. We have *feelings*. I swear sometimes I think if I didn't have bad luck I'd have no luck at all.

Three

"Gloriana, sweetheart. Och now, don't cry."

I was gently lifted off of Valdez and wrapped in strong masculine arms. Definitely an improvement over smoke-tinged dog fur. And don't you love the Scottish thing? I've always had a weakness for it.

"Blade." I sagged against him, for once glad of his need to take care of me. When I'd first met Jeremiah Campbell, I was attracted to his take-charge attitude. Hey, it was 1604. That's what men did back then. I closed my eyes and inhaled. Jerry smelled of male and midnight. One whiff and I was right back at the Globe and the early days of hot sex and his promise of "I'll be here for you forever." It was all I could do not to wrap my legs around his waist and beg him to take me.

I got a grip. Barely. We're friends now, sometimes lovers, but I couldn't or wouldn't just relapse into a quivering mass of female insecurities around him.

"Did you see my shop?" I looked up and saw his teeth clench.

"What was left of it." His arms tightened around me. "Damn Westwood. I'll find him and rip his throat out. Tear him apart. There won't be enough left of him to interest carrion. He'll pay for this, Gloriana."

"What if he didn't do it?" I wiped at my eyes, then leaned against his hard chest for a moment longer.

"Who else?"

"I don't know. I've had headaches. And a voice in my

head. Menacing." I looked up at Blade who was glaring at Valdez. Obviously the dog hadn't mentioned this in his reports. Yeah, he's Jerry's furry spy.

"A voice? What the hell is this?"

"Forget it. Had to be Westwood. The voice has to be another vampire—" I heard Jerry's chest rumble. Had he *growled*? "Come on, Jerry. A vampire wouldn't burn up another one. Plus it was daylight."

"With enough hatred, some would hire it done." Jerry put me from him. "I can't imagine you with such an enemy, but tell me more."

I sank down on the couch. "Not now. I've had a rough night. And quit giving Valdez the evil eye. If it hadn't been for this dog—" My voice broke. Burned in my sleep. The end. No encores. Hey, I'd decided to be immortal, I damned well intended to keep on keeping on.

"Yeah, I really earned my Twinkies today. Dragging four vampires all the way to the roof, up lots of stairs. And I had to knock down doors with double dead bolts." Valdez paused for a weary breath. Oh, yeah, he was pouring on the drama. *"Except for Florence, none of them was exactly a lightweight if you know what I mean."* Valdez bumped my leg with his nose. *"Someone promised to buy me Cheetos."*

Jerry pulled me up to hug me again, before he settled me back on the couch. "Valdez, you've gone a long way toward earning your freedom. But if you ever withhold information again—"

"No way, boss. I was gonna tell you if somebody actually made a move on Glory. Hey, it was just a voice. I never saw anybody." Valdez laid his head on my knee. *"Glory knows I've got her back."*

Jerry frowned, then turned to pick up the door and lean it against the wall. I watched his muscles bulge under his black sweater. Black sweater, dark jeans, black loafers. With his dark eyes and hair, Jerry had the vamp look going on. Not that a mortal would see him that way. All they'd see was a handsome man in his prime. Jerry always could light my fire, and I was feeling an urge to reaffirm life if you know what I mean.

"I heard the fireman tell you to evacuate." Jerry turned back to me. "Come home with me, Glory. Let me take care of you."

I had my mouth open to say hell yes when Flo emerged from her bedroom. She was dressed in one of her favorite outfits. I won't describe it, just know it was cut down to there and up to here. And black. She wore red heels, her current favorites. If we were hosting a cocktail party, she was good to go. She was cradling a pair of Manolo stilettos.

"My poor babies. They have survived, but stink of smoke. So do I." She sighed and stroked the shoes. "I am devastated."

"You'll come home with me, Florence. I have a steam shower that will set you to rights. *Si?*" Damian lounged in the doorway. "You can come too, Gloriana. I've offered all the residents of the building rooms." He winked at me. "Of course it will be a little crowded, *cara*. Some of us may have to double up."

"Back off, Sabatini. Gloriana's coming home with me." Blade slung his arm around my shoulders. "Aren't you, sweetheart?"

How nice. I was still dripping and stinky, but two hunky vamps were fighting over me. Well, maybe not actually fighting. And Jerry had asked instead of ordered. He knew Damian had been pursuing me. Jerry was jealous. Excellent. I threw up a block so Jerry wouldn't be able to tell just how *not* tempted I was by the Italian stud's offer.

"Jerry's right, Damian. I'm going home with him. But thanks for the offer." I glanced at Flo, very aware of my wet jammies, wet sheet, wet blanket . . . you get the picture.

"Leave her alone, Damian. Jeremiah will take care of her." Flo grabbed her brother's hand and dragged him toward her bedroom. "Come help me. I've three suitcases and my shoes, of course, that you must carry downstairs."

"I'm going to hire a restoration company. They'll come

in here. Get rid of the stink. Even clean your clothes." Damian had a hunted look when Flo started filling his hands with shoe boxes. "You two should be able to move back in a day or two, a week at the most."

"No company will touch my shoes, Damian." Flo eyed Jerry. "I don't suppose you'd take down a load for me, Jeremiah."

"He's helping me, Flo. Make two,"—I watched the tower of shoe boxes Damian was balancing wobble—"or six trips."

"Fine." Flo is always practical, and she liked seeing me with Jerry. She's convinced we're probably fated to be together, since we've kept our relationship going on and off for centuries. When Flo's through with a lover, they might as well be dead. She never looks back. I've looked back way too often.

"Maybe I'll ask those cute firemen to help me. This *is* an emergency." Flo picked up a velvet sack with her most expensive ostrich pumps. "Come on, Damian. You'd better have brought one of your big cars."

Damian muttered something vile under his breath as he stalked into the hall. There was a crash, then a slap and Flo shouted Italian insults. I managed a laugh, even though I was more than a little depressed by the smell and the thought of having to pack. I stood and stretched.

"Let me grab some stuff and get dressed and I'll be ready in a minute." I patted Valdez on the head. "Jerry, would you help out by grabbing some of this pup's treats from the kitchen? He'll tell you what to bring."

"*I sure will.*" Valdez trotted toward the kitchen. "*The Twinkies are in the cabinet next to the refrigerator. Glory probably wants some of that bottled stuff she drinks too. And the lights are out. There's a rib eye in the freezer that will ruin if I don't eat it soon.*"

"One moment." Jerry reached out and pulled me back into his arms. He looked at me for a long moment. Probing my mind? Or my heart? "Are you really all right? I almost lost you."

I swallowed. Nobody can do intense like Blade. I reached

up and stroked his cheek, rough because he hadn't shaved. In fact, Valdez's report that we were on the roof had probably sent Jerry straight from his bed to my side.

"You haven't lost me, Jeremiah. And you won't." I pulled his head down and kissed him. Not a little peck either. I was already in life-affirming mode. When I leaned back I glanced at the doorway. Damian was back for another load. He grinned and winked. The man thinks the world revolves around him. I'm sure he interpreted that kiss as an attempt to make him jealous. I smiled back. Whatever.

"Damian, this smell disgusts me. Hurry." Flo pushed him across the room. "Glory, I take the *Sex and the City* DVDs with me. Okay?"

I shrugged. TV was the last thing on my mind right now.

"You expect me to watch your girlie TV shows?" Damian came out loaded like a pack mule. "I'll pay the company double. You'll be back here by tomorrow."

Flo sniffed. "I don't think so. And, *caro*, you could learn a lot about women from that show." She patted his cheek.

"Pah! I know all I need to." He gave me a smoldering look. "I've had no complaints."

"Not to your face anyway, little brother." Flo smiled as two burly firemen appeared in the hall doorway. In minutes she had everything loaded and shouted "Ciao," on her way out the door.

I headed into the bedroom. Boy, did I need a shower. I reeked. To hell with it. The building looked safe enough to me. Sure, with the electricity out, it was dark, but with vamp vision, that was no problem for me.

I hit the bathroom, shut the door and stripped down. Shampoo, that stupid generic cream rinse that left my hair limp and about ten minutes under hot spray had me feeling a thousand times better. No hair dryer, but I combed out the tangles and pulled my hair back. Of course the clothes I had to put on smelled bad, but I didn't plan to keep them on long. When I got back to Jerry's place I was going to thank him very personally for a place to stay and for making Valdez watch over me.

I stared at my rumpled bed. The fire hadn't made it upstairs, but it could have. And I would have . . . The bed blurred and I grabbed a tissue. Damn it, even *it* stunk like smoke. I threw some things into a suitcase and opened the door to the living room. Blade was there talking to a fireman who obviously was anxious for us to vacate the premises.

"We're leaving. Right now." Jerry smiled at me. "You look wonderful, dearling."

"We need to know where to reach you. The arson crew's down there right now. This fire was no accident. An investigator's going to want to question you." The fireman glanced at the door leaning against the wall. "As soon as we get a structural report, we can let you know when it's safe to return here."

"Sure. Fine." I grabbed a magazine, tore off the cover and scribbled my cell phone number on it. "You can reach me here." I thought about shouting accusations along with the name of suspect number one. Brent Westwood couldn't be allowed to get away with this. But Jerry squeezed my hand. He had his own plans for Westwood.

If the billionaire was responsible, the fire was just the latest in the hunter's attacks on vampires. The man had almost killed me more than once, and he wore a necklace made of fangs. I shuddered, remembering. Two of those fangs had belonged to Jerry's best friend.

Valdez woofed and headed for the door, obviously ready to get out of here. Me too. I held on to Jerry's hand and looked around. My home. I wasn't sure if I'd ever feel the same way about it again.

"We're outta here."

"Come here, Gloriana."

I slammed the lid on the washer and turned the knob. At least I'd have clean clothes tomorrow. I smiled at Blade who'd been beyond patient as he waited for me to cook

Valdez's steak, rare of course. Then throw my first load into the dryer.

"Is that an order?" I moved up close and put my hands on his sweater, dark, like his eyes. His hair was wild, like he'd run his hands through it. I reached up to tweak it into place, almost holding my breath while I waited for his answer. This was old territory with us. He ordered, I didn't obey. Splitsville.

"Nay. I may have been slow with ye, Glory, but I finally understand that ye dunna take orders well."

"And you also understand that I melt for the whole Scottish Highlander thing." I grinned and slipped my hand under his sweater. Firm stomach, warm, not cold like people think vampires should be. We have a little heat, though not the same as mortals.

"Are ye? Melting?" He pushed his own hand into the back of my hair and looked into my eyes.

"Aye." I stretched up to kiss his smiling mouth. "Take me to bed, ye lusty Scot. I have a need for—" He kissed me silent, then swung me into his arms. He strode past Valdez who was sacked out on the living room couch, his paw on the remote control as he searched for porn. Have I mentioned that the dog is such a . . . guy?

"Hey, look. We're on the ten o'clock news."

Jerry stopped behind the couch. "You were on the roof."

I felt his arms around me. Good, at least he wasn't dumping me on my ass. Gloriana with a sheet over her head was not a pretty sight.

"Must be a slow news day." The reporter's voice described the scene, but the billowing smoke told the tale. Then we were in front of my shop. The interview. Valdez was by my side looking like a regular dog, a black Labradoodle with a cute face and wagging tail. Amazing that he looked so ordinary. Especially since he'd spent the afternoon dragging vampires up flights of stairs to safety.

The camera panned to my burned-out shop and I swallowed. Would I be able to rebuild? I'd sunk everything I owned into that shop. I'd never let Jerry take care of me, though he'd offered often enough. I could always waitress again. I'd gotten good tips, especially if I showed some cleavage. Forget cleavage. On TV I looked like hell. Wet hair hanging, raccoon eyes because I'd fallen asleep with my makeup on. A bad habit, but my skin will always be twenty-four years old. Don't you hate me? I don't even use moisturizer.

On TV Flo was clinging to me like plastic wrap and all of Austin now thought we were a couple. Though why a hottie like Flo would hook up with a woman who looked four feet wide in her fireman blanket—

"I think you and Florence make a cute couple." Jerry dropped a kiss on my head.

I socked him in the arm. "How about some sympathy here?"

"You have that." A softer kiss this time, close to my ear. "I'm sorry about your business, Gloriana. If you want to rebuild, I'll help."

Help. As in labor? Knowing Jerry, it was help as in throwing money at the situation. Unless he was needed for swordplay, that was his best move. He could afford it. But could I afford the complications?

"Thanks. Let me see what the damage is first. And if Damian had any insurance."

Valdez was doing his thing with the remote again. Forget Valdez. Jerry carried me up the stairs. To his bedroom. I admit I've spent a few nights there. He has a really nice home that he rents from Damian, who is a real estate tycoon. Renting. Like maybe he wouldn't stay in Austin. Jerry had moved here from Shreveport to be near me. But he didn't have any other reason to stay. I had to quit thinking. No problem. Especially when he dropped me on his king-sized bed.

He stripped off his sweater, grinning when I tossed my own across the room. I hadn't bothered with a bra. They were all in the wash. Jerry fell on top of me. I laughed and pretended he'd knocked the wind out of me. Fat chance.

With my vamp strength I could toss him across the room. He obviously read my mind because he shook his head.

"Only if I were unconscious."

"Aw, come on. Let me try." I pushed at him. No go. His face got serious just before he kissed me. He was obviously in life-affirming mode too. When we came up for air, I ran my hands through his thick hair.

"We probably should shut the door."

Blade didn't answer, just nuzzled my breast. The door slammed shut and the lock clicked. Got to love vamp powers. Not that I was really paying that much attention. Not with Blade's mouth on my nipple.

I held on to his hair and just relaxed into the moment. I *saw* his jeans off of him and they hit the floor. I can make things move with my mind. Pretty cool. I concentrated and my skirt and panties landed next to Jerry's jeans. Now we were skin to skin, my favorite way to be with Jerry. He chuckled and looked at me.

"I love your new tricks, lass. Mayhap you'd like to see one of mine." He reached down to stroke my hip.

A new trick? We'd had some amazing sex over the centuries. On mountaintops, in caves, not to mention that tricky time on horseback. I smiled and ran my hands over his firm buttocks.

"Only if it involves you screwing me until I go blind."

Four

"Definitely." Jerry's chuckle rippled through me. God, everything he did was sexy.

"Then go for it."

"First, close your eyes." Jerry rolled over until I was on top of him. "No peeking. Not until I tell you to."

I did as he asked. Four hundred years. You'd think that sex would get boring. And the same old same old might. But with a vampire, there was always a little something extra. Vampire men are like that bunny in the commercial—they keep going and going . . . Boy, could I tell you stories. And then there's the mind reading. Try drawing a mental map for your lover of hot spots that need attention. I took a deep breath. What did I smell? Lilacs? I *love* lilacs.

I kept my eyes closed even though I could tell I was no longer on Blade's pillow-top mattress. I was warm, floating, but not in water. Then I settled onto something hard and slightly scratchy. What?

"Open your eyes, Gloriana."

I did and gasped. We were in an English garden. One very like the one my mother had tended behind our house when I'd been a child. Lilacs were in bloom, bees buzzed and I lay on a blanket under the tree that had been next to the pond. And the sun. The sun was shining, warming my naked body. I looked at Jerry, at the way the light hit his broad chest and the proof that he still wanted me. I leaned on one elbow, striking a pose that pushed out my breasts.

"How—"

"Don't worry about how. Just relax and enjoy." Jerry picked up a ripe strawberry and brought it to my lips. "Eat."

I inhaled and almost cried again. The delicious smell . . . "I . . . I can't."

"Yes, you can. This isn't real, Gloriana. We're living a fantasy. One of yours, I hope." Jerry grinned and pushed the strawberry into my mouth. "Bite. Remember the sweetness. Taste it."

"You're kidding." I admit I'm a little food obsessed. Remember the Cheetos debacle? The berry burst in my mouth. Too divine. I chewed, but hesitated. Okay, I took a chance and swallowed. "Will this hurt me? You know when I ate those Cheetos . . ." I sucked in my tummy. Damned stupid Cheetos bulge.

"Would I do that to you?" He smiled and laid his hand on my tummy. "And you don't have to hold this in. I think you're perfect just as you are."

I put my hand over his. Perfect? Of course. This was my fantasy after all. And I'd just had a *strawberry*.

"Mmmm. Have I told you you're a genius?" I reached for another berry. He'd conjured up a whole bowl of them. God, how I'd missed this. Food. That's why I'd made a fool of myself over Cheetos. I *had* to learn how to do this trick.

"I'll teach you how. Someday." Jerry picked up a pastry. "Smell."

"Oh, my God. Lemon tart?" I dipped a finger into the filling. This felt so real. And when I licked my finger clean, my tastebuds were in full party mode. I sighed with pleasure. "You did this for me?" I scooped up another finger full and wrote a "G" on his bare chest.

"This is amazing. How can I ever repay you?" I leaned forward, my tongue tracing a path down his stomach. Mmm. Blade and lemon. Delicious. I reached for another tart.

"You're doing a pretty good job of it." He gasped when I scooped up more lemon and dropped a dollop of it on his jutting penis. "Of course if you'd like to lick that off . . ."

"That's the plan." I slid down his body. He lay back and groaned when I took him in my mouth. I stroked him, inhaled him and made him arch off the blanket when I swept my tongue around his hot length. Mmm, those vamp powers. I didn't have to look at a clock to know he could stay hard and ready for me for hours. And he'd have to, because it was definitely *my* turn.

I sat up and tossed my hair behind my back. Jerry's eyes had actually rolled back in his head and a fine sheen of sweat glistened on his pecs when he clinched his fists. Birds still sang, bees still buzzed, but my heart seemed to stop as I looked down at him.

"Earth to Jerry."

"I'm here. Barely." He opened his eyes as he leaned up to slide his tongue across one of my nipples. Then his fangs, deliciously sharp and dangerous, traced a path over my breasts.

I reached for another strawberry. "Want one?"

"Nay, lass. I hunger for something much sweeter. But go ahead. I like seeing your pleasure." He held onto my breast and watched me.

Sex with a handsome man? Or strawberries? Okay, so I'm one sick puppy. But for a moment the fruit won. I bit into a berry and the sweetness filled my mouth again. The thrill was almost enough to make me forget Jerry's fingers toying with my nipples. Almost. But I ate another, then rubbed a third across Jerry's smiling lips and kissed him. So delicious. I sat up and ate the last of the strawberries.

Sue me, but I'm full-figured for a reason. I always loved my food. And after I married unwisely, we'd struggled on an actor's pay. Treats like strawberries had been unheard of. Then I'd been widowed. I'd been hungry, a lot. Only Billy Shakespeare's kindness in letting me play an occasional part and repair costumes, had kept me from starving.

Jerry's hands gripped my ass before his fingers drifted between my thighs, finding me ready and then some.

"I'll ne'er forget the night I met you." Jerry smiled and touched me until I gasped. "I knew you were no man on that stage."

I explored his firm chest. "Are you saying I was a poor actor?" I lightly pinched one of his nipples. I'd been a woman pretending to be a man playing a woman. Billy Shakespeare always had loved that type of game.

"Never that. You had the audience convinced. But then I'm no ordinary man, you see." He slipped two fingers inside me and I swear my eyes crossed.

"Yes, I do see, sort of." I put my hand around his cock. "Not ordinary at all."

"You won me twenty guineas that night." He grinned, stroking me just the way I liked.

I returned the favor, moving my hand in a rhythm that had him pushing into my hand.

"So glad I could help." I sent him a mental message. Harder. Deeper. I moaned when he slid his fingers even farther inside me. "You were bold that night."

"Aye, and I got my face slapped for it."

"As you should have." Blade had come backstage and, before I'd known what he was about, he'd thrust his hand down my bodice and up my skirt.

"You held back, lass. I know a love tap when I feel one."

I kissed his cheek, rough with evening beard. "Mayhap I like bold. And you did offer to buy me a late supper. I was a greedy wench." Still am, truth be told. I leaned into his open-mouthed kiss, greedy for *him*.

I'd been *easy* for him too since the moment I'd seen him. He'd fed all my hungers, wining and dining me until I was stuffed like a Christmas goose. I hadn't known he was vampire at first. When he'd finally taken me, I'd been so hot for him, he could have bit off my left tit and I would have begged for him to take the other one. As it was, I found the blood drinking incredibly erotic. Feeding him, feeling the pull from my neck to my womb. My body clenched, remembering.

Little wonder I'd finally begged him to make me vampire. So we could live together forever. Forever is a long, long time.

Jerry pulled me up his body until I sat astride his clever mouth. Oh, God. I leaned back, turning my face to the sun. When he stroked me with his tongue, I shuddered and made those stupid little sounds I make when I'm close to coming. He held me to him. I bucked when his tongue darted inside and his fangs touched me. Then he sucked. Oh, sweet Lord. I held back when I wanted to bounce on him like a pogo stick.

"I . . . I can't. I'll crush you." I felt him smile against me. He lifted me slightly, just to prove he could, I guess.

"You're a feather, lass."

A feather? Don't I wish. You'd think a vamp's liquid diet would make you thin. No such luck. I'd been supersized when he'd turned me. I'd be supersized forever.

"Quit thinking, Gloriana." Of course he'd read my mind. My insecurities. He looked up, his eyes twinkling. "And if you crush me, lass, know that any man would be happy to die with his face buried in—"

"Jeremiah!"

Jerry grinned, then slid me down until I felt his erection between my thighs.

I quivered and opened my legs. I needed him, inside me. *Now.*

"Not yet, lass. Patience." He flipped us until I was beside him on that damned blanket.

"When did you become a tease?" My mood was deteriorating. I nudged his erection with my knee. "I want you, Jerry."

"Of course." Arrogant Scot. "First, tell me something you'd like to taste."

I looked down at his erection. "Well . . ."

He growled and gave me a hot look. "Careful, lass.

You're going to undo me." He took a breath, visibly taking control of himself. "I'm not through with this fantasy. Food. Tell me something you never got to taste when you were mortal."

I grinned. We both knew I'd tasted *him* back in the day. So I took about half a second to think about mortal treats. "Ice cream. Chocolate."

"Ah, a challenge. And a mortal favorite. I've heard a few moaning with pleasure over such a simple food. You'd think they were having great sex."

Before I could blink, he had a double scoop cone of rich deep chocolate ice cream in his hand. I swear my taste buds tingled. I know my thighs did.

"Taste." He held it inches from my mouth.

I inhaled, then sighed. "Forget it. What good would it do? Lemon? Yes. Strawberries? Of course. But chocolate ice cream? It wasn't even thought of when we were alive. You can't possibly know—"

"But I can. When I saw those mortals, usually women, crying out with pleasure over the dish, I probed their minds. A man needs to know these things. What gives a woman such satisfaction." Jerry made a show of stroking his tongue over the ice cream. "Ahh. I think I see the appeal."

"Vicarious eating. Wow. Now *that's* something I have to try."

"But not now." Jerry shifted so that I leaned against his chest. I couldn't take my eyes off the cone in his hands. Chocolate ice cream melted down his fingers. "Come now, lass. You know you want a taste."

I reached out with my tongue. Sweet, dark and as erotic in its own way as the man smiling at me, his eyes sparkling with pleasure. At *my* pleasure. I took a greedy bite, then licked his fingers clean before I tossed the cone aside to kiss him. How could I waste my time on food when I had a man ready to satisfy a much deeper hunger? A dear man who knew how to please me and, better yet, took the time to do it. I wrapped my legs around his hips and finally, finally he let me take him in. I shuddered. He fit me like no else ever did. No one.

"Gloriana," he whispered as he moved over me. "Blind yet?"

I pretended to grope for his face. "Not yet. But everything's going dark." I squealed when he pulled me up until we were face-to-face, still connected. The new position shocked me into an orgasm.

"I think this may be better than chocolate," I whispered.

"You think?" He touched me just right to send another jolt through me.

"Okay," I said when I caught my breath again. "This is better than chocolate, way better." I kissed him and held onto him when we moved together. So good, so good, so incredibly, unbelievably good. I closed my eyes, my world went black and I broke apart.

When I opened my eyes again, I was back in Blade's bed. No sign of chocolate, strawberries or lemon tarts. And no sign of Blade.

"*Finally*, *you're awake.*" Valdez dropped my purse next to my head. "*Your damned cell phone's been ringing all day. I don't know how I'm expected to function as your body guard without my sleep.*"

"Whining's very unattractive, fur face." I pushed my hair out of my eyes and sat up. Oops. Not wearing anything. I held the sheet up to my chin. Valdez and I've been together for five years now. He's probably seen more of me than he wanted to, but that didn't mean I liked to flaunt it. Dog form he may be, but I know he's also something else, something or someone who has a decidedly masculine gleam in his dark brown eyes.

"Where's Blade?" I pushed Valdez off the bed. "Turn your back." When he did, I hightailed it to the bathroom and the robe I knew Jerry kept on the back of the door. It dragged the ground, but was a nice thick terry that covered me from neck to toe.

"Blade's downstairs. He and Mara are having words." Valdez was back on the bed again, glaring at my purse. It was ringing, "Phantom of the Opera." I love Broadway show tunes and you can imagine why Phantom is one of my faves. *"You gonna answer this?"*

I dove for the purse and fished out the phone just as it stopped. A beep and I saw that I had missed ten calls with five voice messages. Scrolling through the system, it was easy to see that most of the calls had been from the fire department. My day employees had called too. And the vamp who filled in some nights for me had just left message number six.

"Blade and Mara? What kind of words?"

"Fighting words. It's a hate-a-thon. Westwood being at the top of their list."

"They're not fighting each other?" Mara MacTavish is the widow of Blade's best friend, the one the vamp hunter had taken out. That fang necklace thing. Mara was not taking her loss well and who could blame her. She's obsessed with making Brent Westwood pay. I have no problem with that. What I do have a problem with is that she seems determined to use Blade, *my* Jeremy Blade, to do her dirty work. Okay, maybe that's not entirely true. Mara is more than capable of ripping Westwood's throat out. But the billionaire is proving to be too damned wily for even a vampire to catch.

"Nope. They're on the same page."

No surprise there. Blade's all for the revenge thing. If Mara weren't super sexy with the whole Scottish lass deal going for her, I would say let them have at it. But, while Jerry and I are on again, off again, that doesn't mean I like his off periods from me to be spent with beautiful women. Yeah, I'm perverse. I've always been happy to spend more than my share of off time with beautiful men when I can get them.

"Hello. Glory, answer the damned phone."

While I'd been lost in my dismal thoughts, the phone had started up again.

"Hello."

"Glory, finally! Are you all right?" Lacy Devereau, my shape-shifter day worker. She's actually a werecat. You can imagine what Valdez, überdog, thinks of her.

"I'm fine, Lacy. I'm at Blade's." I settled back on the pillows. My vamp healing sleep had taken care of any residual aches and pains from being dragged to the roof. "I guess you've seen the shop."

"Yeah." Big sigh. "And I had to fight like hell to get to my apartment to pick up a few things. They're investigating the cause of the fire and are supposed to be inspecting the building, but no one will tell me when we might be able to move back in."

"I've got some messages from the fire department, maybe that will tell me something." I mentally checked my bank balance. How long could I afford to keep my employees on the payroll without any income coming in? Answer: two days, three tops. "In the daylight, what does the shop look like? Do you think we can salvage anything?"

"Windows blown out. Everything soaked with water and some kind of chemicals." Another big sigh. "Burglar bars will keep looters out, but I'm not sure there's anything they'd want anyway. It looks pretty bad to me."

"That's what I thought when I saw it last night." I looked at Valdez who was obviously taking a nap. "You'd better look for another job, Lacy. I hate to lose you, but I don't know when or if we'll be able to reopen." I paid my employees minimum wage plus commission. The kind of people I hired didn't come with references and PhDs.

Lacy is a hard worker, good with customers and a werekitty who knows what I am and understands my weird schedule. I also had another vamp and a college student working for me. The mortal student was a merchandising major who did it for the love of the clothes. She spent more than she earned, maybe because she had a daddy bankrolling her.

"I've got some money saved and Damian is letting me stay at the castle until the apartments are livable again." Lacy giggled. "I have to share a bathroom with Florence. I don't see how you guys do it on a regular basis."

My roomie believes in the power of long soaks in fragrant bath salts. Sharing a bathroom with her is a challenge that I suddenly missed so much tears stung my eyes.

"Are you saying you'll help me fix up the shop? If it can be done?"

"Sure. You're going to need someone to handle the daylight hours. You know any repairs are gonna have to be made then."

"Yeah. My life is complicated." For a moment I missed Las Vegas. I'd spent a few decades there working as a dancer in a club/casino right off The Strip. No one questioned a night owl in Vegas. Austin was a tougher sell. But Austin is full of vamps and other immortals. I'm getting really comfortable being surrounded by my own kind.

"Glory? You do think we can get the shop going again, don't you?" Lacy cleared her throat. "I've had a lot of jobs over the years and working for you—"

"Say no more. We'll figure it out. Together." My phone beeped again, incoming call. "Thanks, Lacy. I'll get back to you as soon as I know anything. Say hi to Flo for me and ask her to loan you some of her brown sugar body scrub. It's to die for." I disconnected and took the other call.

"Ms. St. Clair? This is Steve Fleming with the Austin fire department, arson division."

"Umm, yes. What can I do for you?" I hate dealing with government bureaucracy. I know from experience that they have a nine-to-five kind of mentality. Getting them to wait until the sun goes down is a bitch. I usually have to whammy them into cooperating. Or get a friendly mortal or shifter like Lacy to do the daytime thing for me.

"I need to get a statement from you and ask you some questions. Could you meet me at the site?" Steve had a nice deep voice with a Texas drawl I found interesting. Valdez snorted in his sleep and rubbed his nose on Blade's pillow. Blade. I'd moved to Texas with the idea of hooking up with a cowboy type. But Blade in a Western shirt was close enough for me.

"When? Mr. er, Officer, er, Detective—" What the heck did you call an arson investigator anyway?

"Lieutenant Fleming, but call me Steve, ma'am. I understand from Ms. Devereau that you're a night person. Works for me. I'm on the night shift myself. How about meeting me in about an hour, in front of your shop?"

I glanced at the clock on the bedside table. "Ten o'clock?"

"Right. Is that possible?"

"Sure. And call me Glory. See you there." I lay back and rubbed my forehead. The business meant a lot to me. This fire had been personal and whoever had started it was going to pay. Big time.

Five

🦇

"**Y**ou're frowning." Jerry stood in the doorway with a glass of what looked like my favorite beverage in his hand. "Valdez, get your mangy hide off my bed."

I grinned and gave Valdez a shove. He jumped down quickly. He knew better than to cross Jerry. I don't know what my boyfriend has on the dog, but it must be pretty serious.

"*I'll be downstairs. Call if you need me.*" Valdez stretched, gave Jerry a tail wag as he walked by and disappeared down the hall.

"He never obeys *me* like that."

"Take a firm hand with him, Gloriana. He's here to serve you." Jerry sat on the edge of the bed and handed me the glass.

"Funny how that works. He's here to serve me, but if I want to go out alone . . ." I sniffed. Fangtastic in AB negative, my favorite. I took a sip.

"Not going to happen. He's here to *guard* you. Something he can't do locked in your apartment while you're out God knows where."

"I admit he saved me. But Jerry—"

"No buts."

I gave up for the moment and took a swallow of Fangtastic. Drinking fake blood is probably like drinking a diet decaf when you really want the full shot of caffeine and sugar. Pretty good, but nothing like the real deal straight from the source. Hey, I've evolved enough to survive on it.

"Thanks for the drink anyway. But,"—I held up my hand when he opened his mouth—"if I decide I want to go out alone, or with Flo, or anyone for that matter, I will. Sans dog."

"Promise you won't do anything foolish. Just to prove your independence." He watched me sip my drink. I licked my lips and his eyes narrowed.

"I *am* independent. Get used to the idea." Like that would ever happen. After four hundred years, I'd finally snapped to the fact that Jerry wasn't changing. Period. And this protective thing would really be pretty flattering if it weren't so damned invasive.

"I've been thinking about recent events. Valdez has proved his worth, but now I think he needs help." Jerry frowned.

I sat up. "Of course Valdez has proved himself. He managed fine without any help." The rejuvenating effect of fake blood was doing its thing. I was alert and a little pissed that I'd basically been talking to the hand.

"It's something we can discuss later." Jerry frowned, picked up his pillow and tossed it on the floor. "That damned dog stinks like smoke. We'll send him to a groomer in the morning. Louise will take him."

Jerry's housekeeper. "Warn her that Valdez isn't exactly thrilled to go to those places. I took him once, to an all-night place in Vegas. After he finally quit terrifying the staff, he let a female groomer, a cute young thing, bathe him. Then he got the poor girl fired because she accused him of sexual harassment, claimed he talked to her and made, um, lewd propositions while she was bathing him."

"He won't do that again or he'll answer to me. Until he completes his duties to my satisfaction, he knows I won't tolerate problems." Blade watched me closely when I lay back and stretched. Oops, that pesky robe just wouldn't stay closed. "What kind of lewd propositions?"

"Wouldn't you like to know." Bingo. Jerry's eyes gleamed and he reached for the robe's tie. "Maybe you can make me talk, with the right method of persuasion."

"To hell with the dog. I have my own lewd proposition. Starting with you naked."

"Careful. You'll spill my drink." I took a long swallow. "This is the good stuff. I can only afford O positive."

"I'll buy you a case of the damned stuff if you put down that glass."

I grinned when he opened the robe and laid me bare. I sucked in my stomach. Habit and a good habit at that. No matter what Jerry said, a tummy bulge is not sexy. Jerry ran a hand over it, then teased the curls between my legs.

"You look very good to me, lass. But if the Cheetos gave you pain, I say forget about them." He stroked his hand up to cup one of my breasts.

Easy to forget everything when his hands were on me. He was dressed in a black polo and jeans. Strong, masculine and his smile showed me fangs that had me aching for him. There's nothing better than sex with a vampire. Take my word for it. Feeding from each other while doing the deed is beyond orgasmic. We'd done a little fang action in his secret garden, but I was always up for a rerun.

"I'm supposed to meet an arson investigator at my shop in an hour." I drained my glass, set it on the nightstand, then shrugged out of the robe.

"Then we'll have to hurry." Jerry ripped his shirt off over his head and then stood. Vamp speed had his jeans off and sailing across the room in less time than you could say hot body. I reached for him and brought him down on top of me. I cradled him between my legs and kissed him. We were comfortable lovers together. But last night had proved, to me anyway, that we still had things to show each other. I nipped his ear with my fangs then flipped him off of me.

"What's this?" Jerry grinned up at me.

"Roll over." I gave him a shove and he lay on his stomach, his head on his arms.

"Are you giving me a massage?"

"Huh?" I was a little distracted. Muscular male buns do that to me. Not to mention a strong back that has scars from his warrior days, prevampire. He'd kicked off his shoes and even his feet were sexy. I ran my hands up the backs of his hairy legs, then leaned down to nibble a path up to his backside. His muscles twitched against my tongue. I pushed his legs apart and found those sacs that were firm and warm. I tasted them until he groaned and reached for me.

"Nay, warrior. I would pleasure ye." The actress in me had always been good with an accent.

"You torture me, lass. I want my hands on you." No acting from Jerry. He was in pain.

"Forget it. Hold on to the headboard. This is my treat." I raised his hips and slipped under him. I touched him, stroked him, then pushed my fangs into the sweet spot inside his thigh.

"Good God, Gloriana!" He jerked and I heard the headboard crack.

I tasted his essence, his blood, then his maleness. Before I knew it, he was on top of me in another of his vamp moves, pushing inside me before I offered my neck and he drank. I felt the pull of his mouth all through me. Waves of pleasure curled my toes and had me scoring his back with my nails. By the time we'd collapsed next to each other in a tangle of sheets, I knew I was going to be very late for my date with the arson investigator. And I could not care less.

"Are you ever going to get out of that bed?"

I looked up and met Mara's gaze. I didn't bother to erase the dreamy look I probably still had on my face, along with whisker burns . . . Well, you get it and so did she. She dumped a laundry basket on the bed.

"Louise folded your laundry for you." Mara held up a T-shirt, one of my favorites from the annual Austin Bat Festival. "Are you sure you can fit in this?" She held it up to her B cup chest. "It'll be quite a stretch."

I grabbed the robe that had landed on the floor beside

the bed and slipped into it. "Give that here. What have you done to my clothes?" The last was a wail. My XL shirt had shrunk to a barely medium.

"I didn't put this stuff in the dryer." Mara's smirk was not attractive. "On hot."

"Oh, jeez." I sat on the edge of the bed. I hadn't exactly been firing on all cylinders the night before. And I'd been paying way too much attention to Blade's personal equipment and not nearly enough to his laundry equipment.

"Check out the jeans. I'd pay money to see you fit into these." She tossed my vintage jeans, the well-worn ones that had actually fit like a glove, into my lap.

"I'll make them fit." I ignored Valdez's chuff of amusement. He'd seen me struggle into tight jeans before. Not a pretty picture. "Where's Blade?"

"Out." Mara frowned and sat on the foot of the bed. Obviously Jerry hadn't deigned to include her in his plans.

"I've got to get to the shop. I'm meeting an arson investigator." I stood and fished underwear and a bra out of the basket. They hadn't shrunk, but then a thong doesn't have much to it anyway. The bra looked a little sad, but the double D industrial strength ones I wore most days could take a lot of punishment.

"Arson. You know it had to be Westwood." Mara's hands were fisted on her knees. She had on the kind of low slung skinny jeans I'd have killed to be able to wear and a tank top that almost hit the waist band. Men loved the look. All she needed was a belly ring. But piercings close during vamp sleep. I know, I've tried and ain't that a bitch?

"Yes, probably Westwood." I started to put my hand on her shoulder, but thought better of it. She is an old, old, old acquaintance. We'd never been friends, because I'm a low class actress type and she's practically royalty to hear her tell it. But I've known her since my first visit to Scotland and Campbell Castle. She and MacTavish had been so in love. And Westwood now sported Mac's fangs on his trophy necklace.

"Valdez says you and Jerry were talking about West-wood earlier."

"Talking?" She grimaced at my dog, who sat at her feet as if hoping she'd actually pet him. Did I mention Mara is gorgeous? "We were yelling, more like."

"I know. I hate the hunter too." I sat next to her on the bed. Not touching. She'd not appreciate that kind of famil-iarity from an underling. "What are we going to do about it?"

"Jeremiah and I are going to hunt him down. And . . ." Her green eyes shimmered with unshed tears. One crystal drop slid down her porcelain cheek. Of course she cried prettily. I get a red nose and puffy eyes. It's common among us underlings.

"You have to be careful, Mara. Westwood's got more money than God and all the latest technology." Including a high-tech vamp detector. I hate that thing. I've blended with mortals successfully for centuries. And with one blast of his ray gun, the hunter had seen through all my excellent acting skills.

"We'll be careful. But we *will* destroy him." Mara jumped to her feet. All tears had dried up in the heat of her rage. "But not before we make him suffer."

I watched Valdez scoot out of range when she stomped one foot. Not that Prada sandals could do him much harm.

"Cute shoes." I'd heard these rants before and Westwood wasn't the only one richer than God.

"You are so . . . useless." She gave me a disdainful look and stormed out of the room, slamming the door behind her.

"Low blow." Valdez jumped up on the bed and nosed my jeans. *"These are going to be a challenge."*

"You should have bit her on her skinny ass. She insulted me." I snatched up the jeans and the rest of what I needed and headed for the bathroom.

"Blade wouldn't allow me to hurt her." Valdez stayed on the bed and watched me. *"He's very protective of her."*

"I know." I leaned against the door jamb. "And she's right. I *am* useless."

"Not true. You saved the day or night on Halloween." Valdez licked one paw. *"You would be nothing but a set of fangs on a necklace right now if you hadn't distracted Westwood at the critical moment."*

"That *was* pretty cool." I'd been inches away from being skewered, but I'd practiced a little self-defense and visualization and actually saved myself. Unfortunately, the ensuing chaos had allowed Westwood to get away from Blade. Jerry had wounded him, but Mara wasn't ever going to forget that I'd caused Jerry to focus on me instead of Westwood. I was sorry about the guy getting away, but I *hadn't* been useless that night.

I looked around. My distraction had involved setting a fire. Hey, I could start something right now, just to prove I still had it in me. Forget the bed—brass, and I'd developed a real fondness for it.

"Blade's not gonna like it if you set his stuff on fire, Blondie. Besides, I for one never want to smell smoke again." Valdez snorted and licked his other paw.

I sniffed. Thanks to my sensitive nose, I didn't have to be close to realize Valdez reeked. "You're going to the groomer in the morning. You'd better behave."

"No way. Put me in the shower. Like you do at home." He leaped off the bed and practically knocked me down getting into the bathroom. *"Please, Blondie. You know I hate those places. They leave a guy no dignity."*

He'd managed to get the shower door open and stood looking at me hopefully. I had a handheld showerhead at home and bathing him was a weekly ritual I'd insisted on. I looked at the gleaming glass box with everything from a rain showerhead to multiple body sprays. I couldn't wait to check it out for myself.

"You leave *yourself* no dignity. Propositioning the shampoo girl. You got her fired." I opened a cabinet and found a bottle of shower gel, a manly scent that Valdez would approve of. He hated my flowery gels. Too bad I'd left the flea shampoo at home.

"Not my fault. She got soap in my eyes. I couldn't just bark. *And then when I'd already blown my cover and I could see again, I thought, hey, she's cute. Why waste an opportunity?"* Valdez let me squirt the gel all over him. There was a toe tester and it took a moment to get the temperature to his liking. Then I reached in to turn on the shower, jumped out of the way, and watched him sit under the spray.

"Any woman who would accept a proposition from a dog, sorry, but that's what you are, my friend, is not a woman you would want anything to do with." I sat on the closed toilet and watched as he positioned himself in front of one particular showerhead with what I swear was a smile on his face. "You're grossing me out. Move around or the groomer gets you first thing in the morning."

"Hah! Like you're not going to check out all of these features." Valdez snorted and did his own version of a doggy break dance. *"Satisfied?"*

"Not really. But I guess it'll have to do."

He stuck his head under a showerhead and let it rinse him clean. *"I smell better already. And once we're back home, you can do me over. With the flea shampoo again."*

"Fine. I think you're done." I reached in and turned off the water. By the time I'd rubbed him down with a bath sheet, my robe was as wet as he was. "Out. And don't get on the bed." I pulled the towel off of him. "Go down to the kitchen and lie on the tile."

"Maybe I'll shake a little of this water off on Miss Mara. Would that make you feel better?" Valdez shook, flinging water all over the bathroom. *"Sorry. Couldn't help it. Reflex. It's hell being a dog."*

"Yeah, go spray the wench. Cool her down." I slammed the door in his face and dropped the wet robe on the floor. Useless. I refused to think so. Sure I had a business to put back together, so I couldn't go running off to wherever in search of Westwood. But I was *not* useless. I adjusted the water and stepped into Blade's decadent shower.

Oh, boy, there was one showerhead that hit me right where I was just a little sore. From the gymnastics Blade and I had done. I wondered where he'd gone. I'd love for him to surprise me in the shower. I had lots of ideas for things we could do here. Hey, I was useful for some things. Did that make me a slut? I could live with that.

"You're late."

"No, you said eleven-thirty." I looked into the mortal's eyes and willed him to believe me.

"Right. I forgot." Steve Fleming was a well-built man in his thirties who had a young Hugh Grant look to him. Dark curly hair, twinkling eyes and, hmm, a black cowboy hat. I'd be attracted if I hadn't just had vampire sex with a man who could light every fire a woman never knew she had. Mortals, even hunky ones reeking of AB negative, are so . . . ordinary. This one wore jeans and a plaid western shirt that brought out the color of his eyes, a surprising blue.

He glanced at his watch. "Sorry ma'am." He ripped his hat. How cute was that? "Don't know where my manners went. Can we start over?" He grinned. Great teeth. Some of the older vampires . . . Well, an orthodontist would have made a killing a few centuries ago.

"Uh, sure, Steve, no problem."

"Let me show you what I've found." Steve unlocked the burglar bars. I'd never liked the look of those things, like we were doing business in a prison. But they were saving my shop from vandalism now. Yeah, right. Vandals would be salivating over my burnt offerings.

"Where'd you get the key?" I did not want to go inside.

"Landlord. Watch your step now. There's glass and debris."

Debris. Cute vintage clothing store with stock like

fifties' cocktail dresses reduced to debris. I couldn't avoid it
so I stepped inside.

"Oh, man, this is a disaster!" Despite a vow to be tough,
I felt tears fill my eyes. Piles of filthy, wet clothes, fried furniture and swollen books littered the floor. The plate glass
windows had been shattered. Glass crunched under our feet
as we walked around.

"The fire must have been pretty intense." I sniffled and
rubbed my burning eyes. "Sorry, the smell's getting to me."

Steve patted my arm. "And the damage. I know this is
hard to take."

Yeah, Steve had probably seen this kind of thing dozens
of times. He got down to business, aiming a large flashlight
and using a probe to move a few things around.

My mannequins lay like dead, formerly well-dressed
ladies who lunch in their fifties suits. With their scorched
faces and fried wigs, they stared at a blackened ceiling. A
book shelf had fallen over, the contents scattered.

I love old books and picked up a 1936 edition of *Gone
With the Wind* from a puddle. A total loss. My tears dried up
in a wave of fury. My fangs swelled against my gums and
I barely swallowed a snarl. Valdez was right outside, obviously mind reading. He barked, reminding me I had company. I coughed, like the acrid stench was choking me.

"Hey, you okay?" Steve looked at me with concern.

"No," I croaked. "I'm pissed. Who would do such a thing?"

"That was goin' to be my first question." Steve patted my
shoulder again. "At least no one was hurt. The sprinklers
and alarm system saved the day. Response time was good. It
could have been a lot worse." Steve walked over and opened
the door to the storeroom. "See? Fire didn't penetrate."

I glanced inside. "That's good. Except that everything's
wet." Did I mention that I deal mostly in vintage clothing?
A wet cotton shirtwaist was no problem. But the silk Chanel
suit from the sixties that I'd paid big bucks for . . . ? I
stroked the limp sleeve. Emerald green silk.

I swallowed a sob and looked for a place to sit. No such

luck, unless I wanted a wet butt. I followed Steve back into the main room. My friend and semipartner, the Countess Cecilia von Repsdorf, otherwise known as CiCi, had consigned a few pieces of furniture, but the Queen Anne chairs were Queen Anne kindling now.

Steve pointed to a piece of fluorescent tape. "This is where we found the incendiary device. I reckon someone broke the window and tossed it inside. The place has been processed as a crime scene, but the firebomb's all we found."

"Firebomb." I shuddered. If a vampire has a worst nightmare, it's fire. Consumed while you slept. Steve's arm came around my shoulders. He was looking at me like he felt my pain. He wasn't all that tall, maybe five ten to my five five, but he had a nice face that oozed sympathy. I thought about leaning against him for a moment.

Another bark brought me back to reality. Valdez was up, like he was about to come inside from where I'd ordered him to sit in the doorway.

"You really don't want the dog in here. Broken glass. It's too dangerous for a pet."

My "pet" growled, showing some serious teeth. Steve stiffened.

"Valdez!" I put a foot between me and the fireman and smiled at Steve. "Sorry, he's very protective of me." He was standing in for Jerry too. Blade had a business appointment, so he'd loaned me one of his cars, a Mercedes convertible he'd offered to give me more than once. Then he'd ordered Valdez to keep an eye on me. Apparently arson investigators posed a threat.

"Hey, I love dogs." Steve walked to the door. "Hey, cute fella. What's the breed?"

"Labradoodle." Steve looked a question. "You know a Lab poodle mix." Steve seemed like he was about to offer his hand. "Careful, he's been known to bite." I sent the dog a mental message to play nice. "He's still upset by the whole fire thing. His barking actually alerted the residents and helped save us."

Valdez gave me a look and growled. Steve backed up.

"Yeah, that's in my report. The smoke was pretty dense. The dog definitely saved your lives, especially if you sleep hard."

"Sleep hard? Uh, yeah, you could say that. Several of us in the building work nights."

Steve gave Valdez a final look then turned back to me. "Now why don't you tell me who might want to put you out of business."

Six

"Me? Why do you think I was the target?" Give this girl an Oscar. I really wanted to shout Brent Westwood's name. The vamp killer knew way too much about me and my shop. But the billionaire had made a fortune here in Austin. His high-tech company employed thousands in the area. Pointing the finger at him would get me nothing but a quick trip to the loony bin.

"Doesn't look like random vandalism. But the store next door did get the same treatment." Steve walked over to the door and looked outside. "Vandals, gangs, would have tagged the place. You know, with spray paint. I don't see any graffiti."

"Maybe somebody had a bad coffee at Mugs and Muffins. I sure don't have any enemies." Not that I knew of anyway, other than Westwood. And I was convinced that he would have hired this done, making sure he was far, far away before the whole thing went down.

We'd take care of him anyway. There was nowhere he could hide that a vampire couldn't find him eventually. And take him out. I had to believe that.

"I'll talk to the owner of Mugs and Muffins next. You both seem to be night people." Steve set his high-powered flashlight on the counter, pulled a notebook out of his back pocket and flipped it open. "Diana Marchand."

"Right." My fellow vamp would be just as unhelpful to Steve as I was. Dealing with any kind of government official made me twitchy. Steve was cute, though. And I liked the way he kept giving me looks when he thought I wasn't noticing.

"I'm meeting her in a few minutes. Her store had less damage than this one. Because the workers in the back had fire extinguishers."

"Yeah, they're open twenty-four seven. My shop's closed every Sunday and Monday." I took a step and a shattered porcelain figurine crunched under my feet. A black velvet cloche hat drooped with sodden feathers. I walked over to a soggy pile of silk scarves and picked up a yellow and orange Vera. These could be dry cleaned. And maybe a really genius cleaner could salvage the Chanel suit. "Go, if you want to talk to Diana. I'm going to stay in here for a few minutes. To assess the damage."

"Here. You'll need this." Steve handed me his flashlight. "I've got another one in the car."

"Thanks. I'll get it back to you." I swept the light around like I hadn't already been able to see every excruciating detail perfectly with my vamp vision. The beam settled on the computer we used for everything from sales receipts to inventory. I swallowed. The thing was a melted mass of plastic. At least I had a backup copy of the info, but where? At the moment, I was too rattled to remember.

Steve pressed a card into my hand. "Call me if you think of anyone who might have had a grudge . . ."

I smiled. "Trust me. Women are pretty passionate about their clothes, but I don't think any of them would destroy this many innocent . . . victims."

Steve patted me on the shoulder. "Well, you never know. And I'll probably be calling on you again too. For a progress report." He swept his eyes over me, over my clingy T-shirt and tight jeans that had zipped only after I'd stretched out flat on my back on the bed and sucked in my stomach. Hey, no pain, no gain.

Worth it, apparently, since I was detecting a little male interest from Steve, the fireman. I took a breath. That interest might come in handy if old Steve got too nosy and discovered I never, and I mean never, saw the light of day. Of course there was always the whammy.

"There you are. I'm a little early, but I'm anxious to talk to you, Detective." Diana had poked her head into the doorway. She gasped when she saw my shop. "Oh, Glory! This is horrible. Much worse than my place."

"Thanks, Diana. I needed an outside opinion." I shook my head. No need to act the bitch to Diana. She was my friend and a vampire who'd been a role model as far as creating a successful business goes. "Sorry. I'm reeling."

"Sure you are, honey. The place will come back together, you'll see." Diana frowned as she looked around.

"I could run a sale. Southern fried suits half price." I faked a laugh, then put my hand on Steve's arm. "Let us know when the electricity will be back on. We both want to get in here as soon as possible. And moved back in upstairs, of course."

"Should be soon. Inspectors will be out tomorrow, but it doesn't look like the fire spread enough to do any structural damage to me." Steve squeezed my hand, then walked over to Diana.

"That's great. Come over here and let me know what you think." Diana had cleaned up pretty well and had on a Mugs and Muffins T-shirt that highlighted her assets. Steve was in megaboob heaven.

"I'll talk to you later, Glory." Steve trailed Diana without a backward glance.

"*I'm coming in.*" Valdez stepped across the threshold.

"No, don't. I'm not going to spend the rest of the night picking glass out of your paws." I pushed him back out the door. "I'll be out in a minute. Guard the door."

"Gloriana, honey. I thought I was in the fires of hell yesterday." A figure appeared in front of me. Emmie Lou Nutt and her husband Harvey are my resident ghosts. Emmie's stuck for eternity in what she'd had on when she died, a cute little cowgirl outfit that would have been a big seller in the shop. She'd had it on for the Texas State Fair pie competition. It definitely made you think about what you wore on a daily basis. In case you were run over by a pickup truck.

"I'm sorry, Emmie. I'd say someone with a hate for vampires decided to make a statement."

"Somebody. I'll say. First the window blows out. Then whoosh, fire everywhere." Emmie fanned herself and drifted over to the doorway. "It wasn't kids either. I saw the whole thing."

I put down the laundry basket I'd started filling with everything I thought could be washed.

"Really? You saw who did it?" I don't know why that got me excited. It's not as if I could send a ghost down to pick the perp out of a lineup. I watch cop shows. Obviously.

"I saw him too. He ever sets foot in here, Glory, darlin', we'll get him good." Harvey appeared in front of me. His starched and pressed jeans and western shirt had probably been made that way by his beloved Emmie before the fateful day when they'd headed to the state fair. The day he'd accidentally run over Emmie in the parking lot. Could a ghost still iron?

"You okay, Glory?" Harvey looked at Emmie. "Maybe you should come back later. With some help."

I shook my head. "No, I'm not all right. I think Westwood's behind this." I grabbed some cotton skirts and stuffed them in the basket.

"Wouldn't surprise me none." Emmie hovered over a shattered crystal vase. "Bastard seems determined to make your life a misery."

"Emmie Lou Nutt!" Harvey drifted closer to his wife.

"Well, it's true. He's a bastard. Lacy told us he tried to kill our Glory and that nice Mr. Blade on Halloween."

I sighed and dropped another skirt in the basket. "Blade's going after him."

"Good. Mr. Blade looks like he can handle himself." Emmie shook her head. "You're gonna need starch and a hot iron after you wash those, honey. I always liked the spray starch myself." Emmie sniffled. "Dang it. I never thought I'd miss ironing." She sobbed and disappeared.

Harvey grunted. "Glory, you just be careful. Without Mr. Blade—"

"I can take care of myself." I looked at Valdez. "And I've got some help."

"Talking to yourself, Gloriana?" Richard Mainwaring lounged in the door. Valdez lay calmly by the door and barely twitched.

"No. I'm talking to ghosts." I looked around. Harvey had vanished too. "And what did you do to my guard dog?"

"Valdez is doing his job. He knows I'm no threat to you." Richard stepped inside and looked around. "Ghosts? Whatever you say, my dear."

"Don't patronize me, Mainwaring. I have ghosts here. Nice ones. And they'll make you sorry if you aren't nice to me too." A soggy alligator bag sailed across the room and barely missed Richard's head. "See?"

He reached up and snagged it in midair in a pretty impressive vamp move. "Yes, I see." He set the purse down on the blackened counter. "You've got a mess here. So I guess I'll have to postpone my plans for you."

"Your plans? For me?" Damn it. Wasn't there anywhere I could sit in here? I headed to the back room and sat on the wooden table there. Between the smell and the sheer trauma of the whole fire thing, I was a little weak in the knees. A wet butt was worth it.

"You owe me a debt. I haven't forgotten." Richard pulled a paper from his back pocket. He wore leather pants that should have been illegal, they were so . . . formfitting. I made myself look into his eyes. His brilliant blue eyes that matched the faded ZZ Top T-shirt he wore. Mainwaring and classic rock. The man obviously had depth.

"How much?" I stretched out my hand. Good thing I was sitting, the estimate from a Harley specialty shop was three figures, nearly four. I sighed and handed it back to him. "What are they doing, plating it in diamonds?"

Richard looked down at the paper. "This is a reasonable estimate. The work is delicate. And it's platinum. Diamonds would be too flashy."

He'd made a joke. His sexy grin confirmed it. I smiled back. Maybe he was going to be reasonable. Surely he realized I was ass deep in alligators here, with my livelihood in ruins.

"Ass deep in alligators? Where did you hear that?" Richard was grinning for sure now.

"My ghosts. They have a colorful vocabulary." I leaned closer. "And quit reading my mind. I hate it."

"I know. It's rude." He tucked the paper back in his pocket. "But definitely informative. I consider it a survival skill."

"Yes, well, obviously I'm going to be strapped for cash for a while. Can we work out some kind of payment plan? Say, a dollar a week?" I should *not* be interested in the pull of the leather across his zipper area. "Hey, I'll live long enough to pay it out." Forget the dollar deal. I had a mental picture, just a snatch, of two naked bodies working something out on a wide bed. I threw up a block in case Richard was getting the same X-rated preview. Preview? No way. I was with Blade. Had enjoyed something wonderful with him just hours ago.

"I'll think of something." He was still grinning and he moved closer, until he was almost between my legs. He grunted when a vintage Tony Lama boot whacked him between the shoulder blades. "Hey, I'm Glory's friend. Tell them, Gloriana." He looked down at me, his eyes gleaming.

"He's okay, guys." My ghosts were rooting for Blade. Emmie Lou in particular liked the way he looked out for me. And Harvey saw Blade as a man's man. Which he was. When he was just a man. Now he's a vampire's vampire. Richard is too. Sort of. If said vampire is behaving himself. But let a vampire go rogue, endangering the rest of us with reckless behavior, and Richard is there to see justice done. He considers himself an enforcer, a vamp vigilante. Probably goes back to his stint in the priesthood.

"You *are* okay, aren't you, Richard?" He was an inch from

invading my space but I was *not* leaning away from him. He just stared at me, a little something interesting in his eyes before he stepped back and smiled again.

"Of course I am, Gloriana. I'm your friend, if you'll let me be. Even though you practically destroyed my ride."

"A ride that was parked illegally." Okay, a slight exaggeration. "But I said I'd make things right and I will." Uh-oh. Why did Richard's smile suddenly make me nervous?

"You know I'm staying with Blade now."

"Where else?" He had a look that made me want to get all defensive again. Like I had to run to Blade for every little thing? But a burned-out shop was not a *little* thing.

"I have other friends. Damian offered me a place to stay."

"Yes. Florence is there." He got another look in his eyes. Hard this time, like he had a score to settle there.

"You and Flo—"

"Are done. We go our own ways now." He definitely was nursing some feelings and not warm and fuzzy ones either.

I don't know what went down between the two, but the ending had not been mutual or friendly.

"So I'll call you. When I'm moved back in." I jumped off the table. "I know I owe you. I'm sorry about the damage and I'll make good on it. Somehow."

"That's all I ask." And with a wink, he was gone.

I set about sorting laundry again, but the stench of scorched clothing had my head pounding in about five minutes. I said good-bye to my ghosts, gathered up my dog and headed for Blade's. I needed a bath, a cold glass of Fangtastic and Blade, not necessarily in that order.

"I have a surprise for you, Glory."

I sighed and rubbed Blade's cheek. I was sated, again. And couldn't quite open my eyes. "Surprise? Like the picnic in the garden? I could go for some more strawberries." I felt his smile before I finally looked at him.

"No, something a bit more tangible." He rolled out of

bed and pulled on his jeans. "Cover yourself and I'll show you."

I blatantly stretched, as sensuously as I could make it, and posed at the angle that made the best of my overabundant curves. "You sure you want me to cover myself?"

"Quit distracting me, lass. I'm leaving tomorrow night and we need to get this settled."

Leaving? I snatched up the sheet and held it under my chin. "Where are you going? Why tomorrow? I'm traumatized. I need your . . ." I dropped the sheet again. "Comfort."

Blade was beside me in a flash. "You will always have my . . ." He drew a finger around one of my nipples, making me shiver. "Comfort." He leaned down and kissed me with enough energy to make me pull him down on top of me again. Can we say insatiable? Me, him, maybe all vamps now that I think about it.

"Stop. I'm serious." He leaped off of me and moved to the end of the bed. Like he needed the distance to keep his thoughts together. Excellent.

"Okay, okay." I pulled up the sheet again. "Where are you going? After Westwood?" I'd figured out that it was only a matter of time. I'd had Jerry practically stuck to me like glue for almost a week. He'd even wielded a broom to help me clear out the worst of the mess in my shop.

"Aye. I have a lead. Mara and I need to pursue it."

Of course he'd take Mara with him. She'd insist on it. I should be just as determined to put a period to the hunter's existence. But I had a business to resurrect. And, while revenge is sweet, it's not my be-all and end-all if you know what I mean.

"Where do you think he went?" I found my black lace nightgown and dropped it over my head. It was sexy enough that Blade actually stepped a little closer.

"Africa." He shook his head. "Put on a robe. I'm bringing in your surprise now."

"Africa? That's so far away." I stood and walked up to him. "I'll miss you."

"I'm counting on it." He pulled me to him and held me for a minute.

I felt so close to him. And not just physically. I hugged him and breathed in his essence. Maybe it was because he'd made me what I am, but Jerry was the only man I'd ever felt so *connected* with. At least when I wasn't on the verge of killing him.

"Now." Blade stepped back and pulled the terry robe from the wad of comforter and sheets at the foot of the bed. "Cover yourself. I don't want to start this relationship on the wrong foot."

"*Start* a relationship?" I tied the robe at the waist and sat on the end of the bed. "Who or what are you talking about?"

"You've been in danger, Gloriana. I've had concerns about your security for some time." Blade was looking pretty serious.

"Hey, I've got Valdez. We do pretty well. And I did save myself on Halloween. Or have you already forgotten?"

"I'll never forget that. You almost—" Blade rubbed his face, like he was actually tearing up and didn't want me to see it.

Gee. When he put it like that, I felt a little queasy. I'd had the business end of a stake poking my left breast. One false move . . .

"My heart stopped that night."

You had to love that kind of declaration. I smiled, threw my arms around him and rubbed his back. "Hey, any damage I got healed almost instantly. Remember, I'm tougher than I look."

Blade gripped my shoulders and looked down at me. "I never want to see you in such peril again."

"Now you're sounding like one of those heroes in a romance novel." I love those things. Especially the paranormal ones. The things they think vamps do. What a hoot.

"I mean what I say, Glory. I've decided to double your guard."

Seven

"**Double** . . ." I extracted myself from his arms and sat down again. "Two dogs? Or something else? Come on, Jerry. It's hard enough living with Valdez. We've worked out our relationship pretty well. But it took a while and I'm not in any hurry to go through that again. Besides, I need my privacy."

"You need protection." Blade strode to the door and flung it open. A dog sat in the hall. A cute dog, with wavy white fur and startling green eyes. Green eyes that promised mischief and reminded me . . .

"Who the hell is this . . . this wolf in sheep's clothing?"

"You know him. Doesn't she, Will?" Blade gestured for the dog to pad into the room.

"Aye, though it's been a century or two." The dog sat in front of me and casually scratched behind one ear. "Damned mutt ye've got workin' for her already is loaded with fleas. I'll not be sufferin' this kind of treatment." He didn't talk in my head, like Valdez did. No, this one moved his lips. It was bizarre. And if this was who I thought it was, I was putting up a hell of a fight before I took *him* on as bodyguard.

"You'll suffer what is necessary to take care of Gloriana, Will, if you want to earn your reward."

"You didn't bring William Kilpatrick into this house, did you?" Mara was in the doorway, Valdez right beside her.

"I did." Blade turned to smile at her. "I'd think it would do you good to see your brother as a dog."

"Appropriate perhaps. But I'd rather not lay eyes on him at all. He's a cur who does nothing but disgrace the family."

This from a woman who was a blood-sucking vampire. Made you wonder just what it would take to disgrace a pedigree like that.

"*We don't need Kilpatrick here, Blade. I'm more than capable of taking care of Glory by myself.*" Valdez came close to lean against my leg. "*Tell him, Glory. We do okay, don't we?*"

"Yes, we do. I already told him that." I glared at the dog that had jumped up on his sister, practically knocking her over. He wasn't any bigger than Valdez, but he obviously had some vamp strength going on.

"Down, you oaf." She pushed until he sat at her feet, tail thumping the carpet.

"Where's the love, sis?" He glanced at me. "Hey, Glory, lass, ye're lookin' well rested."

Well rested. Translation: I had a severe case of bed head, no makeup and looked like hell.

"You expect me to let one of the Kilpatricks invade my space?" And this Kilpatrick in particular wasn't exactly on the top of my list for potential roommates. Will was a wild child, Mara was right about that. And he chased anything female. He'd cornered me a time or two when we'd first met at Campbell Castle, treating me like the lightskirt all actresses were thought to be back then. In dog form, he was cute. In human form . . . Well, let's just say he was pretty hard to resist and he knew it. But I'd resisted him. His air of superiority, like I should be honored to do him, had made it easy.

"Aw, now, Gloriana. You know you always had a soft spot for me." Will nudged Valdez and tried to get closer to me. Growls that made the hair stand up on my arms promised an all-out doggy war.

Blade wasn't tolerating it. "Enough. You'll both take care of Gloriana. And she's your mistress in this, as always, Valdez."

"Mistress? Is this a sweet deal or what?" Will laid his muzzle on my knee. "Remember me now, sweetheart?"

"Vividly. And I'm still immune." I pushed his face away and stood. "This is ridiculous. I don't want or need another guard. Send this . . . beast back to whatever rock he crawled out from under."

"Glory's right." Mara was obviously not struck with brotherly love. "Get out, Will. Don't let the door hit your tail on the way out."

"Stop this!" Blade's voice was a thunderclap. "You'll all get along. Or answer to me." He pulled me to his side.

I thought about resisting. Don't you just hate the way he issues orders? But while Blade would never hurt me, he was still one scary dude when he was riled.

"Relax, Jer. We'll get along." I patted his cheek and he did relax his jaw a bit. "But I think this is totally unnecessary."

"I need to know you're safe, Gloriana, or I can't leave." His arm tightened around me and he gave me a tender look that melted any contrariness I'd been building up.

"Okay. Okay." I leaned against him. "Just hurry back. This is temporary."

"Of course." He dropped a kiss on my head. "Will, Glory is in your care. One hair on her head comes to harm and there will be no bailout. Understand?"

"Bailout?" Mara tossed her head. "Surprise, surprise. You've got yourself in another financial bind, haven't you? At least you had the good sense not to come running to me this time."

"Fat lot of good it would do me." Will heaved a sigh. "My own sister wouldn't throw me a bone if I was starving." He sidled up to Blade. "Speaking of bones. We don't have to eat dog food and crap like that, do we? I've got standards."

Valdez perked up, obviously sensing an ally. *"No way. I had a rib eye night before last. You just tell Glory what you like to eat and she's on top of it. Though she doesn't really cook. She can barely panfry a steak without burning it. She just doesn't get the concept of rare."*

"If someone didn't insist on this dog form, I'd cook for both of us. I've studied at the Cordon Bleu in Paris. Night classes. When I get the money together, I plan to open a restaurant."

"You're vampire, aren't you? How can you stand to eat?" Could everybody eat but me? Life is *so* not fair.

"Kilpatrick vampires are born, not made, and can do some things made vamps can't. Didn't you know that, Gloriana?" Mara gave me a sympathetic look, like only an idiot could have been around this crowd for hundreds of years and still not have a clue.

"Sure I knew that." Not. I probably *was* an idiot. But I'd spent most of those hundreds of years trying to be anything *but* vampire.

"Will is to do your bidding, Glory." Jerry gave him a hard look. "If he is too much of a problem, I'll replace him."

Mara shook her head. "Good thing you're poor, Glory. Will goes through cash like Valdez goes through Twinkies."

"Hey, I need my strength. And I want to know why he can talk like that and I have to do it inside people's heads." Valdez leaned against my knee. *"Though if the number two guy tries talking like that in front of mortals, you'll straighten him out, won't you, Glory?"*

I rubbed Valdez behind his ears. "Yes, puppy. He'll have to follow the same rules you do. And you'll always be number one with me."

"Thanks a lot." Blade's arm tightened around my waist. "I thought *I* was number one."

I looked up and smiled. "Let me clarify. Valdez, you're my number one bodyguard. Blade, you're my number one "

"Spare me." Mara rolled her eyes. "I've had quite enough of Gloriana's drama. Westwood killed MacTavish. My husband. I see no reason to wait for tomorrow night. Shift with me now, Jeremiah, and we can be in Africa before sunrise." Mara looked down and gasped. "William Allan Kilpatrick, what do you have in your mouth?"

Will looked up from his new chew toy, one of Mara's

Prada sandals. "There's something very tasty about a high-priced shoe."

"I'll kill you, you hound." Mara charged, Will lunged and the two of them ran out of the room, Mara screeching and Will laughing like a hyena.

"That was a surprise." I sat on the foot of the bed again. "Will Kilpatrick. I don't know if this is going to work out."

"I probably do need backup, Glory. Think about it. I'm on duty twenty-four seven. Sure, I get a nap now and then, but I can tell you that years of that kind of stress takes its toll. I could have slept through the whole fire thing. I was that exhausted." Valdez had obviously decided to join the dark side, especially if it might mean a better menu.

"Two dogs?" I collapsed on the bed. "Jeremiah Campbell you are a wicked, wicked man."

"That's my cue. I'm outta here." Valdez ran out the door, which slammed behind him.

"The dog's learning."

"Yes, but are you? Why do you always have to make these major decisions about my life without consulting me?" I tried hard to hang on to my mad, but Blade never had put on a shirt. And a half-naked Blade did stupid things to my mind. Like wiping out my logical thinking.

"I couldn't consult you. You would have said no."

I stopped just as I was about to untie my robe again. "Damned right." Controlling man. Always. One reason we'd parted as often as we'd gotten together. "Take off those jeans and come back to bed. I'm going to punish you for your impertinence."

"You promise?" Jerry grinned as he shucked his jeans and leaped on top of me.

"Okay, you've distracted me long enough. I've been an idiot long enough. Mara's right about that. Made vampires versus born vampires. What other differences do I need to know about?" I watched Jerry get dressed. He was leaving tonight and I'd given him a send-off guaranteed to help him remember me during those long, hot nights in Africa.

Jerry zipped his jeans. "I'm pretty sure we went over this the first time I took you home to meet mum and dad."

"You probably did." And as an actress from humble beginnings, I'd been too busy trying to please the laird and lady of Castle Campbell to pay much attention. Of course I *hadn't* pleased the parents. Jerry and I never married for one thing. And I was what I was. Not a Scottish heiress like Mara, in other words.

I'd met plenty of vamps over the years but it's not considered polite to ask about one's origins. Some vamps, like me, came to the deal willingly and saved regrets for later. Others had been forced into the life. You think *I* whine. So vamps tend to live in the moment. Usually. Speaking of the moment . . .

Jerry pulled on a snap-front cotton Western shirt. He'd been going for a cowboy look to please me because I had a yen for a cowboy type, now that I lived in Texas and all. The yellow looked good with his dark hair and eyes, really good. He left it open. Even better.

"The Kilpatrick, Mara's father, is the one who made my father vampire in the first place."

"So started the family from hell." I muttered it, but nothing gets past Jerry's vamp hearing.

"Now, Glory, the clan is quite fond of you. If you'd married me, they would have accepted you as part of the family."

A big "if." Jerry had popped that particular question about a century late as far as I was concerned. By then I'd spent way too much time with "the clan," four brothers, all alpha males, and two sisters who could give Joan Rivers bitch lessons. And then there was dear Mama, who'd actually tried to stake me one cold winter night. But, hey, I don't hold it against her. I just don't plan to be in the same continent, let alone the same room, with the woman ever again.

"We had some issues. One being that I wasn't part of a dynasty." Like Mara. Or even MacTavish's sister who Mama Campbell had really wanted for Jerry.

"I would never have married Tess MacTavish." Jerry gave me a look, letting me know he'd really like me to get over this ancient jealousy.

"Quit reading my mind. And tell Tess she's off your potential bride list the next time you see her. Watch her reaction." Tess MacTavish put the vamp in vampire if you know what I mean. Men flocked. And she'd always had a thing for Jerry. Hard to believe he was immune. I got another one of those looks. Time for a subject change.

I watched Jerry run a leather belt through the loops on his jeans. "Is that a Gucci belt?" I know my leather goods.

"So Mara said. It's a gift from her." Jerry buckled it, then picked up his wallet from the dresser and slipped it in his back pocket, like he thought I wouldn't notice it was Gucci too.

"What's she doing giving you expensive presents?" This was serious. I gave Jerry the same thing every Christmas and birthday that we were seeing each other—my own too well-curved body. Hey, I'm on a budget. And I *am* enthusiastic. I usually tie a bow on myself somewhere interesting. Jerry loves it.

"I'm letting her stay with me and won't accept payment. So she gives me gifts. It makes her feel better."

"I'm sure." I was also sure Jerry had no clue what a nice Gucci belt and wallet cost either. I wasn't telling him. "So born vampires can eat. Anything else?"

"They can eat *and* drink. Don't let Will near strong spirits. He's quite fond of whisky and doesn't handle it well." Jerry frowned, as if wondering if he'd done me any favors bringing Will on board. I wondered the same thing.

"I've seen Mara shift, use her strength, the regular vamp powers. Anything else?"

"Born vampires don't turn until thirty or so. Before then they're human and mortal. Can even have children. The

Kilpatricks have lost many a bairn before the change." Jerry was still frowning. "I've heard that every hundred years or so they can get fertile again. And if they mate with a mortal, the babe will be vampire."

"Does Mara have children?" What a concept. The woman had about as much maternal instinct as a rabid bat.

"Aye. A daughter, Lily, with Mac before the change. We've not seen her for years. She and her parents had a falling out." Jerry sat on the edge of the bed. "I've been searching for her. To let her know about her father. No luck so far."

I put my hand on Jerry's knee. "It'll be a shock. Vampires are supposed to live forever."

"Which is why I must go after Westwood. To avenge Mac and pay Westwood back for the harm he has done you."

I couldn't argue. And Jerry was at his best in fierce warrior mode. "Be careful. Westwood's going to be surrounded by stake-happy goons, you know."

"That doesn't mean he might not have left some men here. To finish what he started." Jerry pulled me into his arms and rested his cheek on my hair. Tears filled my eyes. Vampires *were* supposed to live forever, especially this one.

"Don't worry about us. Now I've got two guard dogs." I looked up with a watery smile. "But if Will gets into Flo's shoe collection, I may be down to one again before you get back."

"You won't just stay here while I'm gone?"

"No, I need to get back to my own place. You know how I am about my stuff." I'm a nester with a capital *N*.

"Of course. And Florence will be coming back as well?" Jerry likes Flo, everyone does. And she's pretty powerful. If she wasn't too involved with her lover du jour, she'd be bodyguard number three. Do you get the idea that I'm regarded here as Glory the helpless? My own fault. I'm afraid to shape-shift. Spend most of my waking hours trying to blend by acting more mortal than the average human being.

But I've been changing since I moved to Texas. I'm surrounded by powerful vamps and shifters who know all kinds of neat tricks. I'm determined to start using some of my latent power. I bet I've stored a ton of it since 1604.

There was a knock. Jerry kissed my cheek, then got up and opened the door. Mara stood in the hall, positively humming with impatience.

"We should go now, Jeremiah. Once we get to Namibia, we've got to find a safe place to sleep before dawn."

"All arranged, Mara. I sent a man over yesterday. He called a half hour ago. My shipment arrived. He picked it up at the airport and found us appropriate lodging."

Jerry must have shipped his clothes, Fangtastic and other stuff that he saw as essential for an all-out war with Westwood. Vampires don't exactly make reservations on Continental. He and Mara would shape-shift into hawks or some other bird and fly with preternatural speed from here. Mere mortals wouldn't even be able to see them. The two vamps would be in Africa before dawn.

Jerry jumped when I used my own warp speed, newly learned of course, to slip behind him and wrap my arms around his waist. He put his hands over mine.

"I'll be down in five minutes, Mara. Feed the dogs, why don't you?"

"I tried. Valdez is happy with just about anything, but Will is complaining that his eggs were dry and his toast burned." Mara wrinkled her perfect nose. "Like I should know how to cook. What are servants for, I ask you?"

I sure didn't comment on that. Servants? Yeah, right. "He'd better get used to takeout and microwave meals while he's with me."

"Jeremiah, maybe you should let Will change into human form so he can cook for himself." Mara stared at my hands on Jerry's stomach. Or was she enjoying the view? Jerry's chest was a sight I sure never got tired of.

I gently raked my nails over the hair arrowing into his waistband. Her eyes narrowed. Poor Mara, with the famous vamp libido and no man in her life. I actually felt the urge to fix her up. Maybe when she got back from Africa. Unless she finagled her way into Jerry's bed over there. My hands became claws and Jerry grabbed them.

"Impossible. Glory's going to have her hands full handling Will as a dog." Jerry's hands tightened over mine. "I know what your brother's like. But he's fierce in a fight. And I trust him to stick by Glory's side."

"For a price, of course." Mara made a face. "Whatever. Perhaps Will and Gloriana will suit very well." She gave me the old Glory's a slut look.

"Good-bye, Mara. Now leave us alone." I slipped my fingers into Jerry's waistband.

Mara grimaced. "I'll be downstairs. Five minutes, Jeremiah." She headed down the hall. Only a vampire like Mara would dress for a transatlantic flight in a black leather mini and high-heeled Gucci boots to match. The woman did love her Gucci.

The shape-shifting deal *is* pretty awesome. Whatever you're wearing when you change, that's what you have on when you go humanoid again. I have no idea what physics or whatever you call it are involved. But I've seen it work. Many times. I just don't trust myself not to screw it up. How would *you* like to be stuck as a bird or dog or something equally gross?

"You're crushing the wind out of me, lass." Jerry didn't sound like he minded.

"Yeah, right." But I eased up and turned him around to face me. "Kiss me good-bye and make it a good one."

Jerry smiled and ran his hands over my body. I'd been naked in the bed and I was still naked. Not that I'd let Mara see me like that. She'd never made a secret of the fact that she thought I was fat. Skinny bitch. So I'd been hiding behind Jerry. *He* didn't mind my generous curves.

"I'd like to do more than kiss you, lass, but five minutes wouldn't be nearly enough. I'd—" He leaned down and whispered graphic details of what he'd like to do. The list was long, maybe an hour's worth. And I felt heat pooling between my thighs.

"I love it when you talk dirty. Mara can wait." I dragged his lips to mine and gave him a kiss guaranteed to curl his toes. I whispered some interesting variations on his earlier suggestions in his mind. He growled and grabbed my ass like he'd never let go.

But he did. Let go, that is.

"We've got to leave now or we won't beat the sun to landfall."

I sighed and gave him a final hug. "Be careful. And come back as quick as you can."

"Always." Jerry gave me a hard kiss, then strode out of the room. I flopped on the bed and stared dry-eyed at the ceiling.

There was a scratching at the door and I dove under the covers. Until Blade came back, it was flannel nightgowns for me.

"Come in." Two dogs, one trailing a lime green Prada sandal by its broken strap, came in with concerned looks.

Valdez jumped on the bed. *"You okay?"*

"Yeah." I buried my fingers in his fur. The bed dipped and I figured Will had jumped up on the bed too. Valdez growled and gave him a head butt that sent Will crashing into the nightstand. A brass lamp wobbled then hit the floor.

"Easy there, my canine cohort. I'm only guarding our mistress."

"You can guard her from the floor, asshole." Valdez had obviously decided to be top dog. Which was fine with me. The way Will said mistress made my fangs swell and I had a real strong urge to rip his head off and stuff it up his . . . you know. Good. Anger beat the hell out of all the other emotions that I was set to wallow in.

"He's right, Will. And you touch even one strap on any of *my* shoes and you'll get generic canned dog food for the duration." I almost laughed at the expression on Will's furry face.

"Makes me wonder if I've landed in hell." Will stalked over to the door and lay across the threshold.

Valdez snorted. *"Drama queen."*

"Queen? Queen?"

Who knew a dog could hit high C? I closed my eyes as the insults flew back and forth. All I could think about was Blade, flying over a dark, cold ocean.

Eight

"This is where we're going to live?" Will poked his head into the kitchen. "I liked Blade's place better. State of the art. This is pathetic. Electric stove. Don't you know gas is the way to go?"

"Get over it, Emeril. You're not going to be cooking here and neither is Glory if you don't shape up." Valdez took his top dog role seriously. He looked around and chuffed. *"Still smells a little funky in here, but it's good to be home."*

"Yes, it is." I collapsed on the couch and wrinkled my nose. A restoration company had been through the place and what I smelled wasn't so much smoke as disinfectant used with a liberal hand. Too liberal. I immediately had a headache.

"What's wrong, Glory?" Valdez put his head on my knee. *"Is that vamp trying to communicate again? Bad news if he can get at you here."*

"No. Just the cleaning stuff." But the other headaches hadn't stopped. When we were outside, I still heard someone calling my name. There was a knock on the door and both dogs jumped up and growled.

"Who is it?" I got up and looked through the peephole. No one should have been able to get inside without buzzing from downstairs. But then someone might have let this one in, since he'd been a regular visitor until a few weeks ago.

"Mainwaring. Let me in."

Orders. I felt my usual resistance, then remembered that I owed this guy a debt the size of Montana.

"Sure. Come in." I flipped back the dead bolts and flung open my new door. "Thanks for not knocking the door down. I'm not sure how many Damian is willing to pay for." Mainwaring brushed past me.

"Is Florence here?"

"No. She's moving back in tomorrow. Something about dry cleaning that won't be ready. She wants to move everything at once."

"Right. Not that she'll actually pick up anything herself." Richard stared down at Will. "I don't know this one."

"Will Kilpatrick, Mara's brother. You know Mara Mac-Tavish."

"Yes. The grieving widow."

"Hey. Where's your respect?" Will showed some teeth, but one steely look from Mainwaring and he shut his mouth.

"I have great respect for Mrs. MacTavish." Richard nodded at Valdez. "But I wonder what you're doing *here* and why you're not comforting your sister."

"My sister's in Africa, with Blade. Hellbent on revenge." Will sat down next to the door. "I'm on assignment. Guard duty."

Richard looked at me. "Two dogs? What's the story? Doesn't Blade trust you with a real bodyguard?"

I wanted to smack his handsome face. "He trusts me. He just doesn't trust men not to fall in lust with me and drive me crazy with their unwanted advances." I gave him a head toss. "I'm irresistible."

Richard actually grinned. "I'm not arguing with you." He looked around the living room. "Where's your computer? Was it damaged in the fire?"

"My laptop is in the bedroom. I haven't had time to check it out. Why?" I watched Richard prowl the living room. Something had him worked up. Maybe he'd hoped Flo would be here. For a month, the couple had been hot and heavy. Even short term, which is the way my roomie likes it, it's hard to just turn off that kind of attraction.

"I've thought of a way for you to repay your debt."

"Now this is getting interesting." Will stood and walked closer. "You got debts too, Glory? This guy loans money?"

"Down, boy. Glory had a little accident. She's paying for repairs to Mainwaring's vintage Harley." Valdez pushed between me and Will. *"It's a sweet piece of machinery. Or was until Glory ran right over it."*

"It was an accident. And Richard was at fault too. He'd parked in my spot." I went to get my computer. "If doing some computer work will get me off the hook, I'm all for it."

Richard followed me into the bedroom, Valdez on his heels. "I need you to do some research for me. And maybe it's time I learned to navigate one of these things. You can give me lessons on how to use the Internet."

I grabbed my computer and took it to the table in the breakfast nook.

"You never learned how to operate a computer?" I wasn't about to admit I'd been resistant to new technology myself for way too long. Then I'd discovered I could actually do some bargain shopping online. The rest as they say is history.

I sat down, flipped open the computer and powered it up. To my relief, it seemed to be operating all right. We had good wireless Internet access here. Damian had made sure of that once he'd moved his sister in. Flo supposedly didn't read or write, but she was hell on wheels when it came to online shopping. We'd spent many a fun evening on the Italian shoe sites.

"Let me check my e-mail first." I hadn't done it since the night before the fire. A quick glance showed the usual notices from my favorite shopping sites, some spam (yeah, right, like I want to see a nympho getting up close and personal with livestock) and e-mails from some buds I'd left behind in Las Vegas. Richard leaned over my shoulder, an interested observer. I wished he didn't smell so good.

"Oh, my God!" A message from the Fang Collector. One guess who that might be from.

"What? What is it?" Richard leaned over my shoulder.

"An e-mail from Westwood. I doubt it's a thank you for the lovely time we had on Halloween." Especially since the toad was probably still recovering from the wicked knife wound Jerry had managed to give him. I hope it hurt like hell.

"How could he know how to contact you?" Richard pulled out a chair and sat beside me.

"Westwood's a computer genius. He practically invented the Internet. He probably knows everything about me. From my reading habits to my cup size."

"Cup size?" Richard looked puzzled.

"Bra cup. I shop online a lot." I felt too queasy to be embarrassed. I sucked up my courage and opened the e-mail.

"Listen to this: 'If you're reading this, then I guess my fire failed to send you to hell where you belong. Too bad. Either you have the world's best luck or I'm losing my touch. I choose to think the former. But, trust me, vampire, your luck is about to run out. I may have left the scene, but my men have not. They're paid well to make your life a living hell. But not to kill you. I reserve that pleasure for myself. Soon. *W* '"

"The bastard's got his nerve. But he's an idiot for taunting a vampire." Richard jumped up, looking around like he wanted to tear something apart or maybe smash something. I could definitely relate. "Are you going to answer him, Glory?"

"That might encourage him." Westwood's pen pal? My finger twitched over the delete button, but I knew I had to save this garbage. Evidence of harassment, though going to the police was obviously not an option. I did the next best thing, I forwarded it to Blade. As soon as I did it, I knew it was a big mistake. He'd go ballistic.

I took a shaky breath. I had to trust Blade not to go off half-cocked. Hopefully, he'd use his rage to formulate a plan, a carefully executed plan that would turn Westwood into roadkill.

"Damn it!" I jumped up, fighting my own urge to smash

and trash. I grabbed a bottle of Fangtastic out of the fridge. I offered a bottle to Richard but he shook his head. I took a deep swallow and waited for the jugular juice to do its thing. It did make me feel marginally better, stronger anyway.

"I just hope Blade manages to get to Westwood and takes him out. Problem solved."

"Until the paychecks stop, Westwood's men will be creating a nuisance." Richard glanced at the living room. Valdez and Will had both looked up when they'd heard the refrigerator door open, but when neither Twinkies nor a steak came out of the kitchen, they'd gone back to snoozing, Valdez on the couch, Will on the floor. "At least you have protection of a sort."

I was not comforted. "Damn! Damn! What next? Slashed tires? Another fire in the shop?" This was infuriating. I sure wasn't going to sit calmly by waiting to be attacked.

I sat back in front of the computer and hit reply. Westwood wanted to start a flame war? I was all over it. I'd had centuries to hone my verbal skills. I hit send before I could even reread for typos.

"Take that, you creep with the bad jewelry. Fang necklaces are so not cool."

Richard grinned and pulled out a chair to sit across from me. "What did you say, Gloriana?"

"Plenty. I even threw in a voodoo curse I learned in New Orleans." I smiled in spite of my still simmering rage. "Westwood may need clean underwear after he reads my e-mail."

"I hope you don't regret that, Glory. It could cause things to escalate."

I met Richard's blue, blue eyes. He was actually worried about me. Hey, he could join the club.

I took another swig of Fangtastic. "I can handle a few mortals. Maybe they'll decide Westwood's money isn't worth the risk."

"What are you thinking, Gloriana?"

"Mind reading." I looked at my dogs. "We put the pooches to work. They can read the minds of any and all mortals who get within a hundred feet of this building. They pick up a Westwood vibe and we deal with it."

"Are we talking murder and mayhem?" Will had perked up at the word "money." Now he trotted up to stand next to me.

"Don't look so eager. Murder no. Mayhem definitely." I glanced at Richard who'd raised an eyebrow. "Westwood's sent me an e-mail threatening to harass me with some hired muscle. When they come around I can plant memories, fake memories that make these guys run like hell."

"I like it, Blondie. Mind control." Valdez pushed Will out of the way. *"Not sure we can just run loose outside though. Austin has strict leash laws. And doing mind control on every dog catcher that comes by . . ."*

"You won't need to run loose. Stay with Gloriana and read the minds of anyone nearby." Richard looked thoughtful. "When she's in the shop, you can sit by the windows and do your thing through the glass."

Valdez nodded. *"Sounds like a plan."*

"Wait a minute." I'd just remembered something. "Westwood had those tinted glasses. If his guys all wear those . . ." Trust a techno-freak bastard like Westwood to find and use special eyeglasses that keep us from reading his mind.

"So anybody hanging around at night, wearing tinted glasses, is fair game. We act first, ask questions later. The day I can't knock a pair of glasses off a mere mortal is the day I hang up my dog collar." Valdez bumped against my leg.

"We'll work it out." I rubbed his ears and felt marginally better. I stared at my computer but neither Blade nor Westwood had answered me. Yet. "Let's start the computer lessons."

"Good." Richard got up to lean over my shoulder and study my computer screen. "I see Google dot com there. I've heard of it. What does it do? Show me how you 'Google' something. That is what they say, isn't it?"

"Sure. Hey, knowing the vocabulary is a good start." I began explaining the process and the dogs settled back in the living room. I laughed at the expression on Richard's face when I googled *him*. There were Richard Mainwarings doing everything from rocket science to poetry readings.

"Poetry, Richard?" His warm hand settled on my shoulder.

"Why not? I've always been fond of a well-turned phrase."

"Poetry." Will snorted. "Spare me."

Richard gave the dog a look. " 'O 'tis a foul thing, when a cur cannot keep himself in all companies.' "

Will scratched his ear. "A badass vampire spouting poetry? Now *that's* foul."

"I know that bit from my days at the Globe. *The Two Gentlemen of Verona*." I smiled at Richard. "Nice." You had to like a man who could quote Shakespeare. I looked at the dogs. Valdez had ignored Will and was sleeping on his back, giving us a not so nice view of his stomach and elsewhere. "Unfortunately my dogs think their place is in the middle of my business. I got used to one, but two . . ."

"Now, Mistress." Will wagged his tail. "We but live to serve." He glanced at Valdez who had started snoring. "And a fresh pair of eyes could be the best thing that ever happened to you."

"If I just had to worry about your eyes, I could deal." Will turned to give me his best "I'm a badass" look. Okay, maybe he would pull his weight. "Never mind. I did this to myself. I let Blade saddle me with both of you."

"After that threat from Westwood, I'd think you'd be glad of the extra protection." Richard leaned down, like he was studying the web site I'd been showing him.

I could never read his mind, but I had a feeling . . . Could he see down my V-neck T-shirt?

"Of course I can, Gloriana. Why do you think I'm standing here? You mentioned cup size. I got distracted checking them out for myself." Richard chuckled, then stepped back when I jumped to my feet.

"Mind reading scumbag." I slammed the computer shut. "This lesson's over."

"Temper, temper. You said you were irresistible. I just proved the point." Richard dodged my fist, grinned and headed for the door. "I look forward to our next lesson. And while I'm downstairs, I'll scan the neighborhood for any suspicious characters. It's been a while since I've made a mortal scream. Sounds like fun."

I slammed the door behind him and threw the dead bolts. Then I pushed Valdez off the couch and picked up the remote. I needed something funny. *Two and a Half Men*. When Charlie came on to blond bimbo number sixty-seven, I remembered Richard's hand, warm on my shoulder and the twinkle in his eyes when he'd admitted to copping a peek. Okay, I admit it, I don't mind a little male appreciation from someone besides Blade. Hey, Gloriana's still got it. And I was beginning to understand why Flo had gone for Richard. He had a certain charm . . .

My cell phone rang during the third commercial.

"I got your e-mail."

If the male voice had been Blade's, I would have been glad to hear it. Instead I gripped the phone until the plastic cracked.

"I got yours first." *Nice comeback, Glory.* "For a billionaire, you've got weird hobbies. Has anyone ever suggested therapy?"

"For a vampire, you've got an interesting vocabulary. Has anyone ever suggested a stake through the heart?" He actually laughed.

"Bastard." My extensive vocabulary deserted me.

"You're angry. Are your fangs out?"

"Damn straight."

"I wish I could see them. Run your tongue over them. So sharp, so pretty."

"Sharp enough to suck you dry, you creep."

"I remember how you looked on Halloween. Your very generous breasts thrusting against that wooden stake." Westwood made a sound that creeped me out. "What are you wearing right now, Gloriana? Are you naked?"

My stomach lurched and I stared at the phone for half a second before I snapped it closed and threw it across the room. It hit Flo's collection of Patrick Swayze movies (don't ask), then bounced on the rug.

Valdez's cold nose brushed my face.

I threw my arms around him and laid my cheek on his warm fur.

"Westwood?"

"Yes." I shuddered. "I think we just had phone sex."

The phone rang again and we all stared at it.

"Pick it up. Let me talk to that asshole." Will paced around the phone. "Damn it, this dog form sucks. Answer the damned phone, Glory."

"No." The ringing stopped for a few blessed seconds then started again.

"Check the caller ID." Valdez licked my cheek and I finally let go of him. *"Could be Blade. He'll be worried if you don't answer."*

The phone quit ringing, then beeped to indicate I had voice mail. I made myself rescue the battered phone and check the number. Blade. Thank God. But why did he have to be so far away? I'd give anything to feel his arms around me now. I listened to his voice mail and realized I had to call him back before he flew home to check on me. Times like these, I realized a cell phone is nothing but a long leash. Okay, there were worse things than having a man worried about you. Like having a homicidal maniac as a pen pal. I ignored the rock in the pit of my stomach and hit the speed dial.

I wasn't about to mention Westwood's call. Blade needed to keep his cool and the idea that Westwood . . . Well, let's just say the whole thing was seriously creeping me out. The less said about it, the better.

"It looks good, Glory." Flo threw down her paintbrush and wiped her hands on a burnt orange cotton T-shirt that she'd declared too ugly to be more than a rag. "A little plain, maybe, but I think better than it did before."

I couldn't argue, at least not without whining. I couldn't get over the nagging fear that we'd get this place back together and Westwood's fire bomber would strike again.

"Snap out of it, Glory. Damian's put in extra thick windows and hired security to do drive-bys during the day." Flo put her hand on my shoulder. "And Jeremiah has gone after this Westwood. He'll make him pay for this." Flo gestured at the empty racks beside her. "You'll be back in business in no time."

"Right. I'm snapping out of it right now." Damian's workmen had been quick about getting up new drywall and installing flooring. I'd picked out the wood laminate myself, trying for a space that shouted retro, hip, spend your cash here. But fixtures and stock were up to me. Fortunately, an army of friends had shown up ready to paint, clean, whatever I needed. Most surprising had been Flo, who'd put her manicure at risk to pick up a paint brush.

"Now all we need is some stock." I sat on a stool next to my refurbished counter, which would hold my new cash register. The old one sat in the stock room, a lump of melted plastic that resembled a science experiment gone terribly wrong.

"Here you go." Lacy, my day person and shape-shifting neighbor, pushed in through the door loaded down with dry cleaning bags. "These all came out pretty well. I tried to look them over before I accepted them." She made a face. "Here's the bill. I put it on your credit card like you asked. Major bucks, I'm afraid."

I glanced at the bill and swallowed. Since when did dry cleaning cost more than a small car? "Here, let me help you." I grabbed some bags and began hanging up dresses and suits on the metal racks we'd salvaged by scrubbing off black soot.

"And I have more for you, Glory." Flo hopped up from where she'd settled to do the baseboards. "I cleaned out my closet." She smiled at Lacy. "Come upstairs and give me a hand."

"Sure." Lacy gave me a pinch me, I'm dreaming look behind Flo's back. I love my roomie, but she'd never once considered letting me sell any of her vast collection of shoes, purses or clothes before. She'd always insisted classics never went out of style. And she was right. I'd built a business on that fact.

"Mr. Danger here didn't even bother to look up when that door opened." Valdez followed me to the back room where I picked up a trash can. *"Will's not worth the cost of Alpo."*

I set the can down and began stripping plastic bags off clothes. "He's okay." I looked around the shop. So much to do. I wished the dogs could hold a paint brush. Maybe if I tied one to Valdez's tail . . .

"Oh, no you don't. Not in the job description." Valdez sat with a thump. *"I was making a point here. About the slug otherwise known as Will. The point is, he's dead to the world during the day. Which is when you're most at risk."* Valdez sat near my feet while I stuffed bags into the trash can. *"Then at night, when he should be on high alert, so maybe yours truly could get some rest, he's spending all his time trying to look up Flo's skirt or down your blouse."*

"I resent the implication, though I won't apologize for appreciating fine women, cheese doodle. And I've been by the window scanning the street for mischief makers. I saw Lacy when she was a half block away. I know you don't like cats, but the lady's on your side, you know." Will padded up to sit on my other side. "Nice suit."

"Chanel." I stroked the fine wool. Believe me, if I could

have sucked in my gut enough to get the zipper up, I'd have kept it.

"In Paris I had a girlfriend once who shopped at Chanel. Expensive habit. I had to dump her."

"Yeah, right. You dumped her. And I'm a Labradoodle, not a cheese doodle."

"Oh, puh-leeze. At least I chose to be a purebred Great Pyrenees. A dog known as a faithful friend and fierce guardian. Not a mongrel with questionable ancestors."

"Mongrel!" Valdez growled and moved in on Will. *"Yeah, you're fierce. Especially when you finally get up off your ass to come to the food bowl."*

"Right. Like you're not Twinkie obsessed. And what's with the jones you've got for Cheetos?"

I tuned out the ongoing saga. Between the ick factor of Will playing Peeping Tom and paint fumes, I needed air. I stepped outside and took a deep breath. The air was fresh and I instantly felt better. It was after two in the morning, thank God for all night dry cleaners, and the street was almost deserted. Mugs and Muffins, already back in business, boasted only one customer, a student type hunched over his laptop with his coffee at his elbow. His glasses weren't tinted so I figured he wasn't in the Westwood spy network. God, I was sick of being paranoid.

"Gloriana." Oh, hell. A pain stabbed my forehead. *"Come to me, Gloriana."*

The voice was inside my head. I had to follow it. I headed down the sidewalk toward the corner.

"Yes, darling. Come closer. You're beautiful. Let me see you."

I threw off my sweater and reached for the buttons on my blouse.

"What the hell are you doing?" Valdez head-butted me, knocking me on my ass. *"Glory, look at me."*

I shook my head. "What?" Damn, I was freezing. My blouse was open to the waist giving the world a nice view of my black bra, my sweater a lump on the sidewalk a few feet away.

"Get inside, Gloriana." Will ran to the corner, barking and snarling like he meant business.

I staggered to my feet. "That voice. I swear I know it." I grabbed my sweater and ran to the shop door. "Will. You get anything?"

"Nope. Whoever it was got away."

Valdez pushed me inside. My brain was screaming. Even though the voice was gone, the headache seemed determined to hang on. And what was with the striptease? I buttoned my blouse and threw on my sweater again.

"I'm going to look around some more." Will looked at Valdez. "You stay here with her."

"Like I take orders from you." Valdez looked up at me. *"Sit down, Glory. Flo and Lacy should be back any minute."*

"What's going on here?" The man in the doorway provoked a bark-a-thon that made my head scream.

I collapsed on a stool and leaned my head on the counter. "Nothing."

"Why's the door standing open?" Richard Mainwaring glared at Valdez, then Will when he came trotting inside.

"I left it open. I needed air. My head's killing me."

"Close your eyes."

Sue me, but I did. Because the light was killing me, not just because he *told* me to. I felt his hand on the top of my head. Had I combed my hair in the past few hours? Nope. In fact, I think there were globs of yellow paint decorating my crown. I couldn't get worked up about it. The pain!

"The vampire's been working you again. What happened?"

"It was stupid." I kept my head down, eyes closed. "I followed the voice. Like I was under the whammy or something." Richard's hand on my head had actually made the pain stop. I sat up. "And I started taking off my clothes. Like he told me to. How sick is that?"

Richard nodded toward Will. "Back outside. See if you can find this vampire who wants Glory naked."

"On it." Will smirked at Valdez, I swear it, then headed out the door just before Richard closed it.

"Maybe we should lock the door." Valdez was obviously not happy to see Will given an assignment and not him. *"We don't want that Glory-obsessed vampire in here."*

"Maybe we do." Richard sure looked scary when he was mad.

"Like a door will keep out a vampire." Flo shouted from outside. "Open up."

Nine

Richard flung open the door again and stepped back. He just stared at Flo, his face grim.

"Richard." Flo's look as she walked past him, her arms full of clothes, was equally grim.

"Why do you want to keep out vampires? They're some of our best customers." Lacy had her hands full of shoe boxes! And purses!

No headache can stand up to my love of good accessories. I jumped up to help both of them set the things on a table.

"Some vampires are much more interested in causing trouble than in looking good." Richard stared at Flo for a heartbeat or two. "Some vampires are interested in nothing but looking good."

"Excuse me, but I take pride in my appearance." Flo carefully set a pile of silk blouses on the table. "And I've done the impossible. I've kept my look fresh and up to date in spite of being more than a few centuries older than most of the present company."

I put my hand on Flo's shoulder. She was shaking with anger, her fangs visible at the edges of her Cherries in the Snow lipstick. Her color, but so last century. I sure wasn't about to tell her that. Block, block.

"You're my role model, Flo, my guide to fashion forward thinking." I gave Richard a go away look. "Richard's concerned about some vamp he's hunting."

"No, Richard's concerned about Gloriana being stalked."

At least he wasn't glaring at Flo anymore. Now he was glaring at me.

"Stalked?" Flo looked at me, fangs full out. "Who would dare do that to my roomie? I'll rip his throat out. A vampire? No, his throat would heal. Where's a stake when you need one?" Flo grabbed a paint brush and eyed the wooden end. "A little dull, but with enough pressure—"

"Chill out, vamp girl, I think Richard can handle it." Lacy had stacked the shoe boxes neatly. She leaned against the counter so her tiny tank top rode up to show a slim middle that made my jaw clench. The tall redhead had something of a crush on Richard. She was all for his piercing gaze, broody thing.

"You should all be on guard." He turned to his former mistress. "Florence, I don't suppose you've heard voices in your head lately."

"Voices? Like I'm crazy?" Flo was determined to hate Richard and I'd given up trying to make peace.

"No. *I've* been hearing voices, like someone is inside *my* head, trying to get me to come to them." Okay, so maybe I was an incurable peacemaker. "You hear anything like that?"

"No, no one has done this." Flo studied me with worried green eyes. "Do you recognize the voice? Is it Damian again?"

Flo's brother Damian had done a number or two on me with his little mind games while trying to make me another notch on his bedpost. But I'd made it pretty clear to him that I wasn't playing and I think he'd moved on. "I'd recognize his voice. This one is different. Sounds pure American. Doesn't have the cute little accent you and Damian have."

"Cute, of course. But very little. Whoever is in your head—he's dead meat. Am I right, girlfriend?"

"Right. Now show me some shoes. I can't believe you're letting me sell them."

"Maybe." Flo lifted the top off one of the shoe boxes. "And

maybe I need to keep these. I remember the night I bought them. In New York." She glanced at Richard. "A generous lover and a famous musician, very famous, demanded I have only the best." She picked up a red lizard pump and hummed a few bars of a song I recognized immediately.

"Flo, are you kidding? Was your lover—" Lacy stopped when Flo held up her hand.

"I can't say his name. We did not part well. I had to sign an"—she shuddered—"agreement."

"Surprise. Surprise." Richard's smile made *me* shudder.

Flo looked daggers, then turned her back on him as she stroked the shoe. "You can get a good price for these, Glory. Barely worn." She smiled at me. "I move on. There are many more"—she glanced at Richard—"better shoes out there."

"Hey, why bother with shoes at all? You don't need them when you spend most of your time horizontal."

Whoa. Richard was playing the scorned lover, big time. Clearly Flo had dumped *him*. Now Flo muttered something nasty in Italian and rounded on him, hands on hips. I stepped between them, taking my life in my hands, but what's a girl to do? I needed both of them on my side and I'd just put the shop into some kind of order. Any fight between them was bound to be messy.

"Behave, please." I rubbed my head and came away with yellow paint on my hand. How cute was that? I grabbed a rag, wiping my hands while I smiled at Richard.

"Richard, thanks for the help with my headache. I feel a thousand times better." This did not go over big with Flo. I put my hand on her shoulder again and felt her quivering with the urge to leap over me and go for you know who's throat.

"Flo, I'm dying to see what you brought me. Let's dig in." The door opened and Will trotted in.

"All clear outside. Whoever's after Glory has left." He shot Valdez a smug look. "Too bad. I was fully prepared to take him out."

Flo quit giving Richard a "go to hell" look long enough

to examine me with concern. "If this happens again, do what he says. Go outside. Then we attack, all of us. An ambush."

Lacy gave up on her seductive pose and moved closer. "Right. We'll teach this brain buster to mess with our friend."

"Thanks. It's a thought." I glanced at Richard. "But Richard here is the vamp enforcer. Maybe he can run down this guy. I've got too much to do to waste my time dealing with some vague threat."

"Not so vague if he's trying to get you alone. For sex, do you think?" Flo bit her lip. She didn't like the idea of asking Richard for anything, obviously. But the former priest had a reputation for dealing with rogue vampires in a way that stopped the problems they were causing permanently.

"Not everything is about sex, Florence." Richard winced when Valdez sat on his foot. "Hey, watch it, fella, I'm on Glory's side."

"*Sorry.*" The dog moved a quarter of an inch, max. Not surprising. My dog had a crush on Flo that he didn't bother to hide. He'd obviously decided he had issues with Richard. *"Are you going to help Glory or not?"*

"You sure it's a vampire? You know Westwood's probably got guys keeping tabs on this place. Because he knows vamps work here." Lacy had just made a good point. I hadn't told Flo or Lacy about Westwood's e-mail. I gave them a quick recap.

"Bastard!" Lacy snarled like she wanted to change into cat form and rip someone apart. I hid a smile. She'd confessed once that her form was more lap kitty than saber-toothed tiger. What was she going to do? Purr him to death? Flo was agitated too, muttering in Italian.

"The guy was talking in Glory's head. Unless Westwood's got a paranormal on his payroll, he's not behind this stunt." Valdez got up and stretched. *"I'm going outside for my own look-see. Lacy, do you mind coming with? And use the leash. I figure we'd be well rid of somebody here if animal control had seen him running loose*

out there, but I don't want to be the problem instead of the solution."
High and mighty Valdez stalked to the door.

"Is the little doggy afraid of animal control?" Will
pushed his head under my hand. "Unlike you, doodle bug,
I'm fearless. I'll stay here and take care of the mistress."

Flo and Richard both gave Will a narrow-eyed look. Ho.
So I wasn't the only one who didn't like the "m" word coming from my dog.

"You're both part of the problem if you don't get over
this rivalry. I've got a good mind to call Blade and let him
know what's going on." I rubbed my hair with the rag and
came away with even more paint. There was a mirror in the
dressing room, but it's true that vamps don't reflect. Just as
well. I'd have sent myself screaming into the night. "You
guys are a pain and not in my head."

"I'm going outside with you, Valdez." Richard took the
leash from Lacy. "Ladies, I'll be back shortly. Lock the door
behind me." He was out the door before any of us had time
to react.

"Bossy, isn't he?" Lacy did throw the dead bolts before
she picked up a navy Prada clutch. "Can I borrow this before
you sell it, Glory?" She smiled at Flo. "You have amazing
taste."

"Thanks." Flo gave a shrug. "And yes, he's bossy. Just one
reason why we didn't work as a couple." Her shoulders
sagged for a moment, then she visibly pulled herself together. "I'm meeting my new lover later. I've been seeing
him for a while now. He reminds me of a prince I once knew
in Budapest. So handsome, so caring. And he puts my needs
first. Compared to him, Richard is a . . ." She glanced
around, then grinned. "Toad!"

"Huh?" Lacy looked lost, but I saw what Flo had seen.
One of my well-meaning friends had left a box of clothes
earlier in the evening. On top was an unfortunate pair of
bright green flannel pajamas with frogs and toads leaping
from lily pad to lily pad. Need I mention that said friend,
a female vampire, had absolutely no social life? She was a

project just waiting to be tackled. As soon as I got the shop going again, I was going to see about hooking her up. Maybe Richard . . .

Flo laughed. "I'm reading your mind, roomie. By all means set Richard up with toad girl. They will be like two pods in a pea."

"Peas in a pod." I grinned but couldn't keep it going. The nagging thought that Westwood could have paranormals on his payroll was deeply disturbing for so many reasons. One: Fighting humans was easy compared to combating the bag of tricks a shape shifter or vamp could whip out. Two: A paranormal who would work for a known vamp hunter had no limits when it came to dirty deeds. Three? Well, two were more than enough for me.

Will paced in front of the windows, obviously agitated by the thought that Valdez could be getting action while he was on inside guard duty. I went back to sorting through Flo's fabulous castoffs. My customers would go nuts for these. I happily pushed the whole danger issue to the back of my mind.

I offered to pay Flo for her things, but she acted so insulted that I might think she needed money, that I quickly gave up. She and Lacy got into a debate over my back wall. I liked the plain, but clean digs. Flo obviously thought the wall needed something.

Me, I just needed to reopen before I reached my credit limit. I mentally composed a flyer and decided to get the shop open by next week, come hell or high water. As for the hell . . . What if the freak-a-zoid stalking me created a disturbance and ran off my customers? Or worse, if he or she (women's lib, you know) caught me alone in the shop one night . . . And what was the deal about getting me to take off my clothes? I may have had my wild and free days, but stripping for strangers was not going to happen again. A memory, just a wisp, nagged at me. If I could just grab on to it. Who or what—

Will woofed and Lacy opened the door. The boys were

back and the two dogs immediately began arguing again. Why was I worrying about being alone? I was never alone. Alone might actually be a real treat.

"*Hey, Glory. We've got a present for you.*" Valdez pushed Will out of the way. "*Out back.*"

Richard unclipped Valdez's leash and grinned. "He's right. Open the back door." This was the third night in a row Richard had shown up and taken one or both dogs out for guard duty.

"Be careful out there. Do you need us?" Flo gave me a concerned look.

"She won't be in danger, Florence." Richard lost his smile. "I wouldn't do that."

"Whatever." Flo shrugged, then grabbed Lacy's arm and dragged her to the other side of the shop where she'd started a secret project. She'd even hung a sheet from the ceiling so I couldn't see what she was up to. I didn't push to find out either. I was glad for the company.

"Are you coming?" Richard threw open the back door.

"Sure. What's up?" Will was right behind me. I looked out and saw that for a change the security lights were working. My Suburban, its brown a mud color that was supposed to keep the dirt from showing, sat in my usual spot. A man stood beside it. The man wasn't moving, except his eyes. They darted back and forth.

I walked closer and stared into those hyper eyes. Hmm.

"Westwood sent him." Richard sent both dogs to sit by the back door. He bent down and picked up a pair of tinted glasses. "Valdez caught him skulking back here and took him down."

"Wow. I guess I owe that pup a ribeye." The man was a muscle bound type who was thinking in a panic.

"*Vampires. Blood suckers. I'm cooked. Not worth it. Help. Help. Holy shit, I can't move. Not even my little finger. What are they doing to me?*"

"Poor baby. What were you doing out here by my car?" I squeezed the guy's chin. He needed a shave and not in that cool way that makes a guy look edgy and macho. This one just looked scruffy. My touch sent him into hyperdrive.

"Slash tires, key it, a little sugar in the gas tank. A few harmless hassles. I swear it. Let me go. Let me go. Oh, shit, why can't I talk? She's a hot chick, nice knockers, but look at those fangs. Is it gonna hurt? Maybe she'll have sex with me—" The creep wobbled on his feet when I shoved him, but didn't go over.

"Harmless hassles?" All I could see were dollar signs and being on foot. Not cool in Austin. There's great public transit, but I don't think I'd be welcome with two dogs, especially dogs prepared to knock the tinted glasses off anyone who had a vision problem.

"Do what you wish, Gloriana. Though I doubt you'd want to take his blood." Mainwaring was close to me and I could feel his warmth at my back. "He's right about one thing. You're a hot chick."

"You're wise not to mention my 'knockers,' Richard, but your timing sucks. I'm not exactly in the mood for a flirtation which is probably all about making Flo jealous." Okay, maybe men did go for the too tight jeans and snug green T-shirt, both dried on high heat at Blade's. Blade. Hmm. I missed him, but kind of liked Richard's flirting. Did that make me a slut? Again? Historically, I never went long without some kind of action except for some lean years midnineteenth century. But that's another story. Yeah, slut was pretty accurate.

"Now what delicious torture should I use to punish Westwood's thug?" I stared into the man's still frantic eyes. "What's your name? Talk to me."

"Mitch. Mitch Ellison."

"Listen to me, Mitch. You will not hurt my car. You will not hurt my shop and you will definitely never have sex with me. Probably not with anyone." I looked down at his pants. "Your dick is on fire."

"Aw, Christ!" The man began clawing at his zipper, tears

ran down his cheeks and he fell to the concrete. "The pain! Stop it. Please."

"This is fun." Richard's breath stirred my hair. "I hope this isn't how you feel about all . . . dicks."

I ignored him. "Oops. Sorry, Mitch, but your peter just fell off and rolled under the car."

The man shrieked and scrambled around frantically until all we could see were his brown loafers sticking out from the side of the car, kicking at the concrete.

"I can almost feel sorry for the bastard." Richard didn't sound sorry.

I watched the loafers disappear as the wailing reached a fever pitch.

"Where is it? I can't find it. Oh, God." Loud sobs.

"This isn't as much fun as I thought it would be." I leaned down just as one arm reached out to slap at the ground.

Will and Valdez were laughing their furry butts off. For some reason this irritated the hell out of me.

"Inside, both of you." I strode to the back door and threw it open.

"Aw, Glory, this is just getting good." Will bumped against me.

"Come on, Kilpatrick, let her do her thing." Valdez looked at Richard. *"Stay with her."*

Richard nodded and I slammed the door. I turned to finish things. Mitch's whining was getting to me.

"Come out now, Mitch. I found your teeny weenie. I'll give it back if you show me some respect."

The man slid out and jumped up. "Yes, ma'am." He was shaking and tears ran down his cheeks. "Please, please give back my cock. I'll do anything. Anything."

I looked at Richard but he just raised that damned eyebrow. Like this was my party, my call.

"Mitch, you will never work for Brent Westwood again. You will leave Austin and you will know that vampires don't exist. Westwood made up the whole thing. He's crazy."

"Yes, ma'am." The man held out his shaking hand. "Please. Have pity. My wife—"

"Stop whining." The cheating lowlife had a wife. "You will be a wonderful, loving, *faithful* husband. You will treat your wife like a queen and do whatever she asks as soon as she asks it."

Richard chuckled and put his hand on my back. "You want me to finish this?"

"I'm handling it." I grabbed the man's chin again. "Listen to me, Mitch. You will turn over the remote control to your wife. You will watch whatever she wants and never complain."

"Now you're just being cruel." Richard walked around me and patted the pockets on the man's khakis. "Ah. I think you could use this." He pulled out a wad of bills and began peeling off hundreds. "You can even use it to pay off your debt to me."

Visions of financial freedom brought a lump to my throat. I couldn't feel bad about taking Westwood's blood money. Blood. The dickless wonder here reeked of B positive. I licked my lips but decided to let the urge pass. Biting this creep would put me way closer to him than I wanted to be. If he'd been a more exotic type . . . Hey, I'm a blood-sucking vampire and don't you forget it.

"Here." The man eagerly thrust out his hand. I hit his palm with my fist. "Put your thing back on and get out of here." I ignored his pathetic squeal of happiness. When I heard his zipper go down, I turned away. Rapid footsteps announced his departure.

I felt Richard at my back again. "Eight hundred dollars. Shall we call it even?"

I turned and looked at him. "My debt to you?" Gee, he was awfully eager to be rid of our connection. Oh, hell. The gleam in his eyes meant he was doing the mind reading bit even though I'd told him more than once that I hated it. "If that will satisfy you, I'm all for it." I was pretty sure the Harley bill had been more than that.

"Satisfy me? Not a chance." Richard counted out four bills and stuck them in my jeans' pocket, his fingers sliding down to rest warm against my tummy. "I want more . . . lessons."

Damned tight jeans. If his fingers got stuck in there . . . I sucked in my gut and pulled out his hand. "Fine. I can use the cash and I certainly know how it feels to be technologically challenged."

"You pity me." He held onto my fingers, then lifted them to his lips. "Charming."

I sometimes forgot that Richard and I have the same British roots. His accent was slight, but definitely told of his being more upper crust than I'd ever hoped to be. He'd got the American accent down pretty well, but he'd never completely blend in wherever he went. Not with his almost platinum hair and startling blue eyes. He'd been turned vampire when he'd been deeply tanned, maybe after one of his crusades. Vamp magic kept him that way and the combination was impossibly yummy.

At least I'd remembered to block his mind reading this time. I smiled up at him, not exactly hating the feel of his warm lips on my hand.

"I see you've moved on, Richard."

Oh, crap. Flo stood in the doorway to the shop. She looked brittle, the twist to her lips as close to ugly as my gorgeous roomie would ever get. I jerked my fingers out of his hand.

"Flo, Richard was helping me with a creep sent by Westwood."

Flo laughed and looked around. "The creep has crept away, I guess. Glory, your cell phone has been ringing. You might want to check your voice mail." She nodded, like— See? I didn't just come out here to spy on my ex-lover and my roomie.

"Flo, I—"

"Carry on, *cara*. I couldn't care less what you do with Richard. But why you would be interested in this one when you have Blade . . ." A Gaelic shrug. "Whatever." She turned on her four-inch heels and went back inside. The door slammed behind her.

"That was harsh." I turned to Richard, but he was smiling, apparently not disturbed at all.

"Whatever." He winked and strolled away, the picture of unconcerned male.

Great. I got to go in to a simmering roomie and a voice mail that might be from Westwood again. I'd had two since our phone chat. If I didn't know better, I'd swear Westwood was hot for me. Now there was something useful. I could play along, seduce him back into coming home for a little sack action, then bam!—bye, bye billionaire. I'd love to see Westwood on his knees begging for his dick or his life or whatever.

I opened the back door and met Valdez's glare. I'd been outside alone for exactly fifteen seconds. The lecture lasted ten times longer than that.

Ten

🦇

"I'm going alone and that's all there is to it."

"Blade will kill us if we let you do it."

"Blade will just have to get over it." I stopped brushing my hair and looked at Valdez. "Or he doesn't even have to know about it."

"He'll know." Will had been watching me get ready with interest.

When I'd emerged from my bedroom dressed to kill in a leather mini and red bustier, both dogs had perked up. Because they thought we were all going out. Not.

"I can keep my lips zipped, but the doodle dog won't. He's too whipped." Will gave Valdez a look.

Valdez growled, his ears flat. *"I'll show you whipped."*

"Cool it, Valdez. I have a date. A date. Can you grasp the concept? It does not include taking along my pets, no matter how cute. Or protective. Or insane."

Valdez snorted. *"What do we really know about this fireman? He could be on Westwood's payroll. When he gets you alone—"*

"Steve is an arson investigator and a mortal. I can read his mind. He doesn't wear those special glasses and he's not working for Westwood." He'd come by the shop one night while I'd been putting the finishing touches on pricing my new inventory. The dogs had behaved, barely. Flo had scoped him out, then dismissed him. It didn't take mind reading to know she thought mortals were too ordinary for her attention.

But I'd read Steve's mind and liked what I saw. He

thought I was hot and he admired the way I was putting my business back together. Worked for me. I kind of looked forward to an uncomplicated date. One where I didn't have to block my thoughts. Or take along a pooper scooper.

"We'll be fine. We're going to a club on Sixth Street, just a few blocks from here. There will be other people around." And we were going dancing. My toes tingled just thinking about it. Yeah, I did miss Blade, but he'd never been much for dancing and I absolutely love it. Steve said he was into the country western thing, part of the Texas experience I'd been determined to enjoy when I'd moved to Austin.

The buzzer sounded. He was here. I tied a red scarf around my neck, then hit the button.

"Steve?"

"Right. Should I come up?"

"No." I glanced at the dogs. "I'm ready. I'll be right down."

"I'm going on record. This is a bad idea." Valdez nosed my black leather purse. *"Take your cell, call Mainwaring if you get in a bind. You got him on speed dial?"*

"Call Richard? Why not Blade? He could fly in from Africa to hold my hand." I did have Richard on speed dial. Because we'd been having those computer lessons and needed to set them up. "I can handle myself, Valdez. I know you and Blade don't think so, but get over it." I patted Will on the head. "Thanks for not nagging me."

"No problem. A night off. Why would I object?" He looked at Valdez. "Let the doodle here obsess. I'm taking a nap."

"I'm keeping track of this shit, Kilpatrick. Don't be surprised if Blade docks your pay."

I wasn't about to stay and listen to the dogs yammer at each other. I grabbed my purse and shawl and headed down the stairs. Steve waited at the outside door. He was dressed in jeans and a Western shirt that showed off his lean build. The black cowboy hat looked well worn, like he might actually *be* a cowboy. Very cute.

"Ready?" Steve grinned when he saw me. "You look great." He eyed my high-heeled boots. "You sure you can dance in those?"

I took his arm. "Hey, I danced in Vegas in heels higher than this. Now let's go."

We walked down the street toward the busier, rowdier section of Sixth Street where the clubs were doing a booming business. Saturday night. I was reopening my shop on Tuesday and things had come together pretty well. I'd decided I deserved a night off and had jumped at the chance when Steve suggested it. Steve asked me about my gig in Vegas and I trotted out some of my better stories. By the time we got to the club, we were both laughing.

"What can I get you to drink?"

There it was, the awkward moment when I had to either claim to be AA or offer to be the designated driver or something. Instead, I smiled and let him order a rum and coke for me. Why not? I didn't have to drink it and I was tired of being different. You know?

Before the drinks even arrived, we were on the dance floor. Steve was a great dancer, slow or fast. We did the Cotton-Eyed Joe, the swing, then two-stepped the perimeter of the dance floor, my fingers in Steve's belt loops, his hands warm on my shoulder and waist. The night flew by. I didn't feel a single negative vibe and I wasn't so oblivious that I didn't scan the place a time or two or three looking for thuggish men in tinted glasses. Maybe Westwood hadn't had time to replace Mitch. I didn't care. I was having fun.

I laughed off Steve's concern that the ice had melted in my drink and let him order me a second one. That one I eventually managed to exchange for an empty on another table when Steve hit the men's room. By the time the band played its last set, I felt really comfortable with Steve. Comfortable. Unfortunately, even during slow dances, with his strong arms wrapped around me, there was simply no chemistry. Not on my part, anyway.

Steve rubbed my back and nuzzled my neck when the lights were dim, but I felt *nada*. Well, not exactly *nada*. Fresh blood pulsed through Steve's veins. Hot AB negative! Smelling so utterly delicious that I had to fight to keep my fangs in.

"Time to go home." I smiled and picked up my purse. I'd turned off my cell phone as soon as I'd left the apartment. No way was my complicated life going to intrude on this evening.

"How about breakfast? We can hit an IHOP or Denny's. My car's parked not far from here."

I stepped into the cool night air and wrapped the black shawl I'd brought around my shoulders.

"I'd love to, but I'm pretty tired. Maybe another night."

Steve grinned and grabbed my hand. "That's what I like to hear. Another night." He leaned down and kissed me. Just a sweet, getting to know you kiss. It wasn't bad. Or great. I pulled him toward my end of the street. We had about six long blocks to walk. Nothing for a vamp, but a vamp in high heeled boots . . . ? I was leaning on Steve by block three. Unfortunately he took it as encouragement.

"Come here." He pulled me into a dark parking lot between two cars and pushed me against a black Lexus. Yeah, I wasn't really into the moment if I was noticing the make of car behind me, was I? He kissed me, a deeper kiss that involved tongues and hands roaming a little too freely. I couldn't blame the guy. I'd been sending signals all night that I enjoyed his company. Too bad it was his dancing that turned me on. And his sure to be tasty blood.

I pulled back and looked into his eyes. What I felt was bloodlust. Well, it beat the hell out of no lust at all.

"Steve." My voice was low and I had him under the whammy in seconds. He just stood there, his arms still around me while I leaned in and sniffed. I shouldn't, but who could resist clean male skin, the hint of an aftershave that I liked and that damned AB negative? I was in before you could say, "Bite me."

Ah, the taste, the heat, and that quivering down low that was damned near orgasmic. I felt him slump against me and reluctantly pulled back. The poor guy should at least be able to walk home. I licked the puncture wounds to close them then gave him a thank you kiss on his very yummy neck.

"Well, look who's enjoying a little pre-dawn snack." The male voice spun me around. Familiar. The freaking voice in my head that had given me migraines.

"You." I disentangled myself from Steve and propped him against the Lexus. "Who the hell *are* you?" Head clear. No headache. Feeding had given me a surge of energy, like I could conquer the world or at least this scum-sucking vampire.

"Answer me. Who the hell are you and why are you bugging me?" I stepped away from the car and got into his face. Maybe not my smartest move. He was a big guy. Good looking and much too much my type. Dark hair, dark eyes, great build and a dimple in his chin. There was something about that dimple . . . He didn't touch me, just smiled like I amused him. Okay, now I was really mad.

"I'm not surprised you don't remember me. I made sure you wouldn't. Nothing like dumping a woman and then having her bugging the hell out of you."

"Excuse me?" *I* did the dumping not the other way around. This guy was obviously delusional.

"Let me show you something." He grabbed my hand, strong enough that I couldn't wrench it away even though I damn sure tried.

"Let me go, asshole." For the first time, I wished I'd listened to Valdez. An attack dog would be mighty handy about now.

"Gloriana." I heard the guy's voice in my head and thought about blocking him. But I wanted to know who or what he was and what he wanted. *"Remember this."*

I was up high, on a bed surrounded by . . . flowers. Sweet smell, but the noise! A band played a college fight song.

Thousands cheered. The bed jerked and swayed its way down a corridor between skyscrapers.

"Where are we?"

"New York City, Gloriana. 1969. Macy's Thanksgiving Day Parade. You and I, bed buddies."

Naked bed buddies. He laughed up at me when I sat up and pushed out my breasts. Not happening. But the sunlight, the cold, crisp air and the shouts of the crowd sure as hell *felt* real. So did the rush of doing the wild thing while thousands cheered.

"You'd think they would stop the parade, try to arrest us." A snowflake drifted down and melted on my breast. I shivered and grabbed a blanket just as the float lurched to a stop.

"Do you want to add a cop to the mix?" He grinned and snatched the blanket away. "You won't need that. I can keep you hot." Another man appeared beside the bed, this one in full uniform swinging a nightstick.

"You two are under arrest. Unless I can have a piece of that." The cop's night stick stroked my bare bum. The crowd cheered again, obviously pro-law enforcement.

"No, lover, lose the cop, you're more than enough for me." I kissed him and the policeman disappeared. The crowds groaned and the band segued into "Hail Britannia." "Ooo," I murmured when he grabbed my ass and pushed into me. "You do know how to please a woman."

"Always."

Snow came down harder, *I* came harder. He was right. Who needed a blanket?

"What does this float represent anyway?"

He grinned and pointed upward. A banner waved above us. "Make Love, Not War."

"We're protesting Vietnam?" Now I noticed that our headboard was a giant peace sign made of red roses and white gardenias.

"Got to love the sixties, especially when a vampire flies under the draft radar." His fangs slid across my shoulder.

"Wave at the crowd, baby. We're New York's answer to John and Yoko."

The band broke into a Beatles medley. "All You Need Is Love." The crowd sang along.

A turquoise parakeet landed on the brass footboard and began preening.

"You up for a threesome?" He nodded and the bird morphed into a tall brunette with disgustingly slim hips and perky C cup breasts. She was naked, of course. The crowd went wild and the band started "A Little Help from My Friends."

I dove under the blanket. "No, thanks, I want you all to myself."

He pulled me up for a big kiss, then rolled me under him. I saw the bird disappear into what was practically a snowstorm. Nothing could cool off my lover, though. He surged into me again and again. Orgasm number three hit me, but who was counting?

"How long do you want this to last?" he whispered against my neck. His fangs pierced me and another orgasm rocked me and the float. The band found its groove on "Love Me Do."

"Forever."

I shivered, suddenly back in a dark parking lot in Austin, Texas, in an entirely different century.

"That's when I decided we were over. Hate clingy women." He squeezed my hand. "Even sexually adventurous ones."

"Clingy women? Me?" I jerked my hand from his, my fangs full out. "Like I'd ever need to cling to anyone." The adventurous thing I could live with. Though the fact that I couldn't remember was a real buzz-kill. "That didn't really happen. You made it up."

"Not entirely. We had lots of special times." He grinned. "Want to see another one?"

"Get over yourself." My hands were fisted and I was levitating about a foot off the ground. I kind of liked looking down at the slimeball from my past. "And clingy? I don't think so."

"So you say, so you said then." He still had a grin that I was going to smack right off of him. "But I had to be sure. That's why I did what you call the whammy. Wham, bam, thank you ma'am. You never knew Greg Kaplan. Never heard of him. Never had the best sex of your life with him."

"Delusional creep." I picked him up and threw him across the parking lot. Yep, threw him. He landed on top of a silver Honda and rubbed his shoulder. The car alarm went off, but he silenced it with a look.

"Impressive. That's what I call power. When I saw you on TV the night of your fire, I knew I had to look you up. I figured you never had gotten into shape-shifting, you were so freaked out by it back then. Tried it and totally wimped out." Greg grinned and looked me over. "Which is good for me now. You may not use it much, Glory, but you're a damned power gold mine."

While he'd been carrying on about my power, I'd been building up a head of steam.

"My power is *my* business, Greg. And you looked me up before the fire. I had the headache to prove it."

"So someone mentioned your name. It made me think of old times."

"Get lost, Greg." I shook my head. "Why do you care about my power level anyway?"

"Power is valuable if you know what to do with it. Let's get together and I'll tell you about the possibilities. He actually held out his hand. "I forgot how good-looking you are, Glory. We could—"

"Shut up!" I was going to kill this son of a bitch. "You did the whammy on me? On *me*?" Where the hell was a stake when you needed one?

"Come on, Gloriana. You do the same thing yourself. That's what the whammy's for." He actually laughed. "Check out your midnight supper over there."

I looked around at Steve, still leaning against that Lexus

and totally oblivious. "I won't apologize for using it. But no one does the whammy on me. No one. You want to see my power?" I saw the wooden fence on three sides of the lot and seared it. Flames shot up against the dark night sky, the wood ablaze. I turned to Greg, ready to finish him, but he was morphing into a blackbird, obviously out of there.

"Hot damn. The EVs will love you." Then he was gone.

Well, hell. For a moment I tried the change thing myself. I would let my inner hawk come out and take down that freaking little bird. I concentrated, felt tingling in my hands and feet and shuddered. All right now, was I going to let an asshole like Greg Kaplan call me a wimp? I stared at my hands, *willing* them to grow feathers. Zilch. This was silly. All vampires changed. It was a perk I should make use of. So what if I felt sick and knew if even one feather sprouted I'd probably heave. I could do this. I could. So I stared at my all too humanoid hands until the world spun around me.

I glanced at Steve again. Who was I kidding? I didn't change. I was change challenged. A wimp for sure. And, oops, there was the little matter of the fire I'd started. It just might spread to the buildings on either side of the lot. I came down to earth with a thump.

"Steve." I got in his face and touched his cheek. "Look, the fence is on fire. Maybe you should call for backup."

"Fire?" Steve came alive, his eyes wide. "Hell, yes. What was it, lightning?"

I ignored the clear skies and nodded. "Freakish. Zap, and the fire started. It's spreading. I think the noise dazed you. Are you okay?"

"Yeah, sure." Steve whipped out his cell phone and began talking rapidly while he pulled me out into the street. He wobbled a little, but blamed it on the three beers he'd had since he didn't have a clue he was down a quart.

An interested crowd gathered. More late nighters who'd danced the last dance wondered aloud what could have started the fire. Steve repeated the lightning story and got some looks. I just stayed out of the way and wished I had some of my Vintage Vamp's flyers. I know, but I'm a businesswoman. I know potential customers when I see them.

In minutes a fire truck pulled up and quickly got the fire under control. Steve dragged himself away from the action long enough to walk me back to the door of the apartment building. I felt bad. For the juicy kiss I gave him and the vague promise to go out with him again. I wasn't going to do it.

Sorry, but mortals just didn't seem to cut it for me anymore, at least not romantically. And I felt bad for doing the whammy on him earlier. Also for the temptation to do it again. Plant the suggestion that our date had been a dud. But how wimpy would that be? Now that I knew what it felt like to have your memory erased, I was really hating the whole concept. When and if Steve called, I'd just have to let him down gently.

The lights were on in the shop and I saw Flo inside, a paintbrush in her hand. I unlocked the door and went inside.

"Who are the EVs?"

Flo dropped the loaded paint brush and dark burgundy paint splashed across my brand new fake wood laminate flooring and her shoes.

"Oh, no!" I ran to get a rag from the back and mopped at the floor. "Here. I'm going to get another rag, a bucket and some water." I thrust the rag into her hand. She was being awfully quiet and looked even paler than usual. A fact I'd think about just as soon as I was sure my new floor hadn't been ruined.

Five minutes later I was satisfied that no harm had been done. I tried to sneak a peak at whatever Flo had been painting but she quickly stepped in front of me.

"No. It's a surprise for your big opening night." She smiled and dropped her dirty rag in the bucket. "I think you'll like what I've done." She bit her lip. "I hope so anyway."

"I'm sure I'll love it, whatever it is. I'm thrilled you're so involved." My roomie had largely ignored my business. She likes new, the latest and most up-to-date clothes and accessories mixed with those high-priced classics she'd considered worthy of saving. I like vintage, things with a history and didn't mind if they were "pre-owned." We agreed to disagree.

"It's my gift to you. I feel bad your shop was ruined."

"Not ruined and not your fault. Unless your new secret lover is Westwood."

"Please. I would hate to hurl all over your clean floor." We both laughed. Flo hurling. Her vocabulary was strictly TV sitcom.

"All right. Now back to my original question. Who are the EVs?"

Flo sat on a stool and examined her manicure. "Why do you ask?"

"I finally met my stalking vampire. The one who's been giving me the headaches."

"Really!" The chipped nail couldn't hold a candle to this kind of serious gossip. "Spill, girlfriend. Why was he trying to get you naked?"

"Not sure. Exactly. Though he could definitely qualify as a sexual predator. But the worst, the absolute worst is that he'd done the whammy on me. On *me*." I dumped the dirty water in the sink in the back room and dropped the bucket with a bang. "Apparently we had a wild time together years ago."

"And you didn't remember it?" Flo looked indignant. "I wouldn't stand for that from a lover." She jumped off the stool. "You made him sorry, no?"

"I got a good start on it." I sighed. "But he shape-shifted out of there before I could do any permanent damage."

"And you couldn't follow." Flo patted me on the shoulder. "It's okay, roomie. You have other talents."

"He kept carrying on about my stored power. Like it was something I could sell maybe. The last thing he said was that the EVs would love me." I looked Flo square in the eye. "Who are the EVs and why would they love me?"

Flo looked longingly at the door. I stepped in front of her. She wasn't going to escape without at least a little dish. And it was way too late for her to pretend she didn't have a clue what I was talking about. Hey, she'd splashed paint on her favorite Ferragamos and she hadn't even *noticed*. I let her read that in my eyes.

"Okay, okay. I tell you what I know. The EVs are Energy Vampires. Very powerful. Special. They can take power from a vampire and make it into something else." Flo flushed. Whoa. This was rare enough to make me lean closer.

"What? What do they make with this power?"

"Vampire Viagra."

Eleven

I laughed. "You can't be serious. Why would a vampire need Viagra?" I'd just revisited with Greg one of many sex marathons I'd had with male vamps. The very idea that they needed a boost was a joke.

"I'm reading your mind. I know. Male vampires seem always hard. And can stay that way forever if they want." She made a face. "Sometimes you wish it wasn't so."

I nodded. Yeah, lying under an inept lover who was determined to make you come but just wasn't getting the job done? A *Texas Chainsaw Massacre* marathon would seem shorter.

"So explain this Vampire Viagra. Do they sell it?"

"Oh, yes. And it's very expensive." Flo flushed again. "Not that I'd ever pay for it, you understand."

"Of course not. But who would?" Again. Male vamps are horny toads and ever-ready.

"Very old vampires. Vampires who have been and done everything, maybe thousands of times. The Vampire Viagra, it gives you a jolt, a freshness, an edge." Flo got a faraway look. She might not have paid for it, but my roomie had definitely had a Vamp Viagra experience.

"So why would the EVs love *me*?" I sure wasn't in the market for their drug. Not only did I not need it, but I sure couldn't afford anything that Ms. Moneybags deemed expensive. My roomie thought Louis Vuitton was bargain basement.

"Power, Glory. They use power to make the drug. And

you have never used yours. Not much of it anyway." She touched my hand, held on for a second and shivered. "I have learned how to tell . . . Well, you're full of the kind of power they need. On a scale of one to ten? Girlfriend, you're an eleven."

"Excuse me?" Eleven. No, this had to be a joke. "Vamp Viagra? What next? Vamp Valium for those stressful dry spells when the Fangtastic delivery is late again?"

"You laugh. Fine. But the EVs would love to get their hands on your power. On you. It would not be a good thing, I think." Flo bit her lip again. Obviously these EVs weren't to be taken lightly.

"Flo, honey, how do you know so much about it?"

We both heard the roar in front of the building at the same time. There was no mistaking the sound of a Harley. Flo actually looked relieved and dashed to the back door.

"I don't want you to tell Richard about this. He doesn't like the EVs. They are on his shit list." With that she threw the dead bolts and headed out into the night. I locked the door behind her just as Richard rapped on the front door.

"You're out late." Okay, lame. But I was busy trying to block him from reading my whirling thoughts. Vamp Viagra, EVs, and now Flo running out of here like her panties were on fire. What was up with that?

"I called your cell and it went straight to voice mail. I thought something might be wrong." Richard ran his hand through his hair. It was getting longer, giving him a rough look. The leathers he wore added to the edginess. Compared to my mortal date, he was sex on a stick.

"I turned off my cell because I had a date. With the arson investigator who has our case. No progress. They don't have a clue who set the fire."

"A date with a mortal you hardly know." Richard put his hands on the counter. "Did you at least take the dogs?"

"Are you kidding? I wanted a night of normal, Richard. Taking along canine backup doesn't qualify."

"So you went out without protection? Are you crazy? Westwood's men—"

"Give me a little credit, Richard. I knew Steve wasn't going to be a problem. He works for the fire department for crying out loud. And in the alley you saw that I can defend myself." This whole helpless Glory gig was getting really old. "Flo goes out alone and no one's bugging her."

"Flo can shape-shift and escape if someone comes at her with a stake. You can't or won't." Richard leaned closer and sniffed. "Now I know why you made the date. You drank from him. Are you sleeping with him too?"

"None of your business. And if I did sleep with him," I tried for an arch smile, "honey, we'd still be at it now, wouldn't we?"

Richard's stormy blue eyes bored into me. "What did happen tonight, Gloriana? Why are you blocking me?"

"I met the vamp who's been giving me headaches. Apparently he's an old boyfriend." I still kept up the block and I could tell it was driving Richard crazy.

"What's his name and why has he been bothering you? Did he hurt you?"

"I'm not telling you his name and I'm not hurt. I told you I handled him. And as to why he's been stalking me? Why else? Once a man's had Gloriana St. Clair . . ." I ran my hands down my leather skirt.

"Any reason he didn't just pick up a phone?" Obviously Richard wasn't buying my story.

"He didn't approach me directly before because he's always been into games." I shivered remembering just what kind of games. And I'd be lying if I said his parade scenario hadn't turned me on. Until I'd found out about the whammy.

"Damn it. You never should have gone out alone." Richard grabbed my shoulders and looked into my eyes. "I don't like this. You took a hell of a chance."

"My choice, Richard. So back off. Relax. Don't I look all

right to you?" I patted his cheek, determined to play this light. I liked Richard's look if not his attitude. Clean shave. Part of a nice package with the leather pants and his jacket unzipped over a red "Austin Rocks" T-shirt.

"How am I supposed to relax when you're risking your life for some mortal who couldn't do more than run screaming for his mommy when that vampire came after you?"

"Steve didn't know anything about it. I put him under so I could . . . you know. That's when Greg came along." My cheeks went hot. Richard had already smelled the fresh blood on me. And he hadn't judged me, just figured it for foreplay. It's what vampires did.

"Greg." Richard still held me, trying to read my mind. "What's his last name? I might know him." His hands tightened on my shoulders.

Oops. I was definitely keeping my block up. Maybe he had heard of Greg. If the EVs were on Richard's shit list, he'd obviously been investigating them and didn't like what he'd discovered. Maybe I should ignore Flo's advice and pump him for info. But the way he was freaking out, I figured he'd go nuts if I told him about the power issue. I just didn't feel up to the drama. So I stepped back and Richard let me go.

"Forget him. I let the vampire know I wasn't interested in a rerun. I handled him. *By myself.*" I began turning off lights. "I'm locking up. Do you want to go upstairs for a computer lesson?"

"No." Richard followed me to the door, settling my shawl around my shoulders. His fingers lingered. "You look more than all right, Gloriana. Very sexy. If this mortal male didn't try to jump you, he's a eunuch."

I turned and smiled at him. "Of course, he *tried*. But he just didn't do it for me."

"What or who does it for you, Glory?" Richard brushed his thumbs across my throat, which was suddenly dry as dust.

I managed a laugh. "Wouldn't you like to know?"

"Maybe I already do." Mr. Intensity actually grinned and stepped back. "Where are the dogs now?"

"Still upstairs. I just stopped here for a minute, to check things out." I held up my hand. "And spare me another lecture. I'm not up for it." I locked the door, set the alarm, then looked up at the clear night sky. It was a beautiful night, just a few hours until dawn. I was free for a change and hated to go inside. I glanced at Richard and let him see that last thought.

"Fine. You like to live dangerously. I can relate to that. And, of course, I'm glad you're okay." He nodded toward the bike. "As you can see, the bike's fixed. I was just testing it out. Don't go inside. Go for a ride with me. In the hills."

"I'd love that. I really don't want to go in to all the doggy drama about how reckless I am."

Richard pulled the scarf from around my neck and carefully tied my hair back at the nape of my neck. He studied me for a moment, his eyes gleaming in the light from Mugs and Muffins. "It *was* reckless. A mortal couldn't protect you. And Westwood still has men out there. I encountered one earlier tonight here in the coffee shop."

"Here? Right next door?" Westwood's man calmly drinking coffee only a few feet away? Holy crap. "What was he planning to do?"

"He had a can of spray paint and a wooden stake in his backpack. He was composing a message when I found him."

"Nice. Probably something like, 'Die, vampires' across my new windows and freshly cleaned brick."

"Yeah, something along those lines." Richard looked grim.

Graffiti I could deal with, though it pissed me off. But the stake . . . I shuddered. Westwood had claimed to want to take me out himself, but that boast could have been designed to lull me into a false sense of security.

"Now you see why I was worried about you." Richard gripped my elbow and urged me toward the bike. "Get on."

"Wait. How did you handle the Westwood goon?"

"You don't want to know." He got on the bike and started it with a roar. No talk of helmets of course. Why bother? That healing vamp sleep could take care of any injury short of decapitation.

I let his reticence slide for the moment. While I wasn't exactly dressed for a bike ride, I didn't want to miss the chance to feel the wind in my hair. My leather mini was cute, but tight. When I straddled the bike, I'd be showing some serious thigh. Chubby thigh at that.

"Climb on carefully. The tail pipes get hot."

"I've ridden on the back of a bike before." And I had, though it had been decades. And I'd loved it, feeling wild and free. What the heck. With more energy than grace, I managed to get on, then grabbed Richard's firm middle. He took off with a roar and I leaned against him and held on tight.

Austin's in what Texans call the hill country. Some of those hills are right in town and very steep. The cold air felt great on my cheeks as we flew up and down, a windy roller-coaster ride. I rubbed my cheek against Richard's strong back and probed his mind. He finally let me see how he'd dealt with the Westwood man. It wasn't pretty. And Richard the former priest felt compelled to pray for forgiveness. He hadn't intended to take a life, but when a man comes at you with a stake . . .

I gave Richard a reassuring squeeze and whispered in his mind. *"You did a good thing, Richard. Self-defense. If that man had a vamp detector, he could have staked me or Flo if he'd gotten away."*

He pulled to a stop on a hilltop. When he cut the engine, it was wonderfully quiet. Peaceful. Richard got off the motorcycle then held out his hand.

"Thank you, Gloriana. I knew what I did was necessary. But it never gets easy."

I hopped off with even less finesse than I'd got on with. "I understand, Richard. And I'm grateful." I turned and looked at the lights of the city spread out below us. "It's a beautiful night. Let's try to forget vamp hunters and enjoy the view."

"I'm enjoying the view." Richard put his arm around me, his eyes on the swells of plump breasts above my bustier. Hey, showing cleavage is in style. Compared to some of the stars on the TV shows I watch, I was dressed like a nun. Nope, not even thinking about the fact that Richard had once been a priest.

"Out there, Richard. Aren't the lights beautiful?" We both took a minute to just appreciate the skyline of Austin. Okay, so I also appreciated the vibe between us. I'd had a hellacious night. First biting an innocent mortal, a nice guy, when I really didn't want to be that kind of user vampire. Then Greg Kaplan had cornered me. Oops. I'd almost forgotten to block Richard. He just looked at me, all dangerous male and intensity.

"I'm attracted to you, Gloriana." He brushed my hair back from my cheeks. "I think we could be good together."

Wow. Talk about a subject change. His fingers were rough on my skin, but I couldn't deny that the chemistry so missing with firefighter Steve, was definitely alive and well here. Hey, a kiss couldn't hurt. I pulled his head down and planted one on him. It quickly turned into *him* planting one on *me*.

Oh, my. Oh, crap. This could definitely lead to a whole lot more. Could I do this? What about Blade? Forget Blade. Richard cupped my breast and I realized the naughty girl had escaped from my bustier.

He bent his head to trace my nipple, his fangs brushing the tip over and over until I moaned and held his head to me. Damn, but he was good at this. He eased me down on the ground. A rock stuck me right between my shoulder blades. I moaned louder, pain this time.

"Richard." I shoved at him.

"What? Am I moving too fast for you, Glory?" He looked up, his fangs gleaming in the moonlight.

"No, I mean, yes, I mean, rock!" I sat up and threw the damn boulder across the clearing. Which gave me time to think. What was I doing here making out with Richard?

"Relax, Glory. Just lie back and look at the stars." Richard pulled off his jacket and spread it out behind me.

Stargazing? I let him ease me back and sighed at the beauty of the star-dusted night sky. "I'm sorry, Richard." I grabbed his hand when it roamed up my thigh. "This *is* moving too fast for me."

Richard stared down at me. "I get it. You've been with Blade. I've been with Florence. But unless you're exclusive . . ."

"That's not it. Or maybe it is." I tucked both breasts back into my top. "Anyway, it's close to dawn and the dogs will be going nuts. I need to get home."

Richard stood and pulled me to my feet.

"Another night." Richard kissed me, but it was quickly obvious to me, anyway, that the moment had passed. I'd remembered a few things about him, he'd probably remembered a few things about me. Maybe someday we'd both be ready for something more. His kiss deepened. I held onto him, appreciating his broad shoulders, the slow glide of his tongue against mine. Maybe someday *soon*.

A bird sang and I jumped and quickly scanned the area. If it was a certain blackbird . . . But sometimes a bird is just a bird and a reminder that false dawn had come, warning us that we were running out of time. Hey, there *would* be other nights.

Richard smiled, obviously getting the message loud and clear.

I got back on the bike and we spoiled the quiet night with the roar of the Harley. I held on as we zoomed down the hills toward home. The sky was getting lighter by the minute. By the time I got home, I'd literally have to jump into bed. At my door, I offered Richard my couch, but he took one look at my sulking dogs and assured me he'd make it home in time. I was tempted to go with, especially when Valdez quit sulking and started lecturing.

"Opening night. Finally." I looked around. Except for the sheet that Flo had insisted stay in front of the back wall until the "unveiling," things looked good. Better than they had before the fire actually.

"We throw open the doors at midnight. Right?" Lacy was pumped and, even though she was usually my day manager, she'd insisted on being here for this.

"Right." A knock on the door signaled some early birds. Valdez and Will gave a token bark, but they were still sulking about my night without them. They settled back down on either side of the door, two frowning, furry foo dogs.

"It's CiCi, Frederick and Derek." I let them in and swapped hugs all around. The Countess Cecilia von Repsdorf and her son had been great friends of mine for years. Since I'd moved to Austin, they'd practically adopted me. Derek, Freddy's partner, worked in the shop some nights. They were all vampires, of course.

CiCi had consigned some beautiful pieces from her vast collection of what her son called junk. She'd been furious that most of her porcelain and art glass pieces had been destroyed in the fire. Fortunately, a trip to her attic had refilled the shelves and we were good to go. But if Westwood ever crossed her path, she'd vowed to end up wearing *his* eyeteeth.

"Darling, the store looks wonderful." Cici walked over to a shelf to adjust a winged cherub. "I'm sure you will sell, sell, sell."

"She will, Mother." Frederick dropped a kiss on my cheek. "I have some more clothes for you in the trunk of my car. Old tuxes, a cashmere coat with a mink collar that I really don't need in Texas."

"Twinkie," Will muttered.

"What did you say?" Derek was nose to nose with the dog before I could step between them.

"Will . . ."

"I was talking to the doodle here. Valdez. You know how he is about his treats." Will backed up, his tail between his legs.

I didn't blame him. Derek's fangs glinted in the light from the vintage chandeliers I'd had hung around the shop and he must have seriously worked out in his mortal lifetime.

"Sounded to me like a slur." Derek glanced at Freddy. "I won't stand for it. Especially not from you, dog breath." He poked Will in the shoulder.

Will growled and showed his own canines. "You want to take this outside?"

"Cool it, boys. Sounds like a simple misunderstanding." I gave Will a "shut-the-hell-up" look. "Freddy's coat sounds fabulous." I put a hand on Derek's shoulder. "You want to bring the clothes in?"

Derek gave Will one more look, then shrugged. "Sure. Anything to help the shop get going. I need this job." He ignored Freddy's snort. It was no secret that his partner would have happily supported Derek forever. But Derek was a lot like me. He didn't like to be totally dependent on anyone. His commissions at the shop gave him a much needed freedom from an allowance.

"Derek, I'm just happy you didn't hook up with someone else while I was out of business." I glanced at Freddy. Poor choice of words. Handsome, rich Freddy was more insecure than you'd expect from a man with his assets. But then he'd only been out of the closet a few decades. His earlier liaisons had all ended badly. Hey, I got it. I squeezed his arm and looked at the clock.

"Bring it in later, Derek. It's almost time to open the doors."

Derek nodded. "I've got something for you first." He dug into his leather messenger bag and pulled out his laptop. He was one of those techno-geeks, not surprising since he hadn't been a vampire for even half a century.

He'd put my inventory on computer when I'd first opened the shop.

"Something on the laptop?" I gestured toward the counter. "I've updated our inventory on my new computer." Translation: I'd done a lot of deleting. Thank God Derek had got us all in the habit of downloading everything on a flash drive each morning. A flash drive I'd had tucked in my purse upstairs the day of the fire. Boy, had I been relieved to remember *that* detail.

"A grand opening present." Derek whipped open the laptop and set it on the counter. "Gather around everyone." He booted it up and began typing. "Voilà. Vintagevamp shop.com."

A Web site popped up on the screen. There it was, my shop. Or at least a photo of my shop at night. And all sorts of options including a shopping cart. Derek clicked on an icon and the Chanel suit I so adored came up, complete with price.

"Oh, my God! This is so cool." I hugged him and stepped back so everyone could take a look.

"I tried to get Vintagevamps.com but it was taken. And who can spell emporium? I hope this is all right."

"All right? Are you kidding?" I hugged him again, then clicked on another icon. CiCi's porcelain cherub appeared. Sold, too, apparently, and at a great price. "When did you get this up?"

"A few days ago. I'll have to show you how to access your PayPal account. We've already sold a few pieces." He took the cherub off the shelf. "I'll take care of the shipping and everything if I can have a commission on what we sell online."

"Deal." I was elated. A mantel clock Lacy had picked up at an estate sale chimed twelve and she threw open the doors. Flyers had gone out over the weekend and, even though it was 12:01 on a Tuesday morning, a massive crowd of three shoppers surged through the door.

"I love that poodle skirt in the window. My husband's lodge is having a fifties dance. That would be perfect." A woman with a name tag from a local supermarket had obviously just gotten off work.

"Wait!" Flo had been pretty quiet, but now she was determined to have center stage. She looked great in a blue cashmere sweater and Seven jeans with her high-heeled Christian Dior boots. She tossed her dark hair over her shoulder and stared until everyone, including the mortals, focused on her.

"Are we finally going to get to see what you've been painting?" I moved closer and grabbed my roomie's arm. "I've been dying of curiosity."

Lacy made a sound. Was she choking or—oh, my God—laughing? I braced myself. I'd had no idea that Flo even knew how to paint. Though she'd certainly had her share of artist lovers. All of them famous. Wouldn't it be cool if she'd copied her lover Leonardo's *Mona Lisa* on the wall? No, scratch that. Flo hated Lisa and kept insisting *she* had been a *he*. Flo's version would probably include a mustache.

"Ladies and gentlemen. Welcome to Vintage Vamp's." Flo paused for dramatic effect and I braced myself. She ripped down the sheet.

The room was silent. Well, almost. Poodle Skirt Lady gasped and dropped a vintage twin set.

"Oh, my." CiCi looked at me, then at Flo. "Why I had no idea, Florence, dear, that you had such hidden talents."

"Maybe they should have stayed hidden." Valdez nudged my hip. *"Say something, Blondie."*

"It's . . . it's fabulous."

Flo broke into a smile. "I learned to paint this way from my dear lover Edvard. I thought it was just what this wall needed. For a place called Vintage Vamp's."

"Edvard Munch?" One of the mortals, a tall woman who looked like she'd just left a trendy cocktail party, frowned. "But he's been dead for—"

Frederick was beside her in a flash, literally. He nodded and Derek and CiCi handled the other two mortals. I may not be fond of the whammy anymore, but here it was a necessary evil. Had to feel sorry for the mortals, though, standing there with vacant eyes and gaping mouths, barely breathing mannequins.

"Of course he's been dead for over a century. The fool wouldn't let me turn him. 'Why live forever,' he would say, 'When life is so painful?' He was always sad. I think I only saw him laugh a few times. Sexy of course or I wouldn't have bothered with him." Flo stared at the painting with a wistful smile. "Maybe I should add more yellow. Edvard's paintings were pretty gloomy."

"Yeah. His work wasn't exactly a laugh riot." Will stared at the wall, apparently feeling free to chime in since the mortals were out of action, Lacy had locked the door again and Derek was ignoring him. "You did a good job. I recognized it immediately."

"Thanks. I'm surprised you know it." Flo hadn't exactly fallen in love with Will, not when he'd dragged one of her Ferragamo slides out of her closet. No damage or we'd be talking dead dog here.

"I've seen some of his work." Will looked over at Valdez's snort. "An artistic girlfriend who liked museums. This looks like a combo platter, half *The Scream*, half *Vampire*." He turned to Flo. "And all cool."

"Why, thank you, William." Flo pushed his head away when he nudged her butt. Then she looked around uncertainly. "Is it too . . . dark?"

"I think it's amazing." Derek shook his head. "Hey, let's see what mortals think, I figure it'll be unique to this shop. A conversation piece. Maybe I should take a picture of it and put it on the Web site."

"You did a great job, Flo. This looks completely professional." I stepped closer. The female vamp had flowing red hair and leaned over a man. She looked on the verge of taking a bite. It was weird but, in its own way, beautiful. Now the screamer was a different story. Mouth open, he was probably horrified by the pair occupying the other half of the wall. He stood on a bridge, probably ready to jump because he had this really freaky looking alien head.

"It was fun. I may paint again." Flo looked around the shop.

I had visions of a shop slash spook house that would make a horror director weak with envy. I had to head that off at the pass. "We should hit an art supply store. Maybe you'd like to try your hand at a picture, something smaller to hang on the wall upstairs. Maybe a self-portrait. The vampire in this looks familiar."

"It's me, of course, though why Edvard wouldn't paint in my face, I don't know." Flo wrinkled her perfect nose. "He said I was beautiful, but then he gave my hair red highlights. Do you see red in my hair? Pah! I think he lied when he said it had something to do with the composition. He had a redheaded lover after me."

"No, the color draws attention to the vampire. Makes her the star." Freddy grinned when Flo made one of her Italian gestures. "It's fantastic. I swear this looks just like his stuff. I have a print of *Vampire* in my study." He'd been walking from one end of the wall to the other. "Munch was a little twisted, but brilliant."

"That was Edvard. So tortured. I cheered him up for a little while, but it didn't last." Flo made a dismissive gesture with her hands. "I moved on."

There was a knock on the door. More customers. Which was a good thing. I glanced at the wall. Derek was right. As a conversation piece, this was a doozy. I sent a mental message all around and we jumped back into place. The mortals snapped out of it, back on the scene as if they'd never moved from the spot when they'd first seen the painting. They were exclaiming over it when Lacy opened the door again and two men in their early twenties pushed inside. Richard was right behind them.

"Interesting." He smiled at me, then walked over to look

at the wall. "Florence, you've certainly picked up a trick or two in the years you've been"—he glanced at the mortals—"*studying* the great artists."

"Why, thank you, Richard." Flo picked up her black leather jacket and slipped into it. "Good luck with your opening, Glory. I have a date. I won't be back tonight." She smiled at the group and headed out.

"I'm a little worried about her." Lacy was at my elbow. "Have you met her new man?"

I shook my head. "That's not unusual, though. She kept Richard a secret for a while. Seems like we met him just before she dumped him."

"I think it's weird. She won't even talk about this new guy. And we got pretty close while she was working on"—a sweeping gesture toward the wall—"that."

"Florence always has a new man. He won't last, none of her men do." Richard strolled over to Freddy and they soon had their heads together at the laptop discussing the new Web site.

I was doing my best not to stare at Richard's butt in worn denims that hugged his muscular thighs. For a second there, I'd almost felt sorry for him, the most recent in a long, long line of Florence rejects.

I hadn't heard the Harley roar up so maybe he'd flown or driven in. That was the thing with dating a vampire. They could do and be just about anything. Hold it. Not dating. Paying off a debt. Friends. That's all. Okay, okay, friends with . . . benefits. Like rolling on the ground playing tonsil hockey. Hmm. I checked out his taut butt again. With benefits like those, who needed a relationship? Especially one as complicated as mine was with Blade.

I glanced back at Flo's mural. Maybe highlighting the vamp thing wasn't smart, but it was definitely interesting. The artsy looking woman was talking on her cell phone and I heard her say "amazing painting." Good. Maybe her friend would rush right over and find something to buy while she was here.

The poodle skirt lady had talked Derek into undressing the mannequin in the window and headed for the dressing room. CiCi was showing a bronze to one of the men when the bells on the front door rang. Another man came inside.

I froze. Tinted glasses. But I got closer and relaxed when I could read his mind. He was following the hot guys he'd met at a bar down the street. He was also into butts and hot guy number one had some sweet cheeks. Then he spotted an Armani jacket and was hooked on my "cool" shop. No Westwood thoughts from him at all. I smiled and rang up my first sale, that bronze CiCi had consigned. All right. We were back in business.

Twelve

"I tell you, honeybunch, that wall is giving me nightmares."

"Don't be ridiculous. Ghosts don't sleep. Do they?" I was deep into an argument with my resident ghosts forty-eight hours after our grand opening. Emmie Lou hated Flo's painting and, since I was alone in the shop with just the dogs, she'd come out to speak her piece.

"You know what I mean. How would you like to stare at that thing all day *and* all night? That screaming skull. And, honey, you know I love vampires, but that picture's just flat creepy."

"No, it's not. It's art. The customers love it." And they did. Even wanted to take pictures of it. I'd had Flo sign her name to it to make it clear that this was just a depiction, not a forgery. It took some prodding, but she'd finally printed in da Vinci just big enough to cause even more comment. Can't read or write? I don't think so.

"Let her count her money, Emmie Lou. You know she ain't gonna paint over that mural. People've done nothing but talk about it since the place opened up again." Harvey hitched up his britches and stepped closer to the vampire section of the wall. "I think it's kind of sexy, the way she's biting him right *there*." He looked meaningfully at Emmie Lou's neck. "You used to like a little nibble, honey."

"Nibble this, Harvey Nutt." Emmie took a swing at him with one of Flo's purses and an alligator bag sailed across the room.

"Cool it, you two. And don't throw the merchandise." I rescued the purse and put it back on a shelf. I'd locked the door at five a.m. after sending everyone off so I could count the night's receipts. This was typically our dead time. Oops. Okay, maybe it's always dead time for a vampire. But in a business sense, there wasn't much happening. At six, when Lacy came in, we usually got a few night workers as they came off their shifts.

"Sorry, honey. Earlier it did look like your business was booming again." Emmie Lou turned her back to the painting. "Glad of that. I sure didn't want to go back to the days of biker bars or tattoo parlors. Between the smoke and the loud music, honey, we were in hell."

"We've had a great start." I looked up at the tap on the door. Hmm. The dogs growled and started barking. I thought Valdez was going to go through the safety glass. I moved closer.

"Stop it. I know this guy."

Greg Kaplan grinned at me and gestured, like, let me in. Probably not a good idea, but I wanted to talk to him. Ask him about the EVs since I'd got a little of nothing from Flo. And, yeah, it bugged the hell out of me that I couldn't remember our affair. I wanted details. How long had we been together? *Why* had we been together? I didn't doubt the dogs would make quick work of Greg if he threatened me.

"Don't do it, Blondie. This is the asshole who gave you the headaches." Valdez growled again.

"He's not going to do that again, are you, Greg?" I yelled this through the door and Greg nodded, then crossed his heart. "If he does, you have my permission to rip him a new one, okay?"

"Now you're talking." Will glanced at Valdez. "It's about time we saw some action. I say she lets him in. If you can't handle him, *I* can."

"The day I can't take out a loser like that, is the day I turn in my flea collar." Valdez gave Greg the eye through the glass and showed some teeth.

"Fine. I'm letting him in. But I don't need your permission. Just stay on high alert. I may decide he needs a hurt put on him. For past insults." Emmie Lou and Harvey had vanished, but were probably still lurking about. They didn't miss anything and also liked to do some damage when they felt I was being mistreated.

Feeling like I had backup out the whazoo, I flipped open the dead bolts and let Greg in along with the cold night air. Austin had had a cold front, and the temperature was hovering around forty degrees, about twenty lower than on my date night. Texas weather. Nowhere close to the snow weather during the parade when I'd had some of the best sex . . .

"Stop it, Greg. You're planting memories again." This time I threw up a block. We were going to communicate like mortals, with voices and body language, or not at all.

"You heard her, asshole. I'm watching you." Valdez growled for emphasis.

"We're both watching you." Will growled even louder and I shot him a dirty look to keep things from deteriorating into a contest.

"Sorry, okay? I just wanted to talk, maybe shop a little." Greg studied the dogs. "Glory, anybody ever tell you that you keep weird company? What's with the talking dogs?" He sniffed the air. "Who aren't really dogs."

Will snarled and Valdez grabbed a chunk of Greg's jeans.

"They're my bodyguards. Since I didn't whammy *you*, you should remember that I always had a dog with me, a Valdez to guard me. Now I've got two. So I'd be careful about insulting them. They take their job seriously." I loved the way Greg had gone pale.

"Nice doggies. Please let go of my pants." Greg shot me a frantic look.

"Okay, guys. You've made your point. Let him go, but be ready in case this freak tries his mind control tricks again. These men can and will read your mind, Greg."

"Men?" Greg flinched when Valdez tugged and his jeans

ripped. "Sorry, I get it." He held up his hands in surrender. "You have my utmost respect, both of you."

Valdez reluctantly released the fabric, leaving a damp spot on Greg's hem.

"Finally." Greg stuck his hands in his pockets. "I guess I'm in the right place to buy new jeans. I've heard you have an interesting shop. You always were into clothes." He smiled and strolled around. "That's where I met you. At a sale at Bloomingdale's. I was shopping with a girlfriend, but once I saw you, I dropped her like a bad habit." He grinned and winked, obviously expecting me to be flattered.

"So I'm not the only lucky lady you dumped. You wipe her memory too?"

"Sure." Greg wasn't stupid. He could tell I was on the verge of doing something violent. I let him see it in my eyes. "Come on, Glory. Ancient history." He stopped in front of Flo's mural and whistled. "Now that's what I'm talking about." He glanced at me. "Gutsy, putting the vampire thing right out there. On the sign out front and now on the wall. I remember what you used to call it, blending. When did you stop?"

"I'm still blending. A vamp was a sexy chick during the roaring twenties." I did a hair toss. "Kind of like me back in the day. Mortals don't have a clue it could mean anything else and I make a decent living." I remembered just how decent and carefully locked the night's receipts in the safe under the counter. When I tore the paper off the printing calculator, I took a moment to admire the total.

"They have a clue now." Greg gestured toward Flo's mural. "But I'm impressed. I guess you have people who handle days for you." Greg stopped next to a rack of vintage jeans and checked a price tag. "Good deal."

What was I doing having a civilized conversation with this creep? He'd whammied me, given me headaches, even tried to get me outside and naked. I gave Valdez a look and he moved closer.

Greg moved on to the suit rack and fingered one of

Freddy's tuxes. "Nice. Custom tailored." He glanced at the tag. "And my size." He dropped the tag. "If I buy this, will you go out with me? Thanksgiving's coming up. This isn't New York, but I imagine Austin has a parade of sorts."

"Bastard." I threw Flo's alligator bag at his head but he ducked and it landed next to the book shelf. With this kind of abuse, I was going to have to mark that purse down. That stirred my temper even more.

"Glory, Glory, get over it, darling. Where's your famous sense of humor? We had a lot of laughs in New York."

"I lost my sense of humor when I lost my memory." I picked up an oversized leather tote and swung it over my head like David getting ready to chuck a rock at Goliath. Greg slid behind a rack. I'd really like to whack him, but there were just too many breakables around to take a chance. I dropped the bag with a thump.

"That's my girl." Greg grinned. "New Year's Eve. Dancing at a fancy place. I remember you doing a mean twist." He pulled out a blue sixties cocktail dress with a chiffon skirt. "Come on, Glory. You'd look a treat in this."

"Get your grubby paws off the merchandise."

"You and I made some great moves. On and off the dance floor." Greg moved closer and Valdez growled. "Call off the attack dogs and I'll show you."

"The attack dogs stay *on*." I made sure my block was firmly in place. "Tell me why you've been stalking me or move your butt out of here."

Greg glanced at the dogs. "I'd like you to go somewhere with me."

"I wouldn't go to a Wal-Mart with you, Gregory." I decided to play it cool and began to rearrange a display of vintage necklaces.

"Come on, give me a break. I never should have wiped away your memory. But what's done is done." Greg picked up a rhinestone tiara and dropped it on his head. "We had some great times. You should remember the night we went out as two girlfriends. Halloween in Times Square. I made a hot chick, if I do say so myself." He swayed around a rack of vintage scarves, then draped one around his neck. "Almost as hot as you."

Will snorted and muttered something about lace on Greg's panties.

"Listen, hound, a man who's sure of his masculinity doesn't worry about crap like that. Glory can tell you I don't wear underwear." A sly grin. "Easy access."

"Gag me. And no, Glory can't tell Will anything. Because *Glory can't remember*." I threw down the necklaces. So much for playing it cool. "But I do remember what you said Saturday night. You said the EVs would love me." Greg frowned. "What do you have to do with the EVs?"

"You misheard, obviously. What's an EV? A new cell phone provider?" Greg whipped out a snappy new Razr phone. "My provider's not worth shit. You wouldn't believe how many dropped calls I get." He held up the phone and I'll be damned if he didn't take my picture.

"Stop that!" I grabbed the phone. "What do you need with my picture?" Was this really a phone? I looked it over. Of course it was. Only Westwood had a cell phone that could identify vampires. Greg wouldn't need a detector, he could smell us. Just like I could smell him, though there was something off about his essence. Like he'd fed recently, but not on mortal blood or Fangtastic.

"I was just playing, Gloriana. And why wouldn't I want a picture of you? For my memory book."

Now both Valdez and Will snorted. This was not good. They were dismissing Greg as a harmless flake. I knew better. He grinned at me, his fangs gleaming in the light. I read his mind and saw memories of Greg juggling stakes and throwing one at me. Missing on purpose, of course, but I'd carried on for hours, claiming he'd been trying to kill me. His eyes narrowed and I felt a bad vibe from my head to my heart. If I crossed him now, I didn't doubt he'd take me out without a second thought. The fact that my dogs would make sure he didn't live long after that wasn't exactly comforting.

"Relax, Glory. I wouldn't hurt you." He threw on his Greg the nice guy look again. But I didn't trust it, didn't trust *him*.

"What? Are you trying to reassure me with your cute little memories? Or maybe I'm supposed to be grateful that you didn't kill me when you had the chance." I grabbed a pencil and moved closer, aiming for his so-called heart. "Quit playing dumb. The EVs want my power? Are you working for them?"

"Maybe." Greg picked up a Sevres porcelain and held it up. "Put down the so-called weapon, Glory, or I drop this"—he glanced at the tag—"five hundred dollar tribute to spring." He chuckled. "Think it will break?"

"Sure. And a pencil's not a weapon. This," I picked up the wooden stool we kept behind the counter. "This might do some damage. I could heave it at your head. Think it will break? The stool, that is. Or maybe it'll just knock you out long enough for me to rip off a wooden leg and ram it into the region where your heart is supposed to be." I smiled and held the stool over my head. I had to love the fact that Greg backed up a foot. He acted like I was making him nervous and put the porcelain back where it belonged.

I probed his mind again, but he'd slammed it shut. He was humoring me, trying to lull me into relaxing my guard. Wasn't going to happen.

I balanced the stool on one finger. Will whistled and even Valdez looked impressed. I *did* have a lot of stored power. Four centuries worth of it. The fact that I hardly ever used it was my own fault. Too much blending, not enough vamping. I eased the stool back to the floor and picked up an African fertility god, carved from a piece of beautiful dark mahogany. You wouldn't believe who'd consigned it. Who knew were-zebras even existed? I gripped it tighter.

"Answer my questions, Gregory." I glanced at the god with the enormous phallus, nicely pointed. "This is the perfect way to end your worthless life."

"Now, Glory." Greg made a vamp move toward the door.

My dogs sat up straight, teeth bared. I heard the dead bolts whisk shut. Greg looked from the dogs back to me. "No need for violence here."

"Then answer me. And don't try to shape-shift. Your little birdie would make a tasty snack for Valdez. He needs some protein." Valdez smacked his lips on cue.

"Okay, so I work for the EVs. They'd like to meet you. No big deal." Greg backed away from the dogs.

"Wuss," Will muttered.

I gave him a look. No need to get Greg worked up to prove his macho.

"I think meeting the EVs *would* be a big deal. I think they want more from me than a little chat." I gripped the wooden statue. What had I ever seen in Gregory Kaplan? Sure, he was good looking, but there was something missing. Like a moral compass. I could see that in his eyes, now that I really looked. He'd do anything to get what he wanted. *Anything.*

Obviously I'd made a big mistake ever hooking up with him. But it had been the sixties. Free love and all that. And I was starting to remember how cute he'd looked in a Nehru jacket. Nope, not going there. He was *not* cute, he was dangerous as hell, despite the "scared of Glory" act.

"Power, Glory. You wouldn't believe what the EVs can do with it. Try it. Give them a little of your stuff and then sample their product." Greg got a faraway look for a second, then quickly focused again. "You'll realize it's well worth whatever they have to do to you."

"Whatever they'd *do* to me? To make Vampire Viagra?" Oh, God, both dogs had perked up at that. "You two forget you ever heard this conversation. I mean it."

"*Whatever.*" Valdez settled back down, but I knew he wouldn't forget a thing. He never did. This would be in his next report to Blade.

Will paced in front of the glass windows. "This is why I need money so badly that I do dog duty. Expensive, is it?"

"You have no idea." Greg smiled at me. "Why do you

think I'm working for them? I'm not paid in cash, I'm paid in VV." He stared at Will. "You should try it. The rush is unbelievable."

"Hey, I don't need help in that department." Will gave Valdez a look when he snorted. "I've had no complaints."

"It's not about that. Hell, I could break bricks with my cock when it's in ready position without the VV." Greg gave me a sympathetic look. "I'm really sorry you can't remember that, Glory."

"Oh, please. Spare me." I had a feeling the male bragging could go on and on. "But the next time I need to break a brick, I'll be sure to call you."

"Seriously, Glory, it's a pleasure enhancer. For women as well as men. Honey, it's like comparing a wave to a tsunami."

I let that thought wash over me. "So instead of a big O, I'd get a giant one." I had to smile, men can be such idiots.

"*Lots* of giant ones." Greg focused on Will, obviously sensing a potential customer. "I can tell you're an old vampire. Son, you have no idea what pleasure there is still to be had."

"Cut the sales pitch, Greg." I didn't like this, didn't like the look in Will's squinty green eyes. "I'm not going to give the EVs any of my power. You can tell them that's final."

"Now, Glory. Maybe you should consider—Ow!" Will looked back to where Valdez had taken a chunk out of his tail.

"I think you're forgetting who we work for, son. Our job here. Glory's not going within a hundred miles of an EV." Valdez spit out fur.

"Glory's already much closer to them than she thinks. Maybe she should ask her roommate about the EVs."

"I did, I have. What does Flo have to do with this?"

"Ask Ms. Florence da Vinci." Greg laughed. "Got to love that name. And she paints too." He strolled to the door. "Can I leave now? I'll give them the message. Can't say they'll like it, but hopefully they won't kill the messenger."

Greg looked awfully calm for a man who had just failed in a mission for what amounted to vampire drug dealers. He gave me a wry smile, obviously not needing to read my mind to see what I thought.

"Be warned, Gloriana. The EVs *are* drug dealers, ruthless ones. They'll do anything to get what they want. If I didn't think I could still be useful to them, I'd be three states away by now."

"Three states away is about right." I kept up my brave front, but I was seriously creeped out. Bad enough Westwood wanted me dead, now Energy Vampires wanted my power. What next? Pirates after my earring collection?

"Get out, Greg. Do us all a favor and never come back here again." I nodded and Will and Valdez moved out of the way. Greg turned the dead bolt and then gave me a last lingering look.

"Big mistake. Think about it, Glory. Vamp Viagra could take you to a whole new level. You've been settling, babe. Trust me, the sex, the sensations, you'll never forget them. Even better than New York."

"Trust you? Sure. Like I'd trust Valdez next to an open bag of Cheetos."

"I don't know what the hell you're talking about, gorgeous, but think about what I said. The VV could change your life." He winked and was gone.

"*Creep.*" Valdez moved closer. "*I'm definitely telling Blade about this and you can't stop me. Especially after that Cheetos slam.*"

"Hey, bud, I was just making a point. Be a tattletale. Nothing new there. But did you see me handle Greg?" I stomped back to the counter and my pile of necklaces. "He's gone, we're all okay. Problem solved." If only. This was so not fair. Surely there were other vamps, other sources for this power the EVs were so hungry for. Valdez came over and lay next to my feet. I reached down and buried my fingers in his warm fur.

"I'm sorry, pup. That *was* a low blow. This whole EV

thing has me rattled. And the idea that I have a past I don't remember bugs the hell out of me."

"Forget it. And don't let him get to you, Glory. No EV's getting past me."

I blinked back tears. "Thanks, puppy." Will nudged me from the other side.

"We're both here for you. Like I said, I got no performance issues. That Kaplan dude was blowing smoke. He probably wiped your memory because his dick's as limp as Granny's hanky without the VV."

I laughed and scratched behind his ears. "Okay, I feel better." Will ambled back over to the door, but Valdez just looked at me.

"I'm okay. Really. Guard the door." I *was* okay. *Powerful.* I could start fires with a look, move so fast I was a blur and pick up heavy objects with one finger. I sat on the stool. Okay, so it wasn't all that heavy. And my vamp moves were a few seconds short of a blur. I looked around at my newly redone shop. The fire thing I was pretty good at, but I wasn't about to risk the store to prove it.

I distracted myself sorting silver chains, crystal beads and ropes of pearls, at one point flinging a locket across the room with a look, just to prove I could do it. The first wave of night-shift shoppers came in and I could almost forget the whole Greg thing. Almost. By the time Lacy came in to relieve me, I'd convinced myself that power-hungry EVs didn't freak me out.

Vampire Viagra. Naw. Gloriana St. Clair didn't need any help finding her bliss. But what was the deal with Flo? She was always mysterious about her boyfriends. Nothing new there. But this interest in Vamp Viagra . . . That worried me. If this stuff was addictive and Flo was hooked on tsunamis of pleasure . . .

Ridiculous. My roomie might be heavily into her own fulfillment, but she was also the toughest vampire I knew. I couldn't imagine her addicted to anything beyond shoe shopping. Come to think of it, she hadn't done *any* shopping lately. I shivered as the door opened again, letting in another customer and the chill night air.

Maybe it would be a good idea to call Flo's brother. Damian had to know about this Vamp Viagra. He was into everything sensual, seeing as how he claimed to have been the original Casanova. I'd been avoiding him since he'd pulled some stunts with me. I didn't trust him, but I knew he'd do anything for his sister.

I picked up the phone. Oops. I still had Greg's Razr phone. I was about to punch through his contact list when the customer asked a question. Okay, business first. I dropped the phone into my purse. I definitely was doing *something* about this. Just what, I didn't know.

Thirteen

"Gloriana, I think you're overreacting. Florence has always loved her secrets." Damian strolled around my living room and stopped in front of my loaded book shelves. Self-help books mostly. I know, you'd think I'd have given up by now. He picked one up.

"Put that back." Leave it to Damian to go straight to my copy of *The Sixty Second Orgasm*.

"You're kidding, right?" He thumbed through it.

"Be careful. I stood in line for over an hour to get that autographed." It was a cry for help. I'd had a run of really inept lovers and I just wasn't getting there. You know? And the author was this really hot doctor of something called sensuality studies. I'm a sucker for advice from an expert.

"Satisfaction in sixty seconds?" Damian laughed. "What fun is that?" He smiled knowingly and slid the book back on the shelf. "I can give you an orgasm . . ." He was suddenly right in front of me, his hands on my ass. ". . . that lasts as long as you want it to."

"Chill, Damian. We're here to talk about Flo." I used my own vamp move to put the couch between us. Flo yes. Orgasms no. At least not tonight. And while I didn't doubt Damian could push all the right buttons, I wasn't going there again. "What do you know about the EVs and this Vampire Viagra?"

"Me? You're asking *me* about Viagra?" Damian pushed his hands into his pockets so I could see how he didn't need a boost to spring into action.

"Relax, stud muffin, I know you're not . . ." I swept my eyes down his zipper. "Impaired."

"For vampires it's not about erections anyway." Will was still way too interested in the subject. "It's about heightening pleasure. Who couldn't use a little of that?"

Damian gave Will a look and the dog shut his mouth with a snap. Clearly Damian didn't discuss his love life with furry, four-footed animals, even those with the ability to morph into vampires when they weren't indentured.

I sat on the couch and watched Damian prowl around my living room. Damian was arguably one of the finest looking vampires in the known and unknown world. Of course his personality defects cancelled most of that out. He was full of himself, called himself Casanova, and resorted to mind control when his charm failed to get him what he wanted.

All that didn't stop me from admiring the package and now I had the whole never ending orgasm tape playing in my head. I blocked him even though it gave me a headache. No way was I letting him get a clue that I admired any part of him. He turned for another lap around the couch. Damn, he had a fine butt.

"EVs have been around for centuries, but I didn't know they'd settled in Texas. Stay away from them, Gloriana. They're bad news." Damian picked up a bottle of Fangtastic and sniffed it with a frown. "This is okay, but"—he gave me a wink—"you would taste much better." He put down the bottle and moved closer, fangs glinting in the lamp light. "All this talk of EVs and pleasure is making me . . . hungry."

Both dogs growled, but I silenced them with a look. Since they knew I had steaks thawing for them, they subsided with a grumble.

"Forget it, Damian. We were discussing your sister, remember?"

"Florence is too smart to run with the EVs." Damian sat next to me on the couch, just a few inches too close.

"A man approached me who said he works for the EVs.

Gregory Kaplan. Do you know him?" I watched Damian's face this time. He shook his head.

"Never heard of him. He approached you? Did he threaten you?" Damian's green eyes narrowed.

"No. We were . . . lovers once. Not that I remember it."

Damian put his hand on mine. "Are you telling me he did what you call the whammy on you?"

My fangs popped out, a knee-jerk reaction when I thought about the way Greg had manipulated me. Someday I was going to rip open his lying throat and drain him dry.

"He did, didn't he?" Damian was suddenly all sweet concern. "Bastard. I can punish him for you, Glory. Just say the word."

"The word." Damian looked startled and I found my sense of humor. "Don't bother, Damian. He's a sleaze, obviously. But what worries me is that he insists Flo knows something about the EVs. She didn't come home last night, so I haven't been able to ask her about it."

"Of course Florence knows about the EVs. We both do. There was a time in Madrid . . ." Damian waved his hand. "She knows they're dangerous. They are like, hmm, I guess you could say a cult. They have devoted followers, weak-willed paranormals who are seduced by their promises. But my sister is not so easily swayed. She wouldn't get involved with them."

"I hope not." I got up and headed into the kitchen. Both dogs followed me and looked up hopefully. "What kind of promises? Is it all about sex?"

"No. They can do other things with power." Damian was right behind me. "What are you doing?"

"Cooking for the dogs." I poked the steaks with a fork. "Sorry, guys. Still frozen. Maybe I should stick them in the microwave." I looked down when Will groaned. "Just on defrost. I've got to go downstairs soon."

"Do it, Glory." Valdez was obviously a less discriminating diner than Will.

"If you turn it into some kind of gray crud . . ." Will looked over his shoulder at Damian.

"They're *dogs*. You shouldn't coddle them, Glory." Damian frowned at the steak. "Disgusting. Also disgusting that Blade doesn't trust you to handle your own affairs."

"My relationship with Blade is not up for discussion." I couldn't blame Damian for his attitude. He and I had come *this close* to hooking up. Then Blade had managed to kill the mood. "He only wants to keep me safe."

"I could keep you safe." Damian whispered it next to my ear, his breath sending shivers down to the general area of my G-spot. Which I knew well. Hey, it was in the book.

"Good to know." I stuck the steak in the microwave, setting it for defrost. "But I *do* handle my own affairs. My canine companions are backup."

"Backup, my ass." Valdez had muttered it, but he'd known I would hear. I gave him a look that promised retribution.

"Shut up, Yankee-Doodle. When she's pissed, she might throw down a bowl of Alpo." Will wagged his tail. "You can handle yourself, Glory. We saw it. That Kaplan creep was quaking in his boots."

"Dangerous women fascinate me." Damian rubbed my shoulders.

I thought about fascinating him with an elbow to his stomach, but he'd probably take it as foreplay. Instead, I stared at the microwave until it dinged, then threw the steaks into a pan and turned up the heat.

"About the EVs. Apparently I have lots of power, stored power."

"Of course you have lots of power. The way you refuse to shape-shift, and the way you"—Damian glanced at the dogs—"let others fight your battles for you. Your power is just sitting there, waiting to be tapped." He ran his finger up my arm, under my sleeve. "The EVs would turn it into something they could profit from. Why not use it yourself?" He leaned close again. "Ever made love on a cloud?"

"Who hasn't?" I flipped the steaks and frowned down at

them. If I stabbed Damian with the fork, he'd bleed. More foreplay in the vamp world. I know, we're twisted. But— what can I say?—blood does it for us.

"Rare, Glory. Turn off the fire." Will pressed against my leg. The fact that he'd pushed my tie-dyed skirt up almost to my waist wasn't lost on Damian.

"Step away from the stove, all of you."

Damian just shook his head. "What next? Takeout from a five star restaurant?"

"Good idea, Sabatini. Give Glory the phone number. I've got a craving for Italian. Comes from being around Florence all the time." Valdez was pressing me on the other side and I had to shove him away to reach for a knife. I dropped each steak on a plate.

"They're not even. I just bet Valdez gets the biggest piece." Will had his front paws on the counter. "You never did like me, Glory. Not since I grabbed your tit at Campbell Castle."

I shoved him down and picked up a knife and fork. "Thanks for reminding me. You know I never did tell Blade about that. What do you think he'd do if he knew how you'd disrespected me?"

"What the hell do you mean you grabbed her tit?" Damian was clearly appalled. Otherwise he would never have deigned to speak to a dog directly.

"She was an actress, man. You remember what that meant a few centuries ago? I apologized. Done deal."

"Valdez, you've hit the jackpot." I deliberately trimmed an inch from Will's portion and dropped it on Valdez's plate.

"No!" Will threw back his head and howled.

"Fair is fair." Valdez wagged his tail. *"I'd never grab any part of you, Glory, unless it was to save your life."*

Damian frowned. "Blade has much to answer for, saddling you with this . . . menagerie."

I dropped a bite into Valdez's open mouth. "This one

saved my life and Flo's not long ago." I finished cutting the steaks into bite-sized pieces and set the plates on the floor, a good three feet between them. "Eat. I'm running out of time. I need to relieve Lacy in the shop."

"You really do spoil the beasts." Damian frowned at the dogs. "But I guess they do have their uses."

"Damn right they do." I patted them both on the head, but they were too busy inhaling steak to notice. "I guess it's some latent mothering instinct, but I don't mind doing for them."

"Regrets, Glory?" Damian put his arm around my shoulder and guided me into the living room. "I know I've only planted one kind of fantasy in your mind, but if you've got a notion to play housefrau, I'm up for it." He turned me to look into my eyes, his hands warm on the back of my neck.

I couldn't help it. I looked south. Yep, Damian was up for anything.

"Picture this, Glory. I'm Joe Ordinary, coming home from a hard day at the blood bank, and you've just put little Fang down for his nap." His finger gently stroked the sensitive area behind my ear.

I squeezed my eyes shut. Damian was way too good at the whammy. And I was way too good at jumping right into his fantasies. But then he was a multitalented seducer. The husky voice, the practiced slide of his fingers into my hair. I felt him lean closer and suck my right earlobe into his mouth.

"Stop it, Damian. And don't swallow my earring. It's one of my favorites."

"Come on, Gloriana. Relax. I'm just getting to the good part." He plucked out the earring and tucked it into my hand, the hand which had somehow landed on his nice wide, way too masculine chest.

Okay, this is the part where I should have shoved him away and called a halt. But Damian is nothing if not inventive. So I just stood there, silent, a safe three or four inches

between us. Except for his lips on my earlobe. Was he reading my mind through my block? I admit my ears are one of
my hot spots.

He took my silence as consent and drew me another inch
closer. "You greet me at the door, Gloriana, wearing nothing
but an apron. One of those sheer things. And high heels of
course. Italian stilettos." He hummed and slid his tongue
down to the pulse point in my throat. I braced myself. If he
so much as touched a fang to me, I was shoving him
through the wall and into the next room.

"Gloriana," he whispered. "I'm so stunned by your
beauty that I drop my car keys. You bend over to pick them
up and—"

"Stop it. Right. Now." My face hot, I gripped my self-
control like it was the last life jacket on the *Titanic*. At least
his mention of stilettos had put me back on the Flo track. I
shoved, though not nearly as hard as I could have. I put the
sofa between us and pushed my vintage silver earring back
into my earlobe.

"I got to you. I know I did." Damian stuck his hands in
his pockets again, making it clear that I'd gotten to him
too.

"Remember why you're here, Damian. This could be serious. What about the EVs? And why do I think maybe Flo's
new boyfriend is connected to them somehow?"

Damian's brows hit his hair line. "Do you know this?
That Florence is sleeping with an EV?"

"Not for sure. But I'm pretty positive she's been hitting
the Vamp Viagra." I sat on the couch. "You should have seen
the look on her face when she was telling about that stuff." I
looked up at Damian. "Have you tried it? Do you think it's
addictive?"

"I certainly don't *need* to try it. But I have. A woman I
knew was into it. And I'll admit it. I'll try anything once.
Okay, twice." Damian waggled his eyebrows, then collapsed
on the couch next to me. "This woman was wealthy, beautiful, of course, and she couldn't make love without it. She

was addicted. Not me, of course." He tapped his fingers on his dark jeans. "I won't lie to you. The sex was fantastic and lasted for hours." He looked at me. "But I like being in control, you know?"

"Yeah, I know." I could have launched into a litany of reasons why Damian's mind control bits had hurt me, yada, yada, but he was on to something. "I wouldn't like that. Losing control."

"I did things, felt things. Pleasure, of course. Incredible, endless gratification." Damian smiled. "Now that I remember, maybe I've been hasty. We could try it together, Gloriana."

"I don't want any part of it."

Damian shrugged. "I had to give it a shot. I wasn't serious anyway. That Vamp Viagra. It messes with your mind. I couldn't stop when I wanted to. Couldn't slow down and *think*."

"Thinking is highly overrated. Especially if you're getting great sex." Will had emerged from the kitchen licking his lips. "I'd try that Vampire Viagra in a heartbeat."

"So says a man who lives and acts like a dog." Damian's lip curled. He turned his back on Will. "Now you've got me worried about my sister. She's too easily persuaded to take chances. It comes with having lived so long and so well. Florence is always looking for the next big thing."

"Aren't we all? But Flo's usually satisfied with a shoe sale. This is different." I squeezed Damian's hand. One thing I liked about him was his family loyalty. I didn't have a family. But then, even when they were alive, my parents had ignored me, ashamed of my lifestyle. The whole "actresses are sluts and whores" thing. I'd gotten over it, but sometimes I wished . . . Nope, I wasn't going to start a pity party.

"What should we do? Where do these EVs live? Should we go see them?" I didn't want to, but if Flo was in danger . . . Hey, she *was* my family. All my close vamp friends were. I glanced at Damian. Yeah, even Casanova.

"That's what they want, Glory. For you to hand yourself over

to them. Kaplan told you that. You ain't going within miles of their hideout. Even if we could find it." Valdez stretched and ambled over to collapse at my feet, pretending like he hadn't just waved a red flag at this bull. I gave him a look he couldn't misinterpret.

"The dog has a point. They *are* drug dealers. Vicious drug dealers. They keep a low profile or I would have already known they were in the area." Damian looked scarily serious. "I'm sure they have plenty of customers, though. But I'm sure they screen those carefully. This Vampire Viagra isn't something you can buy on a street corner. Unless things have changed, they control the production and distribution with an iron fist."

"We got that from listening to Kaplan. Can't say I like who they put to work for them." Will was playing Mr. Righteous, trying to get back into my good graces.

As usual, Damian ignored him. "Their security will be extremely tight. They'd be happy to let *you* in, Gloriana, but not your guards. And as for getting out . . ." Damian ran a hand through his dark hair. "Damn it, I don't like the idea of Florence having anything to do with them."

"You could just ask her if her boyfriend is an EV." Valdez yawned.

Will put his head on his paws. "You know that lady keeps her secrets. Hell, Glory didn't have a clue her roommate was painting vampires on her wall downstairs."

"Speaking of downstairs, I've got to relieve Lacy. Maybe Flo will come by later. I'll call her. Leave a message if she doesn't pick up. She doesn't like vintage unless she bought it herself, but a werecat sold me a brand-new pair of Christian Louboutin suede pumps back in the day. Never worn. Flo's size. That should bring her in." I stood and smoothed my sixties skirt. I was a walking advertisement for the shop. Thank God I was a packrat who'd kept my favorite outfits through the years.

Vamp magic that I would forever wear the same size. Sucksville though, that the size was a twelve, not a six like roomie Flo. Tonight I wore a red off-the-shoulder peasant blouse with my long skirt. Oh, shoot, I hoped the sixties look wasn't because I still had Greg Kaplan and his free love era on the brain.

"I'll go down with you." Damian handed me my crocheted hobo bag. "If Florence comes in, we'll both confront her."

I locked up and headed downstairs with my entourage. When I got to the door of the shop, I could see through the glass that things were hopping. A crowd clustered around the counter. Waiting to pay? I smiled and opened the door.

"There she is." Lacy looked harried when the crowd parted. I could see why. "I was just about to call you, Glory. Look who's here." She gestured to a woman I recognized immediately.

"Donna Mitchell, Channel Six News. I interviewed you on the night of the fire." She smiled and held out her hand. "Your shop looks amazing. When I heard you'd reopened, I thought you might agree to a follow-up. Free publicity."

"Sure, sounds good." I shook her hand and read her mind. She also wanted a shot at another feature. And rumor had it this was a slow news night. Then her eyes widened when she saw Damian behind me. He had that effect on women. "Hot bod alert."

"Uh." Donna's mind had gone completely blank. I had to step between them, to block her view of the Italian before I could get her attention again.

"What did you have in mind?" No way was I introducing her to Damian. He was here to help with the Flo situation, not bewitch a new girlfriend.

"Well, first we need to get a shot of this fabulous mural." Donna laughed. "By da Vinci, of course. What a hoot."

"Yeah, hilarious." I saw Lacy roll her eyes. "My roommate painted it. Customers seem to get a kick out of it."

"Let me call my cameraman." She glanced at her watch. "We might be able to get this on the ten o'clock news if they've got a spot open. At the very least, it'll be on the weekend wrap-up and the Web site."

"Web site. Yes. We have one too now. Vintagevampshop
.com." I steered Donna over to the mural, well away from
Damian. "Maybe I could plug it."

Donna had her cell phone to her ear. "Good. See you in
ten." She snapped her phone closed and smiled. "Sure, you
can plug your new site. Let's do a walk through. Tell me
about your business." She kept glancing at Damian, who
lounged next to the counter putting the flirt on one of my
customers.

The fiftyish woman laughed at something he said. Yes, he
could be charming. And useful. Like now, when he picked up
a length of crystal beads and draped them around the
woman's neck. She flushed and I heard her tell Lacy to add
them to her bill.

Donna hadn't missed the exchange either. "Who *is* that
man?" she whispered.

"Nobody. Now where would you like me to stand for the
interview?"

"I don't suppose you could get your partner here. You
two made such a cute couple and she *did* paint the mural."

Damian choked and moved closer, his eyes twinkling.
"I'm Gloriana's 'partner's' brother, Damian Sabatini." He
bowed over Donna's hand, leaving her wide-eyed. "It's a
pleasure to meet a woman who is even more beautiful in
person than she is on television."

Donna's mouth opened and closed but no sound came
out. I knew the feeling.

"Damian, why don't you try calling Flo while Donna and
I discuss the shoot? I know she'd hate to miss this."

"Of course. Excuse me, ladies." He pulled his cell phone
out of his pocket and stepped outside. I saw him speaking
so maybe Flo had actually picked up, even though she had
a policy of turning off her cell during dates.

"What a hunk." Donna clutched my arm. "Tell me he's
not gay."

Hmm. Tempting. And I'd spread that rumor myself
when he'd pissed me off. But he was helping with Flo. "No,

very straight. But I wouldn't get too close if I were you.
He's strictly love 'em and leave 'em—" Donna gave me a
sharp look—"according to his sister."

"He looks like he might be worth the risk. Too bad I'm
in a relationship." It didn't take a mind reader to see that
Donna was reevaluating the whole relationship issue. If her
significant other didn't get back into a gym soon and quit
eating the last of the butter pecan ice cream . . . She eyed
Damian's abs again when he came back inside.

"I can't thank you enough, Donna, for setting this up." I
took her arm and dragged her back to the mural, halfway
between the screamer and the vamp. "Why don't we shoot
here first?"

Now the reporter was all business, pointing out a likely
spot for the camera. Damian caught my eye and shook his
head. Obviously he'd gotten Flo's voice mail.

I excused myself long enough to head to the back room
to freshen my lipstick and fluff my hair. If I'd known I was
going on TV, I would have chosen a different outfit. A fifties
shirtwaist would have really sent the message that we had a
cool shop. Or a forties suit with a cute little hat. I gestured
for Valdez to come back with me, then shut the door.

"How do I look?" What a pain that vamps don't reflect.
"Oh, God, this skirt makes my ass look huge, doesn't it?
I've heard the camera adds ten pounds too."

"You look okay. But you got lipstick on your teeth."

"Thanks." I scrubbed my front teeth with my finger.
"Now?"

"Fine." Valdez cocked his head. *"Not like a vampire at all,
if that's what you're worried about."*

"Yeah, thanks." Actually I'd forgotten all about that part.
I touched my tongue to my fangs. Retracted, just like they
would stay unless someone came in with AB negative. I'm a
slut for AB negative. Especially AB negative men. Remember the firefighter Steve incident?

"I hope I don't forget to mention we carry men's clothing." I sat on a stool for a minute. "Maybe all this publicity isn't such a good idea. You can't tell me Westwood's men won't see it. And then there are the EVs. I wonder if they watch TV. I know Greg did. He said he'd seen me on the news." I was babbling. Nerves.

"Too late for a low profile now, Blondie. You've got a business to run. Let Westwood's men report back to him that you're not intimidated by his tactics."

A knock. "The cameraman's here, Glory." Lacy opened the door. "You look cute. The sixties look is hot right now. But you're a little pale." She handed me a makeup bag. "Throw on some blush."

"She's supposed to be pale." Valdez was obviously defensive. *"She never sees daylight."*

"No need to advertise the fact."

I'd gone through a fake tanning phase. Part of my lifelong obsession with blending. I'd managed to avoid a lot of grief by pretending to be mortal. But since I'd been in Austin, I'd discovered how much better life could be surrounded by my own kind—I glanced at Lacy, the werekitty—and other assorted entities. Lacy gave me a critical look after I brushed a little blush on my cheekbones.

"Perfect. Don't forget to mention the address at least three times. So people will remember it."

"Right." I took a breath, stepped out and ran straight into Donna.

"Ms. St. Clair, please stand over here." Donna had powdered her own nose and slipped on a green silk blazer. "We've already taken some shots around the store and I filmed my intro outside. We'll put it all together later." She nodded to the cameraman and turned to look at me. I almost ran out of the store when I saw her thoughts.

Fourteen

"We're here with Gloriana St. Clair, owner of Vintage Vamp's Emporium. If you remember our previous report several weeks ago, this shop was practically destroyed in a fire that the Austin fire department has determined was arson. Unfortunately there have been no arrests in the case." The microphone shifted to me. "Gloriana, we're glad to see you've reopened."

"Thank you, Donna." I braced myself because I could see what was coming. "It wasn't easy, but I'm glad to say it's business as usual at Vintage Vamp's Emporium, your vintage clothing store in the heart of historic Sixth Street." I smiled and kept smiling. Yeah, I sounded like a commercial and why not? I was about to be ambushed and putting Donna under the whammy wasn't an option, not with a crowd of interested shoppers looking on.

"You've certainly made your shop unique. Right now we're standing in front of a mural your partner painted on one wall inside your shop, a painting of a vampire attacking a man. Are you sending a message?" She thrust her microphone under my mouth, this time close enough to bite in two. And don't think I wasn't tempted.

"No, I mean, it's art."

"I'm sure everyone recognizes *The Scream* by Edvard Munch. And he also painted *Vampire*, though it's not as well known. Aren't you implying that the store's name has a special meaning? Exactly what *is* a vintage vamp?"

That damned microphone was in my face again. I'd love to yell "Cut" and cancel the whole deal. But there's no such thing as bad publicity, right?

"Donna, I'm into fashion history. A vamp was a hottie back in the roaring twenties. Do you really think I believe in vampires?" I laughed, what else could I do? "Give me a break. Fangs? Blood sucking?" I shuddered. "I know it's a popular theme in fiction." I nodded at the mural. "And art. But this is just a vintage clothing store." I looked directly at the camera and grinned like an idiot. Then I got a whiff of the cameraman. AB negative. Oh, God, my fangs!

"Rat! I see a rat!" Someone, I swear it was Will, screamed. Valdez and Will started barking like maniacs and racing around the shop, knocking the cameraman down and starting a general stampede for the door. Donna dropped the microphone and, when she scrambled to pick it up, Valdez head butted her into a rack of vintage hats. Donna shrieked and landed face first on a black straw with a wide brim. She came up spitting ostrich feathers.

"Oh, no! I'm so sorry." I had the fangs well under control now and helped Donna to her feet. I sent the dogs a mental message to cool it. "Give me a minute to lock up my pets. There is no way anyone saw a rat, I had the exterminator in just last week." Truth. I have this thing about bugs. Go figure.

"Dogs in a clothing store. Is that really a good idea?" Donna brushed off her skirt. She was one tough lady, the rat thing hadn't even phased her. "Where's the nearest mirror?"

"Dressing room. The dogs are friendly and sleep through most of the night while I'm working." I smiled and patted Valdez when he sat beside me. "Most customers appreciate our animal friendly policy." I was on solid ground here. Austin is full of animal rights activists. If Donna tried to criticize my pets on the air, she'd have backlash on her hands.

She nodded thoughtfully. "Let me think about whether I got enough or not. Get some more shots of that mural.

Sorry, Ms. St. Clair, but a story's a story. People will groove on the vampire angle."

I glared as she headed for the dressing room, plucking feathers out of her hair.

"Excitement's over, folks. No rat, I promise. Will! Drop that!" The dog looked innocent, but he had something in his mouth.

"Christ! That's the connector wire to the lights." Danny the cameraman tried to snatch the wire, but Will growled and wouldn't let go.

"Oh, no! Will it shock him? If my dog gets hurt, who do I sue?" I gestured and Will dropped the slimy cable.

The cameraman wasn't worried about slime. He grabbed it, looked it over, then wiped it on his jeans. "No harm done. I don't see how it could hurt the dog. But I'm not taking any more pictures in here."

Will groaned, gasped and rolled over, his feet quivering straight up in the air. It was a pretty good imitation of death throes.

"Oh, my God! You've killed him." I clasped Will to my breasts. "Sweet Willy. Come back to me." I felt a wet tongue trace my cleavage and pushed him away. "Someone help."

"Of course, Gloriana." Damian stepped over Will, limp on the carpet. "What can I do?" He gave the cameraman a hard look.

"Mouth to mouth?" It was all I could do not to crack up at Damian's look of horror. Valdez solved the problem by jumping on Will's stomach, his back feet landing solidly on . . . you know. The dog screamed—tough to explain that one—and jumped up to run to the back room.

"He lives!" I clasped my hands to my chest, wiping away dog spit. The few customers left burst into applause, including a woman still standing on a Morris chair, her eyes peeled for rats. "Twenty-five percent off everything!" The woman climbed down and hurried over to the purses. I understood. A sale is a sale.

Donna was out of the dressing room, her blazer over her arm. "Let's go, Danny. We've got enough here."

"No kidding." Danny was busily packing up his equipment.

Damian picked up the hat rack while I gathered up hats and stacked them on the counter.

I could have used the publicity if Donna had played it straight with me, but putting the vampire thing out there? No thanks. This wasn't the first time I wondered if I'd been a little too cute with the name for my shop. I didn't try to stop the reporter when she left without a backward glance.

Damian took me aside. "Now that the entertainment's over, I'm going to look for my sister. I left a message that you were going to be interviewed for TV, but she didn't call back. She wouldn't miss an opportunity to show off her painting to all of Austin unless something was wrong."

I put my hand on his arm. "I doubt she's even checked her voice mail, Damian. If she's with a lover . . ."

"You're probably right. But if he's an EV, she's in over her head. You're a good friend to her, Glory. Thanks for telling me about this." Damian covered my hand with his and gave me one of his intense looks.

I'd relaxed my block, but now I tightened up because Damian was looking better and better to me. I glanced around the shop, like I had things to do. Which I did, truth be told. Stick a dozen hats back on the rack. Help that customer find her size in vintage sweaters. Get the hell away from Damian.

"I'll check in with you later." With that Damian left and I let the dogs out of the back room. I sent Lacy home and settled in for the rest of the night.

I murmured reassurances when one of the customers who'd witnessed the recent chaos gave them a wide berth. I waited on a few customers, including the lady who was happy she hadn't actually *seen* a rat and ecstatic that she'd gotten such a deal on two vintage Gucci bags.

I tried to call Flo and got her voice mail too. So I left my message about the shoes and hung up. The store was empty and the dogs snoozing when my cell phone rang. I grabbed it in case it was Flo, but the caller ID let me know it was Blade. I was happy to talk to him and spent a few minutes telling him about my TV experience. An edited version, but I had him laughing anyway.

"Sounds like Will helped you out in dramatic fashion. Maybe now you'll forgive me for saddling you with him." Blade's voice was low and sexy and I suddenly wanted to wrap my legs around him and make him growl with hunger.

"Maybe." I took a breath. Fresh paint, moth balls from some of the clothing and dog. "Jerry, I miss you." I meant it. I missed his smell, his warmth, his strength. And, yeah, his ever ready lust for me. While I like being in charge of my own life, it was nice to have someone I could always count on to care what happened to me.

"I miss you too."

"Is Mara there with you?"

"No, she's watching Westwood's compound. We're afraid he may have skipped out on us. He's flown in doctors to work on his arm, but he may have left to get further medical treatment." Jerry didn't laugh, but I could hear the satisfaction in his voice.

"You really got him good then." Halloween. Jerry's lethal with a knife, and should have finished the hunter then. He'd let my own antics distract him and Jerry still beat himself up for not killing the bastard when he had the chance.

"We've heard his men talking. Westwood will never pull on a bow again."

"Aw gee. Give me a minute while my heart bleeds." Westwood's olive wood arrows had taken out more than one vampire. Like we're big game or something. Then there's the fangs he takes as a trophy. Obviously Westwood is one brick short of a load.

"I won't let him get away this time."

I'd heard this all before. Hey, I understood. The creep

had killed Jerry's best friend right in front of him. I noticed Will's ears twitching. He was obviously tuned in to our conversation despite closed eyes.

"But if Westwood's left the country, what will you do?"

"Follow him. He's a dead man."

I headed into the back room and closed and locked the door. I would hear the bells on the outside door if a customer came in.

Warrior Blade really did it for me, but Westwood wasn't your ordinary opponent. He had billions at his disposal from his computer empire. And technology. His technology scared the hell out of me. I didn't say that. It would just stir up Blade's macho "I'll show you who's stronger" instincts. Instead, I settled for a warning.

"Don't forget how dangerous Westwood is. He's got all this equipment. And he hates you. Not just because you're vampire either. You bested him on Halloween."

"No, *he* bested *me*. He got away."

"I know you feel like you owe MacTavish this—"

"I owe all vampires Westwood's total destruction. If he starts producing his vampire detectors and sells them to every would-be fang hunter, none of us will be safe, Gloriana."

"You're right. At least his injury has kept him out of commission. And Derek's been monitoring the Internet. If any vamp detectors come on the market, we'll know about it." Leave it to a techno-freak like Westwood to figure out how to spot a vampire and put it into something resembling a cell phone. So, no matter how cute I dressed or normal I seemed I couldn't blend enough to avoid detection.

"Promise me you'll be careful, Jerry."

"I'm being careful. Too damned careful. I want to settle this once and for all. If he's really moved on . . ."

"Speaking of moving on . . . Are we actually alone right now?" I'd had enough of this angst over a problem I sure had no way of solving. And Jerry needed a break. I could hear the tension in his voice. He needed to relieve some stress or he might do something crazy, like storm West-wood's compound. Or jump Mara's way too beautiful bones.

"I'm alone. Why? Do we need privacy?"

"It would probably be a good idea." I smiled into the phone. "I'm taking off my skirt. You take off something."

"Is this phone sex?"

"Why not?" I couldn't hear the smile in his voice yet. It made me even more determined to wipe the thought of Westwood out of Jerry's head for a few minutes. And the memories of the hunter's sleazy call out of mine. How better than to replace them with new and improved memories with a man who made me melt just hearing his deep, sexy voice?

"I kicked off my shoes, Gloriana."

"Aw, no good. I want to see some skin. Take off your shirt." I did drop my skirt to the floor and kicked off my slingbacks. If any customers came in at three thirty in the morning, the dogs would warn me. For once I hoped I didn't have any business for a while. I wanted to find out just how hot phone sex could be with the right man.

"My shirt just hit the wall. Take off yours. What color is it?"

"Red. And I'm not wearing a bra." I tossed the shirt on a chair. "Mmm. It's a little chilly in here. My nipples are all pointy and tingling. I'm warming them with my hands."

"God, Gloriana. What kind of panties are you wearing?" Jerry groaned and I knew I had him revved up. Good.

"Black thong. Oops. I *was* wearing a black thong." I sighed. "Now all I'm wearing are my earrings. Are you naked yet?"

Silence. One thousand one, one thousand two . . .

"Yes." There was that growl I loved so much.

"Are you touching yourself like I'm touching myself?" Who was I kidding? Blade was a man. He probably touched himself when deciding whether to wear the black or brown socks.

"No, I'm touching *you*. Can you feel me, Glory?"

I gasped. Impossible. He was thousands of miles away.

He couldn't possibly . . . But I swear those were his fingers, not mine stroking me. My body wept for him and I quivered from the inside out.

"Now I'm laying you on that big table in your workroom and kissing the curls between your legs. Open for me, sweetheart. That's right. Now my tongue dips inside you, tasting your honey. Delicious."

"Blade." I swear I felt his mouth on me, every sweep of his tongue. Oh, God. Oh, God. Not happening. Mind control across continents. But I was flat on my back on the table and I swear I hadn't climbed up there. Wow, I thought *I* had a lot of power. My body clenched until I arched against the table. I closed my eyes and saw Blade's face, then his naked body where he lay on a cot in a tent. The sounds of Africa were a murmur in the background. Could I touch him?

"Feel my hands on you, Jerry. I'm pulling you up my body to kiss you on the mouth. A soul kiss to show you how much I've missed you. Can you feel it, Jerry?"

"Yes."

"I swear I can taste you. And then I look at you, just look at you. I love your broad shoulders. Can you feel me touching them?" I took a breath and knew his scent, unique and all Blade. "I kiss your chest. I sweep my tongue around your nipples and taste the salt on your skin. Is it hot there, Jerry?" I heard him gasp.

"Hot as hell."

A touch, a pressure then a spasm between my legs. Could he really take me? From so far away?

"I'm pushing inside you, Gloriana. I can't wait. I'm sorry but I've got to have you. Now."

And I felt it. Insane, but he was hard inside me, filling me and touching my womb. Shock waves rippled through me until even my toes tingled.

"God, I can't believe this." I knew I was really alone, flat on my back, legs wide. One hand gripped the phone, the other the wooden table. Blade wasn't here, but this felt so *real*. "You can't be doing this."

"Yes, I can. Come with me, Gloriana."

He pushed into me again, harder, deeper. I gasped and the bells on the shop door rang.

"No!"

"Yes." He thrust again while my body held him inside me. The room swam and I couldn't seem to focus.

"I mean no, there's a customer in the shop."

"Let the dogs handle it." His hands cupped my breasts before his hot mouth burned a path from one nipple to another.

"I . . . can't." I sighed. I had to crash back down to earth. I tried counting ceiling tiles. I'd made it to three when Blade's lips circled my belly, then headed south.

A knock on the door.

"Gloriana? Are you all right?" Derek, here to pick up a commission check.

"I'll be out, uh, in a minute. I'm, oh, on the phone. Would you, um, cover the front for me?" Not a customer. My hips came off the table and I bit back a moan.

"Sure. Take your time. Tell Blade hi for me."

"Eavesdrop on my conversation and you're fired." Damned mind reading vampires. Right now I was, oh yes, the star in my own triple X movie.

"Wouldn't dare, boss. I'll be checking on the Web site. My attention is totally on that." He laughed. "And I'm turning up the radio."

The Doobie Brothers blasted through the door. Whatever. I groaned when hands followed lips over my breasts and down my tummy.

"This will take more than a minute, Gloriana." Blade lifted my hips and pushed into me again. Still hard? Hard again? Obviously this man would never need Vamp Viagra. And, damn, but I didn't want to think about that stuff right now.

"I'm going to have to go in . . ." Gasp, "Maybe five minutes." Could I make him scream his satisfaction? I "saw" his thigh, close to his sacs and imagined my fangs piercing the tender skin.

"God, Gloriana. You're evil."

"Evil?" I could definitely taste him. "I'll show you evil." I squeezed his cock while his essence flooded my mouth. This was all in my mind, of course. Had to be. But the mind is a powerful thing. Had that been a shriek? Couldn't have been. Way too girly for Blade.

"Mara's here." Blade sounded like he was strangling.

Ah, the shrieker. I sat up, suddenly aware of the where and the how. "You'd better be covering yourself." That witch would like nothing better than to take over where I'd left off.

"I told her to get out." Blade sounded like he was in serious pain. "Where were we?"

I sighed. Just the mention of Blade's female companion was enough to bring me crashing back to a hard wooden table in a chilly storage room.

"Gloriana?"

"Sorry. But I'd better go."

"Go?" Blade or something pushed me back on the table. "Not yet."

I felt his fangs on my inner thigh. Pay back.

"Jerry," I moaned. He drew on me and I jerked like I'd been electrocuted. The pleasure/pain went on and on. Talk about tsunamis . . . hands, mouth, teeth. Finally I collapsed, hitting my head on the wooden table.

"This did *not* happen." I looked at the phone I still clutched in one fist. Yep, same old cell. Who knew? And now I figured I needed a camera phone. Jerry and I both did. Hmm. Phone sex with pictures. I took slow even breaths before I started heating up all over again.

"It did happen. I've got Mara sulking outside my tent to prove it." Jerry's voice was low, full of satisfaction.

"Back to reality, big guy." I smiled and sat up. Showing Mara who Blade really wanted was a guaranteed mood enhancer. "Tell me what's going on there besides a Mara meltdown." Did he know about my little confrontation with Greg Kaplan? Apparently not, since he merely gave me a quick rundown of their progress, or lack of, with getting to Westwood.

The billionaire was too smart to go out at night and no amount of shape-shifting or other spy techniques had managed to infiltrate his hideout. The guards, who couldn't be bribed, were armed with vamp detectors and had every entrance, including the windows, well covered.

"Are you sure you're all right, Gloriana? I haven't heard from Valdez this week."

I have no idea how those two communicate. It sure wasn't with e-mail, since Valdez couldn't exactly type in dog form. Or with the phone, same problem with dialing. Mental telepathy. I'd just had a toe-curling example of how *that* worked no matter the distance. Of course we'd also had cell phones . . .

"We've been busy getting the shop back up and running. The TV interview tonight should help get the word out that we're open again. If it actually airs. And if it doesn't make us look like the latest vampire hangout."

"Be careful, Gloriana. Westwood's men are everywhere."

"We're handling it. And I forwarded the e-mail the man himself sent me. Nice to know that he's saving a stake for me that he plans to deliver personally."

"Over my dead body."

"Don't even joke about it." I shuddered. I wasn't about to give Jerry an update on all the e-mails and calls since. "Just stay safe." I scrambled back into my clothes, one handed because I still had him on the phone.

"I will if you will."

"I'll do my best. Say hi to Mara." Am I civilized, or what? Should I tell Jerry about Greg? Ask his advice about the EVs? I heard the bells tinkle again signaling a customer. Derek could handle it, but I took it as a sign that I should leave it alone. Blade had enough worries.

"I'll talk to you again soon." I hung up and sat on a stool to give myself a moment. From sixty to zero in a few minutes wasn't exactly an easy trip. I felt drained, yet still hungry.

That's the problem with virtual sex, virtual anything. It wasn't *real*.

And Blade had no idea when he'd be home. In the meantime, my gut clenched and I still had damp panties. I wanted more than a little, okay, a lot, of phone sex. It made me crazy that I didn't feel satisfied. It was like being all dressed up in your cute new leather mini with nowhere to go. I needed something or someone a little more substantial than my own right hand. The bell tinkled again. I unlocked the storeroom door.

Richard leaned against the counter talking to Derek. I clutched a bottle of Fangtastic I'd pulled from the fridge back there, hoping that would explain the flush I was sure still brightened my face.

A customer picked through my selection of fur jackets. I ignored the men for the moment, my inner saleswoman on high alert.

I spent a few minutes helping the woman pick out a muskrat stroller with curly lamb cuffs. Richard paced the store, obviously impatient.

"Here. Let my associate Derek write you up." I smiled and nodded, sending Derek a mental message that he could have the commission if he'd give me a few minutes in the back room with Richard.

"Sure, Glory. Richard says you have business to discuss. I'll hold down the fort until Lacy comes in if you want to go upstairs."

Did I? Want to go upstairs? I could either go upstairs or drag Richard to the back where, one whiff, and he'd know exactly what I'd been up to back there. Richard's hand on my elbow and Richard's set face made me decide the scene might go better upstairs where I could put a couch between us if I needed to.

I glanced at the clock. Only an hour and a half until dawn. Where did the time go? I guess I'd spent more time in the back room than I thought. But time flies . . .

"Thanks, Derek. Upstairs it is. See you tomorrow night."
I grabbed my purse from Derek's outstretched hand.

"Leave the dogs here." Richard's nostrils flared.

Uh-oh. He'd already smelled sex on me. I'm sure Derek
had told him I was on the phone with Blade. Well, so what?
Rich and I were friends. Blade and I . . ? More than friends
and for a long, long, long time.

"That's fine with me."

Valdez growled but didn't say anything since the customer was still standing there.

"Thanks, Derek, see you." I patted each frustrated dog
on the head as I swept out of the door Richard held open.

He put his hand on my back and steered me to the apartment entry where I punched in the security code. He was
being awfully quiet. Jealous? I didn't have a problem with
that. Once we got inside, I turned on some lamps and hit
the remote for the CD player. Norah Jones. Slow and sexy. I
glanced at Richard and hit stop. He was not in the mood.

"You've been with Blade."

"Talking to him on the phone. So what?" I headed for the
kitchen. I didn't want any more Fangtastic, but needed
something to do with my hands. I opened the fridge. "You
want one? I can heat it if you prefer it that way."

He shook his head. "I know you and Blade have been together. But you're not together. Not physically or otherwise.
Not exclusively. Am I right?"

I gave up on the drink thing and went back into the living room to sit on the couch. Hey, a man was actually talking about relationships. I was riveted. I patted the seat
beside me. "You're right. My connection to Blade is complicated."

"So explain it." He sat close, too close, his thigh brushing mine. Now he could really smell sex on me and I could
tell it had an effect on him. Well, I knew just what to say to
deflate any notion he had that he might be allowed to take
up where Blade had left off.

"Instead, I need you to tell me what you know about the EVs."

You had to give Richard credit. Except for the tightening of his jaw, you'd never know I'd sucker punched him.

"What do *you* know about the EVs?" His blue eyes were the color of an ice flow and just as warm. Yikes.

"I know that they sent someone after me." Richard grabbed my hand and I couldn't bite back a squeal at the pain. "Hey, careful."

"Sorry." He instantly eased his grip. "You want to tell me what you mean?"

So I did. I told him the whole Greg Kaplan, EV thing. When I got to the part where Greg claimed Flo was involved with them, Richard shot to his feet. I'd suspected he still had feelings for my roomie. Now I knew he did.

"Florence wouldn't sleep with an EV. I've told her how they are. What they've done." He paced the small room, making a circle around the couch and coffee table. I glanced longingly at the CD player. Maybe Norah could diffuse the tension that was coming off Richard in waves. He gave me a hard look. Maybe not.

"Clue me in, Richard. You've got to admit Flo's not afraid of anyone or anything." The couch shook when Richard dropped down on it next to me again. "And I'm pretty sure she's enjoying the perks, like the Vamp Viagra."

"Stupid female." He shot me a look. "Sorry, that was unbelievably insensitive." He tried for a smile but failed. "What I meant to say was exasperating bitch."

"Oh, much better." I put my hand on his hard thigh. He was really upset and I had to like that about him. Flo had dumped him badly and not looked back. But he still cared what happened to her. "What *do* you know about the EVs? She warned me not to tell you I'd even heard of them."

"That's because she knows I've been following their activities for decades, no, make that centuries." Richard ran his hand through his platinum hair. When I'd first met him, it had been practically a buzz cut. Now it had grown out and I itched to touch the silky strands. On that hilltop . . . He gave me a hot look. I was either going to have to block my thoughts or accept that he was going to read me. I sent him a mental message to cut me a break and leave my mind the hell alone. He leaned back then slung his arm around me.

"Okay, okay. No more mind reading. But I do care about Florence. As a friend. The EVs are ruthless bastards, always hunting for new power sources." Richard squeezed my shoulders gently and I felt myself sway toward him. Nope. Not going to do it. I wanted to hear this.

"Flo said she could check my power level and that I had a ton of it. How does that work? Can they suck the power from someone and use it to make things?" And does the whole power draining operation hurt? I kept that one to myself. Richard didn't need to hear me whine. Besides, I didn't plan to let an EV within sucking distance.

"The EVs are the reason I came to Austin in the first place. Their unique ability is that they can convert power into other things. Drugs. In the right hands, this could be a good thing, a way to perform miracles." Richard let go of me and jumped to his feet again. The way he said miracles reminded me about the whole former priest thing.

"But they're the wrong hands?"

Richard's fists opened and closed against his strong thighs. Righteous warrior, former crusader, you didn't want to mess with him. I could easily picture him crushing the life out of some bad actor.

"They couldn't be more wrong. The EVs have taken this ability and perverted it. They take advantage of an immortal's boredom, his"—he glanced at me—"or *her* desire for excitement, something different."

"Like being immortal and vampire isn't enough. There has to be more than the same old, same old." I got it. But I didn't see a drug as the answer. There were always new places to go, people to meet. Of course all the drifting got old too. I could vouch for that. Since settling in Austin I felt like I'd finally found a home. I'd hate like hell to leave here.

"I followed the EVs here from Buenos Aires. I want to put them out of business permanently." He had a fierce look. I didn't doubt that if anyone could bring the EVs down it was Richard.

"I don't see how you could do that alone."

"I wasn't alone there. I had allies. And here I was waiting until I knew more about their current setup before involving the locals." Richard glanced at me again and shook his head. "Not you, Glory. Some of the older, stronger vampires."

"But it's me they want, Richard." I bit back a snarky comment. Of course he hadn't considered me in forming his vampire militia. What could a clothes-obsessed vamp with a shifting phobia do for him?

"I'd never use you as bait, Glory. But it will be difficult to get to them. The EVs in Argentina were well guarded. I'm sure they will be here too. I've been searching for their stronghold, but haven't found it yet. Apparently the power supply in Argentina was running low. And then there was a coup, I guess you'd call it. They have a new leader and he decided to change location."

"A coup? Damian said they were like a cult. I assumed they had some kind of charismatic leader." It never failed to amaze me what I didn't know. I'd sure had enough years to learn just about everything. But then the EVs were apparently a secret society. A well-kept secret.

"The EVs' secrets are held by what they call the Demoness, Honoria, the spirit of a Roman princess who was married to Attila the Hun. She's the source of their power and speaks to the current leader. If a leader doesn't keep his followers in line or please her, Honoria devours him, literally."

I shuddered. Devouring female demons. Of course any woman married to Attila the Hun might actually enjoy snacking on hapless men. And Flo was involved with these creeps? "Makes you wonder what the old leader did, doesn't it?"

"There have been rumors . . ." Richard shook his head, like he'd exhausted his knowledge or didn't want to waste any more time on the subject with me. "But I wasn't surprised that the group moved to Texas. Even down there, we heard that Austin is a paranormal playground."

"Yeah. They even print up T-shirts that say 'Keep Austin Weird.'" Okay, so I had one. Pink and very cute, though a little tight since I'd dried it on hot. "I don't think the chamber of commerce realizes just how weird Austin really is though."

"The EVs know. They have spies like Greg Kaplan, fools who will work for their drugs, finding power sources for them." Richard stalked to the kitchen, pulled out a Fangtastic and twisted off the top. He took two deep gulps and his face turned pink. I was so not noticing how cute he looked with that slight flush, not to mention the late night beard, as pale as his hair, that hugged his strong jaw.

"Give me one. You know you still haven't told me how they do their power thing." I was obviously having a sinking spell if I could forget what I'd just had with Blade and have lustful thoughts about Richard. He drained his bottle, then grabbed two more from the fridge. Hey, that stuff wasn't cheap, but one look at his set face and I wasn't going to bring up my budget concerns.

I took the bottle and opened it. The flavor of the month was O positive. On sale and always the cheapest vintage. Remember that budget? I wrinkled my nose, then took a swallow.

"You're stalling, Richard. How do the EVs get power from a vampire?"

"They suck your belly, Glory."

Fifteen

I spewed about two dollars worth of Fangtastic all over the coffee table. "What did you say?" I set the bottle down before I dropped it.

"Your belly, your navel, like where you were attached to your mother. That's where they get your power." Richard headed for the kitchen and came back with a handful of paper towels. He efficiently cleaned off the coffee table, then I heard the thunk of wet towels hitting the bottom of the trash can.

"That is beyond gross." I pressed a hand to my oh-so-generous power base. No wonder the EVs wanted me, especially now that I had the added attraction of the Cheetos bulge.

"It's what they do." Richard sat down beside me.

"How do they convert it, though? And is there a vein there? Do they use blood or . . . something else?" I had visions of lying drained and helpless atop some kind of altar with a straw in my belly button. South America. Maybe they'd also called in Incas or Mayans or, oh, hell, the Devil, for ideas on how to convert power. And Honoria had been married to Attila the Hun. I bet he'd been so busy conquering countries she'd been deprived sexually. Was that why she'd helped the EVs come up with the Vamp Viagra?

"They have a council of twelve. All born vampires. Their secret abilities come from an ancient book that Honoria controls. Only the chosen twelve have access to it."

"An EV manual. How creepy is that? It figures they're

born vampires. Born vamps think they're superior to us made types. And they *can* eat." If Mara ever dared eat a bag of Cheetos in front of me . . . Well, let's just see how she'd like wearing a Cheetos bag thong.

Richard was deep in thought. Obviously eating wasn't on his radar. "I'd like to know how they even knew about you, Glory." Richard plucked my hand off my stomach.

"Greg said someone mentioned my name and he remembered me and my shift aversion. What do you bet my roomie Flo was the one with the loose lips?" I made a face. "I'm sure she didn't intend . . . Oh, hell, Richard, do you think they're sucking Flo's power?" Richard's flush had faded until he was ghostly white.

"I hope to hell not. If they don't kill her," he said, and I saw him swallow, "she can recover some of it. But it leaves a vampire weak and vulnerable. Just about powerless." He looked down at my hand. "Damn it, we need to find her."

The door crashed open. "Find who?" Flo swayed into the room, clearly high on something.

Or was that low? She didn't look right, like she was dreaming, or fading. Or . . . oh, shit. I jumped up and grabbed her when she stumbled. Richard was on her other side and shot me a concerned look over her head.

"We've been worried about you, Flo. Where've you been?" I sent Richard a mental message and we guided Flo down the hall and into her bedroom. Her hair was wild, her face pale sans lipstick and, scariest of all, she'd lost her shoes somewhere. Flo never went anywhere without top of the line footgear.

"Simon and I were together." She reached up and patted Richard's cheek. "Sorry, *caro*, but I move on."

I had to give Richard credit for not dropping Flo right on her cute little butt. Instead he helped me lay Flo gently on her bed, a decadent number complete with gilt cherub headboard. Her red satin comforter slid to the floor and he kicked it aside. I didn't say anything, just adjusted a pillow under Flo's head. Her eyes closed.

"Don't you dare go to sleep." I tapped her cheek lightly and her eyes flew open.

"Did you just hit me?" She sat up, eyes shooting sparks.

"Glory didn't hit you, Florence, but if you don't calm down, I might." Richard fisted his hands and I believed he had a slap or two in him.

Flo's anger dissolved into tears and she clasped me to her bosom. Mood swings. "I'm sorry, Glory. You're my best friend in the world. You must come with me to meet Simon. He will love you as much as I do."

I inhaled and almost choked on the scent of sex, blood and something sickly sweet. I looked at Richard. Vamp Viagra? He nodded. I patted Flo's slim back. Hmm. She'd lost her bra somewhere, but with perky twentysomething breasts, this wasn't a tragedy.

"Flo, tell us about Simon. Is he an EV?"

Flo collapsed back on the pillows. "Not just an EV. The leader. The king of the EVs. I think I'll change my name again. Simon calls me Fantasia. Like the Idol. Isn't that sweet?" She sighed and cuddled the pillow to her.

"Idol?" Richard looked mystified.

"*American Idol*. Third season. Flo and I . . . Never mind." I touched Flo's shoulder. "Wake up, Flo. Tell us about Simon."

She smiled into her pillow. "He promises to make me his queen. But he wants to meet you first, Glory. To get your approval. Isn't that sweet?"

"Seems to me, he should need Damian's approval, not mine." Like I didn't know what Simon really wanted with me. Would he hang me upside down and drain me? Oh, with a siphon at my navel, of course.

"He knows my brother doesn't give me permission for what I do. But you, Glory, my roomie, he knows I care what you think. Simon's so considerate."

"Considerate? Like hell." Richard jerked the pillow from Flo's grasp. "What are you playing at, Florence? Do you want to get Gloriana killed?"

"No, I love her." Flo's lips trembled. "I do, I love you, Glory. I've never had such a good woman friend before." Her eyes closed and a tear streaked down her cheek.

"I love you too, Flo."

I couldn't help it, I pulled up her shirt. Her navel, above her low rise jeans, was bracketed by two angry welts. Damn them, the EVs hadn't even bothered to heal her. I shuddered. Obviously Flo had been giving power. Had the Vamp Viagra been her reward? I checked out Richard's reaction. I'd never seen him more furious. I pulled up a sheet to cover her.

Maybe I should undress her, but we still had an hour before dawn and I wanted to learn more. If not from her, then from Richard. I heard a soft snore. Okay, Richard would have to fill me in. I threw the coverlet over her too, turned off the light and gestured for Richard to follow me back to the living room.

"This is bad, Richard, really bad. What do you think?"

"I think Florence is in way deeper than we realized if she's involved with Simon." Richard paced the worn hardwoods around the area rug, a nice fake Oriental I'd found in a Dumpster out back. The things people throw away . . .

I dragged myself away from the edge of meltdown. I didn't give a damn about the rug. I was terrified. For Flo and, gulp, myself. I looked down at my rounded tummy, which I'd suddenly discovered I loved with a passion and wasn't about to give up. Not to an EV anyway. Now if liposuction worked . . . Never mind. Obviously my thoughts were all over the place.

Right now my stomach was covered by three layers, blouse, skirt and my skimpy excuse for panties. Maybe if I wore one of my vintage panty girdles . . . Those things were like iron. Trust me, you can't even bend in one. Of course a vampire, even an ordinary one, could make quick work of it. I'd had a lover bite one off me once. Of course that had been consensual and not the least bit threatening. But if an EV came at me, fangs drawn . . . Oh, God.

"Glory." Richard spoke next to my ear. "Quit freaking out."

"Why? Obviously Simon, king of the EVs, is trying to use Flo to get to me." A role that normally would've turned my roomie into a shrieking harridan. Flo-slash-Fantasia used men, not vice versa. "Do you think he could really make her his queen?"

"Honoria wouldn't stand for it. She's the only female in charge of that group. If Simon thinks he could use Flo to get to you, he's going to be disappointed. He'll have to go through me and two very angry dogs to get to you." Richard grabbed my arm. "Let's go downstairs and get the beasts. And we need to warn Derek. No powerful vampire is safe with the EVs on the prowl."

Bang. Bang. Bang. Loud noises from Flo's bedroom. We both rushed down the hall and I threw open the door. Flo was standing on the bed, a gold Manolo sandal in her hand.

"Flo, what are you doing?"

"Hanging this picture of Simon." She gave the tack another whack with the stiletto heel. "Isn't he handsome?"

"Uh, Flo."

The shoe heel snapped and Flo tossed it aside without so much as a glance. She dropped back on the bed.

"That's *Simon*?" Richard and I both gaped at the computer generated photo she'd tacked to the wall. "I don't think—"

"So handsome." Flo had a dreamy look on her face. "He should be in movies."

"Uh, he *is* in movies." I glanced at Richard and he shook his head. What? I wasn't supposed to tell Flo that she'd just ruined a very expensive shoe hanging up a picture of Brad Pitt? I looked down at her still unfocused eyes and loopy smile. "I mean, yeah, he's movie star handsome."

"And he's all mine." Flo threw out her arms then was out like a light again. Richard gestured and we stepped back into the hall. He closed the door.

"Are you kidding me? Does Simon really look like that?"

I gave myself a few seconds to live the fantasy. He could suck my belly button, my ear, my big toe for all I cared. Hey, he'd played a vampire in a movie. If Brad really was one . . .

"Snap out of it, Glory. Of course he doesn't really look like that. You've just seen one of the powers an EV has. He can delve into your mind, find your secret fantasy and make you believe you've found it." Richard ground his teeth like maybe he'd hoped *he'd* been Flo's secret fantasy. "He doesn't even have to shape-shift to do it."

"Kind of like the whammy then. With a twist."

"The twist is Flo's been brainwashed. She sees what she wants to see when she looks at Simon."

"So if I met Simon, he'd look like Johnny Depp?" *Chocolat* Johnny, not *Pirates* or, shudder, *Charlie and the Chocolate Factory* Johnny.

Richard snorted. "If that's *your* fantasy."

"Cool. I mean that conniving bastard." Wow. No wonder Flo was so hot and heavy with Simon. Her two favorite hunks were Patrick Swayze in *Dirty Dancing* and Brad Pitt in anything.

"Let's go downstairs."

"Wait." I held onto Richard, stopping him at the door. "What are we going to do about Flo?"

"Leave her to sleep it off. I doubt she'll wake up until tomorrow night. Then you, me, Damian . . ." He shook his head. "Oh, hell, I'm not sure she's going to listen to any of us. Once you've got a taste for the Vampire Viagra, it's almost impossible to give it up. I've seen it before. The withdrawal is a bitch."

"We need to warn Derek about that too. He and Freddy know most of the paranormals in Austin. Maybe we should call a meeting, spread the word." Blade usually headed up vamp meetings. I suddenly wanted him beside me with an ache that made me grab my stomach again. Damn that Westwood. Why'd he have to run all the way to Africa?

"A meeting is a good idea. But if the EVs get wind of it, they're not going to like your interference."

"As if I give a rat's ass what they like. And what about this king? Simon? Can all the EVs do the Brad Pitt whammy or is he something special?" I dug in my purse for my keys and locked the door once we were out in the hall.

"Simon Destiny." Richard shrugged. "Stupid name. Not his real one, of course. Special? Obviously women under his influence think so. I met him once and I wasn't impressed. Of course he didn't turn into Beyoncé for me either."

I stopped and gave him a look. "Beyoncé?" Could he have picked a woman more opposite from me? Tall, dark, with a body to die for versus short, blond and a body . . .

"Gotcha." Richard grinned for the first time all evening.

I muttered a comment on his parentage and Richard actually chuckled. Finally, almost at the bottom of the stairs, he stopped and turned me to face him, serious again.

"Simon's not going to want to give Flo up. Not till he's ready to discard her. And he's got to appear to be a strong leader. He can't risk angering Honoria."

"Too damn bad." Florence da Vinci discarded? This was so not like my roomie, always the power in any relationship. I wanted to run up and hug her, then wake her and try to reason with her again.

"You can't reason with her, Glory. She thinks she's hooked Brad Pitt when Simon actually . . ." Richard put his hands on my shoulders. "I call him Simon the snake. He's got the look of a reptile, complete with a forked tongue."

"Oh, God! I didn't want to hear that." I leaned against Richard for a moment. "We've got to help Flo understand how dangerous this is." I inhaled Richard and thought about how nice it was to feel his arms around me. Yeah, I'm an independent woman, but centuries of male companionship have left me with a case of attention deficit disorder. Male attention, got to have it. With Blade gone, Richard was doing nicely.

I sighed and pushed back. I'd blocked that weak female moment from Richard and he was frowning at me, like he was afraid I'd go off on my own and do something dangerous to get Simon to leave Flo alone. Fat chance. If Simon turned into Johnny Depp for me, I'd probably hop on the altar and hand him the straw myself.

We headed to the shop. Outside, I appreciated the cold air on my face before I unlocked the back door. Inside, the dogs were on high alert. I'm sure Valdez at least could tell I was upset about something. Even Derek lost the twinkle in his eyes when he saw our faces. No customers. So we filled Derek in. He was on his cell phone before we finished. He and Frederick decided to call a vamp meeting. At Freddy's house.

As soon as she heard what they were talking about, CiCi refused to leave home. I didn't blame her. A fortress would be nice right now. With a moat, hungry alligators and rabid bats circling overhead.

I waited on a few customers while Derek and Richard powwowed in the back. I couldn't quit thinking about Flo. She'd acted so unlike the powerful roomie who'd painted strange things on my wall and taught me my best vamp moves. Hell, she hadn't even asked me about the TV interview or, gasp, the Louboutin pumps. I'd give her the benefit of the doubt though. Maybe she'd never bothered to check her messages.

By the time Lacy came in, I was beyond exhausted, mentally and physically. I trudged up the stairs a few minutes before dawn, arguing with Richard that he didn't need to sleep on my couch. Then I saw the door to the apartment. Wide open.

"Glory, get back. Let me check things out."

I leaped over Valdez and ran down the hall to Flo's bedroom. I threw open the door. She was gone.

I was just going through Flo's closet to see if she'd taken any clothes with her when my cell phone rang. I pulled it out of my purse I'd dumped on the floor in my panic. I didn't even bother to look at the caller ID.

"Flo? Is that you?"

"Gloriana, you really need to check your e-mail. I'm waiting to hear from you."

I snapped the phone shut and threw it across the room.

"Who the hell was that?" Richard dug the phone out of Flo's comforter and held it out to me. "Obviously not Florence."

"You don't want to know."

"Yes, I do." Richard was right beside me in a heartbeat. He put his hand on my back. "You're even more upset than when you saw Florence had taken off."

"Taken off or been kidnapped?" I sank on the side of the messy bed. "She didn't take any clothes that I can see. Not even shoes." I gestured toward the usually neatly stacked shoeboxes. Flo is nothing if not meticulous about her wardrobe. And a creature of habit. If she wore a pair of shoes, she set the box on top with the lid off. The only empty shoebox was from the pair she'd worn out of here last night. The pair she *wasn't* wearing when she got home. And then there was the Manolo with the broken heel, the box with its mate casually dumped on the closet floor. Flo *really* hadn't been herself.

Richard sat beside me and my phone rang again.

"Don't answer that." I grabbed the phone and shut it off.

"Who's bothering you? Surely you would talk to Blade."

"It's not Jerry." I felt tears welling and blinked them back. "It's Westwood. He started calling me. After I sent him that e-mail." I took a shaky breath. "I think he has a crush on me. I should probably play along, try to get information for Jerry, but I just . . . can't."

"Bloody hell!" Richard grabbed my phone and ran through the menu. "He left you a message." He put the phone to his ear, his frown becoming a cold, stony rage that scared me, even though I knew he wasn't mad at *me*.

"The bastard won't get away with this. We need to change your number for one thing. This is harassment."

"No kidding. But I won't change my number. I should

get up my nerve and see what I can find out from him. Jerry thinks Westwood may have left Africa. He needs to know where the hunter's going next." I didn't have to listen to know what the message said. Westwood had stuck to one theme, how lovely my dental work would look on the chain around his neck. Or maybe he'd start a charm bracelet. For a future bride. He was thinking of marrying, he owed the world a passel of kids with his superior gray matter. She'd have to be human, of course, and any woman he got serious about would hate vampires as much as he did.

"He's a sicko. I don't know how he made billions." I pushed off the bed and walked back into the living room. Valdez and Will studied me worriedly.

"What's up with Flo?" Valdez nudged my hip.

"I don't know, puppy." I sat down on the couch and put my feet on the coffee table. I got a good look at my Ferragamo slingbacks. Flo had helped me pick them out during a half-price sale. I burst into tears. "I don't know." Noisy sobs. How humiliating, but I couldn't stop them.

"Good God, Glory, I'd hoped you weren't one of those weepy females." Will bumped my foot. "Flo's tough, she'll be okay."

Richard handed me a towel, though I don't remember him going into the bathroom to get it. I blotted my cheeks and sniffled until I felt like I had the waterworks under control.

"Sorry, guys. I guess I'm on sensory overload. Between Westwood, the EVs and Flo, I feel like I've got a full plate." Another tear ran down my cheek and I wiped it away. Full plate. Stupid. I couldn't even eat a bag of Cheetos without suffering stomach cramps that would have made the Marquis de Sade whimper.

"I doubt Flo was kidnapped." Richard was up again, prowling around the apartment. "She wanted to be with Simon. I'm sure she woke up from her nap and decided to go back to the EV compound."

"Without her *shoes?*" My voice rose and I jumped to my

feet. "Damn it, Richard. Didn't you learn anything about my roommate while you were sleeping with her?"

Richard shrugged and I wanted to slap him. "We didn't exactly get together to talk. I never had much conversation with the woman."

"Well, 'the woman' is my best friend. I'm worried about her and I'm going to do something about it." I stalked into Flo's bedroom and grabbed my purse.

"Where the hell do you think you're going? It's almost dawn." Richard grabbed my arm, jerking me to a halt.

"Nowhere. I'm exhausted and I'm going to bed. But first"—I dragged a phone out of my purse—"I'm going to make a call."

"Not Westwood." Richard grabbed for the phone, but I used a vamp move to dodge him.

"Nope. This isn't my phone, it's Greg Kaplan's. And I just bet . . ." I scrolled through his address book. Lots of women. A guy named Lucky and, oh, yes, Simon. I punched the button and heard the phone start ringing.

"Hello."

"Flo?"

"Yes." I heard a big sigh. "I'm okay, Glory. Simon saw this number on the caller ID and made me answer."

"*Made* you answer. Are you sure you're all right?" I shoved at Richard who tried to grab the phone again. Of course he was practically breathing down my neck, listening too.

"I'm fine. I just decided I had to come back here. I left my new Calvin Klein stretch suede boots. So foolish of me. I shifted into my favorite bird and flew right out here." She laughed and I heard a male voice in the background. "I know, I know. It's too close to dawn for me to leave now. So I stay. You go to sleep and quit worrying about me. Tell Richard too. Simon is taking good care of me. I'm fine."

"Flo—"

She'd hung up.

"What do you think?" I snapped the phone shut and looked at Richard.

"I'd say she's in no danger yet. Obviously Simon is enjoying her company and she's no worse for wear if she had enough power left to shape-shift." He gestured and I gave him Greg's phone. "Let me look at this. I'll see what I can find out from these numbers." Richard was looking as exhausted as I felt. Valdez and Will had settled on either side of the door, Will obviously out like a light.

"Tomorrow." I took the phone and set it on the coffee table. "You want to crash on Flo's bed?"

"I'd rather crash on yours." Richard ran his hand across my cheek to my ear. "Just sleep. Too close to dawn for anything else."

I knew it wasn't a good idea to sleep in the same bed with him. And I sure wasn't in the mood for sex with anyone, not even Richard who was looking really good to me. Kind of like Spike on *Buffy* good. Have you seen his calendar?

"Fine. But you're sleeping in your clothes." Silly. We'd both be dead to the world as soon as the sun hit the horizon which, according to my body clock, was about three minutes from now. Hey, we both needed to lighten up after all this angst.

Richard played along, though he was obviously still worried. "And what are you sleeping in?"

"You'll see." I strutted to my bedroom and slammed the door. Sexless or sexy? I rummaged in a drawer until I found the perfect thing. By the time I opened the door again, I could hardly keep my eyes open.

"Come to bed, Richard."

He laughed, a full-throated belly laugh that made me smile. Who knew this intense, complicated man could laugh until he cried. I liked him even more, especially when he brushed past me, just close enough for me to feel his interest. The man was obviously insane. He'd have to be to make a pass at a woman in *Smurfs* footie pajamas.

Sixteen

I was hot, stifling, and I couldn't wiggle my toes. My arms were weighed down, pinned to the bed. Not fair. Not with Johnny Depp just inches away and snoring softly. I wanted to wake him with a surprise. Me, wrapped in nothing but my birthday suit.

I pushed and finally managed to get an arm free. If I could just touch him . . .

"Watch where you put that hand, Glory."

I sprang out of bed like I'd been shot from a cannon. "Valdez?"

"The one and only." My dog lay on top of the covers in the center of the bed. The other pillow, where I could have sworn I'd left Richard when I'd closed my eyes, was empty.

"Where's Richard?"

Valdez jumped off the bed and stretched. *"On the phone."* He trotted across the room and nosed open the door. *"Check it out."*

I looked down at what had to be the world's ugliest pajamas and shook my head. "In a minute." I headed for the bathroom, taking my makeup bag and a robe with me. I could see Richard, his back to me as he paced the living room, a cell phone to his ear. I wasn't about to let him see me again until I'd gotten rid of these awful pj's.

Five minutes later I strolled into the living room, the empty living room. I sniffed. Bacon? Had Richard cooked?

"Richard?"

"He's gone." Will came out of the kitchen. Human Will,

not dog Will. Naked except for a frilly pink apron tied around his lean middle. Flo had bought the apron for me as a joke after I'd filled the apartment with smoke trying to cook for Valdez. I'd never worn it. And Will . . . Let's just say it was simply not covering all that it should.

"What the hell do you think you're doing?"

"It was an emergency." Will grinned, way too charming with his red hair, tanned face and, oh, yeah, bare chest and washboard abs. "The doodle and I were starving and Mainwaring sure wasn't going to feed us."

"Will's a decent cook, Glory. What could it hurt to let him shift some while he's here?" Valdez emerged from the kitchen smacking his lips.

I looked past Will to the pile of dirty dishes in the sink. I *would not* look at his bare bum as I headed for the fridge and a Fangtastic.

"What happened to Blade's rules? He's going to flip when he hears about this."

"Does he have to know?" Will slung his arm around me. "Come on, Glory, lass. Where's the harm?" He glanced at the bottle I'd just opened and wrinkled his nose. "You could at least spring for a better quality hooch. There's a new brew out of Czechoslovakia that'll knock your cute little socks off."

"Save the charm for Blade when he hears about this." I took a swallow. A Czechoslovakian synthetic? Hmm. "And I *will* tell him unless you leave this kitchen spotless then shift back pronto." I put some space between us. "And don't touch me." I flashed back to the whole tit-grabbing incident. I'd knocked Will on his ass then. But I'd had the element of surprise. Who knew an *actress* wouldn't have welcomed the Kilpatrick's son's attentions?

"Glory, lass, now don't be hasty." Will was still smiling. I knew that because I simply was not going to look at him below the neck.

"Why are you naked?"

"I'm stuck in dog body for weeks at a time and you expect

me to wear *clothes*?" Will turned on the faucet and squirted dish washing liquid into the sink.

I gave his toned butt a five second, okay, a ten second, appraisal then turned my back to him.

"Ask Valdez. I'll bet he's naked under that fur coat. Am I right?"

"Too much information." Dogs. I had dog bodyguards. Not hunky men who looked like extras in a gladiator movie. "Clean up." Oh, what the hell. "Do the bathroom too, then shift back. And stay that way unless I ask you to change."

"Fine. Whatever. You're the boss." I heard more grumbling as I headed to the bedroom to get dressed for the night.

"Don't let him shift too often, Glory." Valdez was right on my heels. *"Shifting takes a lot of power. He needs to save it for defense."*

I paused and studied Valdez's soft brown eyes. What did he look like in human form? Dark haired, with the Latin look the name suggested? But he was the latest in a long line of Valdezes. So the name didn't have that kind of significance. His eyes gleamed and I knew he was reading my mind.

"You want me to shift, Glory? Blade forbids it, but I'm willing to keep it our secret." He wagged his tail and I swear he grinned. *"Got to warn you, though, that Will's right. I* am *naked."*

I slammed the door in his furry face. Not thinking about Valdez. Definitely not thinking about Valdez as naked man. I concentrated on the contents of my closet. What to wear to a vamp meeting? A form-fitting, black, seventies jump suit. Loved the bell-bottoms and it had a cute chain belt I could whack Will with if he dared shift in public. Will was a loose cannon and now he'd given Valdez ideas.

Should I call Blade and tell him my canines were going cowboy on me? But Blade was busy following Westwood and he really didn't need to hear me whine about how I couldn't control my own dogs. Besides, I could always threaten to get Blade to dock Will's pay. And Will could cook, take on more housework. I should bring a pair of jeans up from the shop for him to wear. He looked like he took a thirty-four long.

By the time the three of us trooped downstairs, a sulky Will was safely back in dog form and complaining that scrubbing the shower had ruined his hands. I'd convinced myself that having him shift on command might not be a bad thing. He bumped against my leg, dotting the black gabardine with white dog hair. I had visions of Will on his knees with a lint roller. Not a bad thing at all.

"You see? I'm fine. Nothing to worry about." Flo had zipped into the shop a few minutes after I'd taken over from my mortal part-timer. "I finally checked my voice mail. Where are those shoes?"

So far no customers had mentioned that we'd made the TV news but the weekend roundup was still a possibility. Melanie, the part-timer, had let me know an art student was interested in the mural and wanted permission to photograph it. Something about a dissertation. I wasn't sure it was a good idea, but had agreed to meet with the man later. Now I told Flo about the TV interview and the art student right after we made a deal on the suede pumps. She'd loved them and, even after giving her the family discount, I'd made a tidy profit.

Flo cradled the shoe box to her chest and grinned. "So my mural will be famous. Edvard would be pleased."

"It's not exactly the Sistine Chapel. You really think decorating the wall of a vintage clothing shop would please Edvard?" I smiled, though, because Flo did seem like her old self, complete with fresh outfit and matching Stuart Weitzman pumps. Her hair was pulled back into a ponytail, showing off her high cheekbones and porcelain skin.

One male customer was lingering by the suits just to watch her breathe. I gave him a questioning look and he left. I almost called him back. I didn't mean to run off a potential customer, but I also didn't need someone eavesdropping on my conversation with Flo either.

"Edvard wouldn't mind." Flo trailed a finger across the

wall just where the man's neck met the vampire's lips. "He didn't mind anything I did."

"Speaking of things you do . . ." I checked out another pair of customers flipping through a dress rack. Okay, I had my limits. "Forget it. I've arranged for Lacy to take over at midnight. Will you meet me at the apartment then?"

Flo glanced at her watch. "I guess I could watch a DVD for a while, but don't keep me waiting. I have a date later."

"With Simon?" I wished Flo would move on like she usually did. If she stayed with her normal pattern, Simon probably had only another week or two at the most anyway. But would he let her go? And now there was this whole Brad Pitt thing going on. I kept up a block so Flo couldn't read my mind and start an argument I didn't feel like finishing.

"Yes, with Simon." Flo picked up a pearl necklace, ran it across her teeth, then put it back. "Fake. Simon has promised me a special gift. Remember, I told you I wanted a man who would give me good jewelry." She sighed. "I think I finally found him."

"Swell." This was the pits. Of course Simon could afford real pearls, diamonds, whatever. He was a damned drug dealer. I glanced at the women again and was relieved to see them head for the dressing rooms. I grabbed Flo's arm and pulled her toward the back.

"Honey, do you remember what happened last night?"

Flo looked down at where I gripped her arm. "Careful, Glory, this is my favorite cashmere sweater. Don't you love the color? Apple green." She smoothed the soft knit. "Simon says it makes my eyes sparkle like emeralds. He is always saying things like that. Sweet compliments. He'll be sure to notice how these brown suede jeans fit me." She turned to show me. "What do you think? Does my butt look too big?"

"Flo, a size six butt is not considered big by anyone's standards other than someone size zero and you know how we feel about *those* people." I bet Beyoncé had a size zero butt and I really didn't want to think about that now.

"Please concentrate, Flo. You were zonked last night. You acted . . . drugged."

Flo just waved her hand. "Nonsense. It was near dawn. I was exhausted from a night of very intense lovemaking." She glanced toward the dressing rooms. "Simon is a stallion. My God. And his tongue . . ." She shivered and I fought back a gag.

"Did you take any of that Vampire Viagra?"

"Of course. Why not? Simon passes it out like it's candy." She ran her hand down the pearl buttons on her cardigan, "I surpassed myself." She leaned closer. "I had him weeping, Glory. The king of the EVs. Simon Destiny. Kissing my feet and declaring that I was the best lover he had ever had." She had a dreamy look that gave me chills. "Isn't that incredible? You should try it."

"Try what?"

"The VV of course." Flo laughed merrily and patted my cheek. "Not Simon. He's mine."

As if I wanted to go within a mile of the reptilian creep. "About Simon." I poked my roommate in the general location of her navel. "You've been giving him your power, haven't you? To make the VV."

"Don't be ridiculous. I don't give my power to anyone."

I reached out and pulled up Flo's sweater. Flat tummy, damn her, but no telltale marks. Obviously the evidence faded with the healing vampire sleep.

"What are you looking for, Glory? I'm not giving him my power. Simon has drones for that. Stupid vampires who are hooked on his drugs. He's a businessman, Glory. He sells things, just like you do." Flo jerked down her sweater, careful to smooth it.

"You're comparing me to a drug dealer?" I didn't appreciate that comparison one damned bit and let her see how much in my eyes.

"Now, Glory. You know what I meant. We're best friends. Right?" Flo backed away from me and smoothed her sweater again. "I think your customers need you. I'll see you later. I think I'll watch *Ocean's Eleven*." She turned on her heel and waved from the door, the bells tinkling as the door closed behind her.

I just stared. Simon was just like me? I wanted to run after my "best friend" and drag her back by her cute little ponytail. But she'd disappeared, probably already upstairs using her vamp speed. The fact that at least one pedestrian might have seen her apparently hadn't slowed her down. Had to get to that Brad Pitt movie.

Damn it, she *was* out of control. Valdez and Will gave me a look, but didn't speak since the mortals were out of the dressing room and whipping out their charge cards.

After the women left, I seethed. So that was my excuse when I overreacted just a bit at the sight of the art student. Young, academic type, complete with tinted glasses and a stake in his pocket.

"Holy crap, Glory." Will stood on one side of the body, Valdez on the other.

Valdez nudged the glasses lying on the floor beside the unconscious man. *"I hate to tell you this, but these are regular tinted reading glasses. I read the guy's mind. Nothing in there but artsie-fartsie stuff. The guy's really deep into his dissertation on paranormal figures in art."*

Will bit the wooden handle poking out of the man's pocket and pulled, dropping the thing at my feet. "Here's his stake. Disguised as a paint brush." He grinned. "Check out the traces of red on the bristles. Might be the blood of all the vampires he's killed with it."

I didn't waste time with a clever comeback. Instead, I ran to the door and locked it, about a minute later than I should have. At least no customers had witnessed me going completely insane. I dragged the man to the back room. He didn't wake up. I pulled a cold bottle of water from the fridge and dumped some on a paper towel, then knelt down to press it on the man's closed eyes.

"Hello? Are you okay?" What had Melanie said his name was? Larry. Larry LeFevre. "Come on, Larry. Open your eyes." The man's pale blond lashes fluttered. "That's it. Wake up, Larry." I picked up his head and held the water bottle to his trembling lips. "I'm *so* sorry."

"Wha . . . What happened?" Larry took the bottle and held it against his forehead where a lump the size of a dime was rapidly swelling to quarter size.

"Freak accident." I helped him to his feet and watched him sway for a minute. Right. Glory the impulsive freak had accidentally bopped art boy with an art nouveau bronze titled *Reclining Nude*.

"Accident?" Oh, great, he was looking green like maybe he'd puke. I slid a trash can near him, just in case. "I don't remember." Larry groped his face and I remembered to hand him his glasses.

"There you go. Not broken, thank goodness."

"Thanks. Eye strain. Too much time on the computer. But the dissertation's due in a few months." He took a shaky breath and sat on the stool, obviously still wobbly. Him, not the stool. "What kind of accident?"

"I turned and you just walked into this lovely work of art." I pressed the statue I'd used as a weapon into his trembling hands. "Fortunately the piece is undamaged. I don't want to think what *could* have happened."

"Oh . . . good." He stared at the bronze, his thumb absentmindedly stroking the curve of the woman's voluptuous hip. "It's beautiful."

"It's yours. In apology. I'm so, so sorry." I looked into his eyes. Yep. I could read his mind now that I stopped long enough to check. He was still a little dazed. Headache. Confusion. The statue. Wished he had a girlfriend with that kind of figure. Sally didn't have curves, she had angles. But she gave the best—

"Larry!" I'd just read way too much. I do hate to intrude that way.

"Uh, the mural . . . ?"

"Of course you can use the mural for your dissertation. Come back during the day." *When I'm not here.* "I'll leave word to give you full access." I kept a hand under his elbow and walked him to the door, then reached to flip open the dead bolt.

"I can't accept—"

"Nonsense." I grabbed a piece of bubble wrap and a bag and had the statue back in his hands before he knew which way was up. "Here. Take it, please. It's the least I can do after wounding you." I checked in on his scattered thoughts. The man needed aspirin. He looked down and picked up the paint brush and stuck it in his pocket again. Sally's paint brush. He was supposed to stop by her place with it. Now he couldn't wait to show her the statue. It was erotic. Maybe it would inspire her to give him a—

"Larry! Maybe you should go home. Take an aspirin or two."

"Yeah, sure, Ms. St. Clair. Thanks. Really." Larry pulled open the door and took a deep breath of cold air. His head didn't hurt so bad that he couldn't get up for one of Sally's world class bl—

"Bye, Larry. Take care of yourself."

He hurried out the door before I could change my mind. He knew just where he'd put the statue. Right next to his Erté print. Blah, blah, blah, more art stuff. I slammed the door shut and leaned against it. Way too much information. And who knew academic types thought below their belts just like macho vamps did?

"Glad that's over." I smiled at the dogs. "Whoa. I've got to relax. I can't believe I did that."

"Uh, Glory." Will wagged his tail. "There's a woman hiding under the bench in one of the fitting rooms. She ran in there when you turned into a psycho bitch." Will did a dog version of a chuckle, half bark, half snort.

"Just do the whammy on her, Glory. She was looking at that black velvet coat over there when the shit hit the fan." Valdez trotted to the curtain and nudged it aside with his nose.

"You mean when I hit Larry." I pulled the wild-eyed, trembling woman out from under the bench. She had on worn jeans and a pink sweater that was only slightly less fuzzy than her over-processed hair. I stared into her pale blue eyes until she was under then led her to the rack where the velvet coat still hung. I looked into her eyes again.

"You're happy you found the velvet coat you were looking for. And even happier that it's on sale, half price." I reached up and touched one of her split ends. "You'll use the money you saved to get your hair done by a professional." The woman nodded. "Now shop."

The woman smiled and pulled the coat off the rack. "This is just what I was looking for. And half price!" She brought it to the counter and dug in her purse for her wallet. "You know a good hair dresser?" She nodded toward my shoulder length curls. "I'd love a new look before I go home with my new boyfriend at Thanksgiving." She made a face. "Meeting his parents."

I pulled out a business card. "Here, tell Reza that Glory sent you." Reza's a werecat buddy of Lacy's who had a beauty shop a few blocks away. "Good luck with the parents."

I smiled as the woman left and more customers came in. Business was booming, thank God.

I was really glad to see Lacy at midnight. She usually didn't work at night, but when I'd told her about Flo and the meeting at Freddy's, she'd insisted I let her fill in for me.

Now to deal with Flo. I wanted her to go to the meeting with me and GET A CLUE about what she was mixed up in with Simon. I hurried up the stairs, the dogs at my heels. I could hear the television even before I opened the door. And laughter. Flo's merry tinkle and a deeper laugh.

I stopped in front of the door, scared that I was about to meet Simon Destiny. Would my dogs be strong enough to keep me from being dragged away into his den of drug dealing tummy-suckers?

But it was just Damian sitting beside his sister, laughing at an old *Seinfeld* episode. The one where Jerry and Elaine make a vow of abstinence. They were even worse at abstinence than I was. It was a good episode and if I didn't have the meeting to go to, I would have enjoyed sinking down on the couch with a cold glass of Fangtastic in my hand and laughing out loud with them.

"Meeting tonight. Are you going, Flo?" I kept my purse slung over my shoulder. "We need to leave in five minutes or less."

Damian grabbed the remote from Flo and the TV went dark and silent.

"Stop it, Damian. We're just getting to the best part. I want to see who caves first."

"Forget caving, Florence. Glory and I want to talk to you. About your involvement with Simon." Damian pulled his sister to her feet. "Look at me, *cara*."

"Relax, Damian. Simon's fine. I'm fine. I already told Glory that."

"And did Glory tell you the EVs sent a man for her? That he threatened her?"

"Well, I don't know that he actually threatened me." Sometimes I'm stupidly honest. "But Greg wanted me to come with him to the EV headquarters. He's been stalking me. Giving me those headaches. Remember?"

"Greg. Yes, I have met such a one. A drone. Pay him no attention." Flo smiled. "He has no power so he looks for powerful ones to bring to Simon. But Simon would never have him take someone against their will." Flo looked at Damian. "You two are getting worked up for nothing."

"The EVs are drug dealers, Florence. I don't consider that nothing."

"Now, Damian"—Flo patted his cheek—"I remember that you tried the Vampire Viagra yourself before it was called by that silly name. We bought some from Juan Carlos in Madrid. It was not so bad, no? I had my lover El Greco and you." Flo grinned. "I think you had a harem back then."

"Merely six or seven . . ." Damian shook his head. "I hated the drug. I was like a bull, mating any female who would bend over for me."

"And is that such a bad thing?" Florence actually

laughed, while I just stood there with my mouth open. Damian is nothing if not suave and sophisticated, especially when it came to seduction. The VV must have really done a number on him to turn him into a rutting beast.

"Come to the meeting with us, Flo. With the area vampires. About Westwood and about the EVs."

"What? Are we forming a posse? Will you run them out of town?" Flo frowned and picked up her purse. "I'm not interested in your meeting. And as for Westwood, if you want him terminated, you should talk to Simon. I think he could arrange anything."

And Flo was out the door. Damian and I just looked at each other.

"She's out of control."

"She's always out of control." Damian threw the remote control on the couch. "Let's go. I told Richard I would drive you to the meeting. The dogs too. I brought the big Mercedes." He looked down at Valdez. "You two will ride in the back and you'd better not put paw prints on my leather seats."

"Then don't park next to a puddle." Valdez sniffed and followed me out the door. *"I'm worried about Flo, Glory. She's way more into this guy than she usually is."*

"I know." I turned and locked the door after the four of us were in the hall. "But what can we do about it? She's an adult. And she didn't ask for our interference."

"She didn't ask, but she's going to get it." Damian ran down the stairs. "And if it takes a posse to get rid of the EVs, then that's what we'll have. Vigilante justice."

"Obviously you weren't watching *Seinfeld* all night."

"Nope. Flo's got a thing for Brad Pitt. Says Simon reminds her of him. She couldn't find the movie she wanted so we started with *Legends of the Fall*." Damian turned and grinned at me. "Did the posse thing give us away?"

"You know it."

Seventeen

Over a dozen vampires crowded into Freddy and CiCi's living room. Damian had dropped the dogs and me off in front while he'd gone in search of a parking place. The house was near enough to the University of Texas that, even at 1:00 a.m., the street was lined with cars. Music and laughter from a house three doors down probably meant students lived there.

There was no music *or* laughter coming from Freddy's house, but plenty of loud conversation. That stopped when I entered the room, trailed by Will and Valdez.

"What?" I checked out the crowd. CiCi looked distressed. Derek and Freddy amused. The silent majority accusing. Or was I being paranoid? I grabbed a Baccarat crystal goblet of Fangtastic from a silver tray and sniffed appreciatively. AB negative, my favorite.

"There she goes again. I told you I saw fangs." Darren, the professor type Valdez had saved from the fire, pointed at me. "Run it again, Derek. You'll see."

I gingerly touched my tongue to one of my fangs. "So? I'm among . . . friends. If I can't show fang here, where?"

"TV, Glory. The station's Web site has your segment up." Derek gestured toward his laptop set up on the dining room table visible through an archway. "Fang, honey, on TV and on the Internet. We all saw it."

"And that painting!" A female vamp I'd met a few times before was obviously upset. I'm terrible with names, but I remembered her hair, desperately in need of a trim. I mean, the hippie, "hair down to your butt" look was so over.

"What about the painting? My customers love it." I took a sip and sighed. Times like these, I thought about hooking up with a rich vampire (okay, a rich vampire like Blade) and letting him actually take care of me. Imagine AB neg every night.

"A *vampire* painting, Glory." Another woman, a friend this time, Diana from Mugs and Muffins, chimed in. "I love Flo, but how could you let her paint vampires on your wall? Why not just post a sign? 'Stake me.'"

"It's art. Decoration for the shop. No one takes it seriously. Hey, aren't we here to discuss the EVs?"

"Glory's right." Freddy looked at Derek. "We're here because the EVs have invaded Austin."

"That's an exaggeration, isn't it, Frederick?" An older vamp who obviously didn't care that he was playing into the stereotype, stepped forward, one hand in the pocket of his black velvet blazer. He could have been Bela Lugosi's twin with his dead white skin and slicked back hair. He must have left his cape in the car. "There are only a dozen EVs. Hardly an invading horde."

"A dozen or one. What they represent is a danger to all of us. And they have plenty of followers." Freddy glanced at his mother. What was up with CiCi anyway? She'd sunk into a chair, her hand shaking as she drained her goblet.

"What's an EV?" Diana, bless her, hadn't been clued in. It was nice not to be the dumbest blonde in the room for a change.

"Energy Vampires." CiCi shuddered. "They take a vampire's power and use it for the most unspeakable—"

"Vampire Viagra. Can you believe it?" I should have known Will had been quiet long enough.

Diana laughed, obviously thinking this was a huge joke. But a quick glance around the room made it clear the majority of the vamps knew exactly who and what EVs were and what their main product could do.

"Seriously, Di." I took pity on her. "Flo's involved with their leader, Simon Destiny."

"Simon!" CiCi gasped. "Frederick, you didn't tell me Simon was here." She put her hand to her throat and, even across the room, I could see the frantic pounding of her pulse. She was really agitated. Vamp's hearts usually thump along at about half mortal speed.

"No, Mother, I didn't. Even if he moved in next door, neither of us needs to see him." Frederick made a vamp move to his mother's side and held onto her hand.

"But he's your father." Richard spoke from the doorway.

Oh, boy. Talk about your bombshells. I met Richard's gaze. Forget reading his mind. Everywhere I looked vamps' minds snapped shut, tight as the lid on a coffin.

"EVs can reproduce?" Diana was determined to be the voice of ignorance. "Is Freddy an Energy Vampire?"

"EVs must be born vampires. Just like"—CiCi glanced down—"Will here." CiCi held onto Freddy's hand, her knuckles white. "Their special gifts, if you want to call it that, are secrets handed down to members of what they call a council. They're very selective in who they invite to join and limit their membership to twelve."

"The Dirty Dozen." Oh, great, now Valdez felt compelled to speak.

"But, CiCi, I'm sure you didn't know . . ." I hated the accusing looks she was getting. CiCi's like a mother to me, the kind I wish I'd had but never did.

"Simon enchanted me. Our affair was brief, very intense. I knew he was vampire. That was part of his allure, of course." Nods all around. CiCi visibly calmed herself. "I became pregnant. Simon was delighted. Any child of his would be vampire some day. I was merely a convenience for Simon, a worthy vessel." CiCi's mouth had a bitter twist. "I was supposed to be honored and happy to give him my child to raise."

Freddy squeezed his mother's hand. "But you didn't."

"Of course not. Simon miscalculated when he chose me as his brood mare. Once my enchantment with him wore off, I saw how cruel he could be. I ran away before Frederick

Real Vampires Live Large

195

was born. And married Count von Repsdorf who was old
and desperate for an heir. He loved me and was very kind."
CiCi had a sad smile. "But he died soon after Frederick was
born, set upon by footpads. Simon's work, I'm sure of it."

"But Simon didn't claim his child then?" I couldn't keep
my mouth shut. What a story!

"I was terrified that he would, but Simon wasn't really
interested in a baby, only in the man Frederick would become, the vampire he would become. So Simon bided his
time." A tear ran down CiCi's cheek. "When Frederick
turned, I had to become vampire as well. I couldn't leave my
child alone to live forever with such a father."

"I'm sorry, Mother."

CiCi smiled at her son. "No regrets. But I don't want any
of you to underestimate Simon. He's very powerful. And
ruthless. Even then he was involved with the EVs, a mere
follower, not yet on the council. He has worked his way up
in the group." She swept the room with an intense gaze and
no one looked away. "Frederick and I have managed to live
our own lives for centuries, but periodically Simon ap-
proaches Frederick again. I think he is almost proud that his
son is not easily swayed to follow in his footsteps. But he is
convinced Frederick should join the EVs. If you know anything about them, then you know they will do anything
for Honoria, their . . . demon." CiCi shuddered.

"See? I was right to be worried. We need to get Flo away
from him." I sent CiCi a mental sympathy card.

"Yes, indeed. The man works tirelessly to please Honoria. Who do you think invented this"—CiCi wrinkled her
elegant nose—"Vampire Viagra?"

"You can't be serious." Di gave Damian a sideways
glance. They had a history, pretty hot to hear her tell it. But
Damian had fidelity issues. Enough said. "Vampires don't
need Viagra. At least not one I've ever slept with."

"Of course not, my dear." Bela glided closer. "Not unless
they had an unfortunate accident before they were turned."

"Born vampires like me *never* have performance issues."

Will bumped against Diana. "When I get through with this gig, we can hook up and I'll prove it."

"Uh . . ." Diana's glance shouted *save me!*

I just shrugged. When she saw Will in human form, she'd probably be more than happy to give him a spin on her pillow top. He had Mara's beauty and a masculine build I'd just recently been reminded rated a ten on the yummy meter. I looked down to where his tail brushed against me. Even his dog form was cute. Not that I'd ever be interested.

Will wasn't through. "With made vampires"—he sniffed in Bela's direction—"performance is a crap shoot."

I swear I was getting a muzzle for my number two dog.

"Are you implying—" Bela's fangs were suddenly huge in his dead white face. Did he have on *lipstick*?

Valdez jumped between them. *"Are you going to waste your time on a dog?"* He grinned and wagged his tail. *"Obviously, this one's talking out of his ass. Look at him."*

Interesting. I'd never have suspected Valdez would lift a paw to protect Will. Then Valdez looked at me. Oh, yeah, he was doing this for me. Because he felt I needed backup. Hey, I appreciated it. I patted his head when he trotted back to my side.

The room filled with loud discussions and it quickly became obvious it was a made versus born standoff. We were about evenly divided. Valdez, being the only shifter, just stayed by my side and I was happy to rub his ears and watch the escalating arguments. At least I wasn't the cause this time. It was obvious born vamps considered themselves above us "made" types. No news there. Mara had drilled that into me from day one at the Campbell homestead.

Will was nose to nose with Bela again. "You want to make a bet on that? I got five hundred that says I can knock you flat on your ass even in this dog form."

"Relax, you two. No pissing contests in CiCi's living room." I jumped between them. Maybe not my smartest move, but I was surrounded by friends here.

"Can we get back to business?" Damian's raised voice

silenced the crowd. "Richard, will you tell them what you know about the EVs and their work?" Damian looked around the room. "Richard has been on their trail for decades. He followed them here from Argentina."

"Yes, I did." Richard smiled apologetically at Freddy and CiCi. "The EVs will stop at nothing to get the power they need to make their drugs. The Vampire Viagra is the most lucrative, but not the only thing they make. The Demon Honoria has a full bag of tricks."

"What else do they make?" God, could Diana be any more clueless? But I smiled at her because I had the same question. She'd just been faster with it.

"He's been working on a daylight drug. Last I knew, he hadn't succeeded."

"Daylight drug. So a vampire could survive the sun's rays?" Now this was interesting. The Viagra thing didn't do it for me—hey, I'm hot enough without it—but to be able to feel the sun on my face for real . . .

"That's what he claims. But more than one vampire has been killed trying to use it." Richard was beside me, his hand on my shoulder. "It doesn't work. Vampires have given him fortunes and then expired anyway."

"That's harsh." Will stayed close to Diana.

"But get this, Diana. The EVs take power from vampires to make their drugs. And they've been after me." I almost fell back as every eye swung my way. Whoa! Nobody can do intense like a vampire.

"You!" Diana ran to my side. "What happened? Honey, are you all right?" Diana has a southern thing going on. Part of her charm. Will sure thought so. He edged closer and, if he put his shiny black nose under her skirt, it was going to be no shifting and generic dog food for a week. He got my mental message because he eased away from her and gave me a dirty look.

"I'm okay. But they sent someone to try to persuade me to come see them. Since I don't shape-shift, the EVs figure I have lots of stored power." Would I be a greedy slut if I took a third glass of Fangtastic? To hell with it. I picked up a refill and sipped.

"Didn't Florence tell you that too?" Richard was serious on a stick.

"Yes. Simon taught her how to check a vamp's power level. I'm off the charts." I felt Valdez push against my legs. "So I'm being careful. He won't get to me again."

"Who came after you?" Diana was a good friend and she looked really worried.

"Greg Kaplan." I grimaced. "We were . . . together years ago. Now he's hooked on the Vamp Viagra, so he does jobs for the EVs in exchange for the VV. If any of you know him, don't let Greg get anywhere near you. He'll try to lure you back for a little power draining." There were a few nods. So maybe I wasn't the only one Greg had approached.

"And, folks, don't kid yourselves. After a session with the EVs, a vampire can be greatly weakened. No shifting. No preternatural speed." Richard swept his gaze around the room.

"Hell, you'd be pretty defenseless." Diana bit her lip.

"Exactly." Richard nodded. "Frederick, you're Simon's son. And I don't doubt your being here is one reason he chose to come to Austin. Has he approached you to join the council since he got here? I've heard they have an opening. Apparently one of the EVs believed his own hype and met the sun with disastrous results." Richard ignored CiCi's gasp and focused on Freddy.

Darling Freddy, who could make me laugh, was a wonderful friend and had the best mom in the world, didn't crack a smile. Everyone in the room but Freddy's mom and me stared at him like he'd morph into a creepy creature with a forked tongue at any moment.

"No, he hasn't approached me yet. This time." Freddy looked at his mother. "And if he did, Mother, I'd tell him I'm not interested. Just like I have all the other times he's tried to play the 'father' card. Why would I want to join a group that obeys a female demon?"

"Their secrets don't have to be used for evil, Frederick. If you joined them, you could—" Richard winced when CiCi grabbed his arm.

"No, I won't hear any more of this. Frederick will not be your spy. The EVs would kill him, Simon's son or not, if he betrayed them." CiCi faced off with Richard. "Wage your own war, priest, and leave us out of this."

Okay, now Diana was really goggle-eyed. Maybe not everyone knew Richard had been a priest once. Every woman in the room checked out his buff bod, nicely showcased in worn jeans and black T-shirt. He obviously hadn't taken anyone's confession in a long, long time.

"Very well. We'll keep Frederick's relationship with his father out of this." Richard nodded. "But we have to do something. We know they want Gloriana, but any one of you might be powerful enough to interest them."

That made things clear enough. And now I had to sit down. But I jumped up again immediately. The buzz from three glasses of Fangtastic will do that to you.

"I suppose they would trade power for the VV." Will pressed on my other side. "Not that anyone in this room actually needs the stuff."

"You don't have to need it, to want it." Bela spoke up. "I tried it many years ago. Before it took on the trendy name." He shrugged. "This Viagra craze is new. The EVs could enhance pleasure long before mortals realized they could do something about performance issues."

"Why would you want it, if you don't need it?" Thank you, Diana. Now every vamp in the room was on the edge of his or her proverbial seat.

"It takes sex to a whole new level. For a man or a woman. I won't deny it's an unforgettable experience. I'd definitely try it again with the right woman." Bela picked up Diana's hand and I wanted her to jerk it away. His lips brushed her palm and, hello, Damian was right there, between them, before I could blink.

"We get it, Ralph."

Ralph? Bela Lugosi's name was Ralph? I hid a smile. There was nothing funny happening in this room. And nothing concrete being done about our problem either. At least we'd put these vampires on alert. Unfortunately, we'd probably also given them reason to run for the nearest VV supplier. I looked at Richard. He wasn't getting the cooperation he'd hoped for.

"The VV can be addictive, people, and is as expensive as hell. I think it's time to put these drug runners out of business for good. Or at least get them away from here. But I can't do it alone. I need your help. To find the EV headquarters for starters." He nodded at several male vamps who maybe were thinking about jumping on the "run the EVs out of town" bandwagon. It was a start anyway. "I know you'll all spread the word to be careful to any vampire who couldn't be here tonight."

"Are only vampires at risk? Can the EVs take power from other paranormals?" I was thinking about Lacy or even Valdez.

"They seem to prefer vampires. I don't know if they've taken power from a shifter. But I suppose it's possible."

"They'll have to catch me first." Valdez showed some teeth.

"We'll be careful." I rubbed the dog's ear. "What do you want us to do, Richard? Maybe if we all promise not to buy from the EVs, they'll move on." I checked the crowd for reaction. Hmm. Not exactly a groundswell of support. Addictive drug or not, a vamp, always sensual anyway, would hate to pass up a chance at better sex. The EVs were obviously sitting on a gold mine.

"Hoo-kay." I'd had about all the vamp togetherness I could take. Even with top drawer refreshments. These meetings weren't that great without Flo and Blade.

Richard frowned and looked around the room. When no one stepped forward with an "annihilate the EVs" plan, he nodded. "I guess this meeting was a waste of time. But I thought I owed all of you fair warning."

"Some of us appreciate it, Richard." Damian exchanged

hard looks with some of the men. "Ignore this information at your own risk. Richard and I intend to proceed with or without your help. I hope you'll think about how you would feel without your power. Remember, drugs can make anyone careless. We enjoy Austin and intend to stay here. Anyone risking our lifestyle will be dealt with."

That threat was clear enough. I felt antsy, ready to get out of there. Too many vamps together must create a hell of a power surge. Could the EVs sense it? Could they be surrounding the house right now?

"If you need to meet again, meet somewhere else." CiCi must have felt the same way I did. "Damian, they can come to your castle, can't they? You have such excellent security."

"Of course." Damian exchanged looks with Richard. "But I see no reason to meet again. Not unless more of you step up."

I put my hand on Richard's arm. "You two be careful. You can't take on these EVs by yourself. And while Flo didn't take *your* power pulse, I bet both of you've got more than enough to interest the EVs."

Richard squeezed my hand. "I haven't lived this long by being careless, Gloriana. I will do what I can to keep all of us safe." He smiled at me and I got a nice warm feeling in the pit of my stomach.

"You and Damian won't have to do this alone." Frederick stepped forward. "I'll help you, Richard. Stay. Sit down with me. I want to know more about my father's organization."

"Thanks." Richard clapped Frederick on the shoulder, instantly forgetting all about me.

"Damian, will you take me home?" I turned to Damian who, in typical Damian fashion, had morphed from fearless EV fighter to Casanova, to flirt with Diana.

"Of course, Gloriana. Gather the beasts and I'll meet you by the door." Damian whispered something in Di's ear and she nodded. Making a late date? Not my business. Not Will's either and he was sulking about it. He really couldn't

compete for Di's attention in dog form. And Diana wasn't
the only attractive female vampire in the room Will might
have liked to hit on. Bela, no, *Ralph*, had moved on to a redhead who looked like she could handle anything.

I reached for my cell phone and turned it on again. Messages. I scrolled through the numbers. Jerry. Flo. Unknown,
which I was afraid was Westwood. I might not ever listen to
that one. But Jerry and Flo . . .

Jerry first. Westwood had definitely skipped out on them.
He and Mara were headed to Europe. Westwood's arm wasn't
healing well and he was going to a clinic in Switzerland.
Jerry and Mara had cornered one of Westwood's men and
pulled that info out of him. His mind, that is.

My stomach in knots, I listened to Flo's message.

"Glory, Simon is so sorry you've been worried about me.
And that he might have frightened you with that man coming after you." Flo sighed. "Kaplan's been punished, Glory.
And Simon wants to make it up to you. He's sent you a case
of your favorite Fangtastic. Please keep an open mind about
him, Glory. He's not the villain Richard claims he is. Remember, I dumped Ricardo not so long ago. He's jealous of
Simon. I'll talk to you tomorrow night. Ciao."

I stared at the phone for a moment. Well, as a peace offering a case of my favorite was a swell start. But I didn't believe for an instant that Richard was acting out of jealousy. I
glanced at him where he stood listening intently to CiCi.
Flo needed to hear CiCi's version of Simon and the EVs. I'd
have to see that the two women got together.

"Richard, I'll do whatever you need me to." Damian
glanced back at Diana who'd picked up her purse and was
saying her good-byes. "Call me tomorrow." He turned to
me. "Gloriana?"

I nodded, then stopped to hug CiCi. She was looking
overwhelmed. Well, who wouldn't after finding out that
your ex and the father of your only child was in town? The
fact that he was Simon, king of the evil EVs, was just the icing on her crappy cake. Then she looked me in the eye and

sent me a mental message. She was more than a match for Simon Destiny when it came to protecting her darling boy. Hmm. Made me wonder what kind of power rating the lady had.

When we got to the car, I told Damian about Flo's message.

"She's obviously hitting the VV too hard. After what we heard tonight, I'm even more determined to get her away from that creep." Damian drove fast and we were at the shop before either of us had come up with any kind of plan to help his sister.

Damian stopped and shook his head. "No parking places. What the hell is going on at"——he glanced at the glowing clock on the dashboard——"four o'clock in the morning?"

"Looks like a block party." I hopped out and let the dogs out of the back.

"A block party from hell, maybe."

Eighteen

I scanned the crowd. Lots of black lipstick, black clothes and eyeliner, but none of that scared me. I could have done without all the piercings and tattoos, but, hey, maybe that was jealousy talking since I'd had no luck with either. And, trust me, I'd tried. Three hours for a sexy pair of lips in luscious red puckered up on my left butt cheek. After a day of vamp sleep? Nada. Talk about frustration.

"I'll park and then I'm meeting Diana at Mugs and Muffins. Will you be all right?"

"Sure. These look like potential customers to me." I smiled and pushed my way through the crowd. I'm nothing if not open-minded. I mean, I travel with a shape-shifter and a vampire, both of whom were baring their teeth to clear a path for us to the door of the shop.

But why wouldn't these people wear something other than black? Booorrring. I should know. I spent a century or so in black, blending into the night, hiding in the shadows. Trust me, I'm so over the lurking thing. Well, unless an EV or a hunter is on my trail.

I heard the music even before the door opened. My usual oldies station? I don't think so. Not with that bass beat. Obviously the TV Web site got more hits than I'd imagined. Inside, people crowded in front of Flo's mural. Not everyone was in black either. A pair of women who looked like escapees from a PTA meeting elbowed a man in khakis and a pale blue polo shirt, a man who wore . . . tinted glasses.

"Glory, thank God. Could you see what's going on in the

dressing room? The same couple has been in the left one for way too long and don't get me started about the noises coming from there." Lacy, who had three customers in line, looked pretty frayed around the edges. She probably hadn't even noticed the man with the glasses.

I felt a bump against my thigh. My dogs had sure noticed. Valdez nudged me on his way for a closer look, Will right beside him. I moved in to see if I could read the man's mind.

"No! Stop him!" A scuffle, screams and one of the soccer moms had glasses guy on the floor.

"Hah! I haven't sat through three boys taking karate lessons without learning something." She held a can of spray paint she'd plucked from his hand triumphantly over her head. Applause broke out. My dogs barked and leaped on top of the man who had been struggling to get free. Will made a perfect landing and the man squealed and grabbed his privates. When Valdez growled in his face the guy froze, actually teary eyed.

"Help! Get away from me!" The man didn't get any sympathy.

"Look at that. Black spray paint." The crowd was getting agitated.

"We should call the cops."

"No, man, I got a little somethin' in my pocket."

"Cops? I'm outta here."

"He was gonna deface that beautiful painting." Deface. Obviously a college student.

"Not as beautiful as you, angel face. We get the dressing room next." Horny college student.

I pushed my way to the man's side. Several people hurried out the door. That pesky cop rumor. I ripped the glasses off the man's face and took the paint can from the woman still sitting proudly on his chest. Her friend was taking her picture with her cell phone.

"Dave's never going to believe what we did at the state library convention. I told you we couldn't just go to bed after that reception, Pam."

Oops. Not PTA. Two renegade librarians.

"This dog's not going to bite me, is he?" Pam glanced at Valdez uneasily.

Valdez stopped growling long enough to lick her cheek. "Guess not."

Will stepped on the man's zipper again when he started to move. Another yelp.

"Good dog." Pam grinned and threw her arms around both dogs. "Get a picture of this, Sharon."

I locked eyes with the art critic and saw fear and Westwood. I put him under the whammy and reached out to help Pam up.

"Thank you so much. Wow. You really saved our mural. As for you . . ." I leaned down and got in the man's face. "Get out of here and don't come back." I sent him a mental message that had him pale and shaking. Something about ripping off body parts. Will growled at the guy's zipper, just in case the fool was unclear on what body part came off first.

"I ever see you here again, I'll press charges." Don't ask me what charges. Intent to deface, maybe. But my carrying customers weren't the only ones who wanted to avoid law enforcement. The dogs backed off while the man got shakily to his feet and staggered to the door. My growling dogs provided an escort.

The crowd booed.

"She's lettin' him off easy. And he's movin' like some freakin' zombie. Me, I'd run like hell."

"Forget him. The dressing room's empty." A couple, pale and pierced, hurried toward what had apparently been turned into a love nest.

"Oh, no, you don't." I grabbed them by their black sleeves next to the suit rack. "Attention, shoppers." I raised my voice over the blare of rap music and all heads turned toward me. "Only one person at a time in the dressing rooms. To try on clothes. Or I'm shutting the rooms down." There were a few groans and the flushed couple who'd apparently just emerged from the room, the girl's T-shirt on inside out, high-fived each other.

Valdez sent me a mental message that Westwood's man was gone, and I breathed my first easy breath since I'd come inside.

"Check out the vampire."

I slapped a hand over my mouth before I realized a new arrival pointed at the wall. I kept an eye on the dressing room situation and offered the librarians a generous discount. After that I helped Lacy sack and ring up sales. Business really was brisk, especially for the sixties skirts and Nehru jackets, black, of course.

During a short lull, I hit the Internet and the TV station's Web site. Oh, great, my little segment was featured. Had I really flashed fang at all of Austin? No, scratch that, the Internet is a wonderful thing. I'd flashed fang at the whole damned world.

I hit enter and the segment started. They'd reprised the part where Flo and I, wrapped in bed linens, dripped in front of the burned out shop. Flo, my "partner," leaned against me while I ranted about a hate crime. Then Donna, looking perky in her green blazer, stood in front of the freshly painted store, the neon Vintage Vamp's sign above her.

"As you can see, the store is back in business." A customer pushed open the door and Donna followed. The camera spent less than thirty seconds panning the racks of clothes, hats, accessories and vintage knickknacks before stopping at the now-famous mural.

I braced myself. Oh, yeah, there I was, in a skirt and blouse I was selling just as soon as I could run upstairs and get them. Could I look any dumpier? The tiny bit of cleavage helped, but the full skirt did my hips no favors and that print . . . Damn, but I'd never noticed the design was horizontal.

I handled Donna's questions okay—my opinion. And that toothy grin was an unfortunate habit when I'm nervous.

So when I got a whiff of the cameraman . . . Yep, fang, just a hint, but undeniable. Thank God the whole "rat" riot had been cut out. Instead we were back on the sidewalk out front, Donna under the sign again.

"So you see, folks, this business may be simply a vintage clothing store where you can find everything from poodle skirts to zoot suits, or a hangout for vampires. No, don't laugh. Vampires have been the center of bestselling novels"—she waved a hand toward the shop and the mural inside—"art and movies. Why, if they're just a figment of someone's overheated imagination? I didn't see any Dracula capes, but, no matter what the owner claims, you can't deny the message that mural is sending. Vampires welcome here." Donna gave the camera a full-on intense "I'm your woman who'll get the truth" look. "We'll be keeping an eye on the situation. You can count on Donna Mitchell, Channel Six News."

"Well, that wasn't so bad." I looked back at Lacy who'd stopped straightening stock to peer over my shoulder. "Did you see . . ." I leaned close and whispered, "Fang?"

"Naw. Well, maybe just a glimpse. Almost like a trick of light. The reporter didn't even mention it."

"Exactly. And she would have, don't you think?" I looked around. "No one's come in trying to check my bicuspids so that's a good sign."

Lacy smiled. "Great publicity. Even the gay angle with you and Flo as 'partners.' How cute was that?"

"Thanks. Flo and I are just precious together. We should change the name of the building. Slingback Mountain." I sighed, not sure I was ready to be queen of the local vampires. No, wait, Freddy already had that title. Can you tell I was exhausted?

"That reporter's nuts. Dracula capes? So cliché. My boss is nothing if not fashionable." Lacy gave me a reassuring smile. She'd been on duty forever and still had all day Saturday ahead of her. Fortunately she seemed tireless. I'd just popped a black crocheted hobo bag into a sack when I finally asked a customer a question that had been bugging me.

"Did all of you see the mural on the TV Web site?"

"Oh, no. There was a segment on the tube. The weekend wrap-up at midnight. Right before the *Saw* film festival. When *Saw 3* came on, I'd had enough. So we decided to check out the mural." The girl with silver nose, eyebrow and lower lip studs smiled. "Cool place and I love that you're open all night. I usually can't get Ronnie to shop." She glanced at her boyfriend who wasn't shopping but had decided to pet a silently suffering Valdez. Will sat in front of the window, staring out with body language that clearly said "Don't mess with me."

"Well, please come back. I'm sorry you had to wait in line to pay. A crowd this big this late is unusual." I handed her the sack and the receipt. "Mugs and Muffins is open all night too. You can always stash Ronnie next door with a coffee while you shop."

"Excellent. Maybe I'll bring my mom back tomorrow. She'd love the old purses too."

"We close at midnight on Saturday and reopen a little after midnight on Tuesday morning." I grabbed a paper from a stack that had shrunk considerably during the night. "Here, take a flyer, hours are on there."

I checked out the dwindling crowd. It was getting close to dawn and I could feel it in my usual sinking spell. I tapped Lacy on the shoulder.

"Think you can handle things alone until Melanie gets here later?" Melanie, our mortal worker, helped Lacy handle the day crowd, especially on Saturdays.

"Sure. Time flies when you're busy." Lacy leaned closer. "That a Westwood goon with the spray paint? I'm sorry but I didn't even notice the glasses. I was just too busy."

"That's okay. We handled him. And busy is good. Great." I gestured toward the door. "I made sure that particular goon won't be back."

"Good. But a lot of the other people here tonight will be.

That mural is killer." Lacy smiled. "Flo's a genius. I don't mind the type of customers we're getting. Daytime, our usuals will still show up. And the commissions are really adding up."

"Good. You deserve every penny. And as for Flo . . ." I sat down on the stool before I fell down. My Fangtastic had just worn off, big time. "I'm really worried about her. She's gone off the deep end with this new boyfriend."

A customer sighed as she piled a fifties sweater set and pearl collar on the counter. "My girlfriend's got a loser boyfriend too. I'm afraid to say anything because I keep thinking she'll figure it out for herself. And I don't want to mess up our friendship. You know?"

"Yeah, I know." Could our friendship survive if I was part of the posse going after Flo's beloved Simon? I shuddered thinking about reptilian lovemaking. I had to get her away from him.

I was dead on my feet, literally, by the time I unlocked my apartment door. I almost stumbled over the case of Fangtastic sitting just inside. AB negative. Okay, so Simon didn't stint when it came to peace offerings. And I wasn't going to turn it down. Are you kidding? Do you have any idea what that stuff costs? And Simon owed me for sending Greg Kaplan sniffing after me.

I took a moment to wonder what kind of "punishment" Greg had received. Cool if he'd been denied his VV fix. The guy was a mind-controlling creep. I couldn't work up any real concern.

I stuck about half a dozen bottles of the good stuff in the fridge, dumped a bottle of the O positive in a bowl for Will and threw down a half dozen Twinkies for Valdez before I hit the shower. I ignored Will's wheedling when he tried to get me to share the primo Fangtastic with him. No way. I thought about drinking one myself, but I was just too tired to savor it. So I fell into bed. Lights out in more ways than one.

I woke to pounding on the door. I glanced at the bedside

table clock and realized I'd actually slept a little past sunset. My body keeps track of the daylight hours, but I like to check the exact times on the Internet too. I love the long winter nights. We were only a month away from the max.

"Okay, I'm coming." I threw a robe over the cotton nightgown I'd worn to bed and staggered to the door.

"It's Mainwaring." Will yawned and stretched.

"Thanks." I threw open the door and saw Richard on the threshold. He looked tired, like he hadn't slept nearly as well as I had.

"Come in. What happened last night?"

"Nothing but talk." Richard frowned. "I'm frustrated."

Will snorted and I gave him a warning look. "I overslept and I've got to go down to the shop. You want to wait while I brush my teeth and throw on some clothes?"

"Sure. I'm sorry. I didn't think—" He ran his hand through his hair. "I should leave . . ."

"No. Stick around. Walk me downstairs. You want a Fangtastic? Simon sent me some premium brew."

"No. I've already fed."

I stopped next to Richard, then took a deep breath. Oh, yeah, he'd fed. I started to say something snippy, then let it go. Flo had told me he had this rather primitive habit of feeding from mortals, then praying afterward like that made it all right. Hey, maybe it did. He wouldn't *kill* to feed, he gets just enough to take the edge off. Me, I'm usually okay with the bottled substitute.

Usually. I felt a pang for Steve the fireman who'd called me three times since our date. To get rid of him, I'd finally had to invent a committed relationship with an old boyfriend. Hey, it could happen.

"I'm glad to see you in one piece. When I left the gang at Freddy's, I was afraid that, if you and Freddy could find it, you'd try to storm the Bastille." I sounded like an idiot and Richard smiled. "Well, you know what I mean."

"I'd be all for it with the right plan. Problem is, we

haven't found the Bastille yet." Richard sank down on the couch and stared at his black loafers. No socks. A sexy look. Hmm.

"I'll hurry. I've got to relieve the day crew." I grabbed a Fangtastic, some of the ordinary O positive, out of the fridge and headed for the bathroom. I wasn't about to gulp down my dream drink.

"Right." He managed a smile and I remembered hot kisses and clever hands. Whatever Richard wanted, I was interested. Purely for stress release you understand. Right after I closed at midnight. With that in mind, I picked out one of my favorite outfits, a deep blue cashmere twin set (from my flush days as a dancer in Vegas) and matching wool slacks. I quickly did my thing with hair and makeup, by feel of course, then sat down to pull on black suede high-heeled boots.

I looked back at my butt. Too big? Too bad. I sucked in my tummy and threw open the door.

"You look beautiful, Gloriana." Richard jumped to his feet.

"Thanks. Can you wait a sec? Got to feed the dogs." I checked out the cupboard and found two cans of the chili Valdez had seen advertised on TV. I nuked it, then sucked in a lungful of the delicious smell. Okay, so I stuck a finger in it for a taste. Good, but not worth major pain and suffering. At least not while I had a hunky vamp waiting for me. I divided the stuff evenly and set it on the floor. Both dogs fell face first into their bowls and didn't even come up for air when I went back into the living room.

"So how are you going to find the EVs?"

"I got a few recruits who are going to start looking."

"Someone could follow Flo when she leaves here to meet Simon some night."

"They could try. She's pretty difficult to track and I have a feeling Simon asked her to keep his location a secret." His face was hard to read, but obviously Richard had tried to follow Flo and failed. Maybe he *was* jealous.

"I'm not jealous of Florence and Simon's relationship, Glory." Richard's pale blue eyes pierced right through any mind shield I might have belatedly thrown up. "I'm worried about her. As a friend. That's all."

"Sure, me too." I sat down beside him, though I'd have to leave in just a few minutes. I hoped Derek had gotten there right after sunset to relieve Lacy and Melanie. "I had a feeling Bela, I mean Ralph, would be happy to make a buy of the VV if you think that would help."

"He already offered. I wouldn't ask anyone to do it, but it may come to that. I keep thinking that it's only a matter of time before one of their customers leaks their location. They're probably sworn to secrecy too, but someone will eventually tell the wrong person."

"So is this why you stopped by? To give me a lack of progress report?" I finished my Fangtastic then set the empty bottle on the coffee table.

"Not just that. You close the shop at midnight tonight. Right?" He leaned closer and I could see the gleam of male interest in his eyes. When they skimmed down my sweater and checked out the way it clung to my breasts, the sexy lace bra I wore didn't hide the bumps of alert nipples.

"Yes."

"I'd like to take you out. Either on the Harley or in my car if you'd rather not"—he brushed my hair back from my face—"mess up your hair."

"Out where?"

"I know you like dancing. I'm not exactly Patrick Swayze, but I've learned a little over the years. There's a new club on South Congress. Rock and roll. What do you think?"

I think I love you. I didn't say it and I sure as hell didn't let him read it in my mind. Instead I smiled and stood. I picked up my purse, a vintage Chanel bag that Flo had given me to sell, but which couldn't seem to make it past my own closet.

"Let's take the car, then." I grabbed his hand and pulled him to his feet. I'm sure Flo had made him sit through *Dirty Dancing* more than once, so he probably did know a few dance moves. I twirled around him, then laughed. "And midnight can't come fast enough." I reached up and kissed him, full on and nothing shy about it. The man had promised *dancing*.

"Excuse me? Aren't we due downstairs?" Valdez dropped his leash at my feet.

I came up for air and loved the way Richard's eyes stayed half closed. His hands were under the back of my sweater and I felt the warmth of his fingers on my bare skin. He finally opened his eyes and smiled, his hands sliding down to my butt before he released me.

"Pick me up here after the store closes." I looked down at Valdez, Will right behind him. "The dogs will stay home. I think you'll be guard enough, don't you?"

"I'll guard you with my life." Richard took my hand and pulled me closer. He hummed a tune, then swung me away from him in a cool move.

"What is this? *Dancing with the Stars?*"

"Shut up, Will." I smiled as Richard leaned me back over his arm, then jerked me close until we were chest to chest. "Wow, Richard, you have some great moves."

Valdez growled, but I ignored him.

"I've had centuries to perfect my 'moves,' Gloriana." Richard's smile sent sizzles right through me.

I bit back a sigh. I'm a sucker for a man with a good line. This promised to be a very interesting evening.

I was still in the shop when my cell phone rang about eleven. I was deep into a debate with a customer about whether redheads could wear pink. By the time I got to the phone, I saw that I had another message from Flo. Good. She'd be home Sunday night and we'd go to church. Hey, don't freak out. Vampires aren't demons from hell, at least not all of them.

The congregation of the Moonlight Church of Eternal Life and Joy probably didn't realize vampires dug their message. It was an upbeat nondenominational place that featured great music, a positive message and nighttime meetings. What's not to like? Flo and I got a lot out of it and we weren't the only vamps who attended regularly.

Would Flo invite Simon to tag along? I couldn't imagine she would or that Simon would be interested, not with his close association with a demon. I tried to call Flo back, just to give her a heads up about my date with Richard, but no answer. I really didn't want to think about what Flo might be up to with Simon the slimy snake.

After we locked the doors at midnight, I left Derek to put the cash away. Two days off. And tonight . . . I carried a dress upstairs with me that a shifter had brought in to sell and I couldn't resist. Full skirt, one of those stretchy cinch belts, deep vee to show off the girls, and the whole thing in the most fabulous sapphire blue velvet.

I grabbed a bottle of the AB negative out of the fridge—Thank you, Simon—fed the dogs more chili, then headed for the bedroom. I threw off my clothes, took a quick shower using liberal amounts of my lavender shower gel, then found some sexy dark blue underwear to go with the dress.

I finished the Fangtastic with a sigh. Damn, it was good. I had a craving for another bottle. Nope, my expensive stash had to last. Instead, I slipped into the dress and wished for the hundred thousandth time for a mirror. At least the dress *felt* amazing, soft, and it fit perfectly, the full skirt disguising my figure issues.

I spun around, then fell, a little dizzy, on the bed. Umm. Soft. Silky. Cool against my cheek.

"Richard's here. Did you know he has a key?" Valdez stared at me from the doorway.

"Flo probably gave it to him." I rolled over and wiggled my toes. I'd probably need to wear shoes. Silver pumps? Or black suede?

"Glory?" Valdez nudged my foot. *"Aren't you afraid you'll wrinkle your dress?"*

"Whatever." I stretched, the velvet moving with me. I loved this dress. To hell with shoes. I'd just lie here and let Richard come to me. "Send Richard in here."

"Uh, you sure?" Valdez moved closer. *"What's the matter with you?"*

"Nothing. I can invite Richard into my bedroom if I want to." Like I had to explain myself to a dog. I tried to work up a mad, but I felt entirely too relaxed to work up much of anything. "Go out to the hall and close the apartment door. Take Will with you. I'll let you know when you can come back in."

"I thought you were going out." Valdez nudged my foot again and I stroked him with my toes. He had the softest fur. *"Dancing? Remember?"*

Dancing. I sat up. Of course. But first . . . "Send him in, V, now." My answer was a snort. Yeah, Valdez is Blade's minion and his first loyalty is to his boss. Not that Blade expected me to be exclusive. We'd settled that issue centuries ago. And all the Valdezes had learned to ignore the parade of lovers through my bedroom.

Okay, honesty here, it was more like a trickle than a parade. This Valdez would just have to ignore the yummy vamp with electric blue eyes and platinum hair who'd planned to take me dancing.

I smiled when Richard appeared in the doorway. He definitely deserved a reward.

"Valdez is worried about you." He grabbed my hand and pulled me to my feet.

"I'm fine." I put his hand on my breast. "Don't you love this velvet? Isn't it soft?"

"Very." Richard kept his hand there and the slight pressure suddenly seemed like the most erotic touch ever.

"What about this?" I moved his hand to the curve of my breast exposed by the deep vee.

"Even softer." He rubbed his thumb between my breasts and I moaned. "The dogs are out in the hall. Did you tell them to leave?"

"Yes." I popped open the buttons on Richard's dark green silky shirt. Wow. Had I ever seen a better, wider, more beautiful chest? I couldn't remember. This one was sculpted by some strenuous exercise, rowing a galley I guess. And his chest had the most precious brown nipples. I leaned in and licked one before pulling it into my mouth.

"Good God, Gloriana. Where's this coming from?" Not that Richard flew across the room to get away from me. Hell, no. He had one hand in my hair, holding me close. The other circled my waist.

I leaned back and smiled, feeling relaxed, yet antsy too. A weird combo. "It's coming from here." I grabbed his hand and pressed it between my legs. "I want you, Richard." I was wearing way too much. I undid my stretch belt and it popped loose, hit my chest of drawers on the other side of the room and knocked over a picture of me in one of my Vegas costumes. "Oops."

I grinned and picked up the picture. "Look, Richard. I was one of the Indian maidens. Just a few strategically placed feathers. Cute, huh?" I set the picture back on the chest, then wrapped my arms around Richard's waist. "You want to play Columbus? I'll welcome you to the New World." I slid my fingers inside his waistband. "It'll be a warm welcome. And not a feather in sight."

Richard grabbed my hand. "Glory, are you sure you're all right?"

"I will be. Unzip me." I slipped away from him, turned my back and lifted my hair.

"I thought you'd want to go dancing . . . first." But, yeah, the zipper came down and the cool air on my back said any dancing tonight was going to be of the horizontal variety. His hands slid inside my dress, pushing it forward and off my shoulders. I turned and looked at him, then wiggled until the dress pooled at my feet. I kicked it away, not even sparing a thought for the delicate vintage fabric.

"What do you think?" I held out my hands. My bra was a wonder of engineering that pushed my breasts up and out like gifts waiting to be unwrapped. My matching panties were scraps of lace that only reached halfway to my navel. I shivered, then moved in to press against him.

"Richard? Answer me. Am I getting to you?" I rubbed my cheek against his chest. I waited for him to move things along. You know, grab my ass, open my bra, *something*. Instead Richard just stood there. Quiet. Too quiet. I looked up and saw his nostrils flare.

"What? Don't you like what you see?"

"God, Gloriana, of course I do." He put his hands on my shoulders. "What have you gotten into?"

"Into? The mood, baby. Let's play." I stepped back then reached for the front clasp of my bra. My breasts are a man pleaser. Guaranteed. Richard was thinking. That had to stop. I wanted him crazed with lust. I let my breasts loose, slung the bra over my head and into a corner of the room. Another crash, this time a vase I'd never really liked anyway.

"You smell like—"

"Lavender. Don't you like it?" I trailed my fingers down his chest to his belt buckle. One of my vamp moves and the belt and the button beneath it opened. Another move and his shirt hit the wall next to the bedroom door.

"No, it's not lavender I smell." He sniffed again, trapping my hand against his zipper.

"I don't use perfume. Defense. Perfume messes up my sense of smell. The lavender doesn't." His hand on top of mine. Was he saying stop or harder? I curled my fingers around the bulge underneath the cloth and his hand tightened. I took that as a "go." I squeezed, he gasped, then pushed me away to stare into my eyes.

"By God, you've been in the Vampire Viagra."

Nineteen

"**Don't** be silly, where would I get that?" I tried another grab, but he eluded me.

"Maybe Simon sent you a sample."

"I don't need Viagra, Richard. I'm naturally this hot." I ran a fingertip across my nipples and shivered. "And all Simon sent me was a case of Fangtastic. Want some?" I traced the long length pressing against his zipper. "Or do you want some of this?" I wiggled out of my panties and tossed them aside. His eyes darkened to a midnight blue. I dropped to my knees, took the tab of his zipper in my teeth and pulled.

"Jesus Christ, Gloriana."

I swear, if he crossed himself, I was going to hit him. If he had any priestly hang-ups, Flo sure hadn't mentioned them. Saint or sinner? Aha. His hands were in my hair again. Sinner was obviously winning. Would I be struck by lightning if I prayed for Richard to take me sooner rather than later? I started going south with his zipper until his cock sprang free into my hands.

"You would never need the VV, would you, Richard?" I stroked his erection and kissed its pretty head. "I know you'll fill me. And when you come—"

Richard jerked me to my feet and stared into my eyes. "Damn it, Glory, that's not you talking, that's the Vamp Viagra. Simon must have drugged your Fangtastic."

"What? Don't you think I can get hot without some help? Look at you. Strong, virile, all yummy male and ready to go." I smiled down at his cock and gave it a friendly pat, then pulled Richard toward the bed. "Come on, Richard. Ricky. Maybe I'll call you that. Flo calls you Ricardo. Doesn't suit you. You're not Italian. English, like me. Hey, we're homies." I pulled harder when he wouldn't fall on the bed with me.

I rubbed his cock. "Big boy. Come on, big boy. Take me." I pulled his hand to my mouth and sucked his thumb, then bit with just a hint of fang. Oh, yum, his blood was rich, dark and delicious. I sighed and fell back on the bed. Open for him.

"Please, Richard." I wiggled my hips. "Make me scream."

"Gloriana, I can't take advantage—" He tucked in and zipped up.

"Advantage? Like I don't know what I'm doing?" I got up in his face, fighting him off when he tried to wrap me in a robe I'd had slung over a chair. "I thought I knew what I was doing. And don't lie and say you're not a little interested. Your cock says you are." I ran my hands up his bare chest and tweaked his nipples. "And cocks don't lie." I kissed his chin. "Loosen up, Richard. Don't play so . . ." I rubbed his zipper again. "Hard to get. Let Glory ease your pain."

"Stop it." He backed up a step. I stayed right with him.

"Flo says you're not a good lover. But she didn't *always* say that." One of my vamp moves should get his pants off of him. I gave it a shot, really concentrating on sending fabric to the floor. No go. He blocked me somehow.

"Why are you fighting me, Richard? Is it because I'm not a size six like Florence?" I dropped back on the bed. Sure. Why would he go for me after having cute little Flo? I wiped away a stray tear. How stupid to cry over stuff like that though. I mean, what did I want? A pity screw?

"Don't be ridiculous."

"I can't help my size, damn it." A sob. Hello? Is Gloriana even home? I pulled the sheet up to my chin. Yeah, she was home and pulling out every little trick she had. Glory St. Clair can manipulate with the best of them. Most men couldn't handle women's tears. He'd cave, we'd get it on and I'd finally lose this antsy "got to have it" feeling that made me about to crawl out of my skin.

"It's a curse." Sniffle. Sniffle. "I've tried everything to get skinny. Even thought about liposuction. But you know the vamp sleep would just undo it. All pain, no gain." I jumped up again, but wrapped the sheet around me. No use giving him an eyeful if he wasn't going to do something about it. Was he weakening? I swear my skin was on fire.

"You're a perfect size. You have a great body." He reached for me, but I scooted to the light switch by the door.

"Here. I'll turn off the light and you can close your eyes. Okay? Just think. Glory's got all the necessary equipment, just more of it. Wait. Not more actual equipment. I mean what is there, tits, ass, the, um, gate to Heaven, has more padding." I flipped the switch. Of course we both had vamp vision, so it really didn't make much of a difference. I got in front of him again.

"Close your eyes, Richard. Maybe if you pretend I'm Flo on steroids . . ." I brushed against him and dropped the sheet.

"Stop it. You're beautiful, Gloriana. Perfect. But you're not yourself." Richard gave me a good long look, like he was thinking about the gate to Heaven—I knew the religious angle would get to him—then he inhaled again. "No, this isn't going to happen." He stalked into the living room. "Get dressed."

I slipped on a nylon robe, but didn't tie it. "When I was a dancer in Vegas I learned some pretty good moves. Check it out." I picked up the remote and turned on the CD player. I knew just the track I wanted. The slow sultry music filled the apartment, Alicia Keys singing "Fallin." I danced around Richard, ignoring the scratching at the door from the hallway. If those dogs thought I was letting them in now . . . How icky would that be? I stretched, undulated, even tried a high kick. Oops. Something wrong with my balance. Richard grabbed me before I fell and I decided this was a good thing.

"Sorry." I smiled, clung to him and kind of rubbed myself on him. Then I pushed him away. Obviously he liked the chase. So I took another turn around the room. Seven veils would have been nice, but at least I could play with the robe. I knocked over a pile of DVDs and kicked them out of the way. *Dirty Dancing* crunched under my feet. Okay, I could do dirty. A bump and grind. I checked my audience. Richard couldn't look away.

I let the robe slide down my shoulders and fall to the floor and picked up a throw pillow. I held it in front of me like a G-string while I shimmied my boobs. Closer to Richard. Oh, yeah, just brush that hard chest with my nipples. Ooo. My nipples *hurt*. I dropped the pillow to rub my hands over them.

"Help me, Richard. I don't know what's wrong with me, but I need your mouth on me. Right. Now." I practically threw him onto the couch. I think I took him by surprise because he didn't resist. I straddled him and pressed a breast to his lips. "Please."

I closed my eyes when he sucked my nipple into his mouth. Good. Now that I had him distracted, I knew where a male's working parts were by feel. I got him unzipped again then took his cock in my hands. Another inch or two and he'd be inside me. I wiggled my hips into position.

"No!" He grabbed my ass and shifted me off his lap.

"Damn it!" I tried to pry his hands off me. "Why aren't you cooperating?" I leaned over and bit his shoulder and not a love bite either. The blood welled up and I licked it clean. Oh, my. Nothing tastes better than an ancient vampire. More. I needed a lot more. Right after we . . .

"Gloriana." He growled my name, but pushed me off of him.

I prowled the room, desperate to get things going. I was Gloriana Freakin' St. Clair, queen of the Macy's Thanksgiving Day Parade. Didn't Richard get that? He was off the couch and watching me, eyes gleaming, damned zipper up again. But his shirt was still in the bedroom where I'd flung it. Hah!

I swept everything off the wooden coffee table, glad I'd sold the old one with its cold marble top. Magazines, remotes and an empty Fangtastic bottle flew in every direction. I lay back, one leg on either side of the wood, feet on the floor. Could I *look* any more inviting?

"Come here, big boy. Give it to me." I grinned at him and wiggled my hips. Oh, hell. "Ow." I jumped up and looked back at my bum.

"What?" Richard turned me and examined my backside. "Splinter."

"I see it." He gently pulled out the sliver of wood, then dropped to one knee and licked the tiny cut.

"Yes." I sighed. "That's what I want. Lick every inch of me, Richard." I swayed and reached back to thread my fingers through his soft hair. "Keep going, lower." I held on and spread my legs.

"No. I shouldn't have done that. It was the smell of your blood."

I looked back and saw him lick his lips. "Go for it, then. Bite my ass. Though there's a vein a little lower on my inner thigh that would be a whole lot better." For both of us. I shivered thinking about his fangs taking me there. "Please."

"No. This isn't right." He pulled back.

I whirled and threw myself on him, knocking him back on the rug. "This *is* right. Quit teasing me, you son of a bitch." I found his jugular and sank my fangs into his warm skin, sucking hard.

His fingers dug into my hair, holding me tightly against his neck. I swallowed, savored the taste for a moment, then decided I'd had enough. I tried to pull away but he kept his hand on my head, refusing to release me. He was too damned strong for me to muscle away from him. I fisted my hands and hit his chest, sign language for let me go.

"Keep feeding, Glory. Dilute that poison you've got in your system."

Poison? Get real. I was flying high, more aroused than I'd ever been in my life. Wasn't he feeling this chemistry between us? But he *still* hadn't taken me. I couldn't freakin' believe it. He'd even managed to get his zipper back up for the thousandth time. I hit him again, then tried a little mind control, since my mouth was clamped to his neck.

"Let me go, Richard. Make love to me. Or if that's too much commitment for you, call it sex. Let's have hot, no holds barred, sex. We can feed from each other later. Afterward. I'll do anything you want if you'll just take me."

I groaned and pushed, desperate to put some space between my fangs and his vein. I wasn't hungry for *this*. I'd just presented him with an offer that no self-respecting male vampire would ever refuse.

"No, Gloriana. No."

Tears burned my eyes and I collapsed against him. Still he wouldn't let me stop feeding, his damned strong hands holding me firmly. I drank and swallowed and drank again. Until I felt sated, bloated, like I'd gag if I had to take in another drop. Finally, finally, he took his hands from my head. I gasped for air. My head, too heavy to support, fell to his shoulder. He cradled me against his chest.

"Better, Gloriana?" He stroked my naked back, gently. And wasn't that a hell of an attitude? I burrowed closer to him anyway.

"Better?" I mentally went through a check list. Still aroused, but not quite as desperately. Check. Warm from feeding and the pressure of his bare chest against mine. Check. Naked. Me, not him. Okay, now I was hot with embarrassment. Forget lists. My mental state was a mess, part frustration, part hating like hell that I'd, oh, yes, waved my titties at Richard and given him my best lap dance and *still* been rejected.

"I didn't, wouldn't reject you, Gloriana." Richard touched my hair, petting me like a favorite cat. "What I rejected was the drug you had controlling you. You would have hated me tomorrow if I'd taken you up on your offer."

"Hated you? We'll never know now, will we? At least I think I'll stop attacking you now. Sorry. And quit reading my mind." I couldn't quite open my eyes. I was such a fool. Had Vamp Viagra made me throw myself at him?

Oh. My. God. That stuff was awesome. I mean horrible. Oh, hell. I still couldn't think straight. I'd been drugged, damn it. That weasel Simon Destiny. If I ever got my hands on him . . .

But what about the dancing? Tears burned behind my closed eyelids. Had I messed up any chance of having a regular date with Richard? Had I repulsed him?

"I'm really sorry, Richard," I whispered.

He picked me up and walked to the bedroom, staggering a little because I'd taken him down about a quart or maybe even a gallon. When we got to my bed, I wouldn't let him go. Surely there was some way I could make this up to him. I pulled him down beside me. I didn't feel the urgency anymore. Not to mate with him. But I needed his comfort, his warmth and to be close to him.

I'd taken so much of his blood, that I felt part of him inside me. Like we breathed with the same breath, touched with the same hands. He traced a path from my breasts to my hip, then pulled me closer. Yeah, I felt that he *did* want me. I sighed and offered my neck.

"Feed from me, Richard. Please. I want you to." I opened my eyes. "And I do know what I'm saying this time." I was finally coming down from whatever astral plane I'd been on. When his fangs pierced my neck, I groaned. I felt the pull and held him close. My tender breasts scraped against his chest and I felt another surge of desire. Vampire Viagra. How long did it last? How long could *I* last without some kind of big finish?

I reached down, touched myself and screamed. Yep, screamed, shrieked, blew completely apart in a world class orgasm, wilder, more intense than anything I'd ever felt in my entire centuries long life.

Crash! Richard fell on top of me, a vamp sandwich between me and my dogs. You heard me, my *dogs*.

"Son of a bitch. Let me go! That's my leg, damn it."

"I know, asshole. Get off of Glory before I rip you apart. Leg first. Head second." Will had the tough guy act *down*.

"Glory, what's this guy doing to you?" Valdez gave Richard a head butt that knocked him off the bed to hit the floor. *"Say something."*

I grabbed the sheet before I exposed myself even more to all and sundry. "I'm fine. Seriously. Will, let him go."

I stared at Will until he dropped Richard's leg. Blood gushed, a guaranteed mood killer. Who was I kidding? I licked my lips. Even after my recent fill-up I still craved another taste. It had been really *good*.

"You screamed, Blondie. Like he was killing you." Valdez sat on the bed, next to me. He looked me in the eye. *"What happened?"*

"Vampire Viagra. That's what happened." I grabbed a pillow, stripped off the case and wrapped it around Richard's calf. Richard staggered to his feet and wiped at the blood. But he wasn't an ancient vamp for nothing. The flow had already slowed to a trickle.

"Impressive defense." Richard locked eyes with Will, then Valdez. "Your dogs really do take their jobs seriously."

"Damn straight." Will jumped up next to Valdez and I had to grip the sheet when it slipped too low. "We won't let anyone get to our Glory."

"That's sweet. And you were both magnificent. Really. But can we end this standoff now and give me some privacy? Please?" I sighed. "I had a VV experience, but I'm better now. Really. Let me get dressed." I saw Richard grab his shirt and shrug it on. And now I owed him a pair of pants. His were shredded beyond repair.

"VV? Where'd you get it? Did this asshole drug you?" Valdez jumped off the bed, in warrior mode again, his growl making even me shiver.

"No. The Fangtastic Simon sent must have been drugged. It turned me into a horny wild woman."

"You don't need a drug for that. Or at least not with the right

guy." Valdez chuffed and gave Richard a "go to hell" look. Oh, yeah, he'd heard me a time or two or dozen with Blade. Through closed doors, walls, hell, I've been know to shatter glass a half block away when in the throes. (Just kidding.)

"Thanks a lot. But you can critique my love life later. Now get out in the hall. Since I don't have a door now, you'll have to stand guard. I need to take care of Richard's wound."

It was Will's turn to snort. "I expect some combat pay after this. To have to listen to Glory get her groove on . . ." He trotted after Valdez toward the hall door. "Man, I don't know how you've handled it year after year. Valdez, the woman's a screamer."

I jumped up and closed the bedroom door then turned to study Richard. He stared at me, his eyes gleaming, pupils dilated as I'm sure my own were. Oops, still naked. I pulled the sheet off the bed and wrapped it around me.

"You're awfully quiet. Mad at me?" I bent down to check out his leg. A pretty nasty gash, but healing already. "I'm so sorry. Sit down. You'd already given me blood and now—"

"I feel it inside me, Glory. The VV. It plays with your mind and . . ." Richard touched himself. Oh, yes, he was still hard and horny. "Holy Mother of God, but I want you." He grabbed my arms and hauled me up against him. The sheet hit the floor.

"No, Richard, that's the drug talking."

He shut me up with a kiss that stole my breath. Then he backed me toward the bed.

"Stop it. This isn't going to happen." I shoved and Richard stopped. But he still had a wild look in his eyes.

"I don't like it, Glory. This feeling. Don't like that I can't control it. But I need . . . you. Help me."

"I . . . I understand, Richard. But I also know this isn't the way it should happen between us. If it ever does." And maybe I did still have some VV in me, because I was almost willing to martyr myself for the "help Richard get his rocks off" cause. He looked so tempting, standing there with his shirt hanging open and his pants riding low.

I held up my hands when he came toward me again. "No, Richard. I know what you're feeling. You need release. But I can't do it for you."

Richard growled and kept coming. I scrambled over the bed, out of reach, and fell against my dresser. A box of powder hit the floor and flew everywhere. I sneezed, then grabbed a lamp and held it over my head.

"Back off, Richard, or you'll be wearing a lampshade and not in a fun, party way."

Richard finally stopped, took a breath and ran his hands through his hair. "What the hell am I doing?"

"You're not doing anything. The VV is doing it. Drink some Fangtastic, my old stuff, maybe you can dilute the effects."

Richard looked down at the erection straining his pants and glanced at the kitchen. "Son of a bitch. I can't believe that crap."

"I guess Simon hoped I'd get hooked, so he sent me a sample. Then, when his minion came calling again, I'd be hot to trot."

"I've never felt anything like it." Richard limped toward the kitchen. "No wonder people get addicted."

"Do you think it's all tainted?" I bit back a moan. Primo Fangtastic polluted. What a waste.

"We'd better pour it down the drain."

I ran after him. "Don't be hasty. Surely not all of the bottles have been tampered with."

He twisted the top off a bottle and sniffed, then wrinkled his nose. "Sorry, Gloriana, but I don't think we can take a chance." He upended it over the sink.

"Wait! Let me see if I can smell the difference. Then I can just do this one at a time. Sniff and drink or sniff and dump." I grabbed the half empty bottle from him and inhaled. I know I'm a broken record on the subject, but is there anything as intoxicating as AB negative? And that's all I could smell. No subversive substance. Just delicious, ready to drink—

"Stop it, Gloriana. Obviously you're too susceptible to this blood type to be objective." He grabbed the bottle and emptied it.

"Maybe you're right, but I swear I can't smell that stupid VV." I grabbed his arm. "Slow down, Richard. Maybe we should—"

He gave me a questioning look. "Hooked already, Glory?"

"I'll show you hooked." I grabbed a bottle and twisted off the top, then watched the rich red flow down the drain. Twenty-two bottles later and *I* felt drained. Richard was acting the self-righteous bastard and I wanted to bash him over the head with the empties. He even rinsed out the sink and checked the fridge, like he thought I'd already become an addict and was holding some back for later. Trust me, the VV had really worn off because *this* Richard was about as appealing as roadkill.

He tossed all the bottles into a trash bag and tied the top closed. What? He didn't trust me not to lick the bottles? Sure enough, he dumped the sack down the garbage chute at the end of the hall.

"I can't believe you did that to us." Will had sniffed the sack, then followed Richard all the way to the chute and back. "First we have to listen to Glory shouting hallelujah, then you toss all the good stuff without giving me so much as a taste? Man, are you twisted."

Valdez nipped Will's ear. *"Shut up. Glory's still not right. That stuff's poison."*

"Poison. Yeah, the VV sure is. But excuse me if I don't do a happy dance that all the AB neg is gone. I know it had to be done, but I can have a moment to mourn, can't I?" I sat on the couch and put my feet up on the coffee table. I had powder between my toes. At least it smelled good, but I'd left footprints from the bedroom to the kitchen and back to the couch. "Will, I hope you know how to run a vacuum." I put a hand to my suddenly aching head. "And Glory's *always* right. You'd both do well to remember that."

"You tossed the VV along with the Fangtastic? You have any idea what that Viagra might go for on the open market?" Will trotted into the kitchen like he hoped to find a forgotten bottle, then out again.

"There *is* no open market for that drug. You try peddling it and Simon Destiny will hand you your tail on a platter, my friend." Richard had his hands in front of him, like maybe he could hide that giant erection he still sported. God, it had to hurt.

I felt sorry for him. At least my ache was inside, not out there for all of us to see. And I also felt a warm rush of gratitude. Until he'd had the VV himself, he'd been a pillar of moral fiber. I couldn't imagine any other male vampire turning down a naked woman begging for it. Of course I'd shown some backbone of my own, turning him down. Hah!

"I could have saved the VV. For when I'm done being dog of the month." Will sat down and scratched.

"A month? Is that all you're signed on for?" I swear Valdez and I would have high-fived if he'd had five. I grinned at him and he wagged his tail.

"I'm not feeling the love here." Will looked at the stereo. "And what's with the sad music? Don't you have any rap or Beyoncé?"

I glared at him. Was the Beyoncé thing a coincidence? I checked out Richard. Yeah, if Beyoncé had waved her breasts in his face he probably would have been shouting his own hallelujah. Whatever. My head was killing me.

"I have a giant headache. A sort of hangover, I guess."

"Close your eyes, Glory. Let me help you feel better." Richard stepped behind me and put his hands on my head. I grabbed the remote, which had landed next to the sofa, and turned off the stereo.

I really was in pain. Both dogs were an interested audience when Richard pressed his fingers over my eyebrows. I sighed as the pain vanished between one breath and the next.

"He's good. I wonder how he does that." Will nudged my knee. "The headache really gone?"

"You bet." I opened my eyes and then reached up to clasp Richard's fingers. "Thanks."

"Am I forgiven?" he said as he held onto my hands but stayed behind me.

"For what? Nothing happened." I let go of his hands and gave the dogs a mental message to make themselves scarce. They both headed down the hallway to Flo's bedroom and I heard the door slam.

"Sorry about the dog attack."

"I'll live. Simon has a hell of a nerve, sending his drugs here. I'm sure Florence has no idea what her lover is up to."

"She's obviously not thinking straight." I watched Richard pick up the apartment door and lean it against the wall.

"You need to get this fixed immediately."

"I'll call Damian. He can send over his handy man during the day tomorrow." I shook my head. "About the dancing . . . Rain check?"

"Definitely." Richard slid his hands around me to snug me up against him. Oh, yeah, he still wanted me *bad*.

I looked down. "Is that the VV or—" He kissed me. It was a hungry, demanding kiss. When he tried to move us toward the bedroom, I pushed him away.

"Answer me, Richard. Is your mind clear? Do you want me or is the drug doing your thinking for you?"

Richard shook his head. "Damn it, Glory. I don't know."

"Wrong answer, Richard." I shoved him out into the hall and wished I had a door I could slam in his face. Would it have killed him to say "Oh, Glory, you're the hottest woman I've ever seen, of course I want you"? He obviously read my mind because he winced and ran his hands through his hair.

"Sorry." He looked sad, yummy and way too easy to forgive. "Of course you're desirable."

"Good night, Richard. Get out of here before we do something we'll both regret."

Richard reached out and touched my hair. "I'm already regretting it." Then he turned and headed down the hall, still limping, torn pants flapping.

I sagged against the doorframe for a moment, then went to give the dogs the all clear. Two hours until dawn. Maybe I'd call Blade. The VV was still inside me in the form of a damp yearning that made my knees wobbly. This restless urge needed to go somewhere and Blade is my go-to guy. Always. Even an ocean and a continent away. And ain't that a bitch?

Twenty

I woke up still feeling slightly hungover and frustrated. I hadn't called Blade after all. I'd had just enough snap left in my overstimulated brain to figure out that wouldn't be a good idea. Even long distance, he could read me way too well.

It had been bad enough having to call Damian about another broken door. He'd wanted explanations I wasn't about to give. And what about Richard? Would I ever be able to face him again? Oh, God, could I have *been* a bigger slut?

"Finally, you're awake." Flo sat on the foot of my bed, disgustingly bright-eyed. "What happened last night? There's powder everywhere and I can't find the remote for the TV."

"Richard and I had a party. Things got a little wild." I watched Flo's face, checking to see if she might still have feelings for Richard. She just shrugged.

"Richard and a party? What? Did he actually loosen up for a change?" Flo frowned down at a chipped nail.

"Loose enough." I even said it with a straight face. "Richard's a decent man. I respect him."

Flo gave me a searching look. For once I didn't want to spill my guts. She didn't press me. A good thing since my anger was on simmer and rapidly coming to a boil.

"Where's the Fangtastic Simon sent you? I know you love the AB negative, but Richard doesn't usually drink it and I doubt you could have finished it off by yourself in one night." She leaned closer. "Though you do look a little ragged around the edges."

"Ragged? Like from a Fangtastic binge? Or maybe I just had a rough night." I leaped out of bed, glad I'd at least had the presence of mind to put on an old nightgown before I'd finally gone to sleep. Not that I'm overly modest—see previous night—but parading naked in front of my roomie with the cute figure wasn't on my top ten list.

"What are you talking about? Too much Fangtastic can't hurt you. And Richard . . . Yes, he has a temper, but he wouldn't—" Flo looked startled when I growled.

"So says the resident expert on men." I stomped a circle around the bed to keep from venting all over her. Not her fault. Not her fault. She obviously didn't have a clue what Simon had done. I took a calming breath and sat on the bed beside her.

"No, Richard wouldn't hurt me, not physically. But he pissed me off when he poured down the drain the Fangtastic Simon sent. I know he did the right thing, but it was hard to take at the time."

"He poured it down the drain? Because he hates Simon?" Flo jumped up and stormed to the living room. "How could you let Richard do that? Simon was making a nice gesture."

"Oh, yeah, really nice. Simon punched it up with a boatload of that stuff he's peddling." I headed to the kitchen and grabbed one of the bottles of O positive.

"What? You had the Vampire Viagra?" Flo shook her head when I offered some of the cheap stuff.

"Yes." I drank, fought off a gag—God, this was swill— then sat on the couch. "Where are the dogs?"

"I asked Lacy to take them for a walk before we go to church." Flo sat on a chair across the room. "How did you like the VV? Wasn't it wonderful? Did Richard try it too? I can't get Simon to use it, but I think—"

"Flo, stop." I took another swallow. I needed to do some kind of whammy on myself so I'd think I was still drinking the wonderful stuff I'd had the night before. "Simon *drugged* me. I drank a bottle laced with VV and ended up attacking the nearest warm male body."

"Richard." Flo settled back like this was going to be good. Regular roomie dish.

"Yeah, Richard." I deliberately blocked Flo from reading my mind. I had some really homicidal urges toward her boyfriend in there. Not to mention the fact that I was close to wrapping my hands around Flo's elegant throat and throttling her for being so clueless.

"Okay, I give. Did you like it? Wasn't the rush fantastic?" Flo grinned like the idiot she was turning out to be.

"No. I felt like I was crawling out of my skin, for one thing. And it was more screaming frantic than rush." I sure wasn't telling Flo that the only satisfaction I'd managed last night had come courtesy of my XTC 3000 vibrator.

"But Richard is a wonderful lover." Flo had the grace to look embarrassed. "I know I said he wasn't, but I lied. I was mad at him, for being so much more into his business than he was into me."

"Yes, he's very intense and still hung up on some of his priestly vows."

Flo laughed. "He's not celibate, Glory. If he told you that, honey, maybe you just don't do it for him."

I paused a moment for a little bitter reflection. Could that be why I'd lost last night's battle? No, I'd definitely gotten to the guy. He'd *struggled* with his decision not to take me. I leaned forward. "I know he's not celibate, Flo, but he has principles."

"Principles? What do you mean?"

"That he wouldn't take advantage of a woman under the influence. Even if that woman did everything but chain him down and force herself on him."

"The chains are in my closet, you should have used them." Flo giggled. "Sorry, I couldn't resist. You should see your face."

"Yeah. Hand me a mirror." I picked up the bottle of Fangtastic and drained it. I'd just let my roommate see how pathetic I was.

"So Richard played hard to get." Flo shrugged. "Not

surprising now that I think about it. But what happened to
the rest of the Fangtastic Simon sent you? Surely not all of it
was laced with the VV. That stuff costs the earth."

"Then your lover was extremely generous." Or didn't
want to take a chance that I wouldn't sample his drug. He'd
probably hoped I'd get hooked and beg him to take my
power. Become one of the drones Flo had mentioned. Simon
must really be in a power crunch to go to so much trouble.
"Richard and I dumped it all out. Maybe it didn't all have
the VV in it, but I wasn't about to take the chance. Richard
even threw away the empty bottles. The man's obviously
not into recycling."

"You should have saved it, Glory. For when Blade comes
home. I bet he would enjoy it. He's not the prude Richard
obviously has become."

I took about a nanosecond to think about the combination of Blade and the VV. "Forget it. Blade and I don't need
it, Flo. And, last I heard, you didn't need help in that department either."

"It's not that I *need* it. But if I enjoy something new,
where's the harm?"

"The harm?" I grappled with the question. "The harm
comes when you take people against their will. Drug them
without their knowledge." Okay, now I was on a roll. "Dan-
gle seeing daylight in front of an ancient vampire, take his or
her money, then watch the vamp fry when the sun comes up."

"Bah. You've been listening to Richard. I have seen none
of that with Simon. You should come see for yourself. I told
you he wants to meet you."

"He wants to meet me so he can drain my power. Even
you admit I'm loaded with it."

"I can see we're wasting our time discussing this, Glory.
We don't agree. I move on." Flo crossed her legs. "How do
you like my new outfit?" She wore a black wool pencil skirt
and black and white sweater that I hadn't seen before.

I decided I might as well "move on" too. "New? It's cute.
Did Simon take you shopping?" I'd gotten the impression

the EVs were practically hermits. I couldn't imagine Simon strolling through a mall with his girlfriend. If Simon did go out with Flo, Richard might have a chance to launch an attack. Of course we'd have to get Flo out of the way first.

"No. Simon doesn't go out much. Typical man. Hates shopping. But he insisted I order something online, then he paid for express shipping. He really is generous."

So much for the mall theory. "Generous? I thought it was a cheap shot, trying to drug me like that."

"But didn't you like the Vamp Viagra? I mean, it makes you feel . . . amazing." Flo ran her hands over her breasts. "Very hot."

I tried to analyze just how I'd felt the night before. Mainly I'd been out of control. Damian had complained about the same thing. Richard too once he'd had it in his system after barely tasting me. It obviously took iron will to not have sex once you were into the VV. Iron. Oh, boy, speaking of iron . . . Richard had been incredibly hard. Side effect? Or was that typical for him? No assist from VV needed.

"You're getting a dreamy look, Glory. I think something did happen with Richard last night. Maybe you're cranky because you feel guilty. Taking a lover while Blade is away. Just blame it on the VV and move on." Flo bent down to pluck a white dog hair from her skirt. "Will sheds all the time. You should brush him."

"Move on. That's always your philosophy, Florence." I saw that I'd upset her. "Look, I'm sorry. I'm hungover. Too much VV and not enough action. And I wouldn't brush Will on a bet. He's been shifting into human form."

"Oh?" Flo looked interested. "Is he handsome?"

"Very. And arrogant. Think Mara as a macho male." I got up and stopped next to Flo. I put my hand on her shoulder. "I'm sorry if I snapped at you. But tell your boyfriend not to do me any more favors."

"That's exactly what Simon thought. That he was doing you a favor. The VV is highly prized. He made a generous gift." Flo looked around and grabbed the lint roller from the table next to the TV. "I love black, but this is ridiculous." She attacked her skirt. "I should make Will shift and clean this for me."

I wasn't going to touch that one. The image of Will, toned muscles flexing while he wielded a lint roller, suddenly got to me. Obviously the VV still lingered in my system. No way was I attracted to him in any form.

"Let me get dressed or we'll be late for church." I headed for my bedroom. "Did you invite Simon to come with us?"

"Yes, but he wasn't interested."

"Too bad. Church would be good for his soul." I stopped in front of my closet and decided I hated all my choices. I'd remembered to hang up the velvet dress I'd worn the night before. I pulled out the full skirt and rubbed the soft material between my fingers. It would have moved so well on the dance floor.

If that damned VV hadn't messed up the evening, would I have ended up in bed with Richard afterward? I knew we had chemistry, even without the VV boost. But I'm not a slave to my hormones. I needed a connection with a man before I allowed him sleepover privileges. And Flo was right about one thing, Richard put his "mission" ahead of everything else. Unusual in a vampire. We're pretty heavily into self-indulgence. Yeah, even me. Okay, okay, especially me.

"Pretty dress." Flo was right behind me. "What do you mean, Simon needs church for his soul? I told you Richard is wrong about him. Simon doesn't send vampires into the sun and the VV is a good thing. What do you know that I don't?"

"I don't know what you know, Flo. For example, did you know Simon is Freddy's father?" I pulled a red corduroy shirtwaist out of the closet and threw it on the bed.

"Freddy? Frederick von Repsdorf?" Flo sat on the bed, careful not to wrinkle my dress.

"The one and only."

"So Simon and CiCi . . ." Flo and CiCi have a bit of a rivalry going. Over men naturally.

"Centuries ago. She knew he was a vampire, but had no idea Simon could give her a baby vampire until after the deed was done. Kind of a nasty trick, don't you think?" I pulled out some cute black patent peep-toe heels and a patent belt to go with the dress and tossed them on the bed.

"I'm sure Simon didn't intend . . ." Flo picked up the belt and hit her thigh with it. "I've heard born vampires are only fertile every hundred years or so after they turn. He probably didn't know—"

"He knew. He considered CiCi a 'worthy vessel,' and I quote the great man himself."

"CiCi *is* a countess." Flo hit the bed this time, a good whack. "So Freddy's a born vampire. Simon's son. And gay." She smiled. "I wonder what Simon thinks of that. Frederick may be the end of his line."

"Who knows? If Simon could get CiCi pregnant, he probably left baby vamps all over the world. Unless the fertility thing is a one shot deal. Maybe you should ask him about it." I concentrated on accessories, since the idea of baby Simons populating the vampire world seriously creeped me out. Would some be fork-tongued like their father? At least Freddy had dodged that bullet. I shuddered and dug out a black purse. Nope. I was getting into dowdy territory. I settled on a black and red tapestry. Definitely more interesting.

"Glory, look at me for a minute, will you?" Flo nudged me with the toe of her black suede boot.

"What?" I looked back, saw her expression and shoved the stuff aside to sit next to her. "Okay. I'm focused. What's up?"

"Simon. He's really important to me."

"Oh, yeah?" I took my belt out of her hands so she wouldn't have a weapon. "Is he important or is it the drug he's plying you with night after night that's important?"

"What? You think I'm . . . addicted?" She looked indignant, then thoughtful. "I could skip a night without the drug. Maybe not even make love at all one night." Flo made this sound like the worst kind of depravation.

Frankly, coming off my own dry spell except for the virtual variety, I didn't get it. Hey, I'd gone years without sex. Don't get me started about my life during Queen Victoria's mourning period. And I look great in black. Really. I'd gone back to England for a little trip down memory lane and got stuck there for decades. It's not easy going transatlantic when you won't shape-shift.

"Don't go to the EV compound after church. Come out with me. We'll do something fun."

"What?" Flo was actually wringing her hands at the thought.

I wracked my brain. Fun. What did we do for fun besides shop? And the kind of stores we liked closed early on Sunday nights. We could watch a DVD or two or six, but even a chick flick filmfest can get old. In Vegas I could always catch a show or, before the intervention, play poker. No gambling in Austin.

"We can troll the Sixth Street clubs. Maybe pick up some guys to dance with." Even I could hear my lack of enthusiasm for that prospect.

Flo grimaced. "I'm not in the mood to deal with mortals. And I thought you still had Westwood's people after you. Jeremiah wouldn't like you going out without the dogs. And I'm *really* not in the mood to drag those two around to the clubs."

"Yeah, and what if Simon sent Greg Kaplan out with reinforcements to get me? Jerry *really* wouldn't like that."

"Are we going to fight about Simon all night?"

I could tell I was stressing Flo out. Was it because I'd suggested she avoid Simon for a night? Hey, she didn't have to avoid him.

"No. He's your boyfriend. You sure don't need my permission to go see him. But do us both a favor and tell him you're taking a night off from the VV. See if he can think of something fun you can do together. Does he ever go out?" He must, he'd met Flo hadn't he? And come to think of it . . . "How'd you meet Simon anyway? Where were you?"

I made sure I was still blocking any mind probe Flo might try. This info could be useful to Richard and the EV posse.

"We met in the park one night. I was a beautiful bird, just enjoying the fresh night air and he landed next to me." Flo sighed. "I knew he was a vampire immediately of course. He smells delicious."

"Which park? Do you ever go there together?" I had to make this interrogation seem casual, so I looked at the clock and jumped up. "Wow. I'd better get moving if we're going to make the opening hymn." We both loved the music at Moonlight.

Flo watched me gather underwear and head toward the bathroom. "No, we never have gone back there. It's the one by Barton Springs. Very quiet at night. Maybe I'll have him take me there tonight. It will be romantic. We won't need the VV."

"You might not need it, but are you sure Simon doesn't need for you to be under the influence?"

"Don't be silly. He never uses it himself and he's certainly never insisted I take it." Flo smiled and headed for the living room. "He has an amazing capacity without it. Of course so do I."

"Think about it for a minute, Flo. *Why* does Simon avoid it? Could it be because it's addictive?"

"I'll prove to you that I'm not addicted. Tonight." Flo grabbed her purse and pulled out her cell phone. "I'm calling Simon right now to set up our date. I'll meet him in the park after church. No VV. Just a romantic setting and us together."

"Good." I went into the bathroom. Maybe I should call Richard with this information. If he was determined to put Simon out of business, this would be a prime opportunity to get the king of the EVs alone. Of course he wouldn't be alone, Flo would be with him. And she'd probably defend him, since that seemed to be her knee-jerk reaction lately. It wasn't like me to rat out a friend. But if telling Richard where he could ambush Simon would get Flo away from the EV, I could deal with the guilt.

I jumped in the shower still not sure what I should do. Maybe just finding out if Flo was addicted to the VV would be enough for tonight.

When I came out of the bedroom, dressed and ready to go, Lacy was back with the dogs.

"No way am I splitting it with you fifty-fifty. My money, my human form buying the tickets." Lacy was eating some of the Cheetos I'd bought for Valdez after the fire. I'd gotten a little carried away with gratitude and had sprung for a case of Big Grabs. She was tossing every other bite into Valdez's mouth.

"My idea, sweetheart. We hit, we split." Will paced around the living room.

"Would someone clue me in?" I picked up my purse and checked to make sure I had my cell phone. "What are you arguing about?"

"*Lottery tickets, Blondie.*" Valdez caught another Cheetos with a snap of his jaws. "*Someone here seems to have a little gambling problem.*"

"It's not a problem." Will put his head on Lacy's knee. He frowned when she tried to give him a Cheetos. "I don't want your cheap snacks. I want champagne, caviar, a winning lottery ticket."

Lacy grinned and looked at me. "He talks me into going into the mini-mart around the corner and buying a few tickets, then he thinks I'm going to split the fortune with him."

"Do you actually think you have a chance of winning? I don't waste my money on such as that." Flo came up behind me and slung an arm around my shoulders, like she wanted to forget our earlier fight. Which was good for me. I hate living in a war zone. And Simon was bound to be a temporary blip on the Florence Da Vinci radar. No man lasted long with her.

"I gave her my lucky numbers. And she bought quick picks with the rest. I say we have a pretty good shot." Will nudged Lacy's knees. "Come on, pretty lady. Agree to a split and I'll make it worth your while." I swear if a dog could leer, Will was doing it with a wiggle of his furry eyebrows.

"What makes you think I'd be interested, dog boy?" Lacy grinned at me. "What do you say, Glory? Is the fur face here worth half a jackpot?"

"See for yourself, lass." Will was suddenly in human form, naked, of course, and too close to Lacy.

"Will! You know that's against the rules." I looked, of course. A fine looking male body is always a treat, even if it is a Kilpatrick male.

Flo's arm dropped off my shoulders. "*Dio mio.* You are in excellent shape, William."

"Of course I am. That's why Blade asked me to do this gig."

"*Blade is doing you a favor, asshole. Get back in dog form before I tell him to dock your pay.*" Valdez looked like he was itching to take a chunk out of Will's well-toned ass.

"Yeah, you'd be a bloody snitch, now, wouldn't you?" Will strutted around the room, not the least bit self-conscious while three women looked him over. I tossed him a throw pillow.

"Cover yourself. Valdez is right. You're supposed to stay in dog form for the duration."

"Just giving Lacy here a preview of things to come." Will grinned and held the pillow over his impressive package. "And if we win together, Lacy my love, there's a little boutique hotel in Paris that has a rooftop hot tub. You and me and the Eiffel Tower in the background, baby." He dropped to his knees in front of Lacy. She was flushed and no longer smiling. "What do you say, lass? Fifty-fifty?"

"Half of nothing is nothing." Flo had lost interest since Lacy was getting the male attention. "You won't win."

"I agree. Fifty-fifty." Lacy reached out to touch Will's handsome face, like to check if she was really seeing what she was seeing. Then Will was back in dog form. "God, but you're fast at that. It takes me a full minute to shift."

"I got the knack, baby. Wait until Paris. You'll see what else I've got the knack for." Will trotted up to me, a grin on his furry face. "As for Blade, his little paycheck won't matter if I hit the jackpot."

Valdez was by my side, his leash in his mouth. *"Will's lying low, Glory. Gambling debts. Like someone else we know, he's got a serious problem. We need to take him to a GA meeting."*

"Yeah, I figured that out." Gamblers Anonymous. I'd spent a lot of time in those meetings. I hadn't even checked them out since I'd arrived in Austin, but talk of winning the lottery reminded me of the lure of easy money. Not that money had *ever* come easy to me.

I clipped on the leash, then grabbed another one for Will. "Behave, Will. Lacy, you want to go to church with us?"

Lacy was still a little bemused. I wasn't sure if it was Will's shifting speed or his human form that had her that way. "No, thanks, I'm staying home and catching some things. I mean catching up."

"Hey, cat girl, you do what you got to do to survive. Right, Valdez?" Will looked at Flo. "And, Florence, if Paris doesn't work out, I've got a line on a villa on Capri that you and I could check out together."

Flo looked thoughtful. "I love Capri."

"Would you women snap out of it? The guy's a loser, in debt to some serious muscle, and shedding fur on your clothes." Valdez chuffed and bumped against me. *"Glory, tell me you're not falling for Prince Charming here."*

"No way." Blame it on VV hangover, but Will's naked body was burned into my brain. A hot tub in Paris, a villa in Capri. He did have interesting ideas. "I say Will needs an intervention and a twelve-step program. And I should know."

Twenty-one

The entrance to the church was crowded as always. Flo and I nodded to acquaintances, sniffed out a few fellow vampires, then settled into seats near the back. I have an unfortunate habit of levitating when I get into singing along with the choir. It's like Heaven is calling me. I rise, literally. A female vampire about CiCi's age sat next to me. She'd helped me before when I'd had liftoff during a song. She was English, wore pretty hats and expensive suits, and smelled vaguely familiar and not just in a vampire way. I pondered the smell during the first songs, then forgot all about it.

Flo and I dig this church because of the message. Happiness, making the most of life, the fact that God loves you no matter what you might have done in the past. The hunky charismatic Pastor John seemed to look right at us even from the big screen TVs placed around the huge sanctuary. He exhorted us to look forward, not back, for the source of satisfaction in our life. Good idea. Back was not so great.

I glanced at Flo and wondered what her forward looked like. The preacher asked us to bow our heads and try to focus on what we really wanted in our future. I closed my eyes and saw a successful shop, good friends and Blade. Richard drifted in there too. Probably because we'd seen so much of each other the night before. He did have an incredible body and—

The woman next to me gave me a sharp elbow in the ribs. Oh, yeah, one of those damned, excuse me, darned mind reading vampires. She sent me a mental message to re-

member where I was. Church. Not the place for thoughts of
hot male bodies and—

Oops. Another elbow. Flo looked over at me and grinned.
She hadn't missed the byplay. She met the woman's eyes,
lost her smile, but nodded. Like maybe she really did know
her. I tried to read elbow lady's mind, but had no luck. The
music started again and I was off and running. I fought the
urge to fly up toward the ceiling and had to concentrate to
stay down and inconspicuous.

The service was over and we were shaking hands with
those around us when elbow lady finally spoke.

"Gloriana, I'm Sarah Mainwaring." She smiled. "I believe
you know my son."

"You're Richard's mother?" My mouth dropped open.
Wow. If Richard had been a crusader and this was his
mother . . .

"A lady never reveals her age, right, Florence?" Sarah
smiled at Flo who wasn't looking all that thrilled.

"Signora." Flo bobbed her head and made a move like she
was ready to leave.

"Wait! I'm surprised I haven't seen you at some of the
vampire meetings, Mrs. Mainwaring. Or with Richard."

"Please call me Sarah, Gloriana. I'm afraid my son and I
don't always agree on things." Sarah gave Flo a look, like
maybe his fling with the Italian bombshell had been one of
those not agreeing issues. "We usually go our separate
ways." She gestured, her hands graceful. "You don't see him
here, for example. I think he's worried I've become a heretic.
We were Catholics so very long ago."

"Weren't we all." Flo muttered, putting her hand on my
elbow. "We left Glory's dogs outside, Sarah. See you around."

"Please come by my shop sometime." When I'd first seen
this lady, I'd felt drawn to her. Like CiCi, she was a moth-
erly type, one of the few female vampires not still twentysomething. I know, I'm hopeless thinking I could have a
mother figure in my life, but Sarah was English, from the

feather in her black felt hat, to the tips of her sensible leather pumps. She reminded me of my roots.

"Thank you, Gloriana. You're most gracious." Sarah held out her hand and I took it.

Whoa. What kind of trick was this? I felt the zing from my palm to my toes as Sarah probed my mind, digging in my dark corners like a miner looking for gold. I was afraid all she'd find was bat guano. I threw up a block, but it crashed against a brick wall. Finally I managed to wrench my hand from hers. I breathed a sigh of relief when the connection was broken.

"That was intense. Next time you drive your back hoe into my brain, try asking permission."

"Then I'd never learn anything interesting, Gloriana." Sarah ignored Flo and focused on me.

"Did you see what you were looking for?" Behind me, Flo said something under her breath about nosy bitches.

"What I found, was that you don't know your own heart, my dear. I saw Jeremiah Campbell." I gaped at her and she smiled. "Oh, yes, I know him and his parents."

"Lucky you." Now it was my turn to mutter nasties.

"I like to think so. But my son is not so lucky. He has a habit of becoming attached to unavailable women." She lasered a look at Flo that could have melted steel. "I hope you'll think long and hard before you lead him to believe you could have real feelings for him."

"They've had one date, Sarah. I hardly think you need to jump in and do the 'mommie dearest' thing yet." Obviously Flo had been on the receiving end of that treatment.

Sarah just smiled. "Richard never allows my interference. And in your case, Florence, dear, it was hardly necessary. He saw through your tricks soon enough."

I stepped between Flo and Sarah and prayed for some kind of distraction. It came in the form of my dog, one of them anyway. Will, trailing his leash, staggered into the sanctuary, an absolute no-no, and fell at my feet.

"Will! What happened? Are you hurt?" I dropped to my

knees and put my arm around him. Then I sniffed. "You've been drinking!"

"Fine Scotch whiskey, lassie." Will licked my cheek, then rested his head on his paws. "My lucky day."

"Where's Valdez?" I jumped up and looked around. No sign of him.

"Gone. Told me left a message. On cell phone. Don't know how. Dumb dog." Will snorted, then fell into a stupor.

I dug in my purse and found my phone. I'd turned it off in church of course. Now I switched it on and saw I had a message.

"Blade's called me off, Glory. Guess he's decided Mara does it for him and you can take care of yourself. Sorry to stick you with Will, but he's paid till the end of the month. I figure I'm due some vacation time and I'm more than ready to be out of this dog body. See ya."

This voice was smoother, more hip than the Valdez who talked in my head. It didn't fit with what I'd imagined he'd really sound like. I hit a button and listened to it again. Blade was dumping me? Like this? I didn't believe it. Something was off here. Had to be.

"Flo, listen to this."

My roomie held the phone, then reared back like someone had spit in her ear. "I don't believe it. That doesn't sound like Valdez anyway."

"We never heard Valdez's real voice. Blade likes to play tricks. The Valdez before this one sounded like the Taco Bell Chihuahua."

"Still. This voice does sound familiar. Maybe . . ." Flo handed back the phone. "Call Jeremiah."

"I was planning to." I hit speed dial but went straight to Blade's voice mail.

"Jerry, Valdez is missing. If you called him off I need to know. Call me back immediately." I broke the connection, then my insecurities hit me like a body blow. I'd been after Jerry for decades to let me live my own life. To take away the guards and trust me to survive on my own. Had he finally decided to take me seriously? I felt hollow and wanted to throw up.

I hit speed dial again. "Uh, Jerry, I'm okay with it, if you've moved on. Just do me the courtesy of telling me to my face, okay?" Not okay. The enormous sanctuary blurred and I sank down on one of the pews.

"This is ridiculous. Blade would never dump you like this." Flo stomped her foot and got in Will's face. "Look at me, you worthless hound. Wake up."

Will raised red-rimmed eyes to her face. "Hey, beautiful. Let's you and me hook up after this is over. I've been watching you. I think we could be good together. *Que bella. Sì?*"

"Concentrate on the problem, signor." Flo pulled back her foot like she was going to kick him then realized where she was. "Where is Valdez? What have you done to him?"

"Nothin' I tell ya." His head sagged again.

"Will, where did you get the booze?" I squatted next to him and raised his muzzle to look him in the eye. "Did you shift?"

"Naw. Some guy put a big bowl of Glenlivet down in front of me." Will belched, then reached out to lick my face.

I jumped back out of range. "Someone wanted you out of the way. What did he look like?"

"Brown shoes." Hiccup. "I never looked higher than that beautiful bowl of fine Scot's whiskey." Snort. Snore.

Sarah had her cell phone to her ear. "That's right. We're at the Moonlight church. Valdez has disappeared. Gloriana's . . . bodyguard." Sarah looked at me as she snapped the phone shut. "Richard's on his way."

"Why do we need him? We haven't even gone outside to look for Valdez yet." I grabbed a showy flower arrangement, tossed the flowers on a nearby pew and dumped water on Will's head.

"Hey, what'd I do?" Will staggered to his feet, then shook water all over us. An usher hurried up.

"Ladies, ladies, please respect the sanctuary. And the dog, unless he's a Seeing Eye dog, should stay outside."

"Sorry." I grabbed Will's leash and dragged him toward the door. I'd played blind a time or two and still felt guilty about it. Will was dead weight, barely able to walk. Finally, I picked him up. And didn't that raise some eyebrows. Will's no lightweight.

Outside, I dumped him on the grass. Where was Valdez? I looked around, called him. He couldn't have come up with a bowl of fine Scotch or brown shoes. I figure if he shape-shifted he'd still be naked and there would have been at least some kind of commotion, even at this liberal church. So I asked strangers if they'd seen a black Labradoodle with a red and white bandana around his neck, his church attire. Okay, that did it. Tears filled my eyes again and I sat on a stone bench in the garden in front of the church.

"He wouldn't just leave like that, Glory. He's really attached to you." Flo sat beside me and put her arm around me.

"I . . . I thought so. We've been together for *years*." I took the pristine white hanky Sarah pressed into my hand and dabbed at my eyes. "And what's with Jerry? If he wanted to cut me loose, all he had to do was say so. I'm not going to force myself on him." At least not unless I'd had a good dose of the Vamp Viagra when he was in the room.

"Here's Richard." Sarah smiled at her tall son.

I felt warmth in my cheeks, remembering the fiasco from last night, how I'd exposed myself in more ways than one to Richard. But any embarrassment could take a backseat today. Valdez was missing. He had to be my first priority.

I looked up and met Richard's gaze. I could see his resemblance to his mother now that they were side by side. Sarah's hair wasn't nearly as white blond as Richard's but she was fair. And they both had the same aristocratic air about them. Richard had probably shifted somewhere else then just walked up. He obviously hadn't arrived that fast by car or motorcycle unless he'd been following me.

Nope. He had better things to do, like obsess over finding

the EV stronghold. That obsession just might come in very handy. I had that hollow feeling again, this time because the problem with Valdez had EV trick written all over it. I had no proof of course, just my gut.

"Did you see Valdez when you came in?" I jumped up and grabbed Richard's hands. I glanced around and saw more people come out of the sanctuary.

"No sign of him." Richard squeezed my hands. "I see you've met my mother."

"Yes. A pleasant surprise." I ignored Flo's snort. "We've got to find Valdez. He left a kiss-off message on my phone, but I don't believe it's him talking. Not that I have a clue what his real voice sounds like, but—"

"Let me hear it."

I hit the button then handed Richard the phone. He listened then handed it back. "Blade dumping you? What do you think?"

He watched me carefully. I really didn't want this to turn into a drama all about my broken heart, which wasn't, by the way, broken. Okay, maybe slightly cracked. "No way. Jerry and I have a complicated relationship, but we're always honest with each other. Jerry would never let one of his minions do his talking for him."

"It's not like Valdez either. He seems loyal. I can't see him taking off like that." Richard squeezed my hand holding the phone. "Try Blade again. Let's spread out and see if we can find the dog."

Richard approached a small group of people while I redialed Blade. More voice mail. I hung up and looked inside the sanctuary again. The place was huge. I ran down the aisles until that same long-suffering usher stepped in front of me.

"Ma'am? Can I help you with something?"

"My dog. I lost my dog."

"The big one that came in here?" The usher looked toward the hastily rearranged flowers and the wet spot on the carpet.

"No, this was a black dog, with a bandana tied around his neck. He always waits for me right outside the sanctuary, by the door." I felt a tear run down my cheek and the usher patted my back.

"Check over by the fellowship hall. They always have cake and coffee after the service. Maybe he smelled the food and headed that way." The man smiled and I wanted to wail against his starched white shirt.

Instead, I sniffed. Ordinary human, who definitely needed his cholesterol checked. "Go see a doctor. Get some blood work."

The man stared at me. "What do you mean?"

"I'm, uh . . ." What had I seen on the Health Channel? "I'm a medical empath. I sense a thickening in your blood. Take care of yourself or you're going to have a heart attack."

"Wow. You sense that? Just by looking at me?"

I shrugged. "It's more of a sniff than a look. Take care." I patted his hand then raced to the door.

"Wait! What's your name? I want you to look at my wife and my mother. Not my mother-in-law, the heck with her."

"Maybe next Sunday." I didn't look back, afraid he would follow me. I sure wasn't waiting around to find out. I scooted to a stop next to Flo who stood in the doorway.

"Fellowship Hall. They have cake and you know how Valdez is about sweets." I headed down the sidewalk, pulling Flo along behind me.

"Cake. Yeah, he'd go for that." Flo hurried to keep up with me.

I can run pretty damn fast in heels. We rounded the corner and saw a crowd coming out of the square building dubbed Fellowship Hall. Many of them were laughing and one woman was dabbing at her skirt. Pink and white icing.

"Who let that dog in there, anyway?"

I pushed through the crowd. What had been a nice sheet cake lay in clumps on the tile in front of the long table. A pretty tablecloth had obviously been used to pull the cake off the table. Valdez had his mouth full, oblivious to the dirty looks people were giving him.

"Valdez! Come here! Bad dog!" I dove for his leash. He danced away then shook his head. Frosting and cake flew everywhere. "Stop it! Come here." I stomped my foot, slipped on icing and almost sat in the middle of it.

He ignored me to take another bite of cake. While he chewed, I grabbed the leash. I tugged, but he just sat down and started licking pink icing off one paw. I finally knelt down and put my hand on his head.

"Valdez, puppy. I was worried about you."

He barked and leaped, paws landing on my shoulders, raking pink and white frosting down my corduroy dress. I pushed him back and sent him a mental message to cool it. My answer was a tail wag, another bark and a lick in the direction of my face.

"Sit. Sit. Bad dog." I pushed him until he sat in front of me. A stranger handed me a pile of paper towels.

"I'm afraid he's not invited back to Sunday service, miss, unless you can tie him up somewhere."

"No! The Lord loves dogs." A woman with a broom and dustpan in her hand spoke up. Several parishioners nodded.

"We need a dog park, a fenced area where we can leave our pets while we worship." A man knelt down and held the dustpan while the woman swept chunks of cake into it.

"You bet we do." Another man whipped out his cell phone. "I'm calling Pastor John right now. He'll love the idea. Maybe we could have a bake sale"—laughter from the crowd—"to raise funds for it."

I guess the church's happiness message worked because no one threatened to call the dogcatcher. And Valdez had made a huge mess.

I plucked a pink frosting rose from the top of his head and, sue me, but I tasted it. What, you think I worry about *germs?* Mmm. Sweet. I resisted downing the whole thing, especially when I felt someone watching me. I turned and

saw Richard standing in the doorway, his mother right beside him. Flo stayed on the other side of the room, as far
away from flying frosting as she could get.

"Uh, I'm really, really sorry. My dog is usually very well
behaved."

"That's okay, honey. If you're single, you should join the
group in the Twilight Room. After you clean up the dog,
that is. The singles are enjoying a late supper. Nice group
of folks, some men and women about your age and some
older."

My age? If she only knew. "Thanks, maybe next week."

Richard was beside me in a flash. "We're both really sorry
about the mess." He slung an arm around me, implying we
were a couple. Hmm.

The woman wadded up the dirty tablecloth and shook
her head. "A shame about the cake, though. It was going to
be dessert for the singles later."

"Wait. Let me pay—" I dug in my purse.

"I've got it, Gloriana." Richard's mother pressed a wad of
cash into the woman's hand. "Please. Accept a donation for
the group. For future desserts."

"Wow. Thanks." The dazed woman's eyes widened when
she realized what she held. "Next week I'll order chocolate
cake. That's the group's favorite. Just don't let the dog in
here. I've heard chocolate is bad for dogs."

"Of course. The dog should stay in the car, shouldn't he?"
Sarah gave Richard a speaking look and he dragged Valdez
out the door.

"Ready to go?" Flo was by my side.

"I really need to wash my hands." I headed for the door
clearly marked "Ladies" near the back wall.

Once inside, I dabbed at pink and white frosting until
I finally gave up and just licked my fingers. Delicious.

"What a disaster." Flo pushed inside, then looked around
the bathroom to make sure we were alone while I washed my
hands. "Those people were giving you the evil eye out there."

"Yeah. Wonder if there's another church with night

services. I'm afraid we'll be blackballed after this." I dried my hands on a paper towel then stared at the large mirror in front of me. Of course I wasn't seeing either one of us.

"Glory?" Flo put her hand on my shoulder.

"Valdez. What's wrong with him? Do you think he really left that message?"

"Only if Blade told him to." Flo reached up and pulled a piece of cake out of my hair. She sniffed, then dropped it in the trash can.

The very possibility hit me like a body blow. "What? And then Blade said 'Let them eat cake'?" I rubbed at a spot on my skirt. "Did you see the mess Valdez just made? Our Valdez knows we try to keep a low profile." I gave up on the skirt.

"But, Glory, if Valdez didn't leave that message, who did? And why?"

"Someone's pulling my chain, Flo. Who and why? One guess."

"Here we go again. Simon, always Simon." Flo put her hands on her hips. "I won't hear this."

"Are you sure that dog is your bodyguard?" Sarah Mainwaring swept into the room, white frosting paw prints on her skirt. "Richard says Valdez is not himself."

"He's right. This is totally out of character." I wasn't just *worried* about my dog. I was getting frantic. Sure, we'd been surrounded by people, but he was acting like a . . . dog. I handed Sarah a paper towel. "Thanks, Sarah, for taking care of the cake. I insist on reimbursing you."

"Forget it. I'm quite able to afford it. Who knows? Maybe I'll check out the singles group myself some Sunday night." Sarah smiled at me, turning at Flo's barely stifled snicker. "Perhaps you should try it as well, Florence. Richard seems to feel that your current 'friend' is an unsavory character." Sarah wet the paper towel and carefully dabbed at her skirt.

Flo jerked her chin up. "I can't imagine why you care who I see, Sarah."

"I don't, of course. But Richard has shared his concerns

about the company you've been keeping." Sarah sniffed. "Not that it should be his concern."

Flo muttered something in Italian. Sarah muttered something back in the same language and I stepped between them.

"Maybe you *should* ask Simon about Valdez. If he wants to get my attention, Flo, taking out one of my guards would be a heck of a start."

Flo turned her back on Sarah. "You always blame Simon for everything. Maybe Jeremiah tires of you. That she-devil Mara has probably been throwing herself at him. You should shape-shift. Go after your man, if you want to keep him."

"Gee, say what you think, why don't you?" This was my best friend? Where was the support? But then I'd done nothing but slam Simon since Flo had started going out with him. Maybe it was time for me to get smart, use some psychology. I put my hand on her shoulder.

"You're my role model, Flo. I don't see you chasing after a man to keep him. Am I right?"

"Of course." Flo's eyes shimmered and I thought she might be working up to shed a tear or two. "I'm sorry I bitched at you about this. It's just that I'm worried about Valdez too. The phone call. Then going so crazy. This is not *our* Valdez. Something's wrong with him. And if Simon did this—" Tears gone, she clenched her fists and turned to face Sarah again. "I'll find out if Simon had anything to do with this. And if he did, he'll make things right. I'm sure of it." Flo turned back to me. "Will you be okay, Glory, if I leave you now?"

"Sure." Flo was going to confront Simon? Was this a good idea? What if he punished her like he'd punished Greg Kaplan? "But, Flo, be careful." We stepped out of the bathroom and I looked around. The place was clean again, and didn't that make me feel guilty? It was deserted, but I could hear laughter coming from the Twilight Room.

Sarah frowned down at her damp skirt. "I'm late for my

book club and, after wading through that boring literary novel, I'm not going to miss it. Richard can give you my telephone number, Gloriana. Call me sometime and we'll talk."

"Book club?" Flo and I stared after her as she breezed out the door.

"Of course. Lady Sarah Mainwaring has a club for everything." Flo shook her head. "That woman's a barracuda, Glory. She'll take a chunk out of you if she thinks you're hurting her baby boy."

I laughed. Now that I had my dog back, a dog who'd probably just been indulging his food obsession, I felt like I could deal with anything.

"Come on, Flo. Richard doesn't strike me as a mama's boy." The idea of Richard being anyone's baby boy was ludicrous.

"Maybe not. But Sarah can afford to spring for a few cakes. While Richard goes around saving the world from bad vampires, who do you think pays the bills? She has an investment club too." Flo sighed. "Look at you. Your dress is a disaster." She ran a hand through her hair. "I'd better not have cake in my hair."

"You don't. What about my hair?" Not that I really cared. For once how I looked meant zilch. Flo knew it too. She put her own dress at risk to give me a hug.

"You look good considering what you've just been through. The dog has much to answer for. But if Simon did something to him . . ."

"Don't go throwing around accusations, Flo." I grabbed her arm. "Be careful how you handle Simon. He's got some powerful stuff going on out there. He ever mention Honoria?"

"Another woman?" Flo laughed. "Of course not. Relax, Glory. I've been handling men for centuries." Flo pulled a lipstick from her purse and expertly reapplied it. "I will get the truth from him." She winked. "One way or another."

"No VV tonight?" I know, I know. I'm not her mother.

But I have a little experience with addiction. And my best bud was showing some signs . . .

"I said I would do without it, didn't I?" She sighed. "I don't like seeing you worried about Jeremiah. Do you really think he would just dump you? Get real, Glory. And for Mara, the ice queen? That woman would freeze a man's balls off."

Hmm. If Blade *had* dumped me for Mara, I hoped his balls spent eternity in permafrost. My stomach rumbled and I didn't think it was from icing. None of this added up. No way did Valdez leave that message. Someone else had to have done it. Otherwise, why was there still a black Labradoodle outside waiting for me?

"I think it *was* a prank. Someone's trying to upset me. The last time we talked, Jerry and I were getting along very well." Like orgasmically well.

"Now you make sense. No silly doubts about Jeremiah. He adores you." Flo looked down at my skirt and frowned. "I'll miss this church. Nice people. I think I saw a vampire in the singles group too." She pulled open the door and headed out.

I followed her. Richard stood outside the door, a subdued Valdez beside him. A few people still talked nearby, single smokers who wanted a last drag before they went inside to mix and mingle.

"Bad dog. You know how to stay." I said this for our audience. "Let's go. No treat for you tonight."

"You'll be lucky if he doesn't toss his cookies, I mean cake, when he's in the car." The smokers laughed.

"Sorry for ruining social hour, folks. I'd better get this dog home." I took the leash from Richard and pulled Valdez along to the car. When we got there, Richard opened the back door and Valdez hopped in to settle beside a snoring Will.

I grabbed Richard's arm. "Did Valdez talk to you while I was inside?"

"No. And I tried to send him a mental message, but he either ignored it or didn't understand it."

"Didn't understand . . . ?" My stomach rolled over. I opened the back door again, picked up Valdez's head and stared into his brown eyes. "Valdez! Say something."

Nothing. Not even a whimper. He did lick my fingers though, as if hoping for some more frosting. I grabbed both his ears and stared harder, like I could *make* him respond. "Please, puppy. Say something. Anything. Call me Blondie."

He just shook his head like he was ready for me to let him go if I wasn't going to pet him. I released him and turned to Richard.

"What the hell is wrong with my dog?"

Twenty-two

We were back at my place before I remembered to tell Richard about Flo's meeting with Simon in the park.

"This is huge, Glory. Maybe we can catch him alone."

"What are you going to do to him, Richard? Try to take him out?" In other words, stake him. I shuddered just thinking about it. I knew Simon was a bad man, but killing any vampire seemed almost sacrilegious to me. And Flo. Would she ever forgive me for sending the troops in after her lover? I hoped once she'd had time to think about how she'd been acting, she'd realize she'd needed to move on.

"You think I'm being too tough on him? Roll Valdez over, Glory." Richard stared down at my pair of dogs, both snoring near the door.

"What do you mean?"

"Look at his tummy, Glory. See if the reason he won't talk is because he *can't*." Richard didn't wait. He knelt down and rolled a snoozing Valdez over until we could see his swollen stomach. Sure enough there were two angry red marks on his belly.

I gasped. "You think—"

"That an EV did this? Yes, I do. I'd say that while you were in church and Will was nose deep in whiskey someone conveniently put in front of him, Valdez had an encounter with Simon or another EV and he obviously lost the fight and his power."

I sat down hard on the floor and rubbed Valdez's tummy. "You mean—"

"I mean right now Valdez is just a dog. Not a shape-shifter. Unless there's some way for the EVs to reverse the process, Valdez may never be able to shift again."

I leaned over and rubbed my face against the dog's soft fur. He smiled and licked a tear from my face. I breathed in his scent, a scent I knew as well as my own.

"Damn it. I knew there was something wrong with Valdez when he didn't ask for ice cream with his cake."

Richard smiled and patted my shoulder. "He would, wouldn't he?" He left me sitting there and started to work his phone, calling on fellow vamps and making plans to ambush Simon at the park.

"I'm going, Glory." Richard dropped a kiss on the top of my head. Yeah, I was still on the floor, Valdez's head in my lap.

"Wait. Simon has to be behind Valdez's condition. If there's any hope of getting my dog restored to his old pain-in-the-butt self, Simon or Honoria holds the key."

"I can't promise not to destroy Simon if I get the chance, Glory. I've been after him for a long time." He rubbed Valdez's ear. "Maybe Valdez will recover his power on his own. Eventually." Richard looked at me and wiped away a tear that had leaked down my cheek. "I know you love him. I'll do what I can to find out how to fix this."

"Thanks." I held on to his hand for a moment. "I know what getting Simon means to you. Do what you have to."

He stood, tall, powerful and determined. If he got a chance at Simon, he'd take it. And Valdez . . . ? He would have cheered Richard on.

I sat there on the floor for a long time after Richard left, stroking Valdez's soft fur. An EV had done this. Which meant Jerry hadn't dumped me after all. I was so relieved I would have laughed, if I hadn't felt more like crying. Was there any hope of getting the old Valdez back? I had to find out.

The phone rang. I got up and pulled my cell phone out of my purse. I glanced at the caller ID and caught my breath. Blade.

"Hello."

"Gloriana, what the hell is going on there? Why do you think I called Valdez off?" Jerry was shouting, like maybe I couldn't hear him across the ocean. Or like maybe he was really upset.

"Valdez is here. I found him. But he or someone left a message that you'd called him off. Because you'd hooked up with Mara. Which is allowed, of course. We do our own thing when we're apart, always have." I took a breath and looked at Valdez, snoring softly by the door. The old Valdez would have been up at the first notes of "Phantom of the Opera," my ring tone. He'd have been listening in, like that was in his job description. He really was just a nosy . . . I sobbed.

"Son of a bitch! Gloriana, tell me everything. And I'm not hooked up with anyone. I'm living like a monk outside a clinic in Switzerland so I can watch Westwood. He's more vulnerable here, outside of his own place."

"Good." I took a watery breath. A monk, huh? Good news for me, bad for Mara. "I mean, you should stay there. That bastard is a threat to every vampire." If Simon was allowed to just suck power from anyone or thing he wanted, then *he* was an enormous threat too. God, when did my life get so *complicated*?

"Tell me what's happened. What about Valdez?" Blade's calm voice soothed me.

I took a breath then filled him in on recent events at the church. By the time I got through with the story, Blade was cursing and swearing to be by my side by morning.

"No, you should stay there. Flo and Richard are looking into it."

"I've heard of Simon Destiny and his EV crew. I had a friend who tried their daylight drug." Blade was silent for a moment. "Liam paid them a fortune. He was so excited to see the sun again. But it was the *last* thing he saw."

"Oh, Jerry. Maybe he thought it was worth it." I'd had those yearnings.

"We'll never know the answer to that, now, will we? Thanks to Simon Destiny." Jerry cleared his throat.

"I'm really worried about Valdez, Jerry. He's a . . . dog. What if he's lost all his powers?"

"Rafael is a very strong shape-shifter. That's why I hired him. He may be temporarily out of commission, but that doesn't mean it's permanent." Jerry said something to someone else and I heard a female voice in the background.

"Is Mara with you?"

"She just came in. I'm going to leave her here and come home to you, Glory. I don't like the fact that Simon's been trying to lure you to his den of drug dealers. Or that he's managed to temporarily take out one of your guards. We will resolve this and Simon Destiny will get what he deserves once and for all." Jerry sounded so damned sure of himself. That kind of confidence made me actually hope that things would come out all right.

"You shouldn't come. I'll be fine." I looked at Valdez, then at Will who was still sleeping off his bender. Well, I'd always said I could look out for myself. Time to test that theory.

"No, I've made up my mind. I'm coming."

Of course I was relieved. "It's too late to leave there tonight. Wait until tomorrow night. It's a long, long way from Switzerland to Texas."

"It is a long way. But I'll leave here tonight, see how far I get, then spend the day somewhere safe and be there sometime tomorrow night. Wait for me, Gloriana, before you do anything about Simon."

"I hear and obey, master." I knew he was just being cautious. It was sweet. Dictatorial, but sweet.

"Come on, sweetheart. Humor me. I'm so damned far away. I want to hold you and tell you that everything will be all right."

I closed my eyes. "Then do it. Like you did the other night. Hold me. Put your arms around me and your lips on my hair." I concentrated. "And I'm holding onto you, Jerry. Just breathing, not trying to get you naked or anything like that." Though now that I thought about it, there was nothing more comforting than lying skin to skin in Jerry's strong arms.

"Sorry, Glory. What did you say? Mara was telling me we have an opportunity to get to Westwood later tonight. He's going into surgery in the morning to try to get his arm fixed. He'll be in a regular hospital room. If we can get inside, we might have a shot at him."

I gave up. The mood wasn't happening. "Then go get him. I'll be fine. Will's going to sober up. Flo's investigating Simon and maybe Richard and his vigilantes will manage to get to Simon anyway." I hung up before I said something bitchy. Trust Mara to come up with a plan just when Jerry was ready to fly to my side.

I sat down beside Valdez again. "You never told me your name is Rafael. Rafe. I like it. Wonder what your last name is. Is it Spanish too? Are you tall, dark and handsome out of that dog body?" I patted his head, but he just stared up at me with big brown eyes, his tail thumping on the hardwood floor.

I sighed and got up. A few hours until dawn. Did I just sit here and wait for something to happen? Would Flo call me? Would Richard? Will snored, obviously still useless. What good would it do Valdez if I ran off and did something foolish, like storm the park myself? I sat on the couch and picked up my latest book, a bestseller on assertiveness.

Half a page and I was heaving it across the room. What did a mortal know about the kind of assertiveness I needed? I wasn't thinking about asking the boss for a raise or a boyfriend to commit. Hell, I just wanted the leader of the EVs to restore my dog's powers. Assertiveness in this situation would get me nothing but trouble.

But then I'm a badass vampire. I don't run from trouble, I start it.

When the phone rang close to dawn, I almost jumped out of my skin. I couldn't believe I'd actually dozed off on the couch.

"Hello."

"Glory, it's Flo. I'm with Simon."

"Enjoying your date?" I glanced at my dogs, sleeping peacefully.

"No."

"Flo, honey, are you in trouble?" I couldn't sit still and carried the phone to the fridge for a bottle of Fangtastic. "Where are you two?" I hoped at the park surrounded by angry vamps with stakes. They wouldn't hurt Flo and surely she wouldn't risk her own life for Simon. Unless he'd done some kind of whammy on her . . . I leaned against the fridge.

"We're at Simon's headquarters. We didn't go to the park after all." Flo took a shaky breath. "I'm sorry, Glory, but Simon is the one who took Valdez's power. He says if you want your dog back like he used to be, you'll have to come here and give the EVs something they need." Flo sobbed. "Don't do it, Glory! We'll figure something out. He'll make you a drone." There was a crash.

"Gloriana, your friend is hysterical. Please understand that no lasting harm will come to either you or Florence if you follow my instructions." The male voice was smooth, unaccented, with a mesmerizing quality that I felt even over the phone.

The room swam and I staggered back to the couch. "Don't hurt Florence, Simon."

"Florence is my lover. Why would I hurt her? We don't need to play those games." He actually chuckled.

I wanted to throw up. "Why did you hurt my dog, Simon?"

"To get to you, Gloriana. I think you have an enormous amount of power just going to waste. I can take what I need and then I will happily restore your 'dog' to his former abilities." He laughed again. "This foolish attachment amuses me. Even Florence is moved to tears over the animal's plight. I found him to be quite ordinary. Shifters are never as interesting as ancient vampires."

"That shifter was *my* shifter. And by vamp standards I'm not ancient. I'm practically a kid. Born way after the Crusades."

"You're old enough to have developed some interesting power. Florence has told me how you've been experimenting with it. You've been delightfully original."

"Cut the compliments, Simon. I don't see how you can be so sure I have the kind of power you need."

"You won't shape-shift, my dear. Sad for you, but excellent for my purposes. Shifting really drains a lot of power from a vampire. And your . . . dog. He hardly provided enough to make one dose of the VV. Pathetic, really."

"Valdez, pathetic? Listen, Destiny. That shifter is worth a dozen of you. I can't tell you how many times he's saved my butt over the years." My voice cracked and I swiped at tears. Will was up and had his head in my lap. Valdez still sat near the door, ew, licking himself. That did it. I couldn't hold back a sob.

"Now, Gloriana. Calm yourself. You can take care of Mr. Valdez's problem. Come see me and I'll explain everything."

"How could I possibly trust you to keep your word?" I found a tissue and blew my nose. Weeping could wait. I had to do something. But I could see it now. Valdez and I would head out to the EV stronghold, wherever that was, and become zombielike creatures, tubes hanging out of our belly buttons for easy access. I gripped the phone.

"I'm the king of the EVs, Gloriana. Of course you can trust me." The very arrogance of that statement convinced me he'd lie like a cheap watch if it suited his purposes. Or to get what he wanted. And what he wanted was, gulp, my power.

"No freakin' way. Maybe I can figure out how to give power to my pup without you."

"Impossible, my dear. Exchanging power is an ancient art that only an Energy Vampire has mastered."

"An ancient art? Get over yourself, Destiny. Flo can tell you about real art. Sucking tummies doesn't qualify. Does Honoria think you're an artist?"

"You will not speak the Demoness's name, woman."

Boy, had I struck a nerve. "Maybe she'd be disappointed in how you're handling things here in Austin. You've got the whole vampire community stirred up against you."

"Now you're being foolish. Vampires are my customers. Honoria is well pleased with my progress here."

"Yeah, right. Then swear on her name that you'll restore my dog and let me go after you get what you want from me. I won't turn into a drone for you, Simon." I jumped up and went to sit on the floor next to Valdez. There had to be a way to help Valdez without going through the EVs. The marks where his power had been drained were gone. And even if I bit him on his hairy belly—ew—I would be taking blood, not giving him anything. And Valdez wasn't a vampire. Biting me would provide him with nothing but a creepy snack.

"I don't swear on the Demoness's name for such trivial matters. I know you're distraught or you wouldn't try issuing orders when I hold all the cards here. Do you really want to alienate the one person who can give you what you want? I'll hang up now. Perhaps you'll be more rational tomorrow."

"No, wait!" I had to deal with this creep-a-zoid, he was the only game in town. "Send Flo home, let her tell me about your operation. Maybe we can work something out. I don't have a lot of money, but I have friends—"

"I'm afraid you're not in a position to bargain, Gloriana. Florence stays here. I believe you're quite attached to her as well. And your dog is useless to you as he is. If you want your roommate and your dog restored to you in good . . . condition, I suggest you do as I ask."

I heard a scuffle in the background. You can bet Flo didn't like being used as a bargaining chip. I hope she'd flown out of there while she had the chance.

"I'll give you time to think this over. I'll call back tomorrow night at sunset."

"Wait! I don't even know how to find you."

"Don't worry. Someone will pick you up, if you decide your friends are worth the effort."

He'd hung up. I closed my eyes and took a deep breath. Worth the effort? Flo and Valdez were worth everything to me. But I dreaded the whole idea of even meeting Simon, much less dealing with him. One thing was certain. I wasn't about to get within a hundred yards of Simon Destiny alone. I was taking a freakin' army with me.

"**Y**ou will come alone, Gloriana, except for the dog. The car is outside as we speak. Try any tricks and you'll never see Florence again."

Crap. Double crap. Did I dare go see the EVs alone? I looked up at Richard who'd arrived before sunrise and slept on my couch. No hanky-panky had been attempted or even mentioned. We were both too wrung out by the thought that Flo could be drained dry, then left out in the sun by that ruthless bastard Simon Destiny.

"I want to talk to Flo, make sure she's all right. Otherwise, no deal."

Richard nodded and put his hand on my shoulder. He didn't need to lean closer to hear my phone conversation, vamp hearing and all. He was really grim, like destroyed grim. Poor guy obviously still had feelings for Flo. Of course I had feelings for my roomie too. If Simon hurt her . . .

"Glory." Flo sounded weak.

"How are you, honey? Is that bastard mistreating you?"

"I'm okay. Just tired. Simon won't give me any Vamp Viagra. I need it." She sobbed and the phone rattled, like maybe she'd dropped it.

"You see, Gloriana, Florence is just suffering from withdrawal. I haven't hurt her, she hurt herself when she got dependent on my product."

"Your product. Gee, you know Flo thinks you and I are alike, Simon. Both businesspeople. But at least what I sell doesn't turn my customers into addicts."

"So you say." Simon chuckled. "And how many shoes does Florence own? How many handbags? Sounds like shopping can be an addiction to me."

I'd had just about enough of this chitchat. Flo was suffering, Valdez was a dog and Richard was practically foaming at the mouth. But we'd agreed I'd handle this. Simon wouldn't deal with a man he knew had been after him for years.

"You say the car's already downstairs?" I walked over to lift the blackout drapes and saw a Honda Accord idling at the curb with its lights on. "A silver Honda? Business must be bad if that's the best you can do. Where's the Mercedes, Simon? The Beemer?"

"Make your jokes, Gloriana. Obviously Florence and Valdez mean little to you."

"No! I mean, I'm coming. Just give me a few minutes to get dressed. Tell your driver I'll be down in ten."

"Good. But no more than ten minutes, Gloriana, or he'll leave and you'll have lost your chance to save your friends."

He hung up.

I looked at Richard. "Now what? I need a weapon, a nice sharp stake. But what do you bet the driver searches me before he lets me in the car?"

"Of course he will. I have a plan." Richard pulled a bottle out of his pocket.

"Are you going to drug someone? What will that do? I need the driver to take me to the EV hideout." I'd dressed in jeans and running shoes, my hot pink "Weird Austin" T-shirt and a hoodie. "I've got pockets in my jeans, but . . ." I knew from experience that only a credit card could fit in that space. I know, but I like them tight.

"This is perfume. Smell." He uncapped the bottle and I didn't need to move closer to get a whiff.

"Whoa! I told you, I don't wear perfume because it messes up my sense of smell, but that smells wonderful. Where did you get it?"

"It's my mother's Joy, I think. It was the strongest-smelling perfume she had." He dipped the stopper inside and then waved it around. "Sexy. Which is deeply disturbing on so many levels."

"Okay, so Mummy has excellent taste. Why'd you bring it here?"

"Because I'm going with you, Glory. And I don't want any of the other vampires to smell me on you." He reached forward and dabbed it behind my ears.

I inhaled. Absolutely delicious. "Wait. You can't go with me. I have to go alone. Or alone except for Valdez. You know he has to come with me."

"I'm coming too. I'm shifting into something very small. I'll be where they won't see me and now they won't be able to smell me either."

Before I knew what he was going to do, he lifted my T-shirt and exposed my Kevlar bra. My Wonder Woman bra had a bright yellow "W" on gray since Kevlar didn't come in red. Kevlar was good defense and just about impenetrable. The Wonder Woman thing had been Blade's idea. And wearing the bra always reminded me that I *was* powerful. Maybe too powerful since Simon wanted a piece of me.

"I approve. You're well prepared." He ripped open the Velcro fastening between my breasts and they sprang free.

"Hey, we're in the middle of something serious here, Romeo. Get a grip." I grabbed the edges of the bra.

"Let me put some perfume here." He slid the cold stopper between my breasts, then leaned forward and sniffed. "A little more, I think."

Okay, this was ridiculous. I needed to focus and his little games were wearing on my last nerve. "Hand me the stopper, Richard. I can do it." I grabbed the stopper, dipped it in the pretty bottle, then swabbed my cleavage. Oh, boy, now I felt surrounded by a cloud of expensive scent. Too much, because my head started to throb. I pulled my bra back together.

"Here, let me help." Richard took the stopper and set the bottle on a table. Then he moved behind me to press his hands on my temples. "Relax, Gloriana. Focus on what I'm about to tell you."

The pressure in my head eased, but I sure couldn't relax. "What is this plan, Richard? I'm not going to just give up my power, or let Valdez spend eternity as a dick-licking—sorry fella, but that's all you've been doing lately—dog." I put my hand on Valdez's head.

"I'm going with you. When the time is right, I'll shift into my human form and we'll take care of Simon. And I know you want Valdez restored. I'll try to make that happen."

"We. You. *I'm* the one with the most at stake here, Richard. And I want to handle Simon. Maybe I'll give him some power. You said it can come back. I'll recover." I pulled down my T-shirt. "And where you think you can hide, I don't know. They're going to search my purse. My hoodie has pockets, but they'll check those too."

"Here, Glory." Richard pulled up my shirt and touched the cleavage bulging over the top. "I'll be right here. Over your heart. After I change, you can put me between your breasts."

"Pervert. What could you possibly turn into—" I gasped when Richard disappeared. Poof. Just like that. Valdez growled and I looked down. A mouse. A little white, albino mouse. Valdez leaped and the race was on. The mouse, uh, Richard ran under the table and Valdez knocked over the lamp trying to get at him. I shouted at Valdez to stop, but he wasn't listening.

I grabbed his collar and worked on hauling him into the bedroom. At least without power he didn't have his super strength. I dragged him, still barking, into the bedroom and slammed the door.

"You can come out now."

The mouse crawled out from under the couch and hurried to sit next to my left foot. I shuddered, but leaned down to put out my hand. He crawled onto my palm.

"Thanks for not becoming a cockroach. I don't think I could have handled that between my boobs." I have a thing about bugs, go figure.

"*Loosen the Velcro, Glory. And see if you can push your breasts apart a little.*"

"Serve you right if you suffocated in there." But of course I did what he said. I made a nice little cave. His nose twitched and his little beady eyes, blue, of course, didn't miss a thing. But I finally got the Velcro closed without damaging either him or my boobs.

This was a good, if awkward, thing. I needed backup. Richard was powerful. And a cute little mouse.

"*I have to warn you right now, Glory. You've got to keep up your mind shield. I can read you so easily. Simon will be able to read you, too. Block everyone but me. Can you do that?*"

"Gee, now I'll really have a headache." I hoped to hell I could manage it. Selective blocking is quite a trick. Of course I'd blocked before, but now I'd have to be really careful. Another headache bloomed when I tried. It didn't help that Valdez was still barking behind the bedroom door. He was making a mess, too. I heard paws scratching at the wood, then breaking glass.

"*Don't let him out yet, Glory. And don't block me. Can you hear me?*"

"Yes, yes, I get it. You're talking in my mind. Fine."

"*I won't say anything after we go downstairs. In case the person they send can hear me. Here's the plan.*" His whiskers tickled and I fought the urge to scratch.

"Settle down, will you?"

"*Sorry, it's crowded in here.*" Another wiggle. "*As soon as you've been searched, I'll crawl out of your bra and hide somewhere else under your T-shirt. For God's sake keep your shirt on.*"

"Okay, okay, I get it. And once we get to the EV headquarters promise you won't do anything rash. Let me handle things."

"*I'll try. But if you're in danger, all bets are off.*"

I pulled out the T-shirt neckline and peeked. His cute little head was hardly visible. Poor guy. Riding in my bra and not even a whisker of a chance at a sexy outcome.

"Be careful, Richard. Time's running out. Let's go." I

picked up my purse and Valdez's leash. When I let him out of the bedroom, he raced around the room, sniffing and carrying on like he was on rat patrol. I guess my perfume was working because he didn't even pause next to me. "We'd better get downstairs. Are we going to have other backup?"

"Damian, Derek and some others are going to follow the car. They know to be careful and stay out of sight. I'm afraid Simon must know you'll be followed, though, so there might be some kind of security along the way."

"Security? Like stake wielding thugs who'll hurt my friends?" I was so going to take out this damned Simon Destiny if it was the last thing I did. Gulp. Tough talk.

The hall door opened and I jumped a foot.

"We're going with you." Will was in human form and had on jeans and a University of Texas T-shirt that I knew Lacy slept in. Lacy had on a fierce look but I could tell she wasn't as into the "save Flo" thing as Will was.

"You can't go. Simon was very specific. If I have any chance of getting to the EV hideout, I've got to go alone."

"Where's Mainwaring?" Will sniffed. "What did you do? Bathe in perfume? Not very smart, Glory. How're you going to use your sense of smell?"

"Don't worry about my sense of anything. If you want to go with me, you'll have to shape-shift and just follow the car. At a respectful distance. I don't want the driver turning around and coming back because he sees he's being tailed." I patted my chest gently. "Lacy, you don't need to come. Your cat would be too easy to spot."

"I want to help. Diana's going. Damian called her to meet him and the rest of the rescue squad." Lacy put her hand on Will's muscular forearm, obviously more than a little interested in him. Not surprising. She had a history for falling hard and fast for good-looking and impossibly wrong men.

"But I told Will my cat probably can't keep up with the vampires." She wrinkled her nose. "Do I smell mouse?" She flipped her long red hair over her shoulder and stalked around the room. "There shouldn't be one within a mile of this building." She sniffed again. "That damned perfume is screwing with my senses, Will's right about that. You should go wash it off."

We all turned when we heard a horn honk down below.

"I've got to go." I grabbed my purse and Valdez's leash. "Do what you want, just don't interfere with what I've got to do."

"Glory!" Will put his hand on my arm. "Be careful, lass. Blade's on his way. You should wait—"

"I'm not waiting. Simon's got Flo. And Valdez needs his power back." I frowned down at Will's hand. "And Blade's going to have your hide for breaking his rules."

"This is an emergency."

"You're right about that anyway." I ran down the stairs, Valdez at my side.

"Good work, Glory. Neither of them figured out I was there and your block must have held up pretty well."

"Yep, and I've got the headache to prove it." I pushed open the outer door and stepped out into the chilly night air. It had rained earlier and the pavement was wet and glistening under the streetlight. The driver's door to the Honda popped open and Greg Kaplan got out.

Twenty-three

"Glory, sweetheart. Glad you could make it." Greg came up to me, glanced meaningfully at a couple window shopping in front of my store, then put his arms around me. I stiffened.

"Relax," he whispered. "Got to check you for any concealed weapons." He ran his hands under my T-shirt and around my middle, then patted me down from my rump to my hips. "Good girl." He stepped back and opened the backseat passenger door. "Put the dog back here and then hand me your purse."

"Valdez, hop in." The dog actually obeyed, seemingly happy to go for a ride. Greg slammed the door, took my purse, then opened the front passenger door.

"Get in." He glanced at the coffee shop two doors down. A man had come out and looked at us curiously. Both of us sniffed. Mortal. Tinted glasses. Oh, hell. What a great time for one of Westwood's goons to make a move. I jerked away from Greg and checked out the man. To my relief I could read his mind through the glasses. Seems he didn't like the way Greg had almost pushed me into the car. I smiled and nodded.

"Let's go, honey." I turned to Greg. "I can't wait to see your surprise."

"You'll be surprised all right." Greg waited until I was in, then slammed the car door.

I felt Richard move inside my shirt. At least my loose T-shirt kept me well covered. Greg got in the car and quickly and efficiently went through my purse. He tossed it back in my lap after keeping my cell phone and his own. He turned mine off, then stuck it in the glove compartment. He looked his over.

"Battery's dead."

"Sorry, I didn't have your charger. What about my phone? Will I get it back?" Not that I cared, but with Richard moving under my shirt, I had to keep Greg focused on something besides my chest.

"Maybe. After this is over, if you play your cards right." He pulled a thing that looked like a flashlight out of the compartment and ran it up and over me. "Scanning for listening and tracking devices. Good girl, you're clean." He tossed it back inside and slammed the door.

"Of course I'm clean. I don't want to take any chances with my friends in danger. How's Flo? What has Simon done to her?"

"She's as okay as she can be without her VV. Simon's got her locked up for her own safety. He could put her out of her misery with a shot of antidote, but"—Greg shrugged— "it obviously suits him to let her suffer a while. I hear she demanded he fix the dog here. Baby, nobody demands anything of Simon Destiny."

"He's a real tyrant, isn't he?" Making Flo suffer . . . A grade A son of a bitch.

"Honey, he's the boss. He can give the orders." Greg put the car in gear, then checked the rearview mirror. "I'd better not see anyone tail us or back we go."

"I want Flo and my dog restored to the way they belong. I wouldn't let anyone screw that up." I looked back at Valdez. He was checking out the scenery. "Why don't you crack the back window so he can get some air back there?"

"Sure. That perfume's pretty hot, by the way. I don't remember you wearing perfume in New York." Greg glanced at me. "Or shapeless T-shirts." He reached out and touched the cotton. "Did I feel one of your Kevlar bras under there? Flo told Simon all about them."

"Sure. I'm not stupid, Greg. I've had some hunters after me. The kind with stakes, not just siphons. So I never go out without my protective gear."

"Take off your shirt. Let me see it."

"I don't think so." I sniffed like he reeked of sewage. "You're just a drone, Greg. Your job is to take me to Simon. I'm sure you don't want to get in trouble with your boss again and get 'punished.'"

Greg laughed. "Know how Simon punished me? He let me spend a night in his special room. Wait till you see it, Glory. You may want to just stay out there and become a drone yourself."

"Special room?" I felt Richard's whiskers twitch. "What's so special about it? Is it like a torture chamber?"

"In a way." Greg reached over to pat my knee. He was on the freeway, headed south. There were a lot of isolated areas outside of town in that direction. As long as we were still surrounded by suburbs, I felt pretty safe, but as the subdivisions turned into stretches of dark undeveloped land, I got more and more uneasy.

"Tell me about this special room." I was afraid any contingent of vamps following us might be spotted. We were off the freeway now and on a highway that wound through hills. We bumped through a low water crossing, mud splashing as Greg drove through it.

"Daylight, Glory. You'd swear you were on a beach on a tropical island." Greg sighed. "I would do anything for time in that room." He looked at me and winked. "You'd love it. Special lights that are just like the sun, only not lethal. White sand, a pool and palm trees." He chuckled. "You and I could have a lot of fun on a towel on the sand."

I sighed and felt Richard warm against my skin. "Sun? Sand? Palm trees?" I looked back at Valdez. "And a lizard sunning himself on a rock. That's you, Greg. Get a clue. I've moved on from my New York days. My men don't conspire to suck the life out of me."

Greg just laughed. "Yeah, right. Except at the old neck or thigh, huh, baby? I remember what you like."

I felt a flush heat my chest and cheeks and Richard stirred. He wasn't sending me any messages and I knew that was the deal. I had my own block up and a probe of Greg's mind yielded zilch.

The car pulled onto a scenic overlook and Greg stopped. "We get out here." He walked around and opened both passenger doors. Valdez hopped out and rushed to the edge of the brush to take care of business. I fought tears. He never would have been that blatant about using a tree around me if he'd been himself.

The overlook had a pretty view of Austin in the distance. I could see the moonlight reflecting off a lake, but no lights anywhere close to where we were. I flinched when a man stepped out of the shadows. He silently got in the Honda and drove off. I hoped my followers realized I wasn't in the car.

"Our ride's here." Greg picked up Valdez's leash and led him to a black Hummer parked under a tree. He shoved the dog in the backseat and waited for me to get in, then quietly shut the door.

"Gee, this is really spylike, Greg. I've never been in a Hummer before. It's huge. And black like the night. Is Simon scared I'll lead a few angry friends to his place?" I'd said it all out loud in case someone up above us could hear.

"Simon's not scared of anything, Glory. You'd do well to remember that. He's king of the EVs, Honoria's right-hand man." Greg put the car in gear, but didn't turn on the headlights, just used his vamp night vision to steer the car down a rough road that ran through a tunnel of trees. Someone flying high overhead would have a hell of a time spotting us. I swallowed.

"Sounds like Simon's stuck in some earlier centuries. When monarchies were the thing. Where are we going, to some feudal castle in the woods?"

"Simon has respect for old traditions, but he's also hip to

new technology. Brent Westwood's got nothing on Simon. The king can afford to buy whatever he needs. You'll see at headquarters." Greg shifted a gear and we bumped up a rocky hill, well off the road now. "I probably should have blindfolded you, but I doubt you'd ever be able to retrace our path anyway. As I remember, you were too much into blending to hone your vamp skills."

"Thanks a lot." I felt a tickle on my chest and tried to scratch without hurting Richard or alerting Greg. It wasn't easy. "Back then, I'd say you were right, but I've been surrounded by strong vampires lately. I'd have to be stupid not to pick up a few tricks."

"Save them, Glory. Tricks like shifting sap your power. Simon will do what you want to your furry friend back there, as long as he feels you've got something he wants. Waste it, and I'm afraid you'll have lost your bargaining chip."

"And what about Flo?" I couldn't imagine my roomie slobbering somewhere in the throes of drug withdrawal. A sex drug. I had visions of her lusting after the handle of her hairbrush and shuddered. Richard had crawled out of his cave and was on my shoulder under my T-shirt. Valdez stuck his head between the seats and growled.

"Flo's okay. Simon can cure her with a shot of the antidote." Greg glanced at Valdez. "Call off your dog or I dump him right here, in the middle of nowhere."

"Dump my dog and I'll—" I reached out and grabbed Greg's crotch. Yeah, right *there*. "Squeeze this puppy until you hit high C." I tightened my grip. "Want to test my vamp strength?"

"Damn it, Glory!" Greg slammed on the brakes and the car fishtailed then rocked to a stop. He looked down, his face pale. "Let go. Right. Now." He pulled a gun from a pocket in the door and aimed it at Valdez's head. "Now or I blow fur face here to hell."

I let go, sorry I hadn't really hurt Greg when I had the chance. Unfortunately, I needed him to find the EV stronghold.

"Now kiss it and make it better." Greg kept the gun in his left hand and grabbed my hand with his right. He tried to pull me closer.

"In your dreams, asshole. Isn't your boss waiting?" I glanced at the clock on the dashboard. "We've already wasted over an hour getting wherever we're going. Is Simon a patient man? Would he like to hear that we were late so you could get your rocks off?"

Greg dropped my hand and stuck the gun back in the door. "We're here. Or I *would* make you kiss it." Greg gave me a warning look. "And you don't want to make either of us mad. I can help you, if you'll let me. Once Simon has your power, you'll need someone—"

"I'd rather lie in the sun, waiting to die, than let *you* help me, Gregory. And, news flash, since New York I've learned to help myself."

Greg glanced back at Valdez, then hit me with his best "I'm a rough, tough vampire" look. "Last warning, Glory. Don't screw around like this with Simon or anyone here, or you'll regret it. And so will Valdez and Florence. You hear me?"

Oh, yeah, I'd definitely heard Greg. So I was fighting terror and a sick feeling in the pit of my stomach as I followed Greg down a path, Valdez at my side. When we finally came to a clearing, I stopped and gawked. A gold dome sparkled in the light from a full moon. Yep, a genuine dome with a spire pointing toward Heaven, like on a cathedral or mosque or some other holy place.

"Impressive."

"Thank you, Gloriana." A man strolled out of the shadows.

"Simon? Or should I curtsy and call you 'Your majesty'?" I held onto the leash when Valdez started barking and lunged. Brad Pitt? I think not. I did a double take. If it hadn't been for his voice, I would have sworn . . . Obviously Simon really could make you think . . .

"Show a little respect, Glory." Greg backed away at a look from Simon. "But not my business. Call me when you need me to drive her home, sir." Simon just stared and Greg scurried away.

"So this is the dog you're so attached to." Simon turned his attention to Valdez. The dog whimpered, tucked his tail between his legs and lay next to my feet. And wasn't that a creep-out?

"And you're the man Florence is so attached to. Funny, but you don't look like Brad Pitt to me. More like Jeremy Blade."

Simon smiled. "It's one of my many gifts, Gloriana. I can sense a woman's hidden desires and become the man she wants." He stared at me for a moment. "You're very busy blocking your thoughts, Glory. Hiding something?" He walked closer and touched my shirt. "Take this off. Kaplan might have missed something."

I shrugged and tore the T-shirt off over my head and tossed it aside. I knew from the tiny movements under it, that I'd flung Richard away with it. He was a vamp. He'd land on his feet and figure out what to do.

"Wonder Woman." Simon actually licked his lips and I got a glimpse of forked tongue that made me shudder. "I'd enjoy a little hand-to-hand with a superheroine."

"Hand-to-hand?" I felt strangely disconcerted, talking to a Jerry clone, a man I'd lusted for since my Globe days. Hidden desires? I'd need to mull that over later. "Or did you have something a little more personal in mind?"

Simon laughed and took my arm. "Come now, you wouldn't think to barter your body for your dog's power, would you?" He led me toward the mosque. "I have much more interesting uses for you than sex." He stopped and looked me over. "Though I like a woman with curves. That Kevlar definitely piques my interest."

He smiled and I almost threw up on his brown suede loafers. Another way I knew it wasn't Jerry. Jerry didn't own a pair of Gucci loafers. Yet. I looked back at my dog lying with his head on his paws. Worth it? I hoped to hell I didn't have to find out.

"Relax, Gloriana. I've plenty of willing women if I'm in the mood to indulge my . . . appetites." He focused on my chest and I wondered if he had X-ray vision. "Like your friend Florence. A most interesting woman. But troublesome. She's convinced me I'd be wise to pay more attention to my business and less to my own urges for a while. Come along." He pulled me toward a gold door.

"Wait! How troublesome? I want to be sure Flo's all right." Smiling Simon was seriously creeping me out and that gold door looked like the portal to hell or a little shop of horrors or something. No way was I going inside. I just bet that Honoria was in there, ready to gobble my power, then snack on my lifeless body for dessert.

Simon squeezed my arm and smiled. "I can sense it, Glory. All your untapped power. You will be a wonderful source. Because you won't shape-shift."

I looked at Valdez who'd stayed on the ground next to my shirt. Now he was sniffing it and rooting around like he'd got a whiff of mouse.

Simon rubbed my arm, tightening his grip when I tried to wrench it away. "I understand your fear of shifting. What if you were injured while in another form? Or"—he nodded toward Valdez—"met with an unfortunate accident and lost your power." He smiled. "You'd be stuck forever as something less than human."

I shuddered and looked away from Simon's gleaming eyes. He had a mesmerizing voice and a knack for ferreting out my deepest desires *and* fears. And—hell's bells—I felt a pull. Oh, God. I'd almost leaned toward him.

"I want to see Flo."

"Of course. I admire your loyalty." He snapped his fingers and a man emerged from one of the smaller buildings on the edge of the clearing. Flo sagged against him.

"Glory?" She shoved away from the man and ran to me.

"Honey, what are you doing here? I'd hoped you wouldn't—" She turned on Simon. "Bastard! Why are you doing this? Leave my friend alone."

"Do you feel bad, Florence? Do you want something from me, perhaps?" Simon reached out the hand not gripping me.

Flo whimpered, sounding way too much like Valdez had a few moments before. "Simon, honey, please. I'm hurting." She actually ran to his side and clutched his hand. "I can make you feel good, baby." She leaned close and whispered, then rubbed herself against him.

"Not interested." He released me and snapped his fingers again. The man who'd stood silently by came forward to drag Flo off of him.

"Simon! Why?"

"You bore me, Florence." Simon smiled at me. "I have someone more interesting here now. We're about to arrange a trade."

Flo screeched. Yep, like a smoke detector during a four alarm. In her vocabulary Simon had just insulted her in the worst possible way. "Bore you? Why, I'll rip out your heart, *bastardo*. I hate you." Flo sank to the ground, sobbing and muttering in Italian. Obviously she didn't have enough strength to rip out anything.

I wanted to run to her and comfort her, but one look at Simon and I knew what I had to do.

"Like I should trust you to make a fair trade." I looked around. More men had come out of the scattered outbuildings. Women too. Even Greg had made an appearance. Some were armed too. With stakes sharpened to a chilling point.

"You don't have to trust me, Glory. Now that you're here, you're mine."

"I don't think so." I concentrated. Shape-shifting. I hated it. Was terrified of it. And the last time I'd tried it, I'd failed miserably. But the stakes were higher this time. Every other vampire I knew did it without a second thought. I had to concentrate. *Will* myself to change. If ever I was going to do it, now was the time. And not some puny bird or bat. Nope. I needed to go for broke. Something enormous. That would drain my power and keep me safe from EV siphons and give me some leverage with Simon the *bastardo*.

I concentrated harder. With a scream that made even me flinch, I morphed into . . . a creature I'd seen on the Discovery Channel.

"Now you've done it, Gloriana. You'll never see your friend cured or your dog restored."

"Oh, won't I?" I flapped my wings—got to love that wing span—and rose in the air above Simon. Before he could move, I had him in my talons and carried him high above that shiny gold dome of his.

"Bad choice of homestead, Simon. That pointy thing on the top *is* gilded wood, isn't it?"

"Put me down. Help!"

His army stared up at us, then a veritable bat brigade swooped in from the night sky. My shirt jumped. Richard was a man again and beside Flo, pulling her into his arms. One by one, the bats became men and women I recognized. With the advantage of surprise, they managed to disarm Simon's band.

"Cowards. Take them down. Don't just stand there." Simon was trying to grab my claws. "Do you want to feel Honoria's wrath?"

"Careful, Simon. Look down. If I drop you now, you'll be skewered. I don't think EV power means much if you have a stake through the heart, does it?"

He stopped moving. I had him by his jacket. A nice Versace that would have sold in my shop in a heartbeat. That is if it didn't have those rips where my talons were clutching it. I felt it rip some more.

"Oh, hell. I may drop you anyway."

"Don't be hasty, my dear. I can help your dog friend, you know. And I doubt anyone else can."

"Prove it." I swooped over the clearing, then hovered

over the dome again. I could see Valdez next to Flo. She'd calmed down, Richard's arms around her. One by one, I identified my friends who had come to help. No sign of Frederick. But Derek was there, Bela, Will, Damian, Diana and . . . Blade, the real one, not the Blade look-alike. He stood by the gold doors and looked up at me like he wanted to throttle me or kiss me or both.

"Kaplan. Get your ass out here and give Valdez your power." Simon in command mode was apparently hard if not impossible to resist.

"You sure, boss? What's to keep Glory from dropping you anyway?"

Simon looked up at me. He didn't look like Jerry now. More like a weasel with a receding hairline. "Good question. I want some guarantees."

"So do I." I made another swoop, this time letting the top of the spike brush Simon's loafers.

"I guarantee to give Florence the antidote and to release her." Simon looked down. "I think her former lover may be willing to take her back."

Richard was holding Flo like he'd never let her go and she seemed to be taking a lot of comfort from him. He looked up at me and sent me a mental message to be careful. Yeah, right. *Now* he remembered me.

"And Valdez? I want a show of faith. Have Greg fix him first."

"Gloriana, drop him. I'll take care of the worthless bastard." Blade stared up at me, his hands fisted by his sides. I checked out the area. I couldn't believe it, Mara wasn't with him.

"No, I've got to get Valdez back to normal." I swooped again, but I felt tired, like this really had drained me in a new and not-so-nice way. I wiggled a talon and Simon shrieked.

"Don't drop me!" He looked up and tried to whammy me. I could tell. I just brushed past the dome again.

"Fix Valdez."

"Kaplan, do it."

Greg grabbed Valdez's leash and pulled him into the domed building. I heard a humming sound. God knows what kind of device the EVs had in there. A fistfight broke out between Blade and one of Simon's followers. Maybe an EV. I didn't know or care, but I was relieved when Blade managed to knock out the other guy.

Obviously the EVs were so busy turning their power into saleable commodities, they didn't reserve a whole lot of power for themselves. Take Simon, for instance. No way could I have held a vamp like Jerry this way. No matter what form I took, he'd have managed to do me one better and overpower me.

The door opened and Valdez pranced out.

Shit, Glory. Look at you. That a pterodactyl? Got to love a dog who'll watch the Discovery Channel with you.

"Yes, puppy." The ground blurred and I heard Simon yelp. I'd swooped a little too low and he'd scraped his leg on the spire. I saw blood drip on the gold dome. I sniffed. Sarah's perfume had been swept away in my change and I could smell Simon's very rich, very potent blood. For a moment I wavered, feeling a pull deep in my gut. Feed from Simon? No way. No how.

"Final guarantee, Simon. You let us all leave here, safe and in one piece, power intact." I swooped again, this time shredding his pants. More blood. God, the smell. This was a bad idea. My fangs were full out and I could almost taste him.

"Put me down, Gloriana. I'll let you taste me. You can feed from me. It will give you a rush unlike any you've ever known."

I jerked when something brushed my cheek.

"Don't do it, Glory." Blade was in blackbird form, flying next to me. "He's a liar."

"Swear a solemn oath. You capable of that, Simon?"

"Drop him, Glory. I'll be all right." Flo had managed to pull herself together. She stared up at me. "But he has to keep his word if he swears in Honoria's name or no one will follow him. These people will do anything for that demon."

"Sounds like a plan. Swear away, Simon."

"Ungrateful, bitch!" Simon shouted down at Flo. "You were never as great as you thought you were. I've had better sex with a were-duck."

Flo screamed and hurled herself into the air. No power though. Instead of changing as she'd obviously planned, she fell to the ground at Richard's feet. He picked her up and cradled her against his chest.

That did it for me. I swooped again. "I think I'd do better to skewer you here and now. Honoria would probably be grateful."

"I wouldn't anger Honoria if I were you. And I have fellow EVs on the Council. Kill me and they'll never stop hunting you. You'll not live long enough to enjoy your mangy dog."

"Hey, asshole. I'm not mangy. I could whip your skinny ass."

I grinned to hear Valdez back in top form. Blade hovered near me.

"Drop him, sweetheart. We'll figure things out."

"No, I think we can make a deal." Simon said it quietly, like he didn't want the guys down below to know he was scared.

"Deal? Flo needs an antidote and we need to be able to get the hell out of here in one piece." I was so damned tired. These leathery wings were unbelievably heavy and every flap took a lot out of me. I barely scraped above the top of the dome.

"That can be arranged. First, call off your people. We don't need a war now, do we?"

I looked down at my friends, seemingly in control of any ground war. My people. Like I was in charge? I felt a surge of energy.

"What's the matter, Simon? You afraid Honoria will gobble you up if you lose too many men? I'll get my people to back off if you—" Simon tried to grab one of my talons and I saw his coat rip some more. "Keep squirming and this discussion won't matter. You're hanging by a shred, King."

"All right. Name your terms. But keep it quiet. There's no reason the peasants need to hear our agreement." His voice was barely a whisper.

"This whole deal is really bad for your image, isn't it? Wonder if the 'peasants' know that's how you think of them." God, but I was exhausted. I felt Blade beside me, willing me to be strong. It helped and I gained altitude. "Swear that you will leave me, my friends and my dog alone from now on."

"I swear that I will not harm you, your friends or your dog."

"Louder." I swept my beak toward the crowd gawking up at us.

"Honoria won't like—"

"Screw Honoria." Oh, boy. Thunder clapped, lightning sizzled nearby and the golden dome actually glowed. Most of the "peasants" fell to their knees and started praying frantically. I felt the electricity in the air and was tempted to skewer Simon and fly out of there as fast as my leathery wings could carry me.

"Say it, Simon. Loud and proud. You will not harm me, my friends or my dog. Not now, not ever. And swear it on Honoria's sacred bible." More thunder. Wind whipped around me, making it hard to keep altitude. I flapped my wings, gripped Simon tighter and felt him shaking. Maybe Honoria *would* gobble him up for making such a poor showing here. I couldn't stress over it, I had a little thing like survival on my mind.

"I swear that I will not harm you, your friends or your dog. Not now and not ever. I swear it on Honoria's sacred bible." Twin bolts of lightning shot from the dome, barely missing both of us.

"Hmm. I'd say the lady's pissed. But it works for me."

"Then put me down now, you bitch."

"Potty mouth." I looked at Blade. "What do you think? Is it a done deal?"

"If you aren't going to drop him, then end this. Put him down, Glory, and let's get you the hell back to human form." Blade dove toward the ground.

Oh, shit. Back to human form. All my old fears rushed right past the adrenaline that had helped me change in the first place. I dropped toward the ground, so hard and fast that Simon actually bounced when we landed.

"Son of a bitch!" He gestured and two of his men ran to help him to his feet.

"Concentrate, Glory. You can do it. Change back." Blade, Flo, Richard, all my friends crowded around me. Or as close to me as they could get with my twenty-foot wing span. Some faced out, like they were guarding me. Sweet.

"I'm so tired." My wings lay on the ground and I felt mud beneath my cheek. A pterodactyl. If I got stuck with a beak that made Cyrano de Bergerac look snub-nosed, I'd . . .

"You're Gloriana St. Clair, a blood-sucking vampire. Let me see you, Blondie." Valdez licked my cheek.

My cheek. My human cheek. "I did it!" I laughed, sat up and looked down. Yep, I was back to my old, slightly chubby self, complete with muddy running shoes instead of some really wicked talons. Wonder Freakin' Woman.

Simon Destiny had disappeared inside his domed building. I heard the sound that probably meant he was being powered up. His word or not, I wasn't waiting around to find out.

"Let's go." I grabbed my T-shirt, but Blade took it and gently wiped mud off my cheek before he handed it to me again.

"I like the way you look in the Kevlar, Gloriana. Today you proved you really are amazing."

I soaked in the praise, then looked around. "Thanks, love, but would someone drive us the hell out of here?" I was all for the juicy reunion thing, but not while surrounded by EVs

giving me the hairy eyeball. I hopped in the Hummer,
Valdez right behind me. He leaped into the backseat.

"I can drive us, Glory." Richard helped Flo into the back.
"I saw the way we came in, I can get us out of here."

"Wait! What about Flo's antidote?"

"Go. I don't want it." Flo leaned against Valdez. "I don't
trust Simon to give me the right thing anyway. Let's go. I
can beat this by myself."

"Get in, Jerry." I hopped out again. "Flo can ride up here.
We can sit in the back."

"No, I want to make sure you're well away from here
before Simon comes out. I'll meet you back at your place,
Glory." Blade leaned into the car and gave me a soul searching, heart melting kiss.

God, but I'd missed him. I grabbed his hair and kissed
him back, letting him read that. Then I glanced around the
clearing. "Promise me you'll go ahead and leave here. Don't
try to do anything stupid, like take on these EVs and their
drones."

Blade frowned. "They need to pay, Gloriana."

"You're seriously outnumbered. Even if their power levels are low, they're bound to launch a counterattack as soon
as they get over their shock at being invaded. Get our friends
to safety." Yep, I'd read him right. It wasn't like Jerry just to
let a woman save the day. And I had, hadn't I? I looked at
him for a long moment, until he nodded and gestured toward the rest of the troops.

"As you wish. Now get out of here." He slammed the car
door. Richard put the car in gear and we lurched forward.

"I'm sorry, Glory. This is all my fault." Even Flo's voice
was weak.

"Nonsense, Florence. Simon came to Austin to be with
his son. You didn't see Frederick there just now, did you,
Glory?" Richard kept his eyes on the rough track, expertly
driving the Hummer through mud and over rocks. I was
glad he knew how to get home, because I was totally lost.

"No, Freddy wasn't there. But I can't say I blame him.

His father is a powerful man. He'd probably be reluctant to declare open war on him. And we did okay without him. We had plenty of help."

"I'm sure as shit glad to be back. What the hell happened to me? One minute I'm outside the church, eyes peeled for trouble and then zilch." Valdez sighed and laid his head on Flo's lap. *"I woke up with that machine stuck on me. Like a freakin' shop vac, only more like a leaf blower. Whomp! I'm me again."*

"I know, puppy." Flo rubbed his ears and looked at me. "Will you ever forgive me, Glory? You had to change! I know you hated that." Her eyes shimmered with unshed tears. "I got us all into this because of my involvement with Simon. I think . . ." She stared at the back of Richard's head. "I think he did a, what you call, whammy on me."

"Of course he did. You acted totally out of character." I reached back and squeezed Flo's hand. "I felt it, the pull. And then there's the whole Brad Pitt thing. I know he's your dream guy."

"Yes, Simon's very handsome." Flo pulled her hand away. "And sometimes generous." She showed me a nice size emerald ring on her left hand. "I have a souvenir at least." She held out her hand, which was shaking, by the way, and admired the beautiful green stone. "I guess I should have thrown it in his face as a 'screw you' gesture. But he picked out my fantasy ring. Hard to give up."

Throw it in his face? Yeah, right. Ever read "The Girl's Guide to Immortality"? A book I really should write some-day. Rule number one: Never return gifts, especially expensive jewelry. A woman who may have to support herself forever needs all the help she can get. Okay, so I'd turned down that Mercedes Blade kept dangling in front of me. For purely practical reasons. Do you know what the insurance and upkeep would have cost me?

I smiled at Flo. "You should definitely keep it. Or sell it and keep the money if looking at it creeps you out."

Flo slipped it off her finger and put it in my hand. "Sell it. I don't want anything to remind me of that gut-sucking bastard. And I'll use the money to buy something completely different."

I jammed the ring into my pocket. "How are you feeling, Flo? Still in VV withdrawal?"

She nodded. "I'm really, really weak, like I want to just lie down and die. And yet when I lie down, I crave—" She looked at Richard again. "I hope this gets out of my system soon. I can't stand feeling so out of control."

"We'll help you, Florence. Won't we, Glory?" Richard turned the car onto a paved road. "We'll be home in about an hour, with a few minutes to spare before sunrise. Lie back and close your eyes. Rest. You too, Glory."

I was glad to close my eyes. Shape-shifting had really taken it out of me. Like I was drained, energy wise. Well, that was a good thing. Vow or not, it was okay to be too powerless for Simon to want me. I heard a soft snore. Valdez? I grinned. No, it was Flo. And wouldn't she be mortified to know that? I closed my eyes and dreamed of Blade waiting for me at home. It had been a hell of a day.

Twenty-four

"I think Kelly must have had an EV lover." Flo lay on the couch, a soft throw over her.

"Kelly?" Blade looked at me.

I nodded toward the stereo. "Kelly Clarkson, *American Idol Season One*."

"Listen to this CD. The lyrics. 'You're like a drug . . .' Not to mention 'Beautiful Disaster.' Simon. She must know Simon." Flo picked up a bottle of Fangtastic, frowned, then put it back on the coffee table without tasting it. "Where's Richard?"

"He's googling."

"What?" Flo sat up.

"He bought a new laptop, Flo. He took it home to do research on that building where the EVs are headquartered." I picked up a map. "He's found out a lot so far. It used to be a compound. A maharishi something or other built it. His group pulled out of Texas after the disaster at Waco."

"Pah! *This* is a disaster. Ricardo should be here. Comforting me." Flo laid a dramatic hand on her forehead. "I don't want to think about Simon or the EVs. Maybe they will go back to Brazil where they belong."

"Argentina." Blade grinned. "You want a cold cloth for your forehead, Florence?"

I frowned at him. I knew good and well who'd have to soak the wash cloth in ice water. Again.

"Flo, honey, don't you think it's time you got off the couch? It's been three days. Time to move on."

"Three days?" Flo sighed. "It seems like three centuries. How did I ever let myself get so caught up—" She shuddered. "Thank God the withdrawal is over."

I nodded. "We're all glad it's over. We hated seeing you suffer that way."

Valdez bumped Flo's arm with his nose. *"You tore up your room pretty bad. I think I saw one of your fancy silver sandals under the bed."*

"My God!" Flo sat up. "I really was out of my head."

"Listen. I've got to go down to the shop tonight. The art student's coming back to study the mural for his dissertation. He would love to meet the artist." I was perched on the arm of Jerry's chair, leaning against him. His hand landed on my thigh. "It's an amazing mural. He really admires your technique."

"I'm a mess." Flo touched her hair, then sniffed and wrinkled her nose. "It will take me at least an hour to pull myself together."

"I'm sure he'll wait."

"Then I'll do it." Flo tossed the throw on the floor and hurried toward her bedroom, muttering something about her shoe collection.

I picked up the remote and turned off the stereo.

"That's a relief. Flo's played that same CD over and over again ever since we got back." Valdez jumped up on the couch and settled into her place.

"Where's Will, Gloriana?" Blade grabbed the bottle of Fangtastic, sniffed it, then took a swallow. "I'm sorry he hasn't worked out better."

"He's across the hall. He and Lacy are whipping up a Thanksgiving dinner. Can't you smell it?" Not working out? He'd made it to the EV showdown, but that was about all I could say he'd done right. Will was a persistent source of irritation with his shape-shifting and cooking. Producing delicious smells for foods that I couldn't taste. I'd even tried the virtual eating with him. No luck yet. He'd taste, I'd probe his brain and yet I couldn't quite pull it off.

"Today was Thanksgiving. I guess the holiday doesn't mean much to me." Blade rubbed my arm.

I threw up a block and remembered a certain Thanksgiving Day parade . . . Wrong man, wrong time. I hadn't even bothered to tape the parade this year, like I'd done every year for decades so I could watch it when I woke up. Now that I knew why I'd been so hooked on it, I was over it. No withdrawal necessary.

"What it means to me is a big shopping day. The day after Thanksgiving. That's why I'm opening at midnight. The holiday's late this year, close to Christmas. We're going to have a big after-Thanksgiving sale."

"You've become quite a businesswoman, Gloriana." Blade pulled me down to his lap and sent Valdez a mental message because he jumped off the couch and disappeared into my bedroom.

"Any word from Mara? Is she any closer to taking out Westwood?"

"No. And I've told her she'd be wise to give up for now. It's become an obsession with her. I'm afraid it will make her careless." Blade ran his hand up under my short plaid skirt and rubbed my knee through my tights.

"You're not going after her, are you?" I wished we had more time and I had on fewer clothes. I could feel Blade's need for me against my hip. Our juicy reunion had been postponed because of Flo's illness, some intense meetings with Frederick and CiCi and Blade's own business interests, which had needed some attention after his long absence.

"No. She'll probably visit her family in Scotland when she gets tired of stalking Westwood. Which should be soon. The man's impossible to get to."

"Any word on Simon and the EVs?"

"You've made a powerful enemy there, Gloriana. I'm worried about you. You humiliated him and Simon's obviously a proud man." Jerry's hand wandered even higher. "Frederick and Richard believe Simon will keep his word for now. Seems swearing on Honoria's bible means more than you'd think. He breaks that vow and the EVs will be looking for a new leader." Jerry frowned. "But he left a loophole, the way he worded it. It didn't hit me until after we had cleared out of there. He said 'I' not 'We' when he was swearing, like maybe he could send a hit squad out after you anyway."

"Will we ever just get to live peacefully? No threats, no problems?" I deliberately put my fear on the back burner. Loophole. Of course. Simon hadn't risen to king by being stupid. But I was not about to let EV worries ruin my reunion with Jerry. I ran my hand over his chest.

"We can dream." He held me close and I felt the slow thud of his heart under my hand.

"Speaking of dreams, Will is upset. Seems he and Lacy didn't win the lottery last night. Did you really saddle me with an addicted gambler?"

"He's a good fighter. And in a way, I was desperate. Hard to find a man who'll play dog these days. And Rafael only has a few more months on his contract. I was hoping Will would work out. He has some serious debt and needs the money."

My stomach churned. I was going to lose my latest Valdez? Do you have any idea how hard it is to break in a new bodyguard? Not to mention that I'd grown really, really fond of my current furry friend.

"Well, my next Valdez will not be William Kilpatrick. For one thing, he won't stay in dog form."

Jerry frowned. "Yes, I noticed that. And have docked his pay accordingly."

"And I also don't fancy having Mara's brother underfoot. He's a wild card. Unpredictable. I need a Valdez I can bond with. I don't see that happening with a man I've seen . . . as a man. Valdez, I mean Rafael . . ." I still had trouble with that name, but it did seem to fit. "Rafael's just a dog with attitude to me because I've never seen him in any other form. I can deal with that." I looked up at Blade. "Of course now that I've demonstrated my own awesome powers, maybe you'll accept that I can take care of myself. No bodyguard necessary."

Jerry shifted me until I sat facing him. "This body should always be guarded carefully." He ran his hands up my hips and around my waist.

"When I think I could have been stuck as a pterodactyl . . ." I shuddered. "Those things are damned ugly. Good defense or not, shape-shifting is still not anything I want to do on a regular basis. Not unless there's a dire need for it."

"But you made an awesome winged dinosaur. Everyone who was there has talked of nothing but your magnificence when you dangled Simon over the dome. I know I'll never forget the sight."

"And I'm afraid Simon will never forget it either, you're right about that." I pushed myself off Jerry's lap and held out my hand. "But that's something to worry about another night." I glanced at the clock. "Valdez, get your furry butt out here."

"You called?" Valdez came out with an empty Twinkie wrapper stuck to his paw. He'd been heavily into the junk food since his return to normal. And I sure wasn't denying him anything.

"Go across the hall and stay with Will and Lacy until time to go downstairs. Tell Will to give you some turkey and dressing. I'll get you both on my way down." I threw open the door and knocked on the one across the hall. I didn't wait for an answer, just slammed my apartment door and locked it. I'd heard the shower go on and knew Flo would be in there at least twenty minutes.

"What's on your mind, Gloriana?" Blade grinned, because he always could read me.

"A juicy reunion. I think we both deserve one. Don't you?"

Twenty minutes was a good start, but not nearly enough time. I was grinning though, when I threw on my clothes again, Jerry a well satisfied and interested observer. I had less than five minutes to get downstairs.

"Um, Jerry. When you looked at Simon, who did you

see?" Okay, a shot in the dark. Maybe Simon had to consciously make a person see him that way. But if Jerry said, "I saw you, Gloriana." Well, wouldn't that be cool?

"I saw an ordinary man, Glory. No one special." He sat up and pulled me to him. "Why? Did he have a power I don't know about?"

"Forget him and his powers." I kissed Jerry and turned to go.

"Wait. I have a present for you." Jerry rolled out of bed and picked up his pants. "I know you lost your cell phone."

"Yes, that damned Greg Kaplan took it." I grinned when I saw what Jerry held in his hand. "Is that what I think it is?"

"A new phone. The latest technology including . . ." He pulled me close again. "A camera. It even takes videos."

"Thank you." I sighed and leaned against him. "Hmm. You got one too?

"You bet." He rubbed my back.

"Call me later?" I grinned, my mind whirling with endless possibilities.

"Count on it." Jerry kissed me and pushed me toward the door.

I stopped in the doorway and gave him my best sultry look. "Call me, Jerry. And don't be surprised if a pterodactyl answers."